Last Summer at Barebones

Last Summer at Barebones

DIANE BAKER MASON

McArthur & Company
Toronto

First paperback edition in 2002 by McArthur & Company

First published in Canada in 2001 by
McArthur & Company
322 King Street West, Suite 402
Toronto, ON M5V 1J2

National Library of Canada Cataloguing in Publication Data

    Mason, Diane Baker
        Last summer at Barebones

    ISBN 1-55278-296-4

    I.Title.

    PS8576.A79537L38 2002   C813'.6   C2002-900676-7
    PR9199.3.M3926L38 2002

Text Design: *Mad Dog Design Inc.*
Cover & F/X: *Mad Dog Design Inc.*
Author Photo: *Gord Jeoffroy, 2001*
Printed in Canada by *Transcontinental Printing Inc.*

The publisher would like to acknowledge the financial
support of the Government of Canada through the Book
Publishing Industry Development Program (BPIDP) and the
Canada Council for our publishing activities. The publisher
further wishes to acknowledge the financial support of the
Ontario Arts Council for our publishing program.

10 9 8 7 6 5 4 3 2 1

This book is dedicated to Bridgid, who never deserted me, and to John Myers, my boundless supporter, who was there at The End.

I would also like to thank Sally Cooper, who was there at the beginning, as well as Stanley Fefferman, who said it was okay. Special thanks to my parents and to my sister Donnamarie (none of whom bear any resemblance to the family in this book). Gratitude always to my sons Ian and Alan, who believe that being a writer is perfectly normal (it isn't), and to Linda Detlor and Margaret Bourdon, who made my childhood years spectacular. Thanks to Andrea Pope, who knows these things do happen, and to Gord Jeoffroy and Lydia Crhak, for being writer friends, and to Peter Kalmeta, who convinced me anything was possible.

I would like to thank as well the writers of my writing workshops: B.C. Holmes, Kevin Lawrence and Edwin Mason, in particular. Thanks, too, to the Humber School for Writers, where I learned so much, and to Paul Lima: a believer who offered practical advice. Finally, I would like to thank Susan McKie and Glynis Kilmartin, who read the manuscript; John Mason, who was a great help in its earlier stages, and Anne McDermid, my long-suffering agent, who fielded the strangest voicemails from me. There are so many other people to thank – the women I ran with, the actors I worked with, and the students I've taught – and I hope they all realize that this is as much their book as it is anyone's.

I am also grateful to the Canada Council for the Arts for their financial support of this book, and to Kim McArthur and all the people from McArthur & Co., my wonderful publishers.

ACKNOWLEDGEMENTS

Excerpt from "Epilogue" from DAY BY DAY by Robert Lowell. Copyright © 1977 by Robert Lowell. Reprinted by permission of Farrar, Straus and Giroux, LLC.

EASY TO BE HARD, by Galt MacDermot, James Rado and Gerome Ragni © 1966, 1967, 1968, 1970 (Copyrights renewed) James Rado, Gerome Ragni, Galt MacDermot, Nat Shapiro and EMI U Catalog Inc. All rights administered by EMI U Catalog Inc. All rights reserved used by permission of WARNER BROS. PUBLICATIONS U.S. INC., Miami, FL. 33014.

Excerpt from THE FEMININE MYSTIQUE by Betty Friedan. Copyright © 1983, 1974, 1973, 1963 by Betty Friedan. Used by permission of W.W. Norton & Company Inc.

LAUGHING. Written by Burton Cummings and Randy Bachman © 1969 ®1997 SHILLELAGH MUSIC (BMI)/Administered by BUG. All rights reserved. Used by permission.

LEAVING ON A JET PLANE. Words and Music by John Denver. Copyright ©1967; Renewed 1995 Anna Kate Deutschendorf, Zachary Deutschendorf and Jesse Belle Denver for the USA. All rights for Anna Kate Deutschendorf and Zachary Deutschendorf administered by Cherry Lane Music Publishing Company, Inc. (ASCAP). All rights for Jesse Belle Denver administered by WB Music Corp. (ASCAP). All rights for the world excluding USA, UK, Eire, Australia and South Africa controlled by Cherry Lane Music Publishing Company Inc. (ASCAP) and DreamWorks Songs (ASCAP). All rights for the UK, Eire, Australia and South Africa controlled by Essex Music (PRS) International Copyright Secured. All rights reserved.

LOVE HER MADLY. Words and Music by The Doors. Copyright © 1971 Doors Music Co. Copyright renewed. All rights reserved. Used by permission.

Excerpt from THE SECOND SEX by Simone de Beauvoir, 1949. Used by permission of Random House, Inc.

"Soar into the 70's," January 1970. Used by permission of Seventeen Magazine.

Toronto Sun excerpt, October 1997. Used with permission of Associated Press.

For three years, Kelly Yeomans, 13, endured taunts of "fatty." Her teenager tormentors threw salt in her school lunch and dumped her clothes in the garbage. Last week, they pelted her house with butter and eggs. The sweet-faced teen told her parents she couldn't stand the abuse anymore. While they slept on a Sunday night, she took a fatal overdose of painkillers...

Toronto Sun
October 1997

Yet why not say what happened?

Robert Lowell

Now

I go back to Barebones Lake, the Wednesday before the Saturday on which I plan to shoot my sister.

The road lopes through the woods, there only by the grace of the forest's indulgence, and the car rides it bareback, spitting gravel from its tires at the turns. At the wheel of the car is me, instead of the Dad, and it's a sporty Mazda instead of a cumbersome, fishtailing, Vistacruiser wagon. My Mazda has a CD player, and an LED digital display for its gauges; the wagon had dials with pointed needles that glowed phosphorescent in the dusk, and a pushbutton radio which, north of Severn River, only brought in static.

It's thirty years since I spent those seven summers on the island. The last was the summer before I turned fourteen. When I round that last turn after the bridge, the blueness of the lake startles me. I had forgotten that feeling. Mackenzie Lodge is under new ownership, and being renovated. There are no clusters of holidayers lying on the little beach and on the greying planks of the government dock; no teenagers skulking around the general store, trying to pilfer Oh Henry! bars. The general store, the boathouse, the whitewashed rental cabins, are all gone. So are the charming two- and three-room log cabins that lined the water's edge, past Ashleigh's Marina, all along the road to Richard's cottage.

I park the car under the oaks, crushing acorns like skulls beneath the tires of the Mazda, and emerge to the sound of their tiny, dying, screams. I can see on the water's edge, at the point where the bay peaks, that Ashleigh's Marina has been boarded up. A large white sign announces that the land has been rezoned, to permit construction of a seasonal condominium resort. Boarded up, its pine-plank exterior blackening with age, its windows empty sockets, the marina hulks like a Carpathian castle, the locus of long-dead nightmares. My personal house of horrors; my evil-ridden, crumbling palace.

Every Gothic castle needs a villain. Theresa is mine.

Even a few short weeks ago, I had not decided. I was still wondering: when will I grow up, grow past, get over? When will I move out of the water, and into the air-breathing life of the adult?

When I see Theresa dead, and not a moment before.

One

**INCREDIBLE VAMPIRE FISH BOY
CANNOT LEAVE BATHTUB!**

"Oh, God! Save my child! He's burning in his own skin!" My prayer burst aloud from my lips as I saw my baby's tender skin rise in a rash, and then into huge red hives! The blisters spread unstoppably to his angelic smiling face! Only when they burst, one at a time like tiny volcanoes, did my boy begin to cry!

My Freddie suffers from lycanthroposis pellidomyasis, an allergy to ultraviolet rays. He was also born without sweat glands! Freddie could easily be cooked alive in his own skin! So my Freddie must stay inside at all times! We have a plastic wading pool in the basement, which we fill with cool water and Epsom salts. Freddie sits there all day sometimes!

We have also nailed tarpaper over the windows...

I suppose you think that's funny.

I look at these paragraphs now (I wrote them; that's what I did for a living – *schadenfreude* for fifty cents a word, slutting my writing for the trash tabloid, the *Tantalizer*) and know that there is something, somehow, funny about this boy, and his hysterical-yet-still-coping mother, and the blacked-out windows, as if they were expecting the Blitz. Happy Freddie peeing in his pool, while his mom brings him lemonade and his dad brings home the bacon.

My editor at the *Tantalizer* once said that I'm good at this job because I'm sensitive. It's actually the opposite: I'm insensitive. I feel the same way about severed limbs as I do about broken teacups: resignation. *These things happen.*

My job was to tell what happened. I had what they called the *personal-interest* beat – stories of individual suffering, *D.E. Graham's Tales of Torture and Triumph.* Where other writers worked on *News of the Weird* (foreign – to North Americans – oddities, from the remote Alpine village whose citizens are all congenitally deaf, to a life-sized crucifix in Spain that is covered in human skin) or the monthly feature, *Killer Konnection* (devoted to the month's most gruesome and/or bizarre slaying), my job involved interviewing people whose story I already knew. Most of the stories were entirely true; only the telling changed. The mainstream headline *Infant Dies in Trailer Park Tornado* became *Twister Rips*

Screaming Babe From Mother's Clutching Hands! Words like *death* and *murder* and *lost* become blanched and invisible in the hands of a conventional journalist. It takes someone like me to really *do* pain.

I used the phone for most interviews, since many, if not most of the stories, were American, and there was often no need at all to drive to the States to see the victims in person. I simply asked *what happened* and *what happened then* and *what happened next.* Then I transformed it into prose according to the rules of my gig: first person, breathless paragraphs, full of agonized declarative bursts, and a peppering of exclamation points. Insert the *de rigueur* heartfelt plea to the Christian almighty – *Oh, God!* – and make sure someone's *eyes welled with tears.* Submit story to editor. Receive cheque. Repeat for more than twenty years.

Good Lord, has it really been that long?

The Dad was so proud, right from the beginning, when my byline first appeared beneath the banner *Woman Angler Hooks Severed Head of Neighbour's Missing Daughter!* He said that he always knew that getting me an education (a Master's degree in Comparative Literature – at least I have the training to appreciate the irony) was the right thing to do. The poor Dad. *Wasted Man Lives Entire Adult Life in Same House, Tended by Bitter Spinster Daughter.* Nope. Not sad enough.

I have never worked for anyone but the *Tantalizer*. I got the gig right out of university, and I never left it. I was made for the job. I could work from home. I could write about the most dreadful pain without flinching. The man in Nebraska whose baler pulled off his arms at the shoulder, but who still walked home across the fields, leaving a double trail of red across the dusting of November snow; the couple whose mastiff ate their toddler, who were bewildered for a moment when the dog trotted into their living room, proudly carrying a tiny arm in its mouth; the man whom a propane explosion left limbless, sightless, speechless and deaf, who communicates by bashing his head against the pillow in Morse code. The baby born with its heart outside its body.

That's one of the few in-person interviews I've done over the last few years – with the parents, not the baby, haha. They lived just outside Montreal, and I could not reach them on the phone. But they were my assigned story, so I drove up to see them, or rather, to see that baby, expecting to meet the sort of stalwart, hopeful, forward-looking sire and dam that one might see on a TV medical show. But none of it. They were shaken to the roots, and they sat together in the hospital ward, digging their fingers into each other's forearms, the skin around their eyes darkened and bruised from wiping.

In my story, they said, "My God! Help us! Our baby's heart is outside her body!" but in reality, they sat in shocked silence, unable to string more than a few words together.

And they let me see the baby. They gave the doctor permission. I said that the publicity might help other babies born this way – that it would bring attention to the cause. I am a fearsome liar, I suppose, for I don't believe anything can be done, about anything. But that baby was startling. Her heart sat on her chest, like an emblem, uncovered and throbbing. She lay crucified in the incubator, hands taped down, tubes in her nose, tubes in her arms, eyes closed like a newborn puppy's. At the world's mercy.

The doctors fixed the baby – put her heart back in her chest – but I wondered at that time what would have had happened if she had lived on, unrepaired? If she had gone to kindergarten that first day, in her new first-day-of-school dress, purchased by her anxious parents and altered to allow for the bloated, tender protuberance? Would she have worn a special shield, to protect her heart? And would the other children have laughed at her, at her amended wardrobe? At the way she couldn't keep up? Would anyone have leapt to her defence, when children followed her home, calling out names, spitting at her, knocking her books from her hands, kicking dirt on her patent leather shoes? Or would there have been not one voice raised to help, because no one seemed to see it, or because everyone thought, privately at least, *she deserves it, she could change if she really tried,*

*it's her own doing that she's this way, why does-
n't she fix herself up?*

Would that girl have walked alone, every day,
ten months of each year, from September to July,
with her heart in her hands, praying to the wicked
god that made her, for just a moment's peace?

As was the case with me?

When David came up from the States for the
Dad's funeral – he spent a total of forty hours here,
alighting and taking off again as if he couldn't bear
the feel of Canada's soil – he said he never would
have recognized me, not in a million years. He
said it as if it were high praise: *you sure don't look
like you used to.*

But I didn't change to get praise. I did it to get
peace. I did the orthodonty and the rhinoplasty,
and I keep my cupboards bare, all so that the creature I once was will never look back at me from
the bathroom mirror.

David asked, "You still write, Dee?" He was
not talking about the *Tantalizer.* He meant the stories I wrote, as a little girl, for Richard.

"No," I said. I realized that to him, I was frozen
in his mind as that huge, fat, freakling, his baby sister, sitting alone on my bed, filling page after page of
my Playtime Doodler with pointless and pitiful
myths.

"And do you ever see that Richard anymore?"
he asked, but then his face went white with the
shock of his *faux pas.* "Oh, Dee, I'm so sorry."

"That's all right," I said, and I heard resentment in my tone: a desire to punish him.

"I *am* sorry, Dee," he said. "It was a long time ago. I really had forgotten what happened."

"I hadn't," I said.

"It wasn't anybody's *fault*," he continued, flailing, trying to fix things. "Just one of those terrible accidents."

"Wasn't it Jung who said, 'there are no accidents'?"

David nodded. "I think it was Freud," he said. "But Dee – it was an accident. Surely you're over it by now."

Yes. Surely. I'm over it. All of it.

After the funeral, and after David flew home again, I stood in the living room of the house on Lindsey Street, and observed its unamended, circa-1970 décor, scrupulously maintained by yours truly through maniacal, daily bouts of cleaning (I am, in many ways, my mother's daughter). And I realized that although I was not a rich woman, I was financially comfortable – who would have thought that the Dad's lifetime as a janitor would have such a lucrative payoff! – and I did not have to live there anymore. I was forty-two years old, and except for my year in the hospital, I had never lived anywhere else.

Through the drapes I peered, and saw a game being played, by children on bicycles, and a fat boy struggling gamely to keep up with the others, as they spun and wheeled like Peter Pan's gang. Peter Pan's gang: those were genuine children. Killers, pirates, hunters. J.M. Barrie got it right.

I did not want to live near children. I closed the drapes again.

Within months, I bought the townhouse downtown, off Wellington Street. Where I believe I may have hoped that things would be different. How different, I could never have guessed.

TWO

TANTALIZER REPORTER STALKS SISTER!
SLAUGHTERS HER IN HONKY TONK!

For week after week, month after month,
Tantalizer correspondent D.E. Graham
followed the woman she knew to be her
estranged sister – the woman who had
ruined her life – waiting for the moment
to wreak her bloody revenge! In a cascade
of bullets, she struck down the witch
who had taken everything from her, all
those years ago!

One afternoon, late November, just after my
forty-third birthday, I was reading a book about
the Nuremberg trials that I'd bought at Seekers'
bookstore on Bloor Street West, along with a
Michael Crichton potboiler that I'd read in four
hours flat. I was in my kitchen, alone with its effi-
cient modernity: its Moën faucets, gas range,
triple-glazed windows overlooking the court, all
so different from the futzy, burnt-orange, frozen-
in-1970 look of the Dad's house, as preserved and
formal as a funeral home. I had received, read, and

thrown out the annual birthday card from my mother. And I had finished my latest story – about a man who tried to kill himself by putting the barrel of a .22 rifle in his mouth, and pulling the trigger. He had only succeeded in blowing off his lower jaw. I had thought that I would surely have to do that interview in person, since obviously the man could no longer talk, but to my relief he had email. He practically wrote his own tale. All I had to do was insert prayer and exclamation points.

I wasn't reading the Nuremberg book for research purposes – the *Tantalizer* doesn't do Holocaust stories; our readers want current pain, not the old stuff – but for personal reasons. I was – as I had the habit of doing – putting my own life into perspective. Other people's pain was a barometer for my own: Dee, your pain weighs *this* much, a grain of sand's worth, and over here is this boulder that is *real* pain. I was telling myself, clearly and didactically, that I had not suffered. There had been Holocausts and forced marches and torture and slaughter and none of it had happened to me. It only *felt* like it had.

I also craved tales of justice. I relished histories of the consequences visited on the perpetrators. Courtroom dramas, true-to-life detective tales, even Zane Greys where the bad guy gets his comeuppance, filled my bookshelves. The institutionalized pogrom of World War II, and the subsequent trials of some of its authors, assured me that genuine pain will be avenged. The only reason *mine* had not been avenged, I believe I thought, was that it was not worthwhile. To me, nothing of consequence had happened.

This calculated construction was a *modus vivendi* that kept me from…well, I suppose, from my anger. Without anger, at God or at humanity or even at Theresa, I could continue to eke out my stalwart little life.

So there I was, eke eke eke, alone in my house, looking over the courtyard, reading a bookful of pain. It had the usual photos, of emaciated survivors, their ribs as clear-cut as the grooves of a washboard (I ran my fingers over my own ribs, counting their ridges below the thin skin with comfort). There were photos of faces, eyes staring up from sunken pits, and photos of ditches filled with bodies, naked asses and genitals exposed, big black wounds in the chest and belly and face. I turned the pages, read the tales, the testimony, the multiple post-mortems, without a grimace. I swallowed them like popcorn.

And then, I choked. My breath left me. I wanted to leap into the page, and stop what I saw; wrest the perpetrator away from his child-victim, save the child, save him! My hand fell flat over the page, as if to push through it. I thought, *it's okay, Dee, the villain got his comeuppance, he died too…they killed him like they killed the others.* I thought this for perhaps as long as a minute, staring at the photo, unable to see (or feel) anything but pain, pain, pain.

What did I see? A photo of a phalanx of children, marching three abreast between two rows of post-and-barbed-wire fences, on their way to be executed at one of the camps. Some of them were skipping, some holding hands and conversing with the kid next to them (*talking in line,* they'd have said in my school – *no talking in line!*). These kids, judging by their expressions and posture, didn't know they were going to die. They thought it was another organized outing; a field trip; an adventure. They were being kids.

But one boy, looking back over his shoulder, had an expression of such desperation, such despair, as he half-turned to his tormentor, who was right behind him, marching on his heels. The tormentor's face was curled into a grin of pure deviltry; he met the victim's eyes with challenge and delight, daring him to make him stop, knowing his prey was helpless. Nowhere around them did anyone even notice; the other children either looked ahead or glanced away, and of course the adults didn't see a thing. But I saw. I pined to be there: to slap away the torturing hand, to shake the little devil in front of my eyes, demanding *don't you know what that feels like, you vicious little bastard?*

And what was the torment, that for me surpassed pits of bodies? The devil-boy was tugging on the other's uniform – pulling the hem of his striped shirt downward. That's all. He was *teasing him. Just teasing.*

But the face of the boy who looked back told more: it told of a lifetime, a short one and one soon to end, but nevertheless a *lifetime*, of one little bastard after another driving him deeper and deeper into misery.

And I thought, *I'm glad they killed that teasing little pest.*

Now, we cannot help from time to time to think obscene thoughts: there is a darker side to the koan, "don't think of a white horse." But this thought, which I at first refused to own, had been such a shout that it seemed more like a blow than a thought. It was as if I'd bit my tongue or turned my ankle, sharp and hard: I knew I didn't like children, and I knew why. But to think such a shocking thing was, I had believed until then, not possible for me. And my panting, weeping, distress over the boy being teased – I had thought I'd driven all of that down, yet here it was, surging up from nowhere like Spielberg's toothy shark. There was no use telling myself I hadn't meant it, that it was a momentary lapse of morals. I *knew* I'd meant it. The megalodon of my anger was alive and well. I might have carved and starved my body, to deny what happened, but I still remembered. I remembered everything they had said, and everything they'd done. And at the spearhead of the memory was Theresa.

I got up and walked around my kitchen, back and forth, and in a circle, I don't know for how long. I couldn't read any more. Outside, the kids were coming home from school, and a demonic chorus was starting, as the afternoon's sessions of street hockey unfolded. I had so hoped there wouldn't be children on this downtown street. But no – they are everywhere.

Clear as a bell, I heard a boy's voice say *fuck off, lardass, we don't want you around.* I don't think it was a real voice; I think I imagined it. Surely God couldn't be that cruel, to throw *that* at me when I was so distressed. But I heard it notwithstanding, and clapped my hands over my ears, screwed my eyes up tight. A raging hunger surged through me – a need for iced cookies, for fried chicken, for crumpets with butter and pot roast and Jell-O pudding with whipped cream and sprinkles, for Peek Freans shortbreads, for homogenized milk. For my mother, my father, my friend Richard, for someone, anyone, who remembered what I went through, and could say, *yes, that hurt.*

In time, I lit a cigarette, and sat down hard in my chair, flipping away the page that showed the two boys. My hands were quaking. To keep myself in my chair, I turned my face back to the book. I was now at the trials themselves, and the testimony of a witness.

I saw something I had never seen before…a fountain of blood. Owing to the gases from the corpses in their shallow grave, the blood was bubbling out of the ground, in a fountain…

A fountain of blood. It was a line from a hymn that we all used to sing at church: *God has a fountain, a fountain of blood.* The sound of it drowned out the kids' game outside (the Dad's voice thundering, my mother's mewling soprano), it brought with it Richard's white body, thin and pale and lying on the rocks at the island, beside a seething pit of flame. He had three eyes, open and watching the sky, watching the stars above him.

I don't know how long I sat there. The cigarette burned itself down to my fingers, and dropped away onto the tabletop, without my noticing. I had a red burn between my first and second fingers, but I didn't feel the pain. When I finally shuddered myself out of it, it was dark outside, and the children had all gone away. The refrigerator hummed. The fridge, empty except for my bottles of diet Coke, my crisper full of celery, my low-fat cheese spread, my boned-and-skinned chicken breast. A single navel orange, from Florida.

I devoured that, tearing it open and nursing it for the sweetness.

That night proved wretched, for I dreamed. It is said that all sane creatures dream. At that point, I had not been a dreamer since I was a child. I was, however, an incorrigible sleepwalker.

The sleepwalking used to cause the Dad some problems, but he used his ingenuity, intervening in a variety of ways. He rolled a blanket up across the floor of my doorway, so that I would trip over it and wake myself up; this worked until my sleeping self began to recognize the blanket and step over it (so we supposed). Then he hung a set of tin wind chimes from the lintel, so that my head would brush against them as I passed. The chimes did not wake me, but they woke him, for he would listen in his sleep for the sound. "You made it halfway down the stairs this time," he'd report to me in the morning, as I made his eggs and consumed my breakfast of half-a-grapefruit and a pot of black coffee. More than once I made it out into the street, where I would stand flailing my arms and screaming *go away*. He also had to put plastic sliding locks on the cupboards and fridge, because I would go rooting around in there and make an awful mess. He said that more than once he was woken by a sound like a raccoon rattling through a campsite, whereas it was just me scrabbling through the pots and pans.

We lived like that for years.

One assignment I turned down – annoying my editor, who put up with a lot from me but who did not know me to turn down assignments, particularly those based in my hometown – was the tale of the man who drove clear across Toronto to murder his mother-in-law, and to beat his father-in-law nearly to death. The twist was, however, that he was sleepwalking when he did it. He was a clockwork automaton, following an untraceable impulse through stoplights and traffic and locked doors. This was far too familiar for me. *Oh God I've killed someone I love in my sleep* was too close to a line that might, one day, appear in my own diary.

Since the Dad died, I had been coping with the sleepwalking on my own. It had not, to that date, caused many problems, although I knew when I had been *up for an outing*, as the Dad used to say, because my alter ego would turn on the stereo and play golden oldies (but never anything after 1970) or it would take everything out of the kitchen cupboards and the fridge, occasionally opening tins and empty jars. There was no point in my putting childproof locks on the cupboards; those were snapped off at the screws.

Occasionally, it would get aggressive: my low-fat, sugar-free yogurt tubs would be fingered and then tossed aside; unleavened flour-and-water crackers were ripped from their cello bag and strewn like bones around the floor. Every single Sun-Maid Raisins packet – I allow myself one or two of these one-inch-square treats a day – would lie gutted on the floor. I felt a little sorry for it, searching the way it did, for things I knew it wanted but would never, ever, have. Nevertheless, it was eating *my* food, and I resented both its mess and its hunger.

As I was saying. That night. That wretched night.

That wretched night, I went to bed determined not to sleepwalk. That tale of the man who drove across town to kill flapped before my closed eyes, a red flag of possibility, although back then I was not sure whom to kill. But nevertheless, before retiring, I locked all the doors downstairs and jammed one of my wooden kitchen chairs under the knob of my bedroom door. I kicked at the legs so that it was thoroughly wedged in, imagining that the effort involved in un-jamming it would short-circuit any sleepwalking. Then, to seal a bargain with Morpheus, I went to bed with Proust, hoping it would knock me out from sheer befuddlement.

The next thing I recall, I woke up on the island.

I could not move, not to lift my hand or raise my head from the pillow. I was in my bunk, and the strings of Theresa's bunk above me groaned; a loon cried and my father snored. I, an adult woman, thirty years away from that time and place, lay wide-eyed, conscious, and paralyzed, seeing not my bureau, my bookshelves, my door, my curtains, my armchair. I saw instead the cabin's bare wood floor with its sheet of worn, green-flecked linoleum, and the glass-panelled front door. Outside, the black pines shifted in the wind, like giants conferring on whom to eat first.

"Please," I said, to the room, to the cabin on Blueberry Island, where I knew I could not be.

Then, something dawned on me: if I was on the island, and it was thirty years ago, then I was thirteen. And I had that *body*.

I had to see, I had to know: was it all back? But I couldn't look down, or move the quilt, or put my hands on my legs and belly, to touch myself. I lay, straining each vestigial proprioreceptor, trying to *feel* how big I was. The hairs on my arm, the skin on my fingers, reached outward, looking for a gauge: where did I end? Where did I start? Was I about to spill over the edges of the bed; was the elastic of my underpants close to popping from the pressure? Was there no way to tell how *big* I was?

A grunt of exertion escaped me, as I struggled to bend my rigid neck, to examine the expanse of my body. Above me, sepulchral despite its high, teenage pitch, came Theresa's voice.

"Quit that noise, you *pig*. I'm trying to sleep."

At the sound of her voice I closed my eyes tight, in case she dropped her head over the edge of the bunk. *Just a dream, just a dream,* I told myself, unconvinced, because although I wasn't a dreamer I knew instinctively that dreams don't work that way. No, I was *not* asleep, I was sure I was not asleep, and although it is never a good idea to doubt one's sanity, I doubted it then. At that moment, my reality was that I had never left the island. I had been trapped there, in a monkey's-paw answer to my long-ago prayer that I be allowed to stay there forever. I had not framed the prayer correctly: I wanted to be there *alone.*

Dream or night terror or hallucination, it eventually ended: I did somehow fall into unconsciousness, and when I awoke (shaken awake by the banging of the garbage men among the neighbourhood cans), I was met by the sight of the chair I had so carefully wedged against my door, not set aside but *thrown* aside, with enough force to dent the drywall beside my bureau. And my bedroom door was open. The room was oddly cold, and the furnace bellowed dully in the basement.

I rose cautiously, as if there had been an intruder in my house; someone who might still be around, hiding behind the shower curtain. My teeth ached oddly, and there was a gummy residue on my palate. Thinking *don't be stupid,* I nevertheless picked up a letter opener from the top of my bureau, and stepped out into the hall. It was even chillier there than in my room. When I started down the stairs, I saw the reason for the icy atmosphere: the front door was wide open, letting in the dawning, wintry day.

I closed the door with a shiver, and glanced to the left, into my kitchen, which was at the front of my home, overlooking the court. All was in order, more or less: a single cupboard door hung open, with my set of Athena dinnerware somewhat rearranged. Whatever had been done while I slept, did not appear to be substantial. I put the letter opener down on the counter, and stood there, listening to the furnace breathe and the garbage truck rumble away. My coffee machine clicked itself on, as I had timed it to do. Eight a.m. The radio, too, came alive. CJRT, the jazz station.

The day was underway, will me, nil me.

I figured the best thing, at that point, was to get to work. I called my editor, looking for an assignment; I hadn't thought of anything myself and was sure *Former Fat Girl Hallucinates* wasn't quite what the doctor ordered. To my distress, however, he didn't offer the usual choice of several leads. Instead, he doggedly insisted I pursue a particular story.

"It's perfect for you, Dee," he said.

"Give me something else. Don't you have a quadriplegic pole-vaulter or something?"

"I'm serious, Dee, these girls are great material. They need your special touch."

"Forget the flattery. I don't want to go to Florida. How about if I phone them?"

"They want an in-person interview. They were really hurt when I suggested you phone it in. They thought you were spooked by their appearance. That you wouldn't want to see them, because they were monstrous or something. Now, that's not true, is it, Dee? That you don't want to see them, because they're monstrous?"

"If they're not monstrous, what are they doing in the *Tantalizer*?"

"Yeah, yeah, of course, but you don't have to rub their noses in it. C'mon, Dee!"

He went on and on, coercing me, even threatening to make me share my beat with another writer, an Ace card he sometimes pulled out when I was recalcitrant. He said the girls were "an example of taking what you've got and working with it, of not hiding from the world." I'm not sure it was a dig, but it felt like one. He told me that despite all their limitations, one of the girls had a college diploma in food preparation and catering. The other had a promising career as a folk singer (she played the accordion, with her hand playing the keyboard while her sister pumped the bellows). And they were captains of their bowling team.

"Wouldn't you like a day at the beach, Dee?" he wheedled. "Daytona Beach is wide and warm. Sand just like sugar."

That was the wrong thing to say to me. I was always seeing food where there was none: brown ceramic plates look like chocolate; Royal Doulton figurines seem to be made of marzipan. Even the spackle on the ceiling swirls like frosting. What would I do with a hundred miles of sugar? I didn't want to know.

So it wasn't the prospect of a day at the beach that got me to say yes, but what I saw as I wandered with the phone to my ear, over to get a mug for my coffee. Behind my stylish island-style counter, spread over the floor in crumpled balls, were sixteen (count 'em) sixteen colourful paper wrappers, from sixteen consumed candy bars, each vacant of so much as a crumb of chocolate. And a Smarties box, peeled open so that its plain brown interior lay exposed. A wasp-yellow Oh Henry! wrapper. The still-sticky cellophane from a demolished package of Twizzlers.

Now I recognized the gummy, unpleasant, pasty residue in my mouth. I had been eating. I put one hand on my thigh. It was no bigger...yet.

The next day, carrying my overnight case, I fled my house as if it were haunted. Which, for all intents and purposes, it was.

Three

Laughing! How could you do this to me!

"Laughing"
The Guess Who

It was a fluke that I found Theresa. I certainly wasn't looking for her. Yet there she appeared, thousands of miles from home, in a Daytona Beach bar where she was performing for a crowd of tosspot teenagers, at least half of them Canadian. I'd interviewed the girls: Siamese twins, linked at the head, with one of their four eyes buried beneath a physiological anomaly of flesh and bone, so that they had only three eyes. I proposed the headline *Sisters Share Brain! Joined Together by Horrible Defect of Birth! Stalwart Sisterly Love Overcomes!*

As usual, my story's subjects had little in common with the story itself. The girls were, yep, they were monstrous; what can I say? One of their four arms was useless – a boneless sausage of flesh – which was strapped around the shoulder of the other twin. When they walked they seemed to be leaning up against each other, their heads squashed together as if by a giant's hand, above two largely separate and functional midsections, tapering to a pair of thick, sturdy, completely capable legs. One twin looked up in the sky, the other at the ground. They had to take turns at watching where they were going.

It was, without a doubt, the most difficult time I've ever had on assignment. Not only did my mind keep playing cat-and-mouse with the bizarre events of the last days – the hallucination, and the candy bar wrappers, and the boy in the photo – but the girls obviously had had another motive for wanting an in-person interview. They were bored, and wanted new meat. And so, they ate me alive.

"You think we're freaks," said Breeanne.

Before I could answer, Leeanne continued. "Get enough freaks, and you'll have a status quo."

"Everyone *else* will become the freaks."

"I agree," I stammered. "Absolutely. Why do you say that…"

"You're a freak," said Breeanne.

"You're *incredibly* skinny." From Leeanne.

"And tall."

"*Freakishly* tall."

"Look at your feet. They're huge. Like shovels."

"Like big shovels."

"Garden spades."

"Okay, enough already," I said. I managed to steer them on to what it was like to be joined to your sister, but that just opened up another can of worms, none of which would go back in their can after the interview ended.

"We hate each other," said Breeanne.

"Yes, that's right," responded Leeanne. "Did you know that if I eat green pepper, she gets indigestion?"

"I can't stop her," said Breeanne. "She buys it, puts it in the shopping cart, eats it, doesn't care how I feel. I try to slap it out of her hand. I can't reach. I can't reach."

"She wears perfume I'm allergic to. My arm breaks out in a rash. I scratch myself bloody, up against the door jamb. But she won't stop."

I wasn't sure they weren't putting me on. "That's not very nice," I said, impotently. "Why can't you get along?"

"We hate each other."

"We do. We hate each other very much."

They trotted out all their beefs and objections. Breeanne was a night owl; she wanted to get laid some day. Oh, yes, many men wanted to fuck her; she got emails from potential partners every time a newspaper did a story about them. But Leeanne was a born-again Christian, and she wanted to save herself for marriage.

"Breeanne farts in church," said Leeanne. "She sings off-key."

"It's not off-key. You just can't hear it properly. The sound is bouncing off your skull. We've been over this a hundred times."

"It's not my skull, it's your *voice*. Fartgirl!"

"*I do not* fart in church," said Breeanne hotly. "Miss Graham, she's a liar like you wouldn't believe."

"You are. Not me. You."

"Maybe," I said, still flabbily trying to force some focus, "This is just sibling rivalry?"

"You have a sister?" they chorused.

"Yes," I said.

"Did you get along?"

"No."

"Were you the problem..."

"...or was she?"

The one finished the other's sentence perfectly. I couldn't tell if they rehearsed it. I attempted one last time to control the process.

"If one of you had to die for the other to survive," I said, in as harsh a voice as I could muster, "would you do it?"

"Do what?"

"Give your life for your sister."

"Look," said Breeanne. "We're joined at the head and torso. We share a brain. Our hearts are merged. When one of us dies, the other will die too."

"Okay," I said. "What about if they could separate you?"

"They can't."

"We're stuck. We're stuck for good."

"But let's *suppose*," I pressed.

"Why should we change..."

"...because someone doesn't like the way we are?"

"But you're changing for *you*," I said. "It would be good for you."

"Who says?"

"Yeah, who says?"

"Maybe we like the way we are."

"Yeah."

"Yeah."

"But, let's just *say* they *could!*" At this point, I was nearly yelling.

Leeanne looked smugly at the ceiling. "You ask the same questions everyone asks," she said.

"You're not a very good reporter," Breeanne told the floor.

"That's right," agreed Leeanne.

"Hey, copycat, shut up," said Breeanne sourly.

"No, *you* shut up."

I shook my head, packing up my pad and tape recorder, beginning the closing process of thanking them for their time and promising the story would be out in a few weeks. They followed me to the door, still interviewing me. Was I friends with my sister now? Why did I hate her? Where did she live? What happened?

We're not friends. I have no friends. She made sure of that. I don't know where she is. I don't want to know.

After they closed the flimsy tin door to their house on my heels, I heard them laughing, very loudly, as if they wanted me to hear. I turned and whipped my tape recorder at the side of their house; it broke against the siding and fell in two pieces into their cactus garden. I debated leaving it there, but after a bit I retrieved the cassette tape and climbed into my rental car, wondering what the hell was wrong with me.

On the drive back to the hotel, I had a sudden moment of imagination: of me, and Theresa, as conjoined twins. Glued together at the breastbone, our faces an inch apart. Her blue eyes looking right into mine, crackling with disgust and hatred. Her button-shaped mouth breathing my breath. I could feel her, right up close to me.

Just how close, I never would have guessed.

So there I was, plopped down for a half-a-day and a night in a tourist town beside a flaccid ocean, flailing around among the college kids and their boom boxes thundering gangsta rap. I took along my notebook and a series of paperback novels, to amuse myself and keep my train of thought on its tracks. Around me, the whole world was drunk. I was beached, like a shark that swam in too close to shore, and found itself gasping on the sand.

I spent the afternoon on the noisy, crowded, sun-umbrella-pocked beach, sucking in the maelstrom of colour and watching the girls and boys, hypnotized by their semi-exposed body parts: their barely concealed breasts and pubises crested with triangles of cloth. I had to wear dark glasses and hold a book before my face, so that I could watch without being cited for ogling (*hey, lady, put yer eyes back in yer head! Geez, what a perv*).

All day I watched: those marvellous tight bottoms, those amazing hard tummies, those grapefruit-firm breasts, wondering that these things could exist for some people without starvation and surgery. I watched the volleyball games, where the girls shrieked and fell in the sand, so that they were frosted with white, the boys glowing caramel beneath their sweat. The girls' ponytailed hair flew like kites' tails as they leaped and spiked. Then over to the concession stand they minced in a troupe, sashaying like Geishas, to get a cherry Coke into which was poured a shot of bourbon.

That night, I passed on my way to my room the hotel's little nightclub, which had on its stand-up sandwich-board-style marquee the promise of COMEDY TONIGHT – LAUGHS GALORE! I nearly passed by, of course, but then I saw the bottom name, an add-on to the list of featured performers – "Toronto's Vagina Dentata."

The idea of my hometown as toothed cunt amused me a little, and I hadn't been amused at all, not for days, not by anything. I was edgy, but also sleepy; I was afraid to go to bed that night in case I sleepwalked and ended up in a Florida prison cell with a half-dozen street people and an army of foot-long cockroaches. I was also, somehow, very very angry. It was a free-floating miasma of anger, lodging at times on the twins, another moment on long-gone Theresa, then off to the Dad, and the kids on the street, then finally settling on my editor for sending me to this misbegotten place.

So, because I was not myself that night, I went into the nightclub to see the comedy show.

I sat there, with my cigarettes and my ashtray and my glass of barely potable red wine. No one shared my table, although all other tables were crowded. Six and seven people clustered around each one, covering the surfaces with beer bottles and plates of nachos. There were beer-swilling and hot-pepper-eating contests, and a puddle of sick in one of the aisles. It was a madhouse – a smoky, squealing madhouse – and outside the beach was dark and so was the water, and the hungry fishes coasted by unnoticed.

I sat and listened to everyone laughing at the jokes and routines, which were all entirely about someone's misfortune, even if it was the comic's own. There were a lot of jokes about crackers and rednecks. But rednecks' necks are red because they toil so long in the sun that their skin boils. I thought of how many of these snickering kids had been crippled this week by a sunburn – had spent two days lying motionless on moistened sheets, their crisped skin slathered in Noxzema – and yet they laughed at people who have to do hard labour in the sun.

I had begun to feel like the textbook Martian anthropologist, watching the creatures about me. The waitress came to update my order, and for a moment I didn't understand her at all. I couldn't find any words to say what I needed: I was unused to going out; to noise and crowds and laughter. Even *more wine please* was hard to say. I thought, as I stared blankly at her, *my God I really am from Mars.*

And I heard a voice say, "Jesus, it's like fuckin' Mars in here."

My voice? No, the comic's. The woman on stage. My doppelgänger – at least, I saw her as that. Fat, loud, and very plain. Her hair was frizzed and dyed black, and she was popping out of her too-small clothes. Her shirt buttons strained across her bosom and stomach. A fat woman, berating the audience. She was no more than five-foot-two.

"Look at all the green complexions. Beer is not four of the five food groups, assholes. Try to ingest a solid – as long as it's not the chunks in your vomit."

She went on a little, about the beach, and the water, which she said felt like swimming in mouthwash, which her mother used to make from salt water for gargling for sore throats, and the joke went flat. But I thought, my mother used to do that too.

Shaking, I waved away the waitress, and looked around the bar, at the other patrons, who were not laughing very hard. The comic was too old for them; she was a fat middle-aged woman with a scold's arrowhead tongue. But she went on gamely, talking about fish and fishing, mention-ing a barracuda attack on a five year old, perfect *Tantalizer* material, and here it was in a comedy routine. She said it was fishy revenge for all the shitty things we do to fish. Hook 'em, spear 'em, drag 'em out of the water in nets. What did fish ever do to deserve that sort of torture? And then there's the fishermen's claim it doesn't hurt the fish.

"'It doesn't hurt the fish.' Jesus H. Fucking Christ, of *course* it hurts the fish. The fish gets its *face* pierced. Okay, okay, lots of you guys have pierced faces too, but remember that fish are a lot smarter..."

Then the comic changed her tack, berating herself, giving them a brief spiel about what a goofy wreck of a child she'd been. How fat. How tormented. How she didn't have any friends.

"I was sooooo out of it," she revealed.

I cringed: the posture was, even after all that time, familiar to me. All of me dragged downward, trying to hide, to crawl, to fawn and beg, as the crowd fell into her hands. They loved her I Was a Fat Kid Routine. They loved the description of trying to run when your legs are so fat they rub together from crotch to calf; they roared at her tale of splitting her pants, not once, but twice, two days in a row, in Grade 2 it was.

I knew the story well.

And then, Vagina Dentata said, "You guys, you Canadians, eh? You know the big Canadian thing, right? You gotta have a cottage. When I was a kid, we had a cottage on this lake. It had the stupidest fucking name."

She didn't have to say it, but she did. *Barebones.*

The next day, I sent my story in by fax, and that was it for the *Tantalizer*. Since then, my job has been following Theresa.

She was in Daytona for two more days, and I was there for her shows, in the front row, with my tape recorder running. Then she went over to St. Pete's, then drove back across Florida's neck and up the coast to do a two-nighter in Myrtle Beach. She had no more gigs until Detroit, where she played three nights in a very dingy and frightening district that had a posse of armed bouncers by the door. The next morning she crossed the border to Windsor. Six weeks she was on the road; I took a loss on my return ticket and drove back, following – more or less – in a rent-a-car. Of course I lost her many times, for she drove very quickly, but like a true Canuck she stayed on the interstates and did a straight Point-A-to-Point-B journey. And when I did lose her, it was of no concern. I knew who she was now, and where she was going. She always said where she was heading next: *Friday I'll be at the Komedy Kavern in St. Pete's, so those of you who haven't lost your licences to a DWI, drop in for a laugh...*

From Windsor all the way to Toronto I never lost her once.

In Toronto she played March of Dames and Just For Laughs and in the Alternative Comedy Lounge, and in the Upper Canada Comedy Night. She had a big following in Toronto; if I'd had any sort of "life," as they say, before that, I would have found her years ago. She played Yuk Yuk's and Second City, and had an ongoing shtick on CITY-TV's voice-of-the-people broadcast, Speaker's Corner. She did a one-woman play in the Fringe Festival which "comprised her routines glued together without proper dramatic adhesive" (or so assessed the *Globe*'s theatre critic, who panned her quite brutally).

She would see me in the audience, and point me out, not knowing to whom she spoke.

Hey, it's my biggest fuckin' fan. How are ya, honey? Love yer suit. Lookit, everybody, this dame here in the front row – she's my stalker. How'dja like someone like her following you around? Who does your hair, Frau Himmler? And like, lady, next time you're downtown, treat yourself to an expression. What happened to you, anyway? Did you try smiling once and not much like it?

She didn't recognize me. But I recognized her. Or at least, I recognized *me*. For if someone – a forensic artist, working in clay – had taken my childhood skull or a photo of me at ten, and *aged* it – if someone had projected what I might look like, and sound like, and be, at forty-odd years of age, then it would be that woman on stage there: that bulbous-bodied, frizzy-haired dumpling, with the multiple chins, and the almost-simian brow. Does she draw in that ridge of hair with a makeup pencil? Or is it menopausal hirsuteness, catching up even with gloriously pretty little Theresa, who was once so blonde, so fair?

Sitting in the audience, grim with recognition, I watched my sister recall – for the debauched entertainment of a roomful of strangers – the tedious and terrible events of the past. Our mother, our father, our brother, me: she took us all in her plump hands and made us fools and freaks again.

And she made it all seem so *funny*.

Do you know how easy it is to buy a gun?

I thought, for weeks, of just confronting her: of standing before her, slapping her face, spitting in her eyes, letting her know that it's *me*. I would sit for hours, thinking about what to do next, now that I knew where she was, and what she was doing. Gurdjieff says that man becomes attached to his own suffering. I was attached to Theresa.

Sometimes I was afraid. Of what she'd say, when I finally introduced myself. Said, "Hello, Theresa. It's me, Dee." I imagined her saying, in the most syrupy of tones, "Why, Dee! You haven't changed a bit!"

I went days without sleeping, days without eating, fainted more than once, didn't answer the phone, didn't wash my hair or do my sit-ups. Poured a bath and a big tumbler of vodka and sat in the steaming hot water with a big Henkels knife in one hand and the tumbler in the other, but of course nothing happened, obviously nothing happened. I went to an Oshawa rod & gun store and tried to buy a shotgun, but the proprietor sniffed at me when I didn't have my fack.

"My what?" I said.

"Your FAC, your FAC. Firearms acquisition certificate. This isn't the States. You gotta have permission. And you gotta register it, and…"

I thought about alternatives. Push her in front of a subway train (but she drove a car). Run her off the road, into a guardrail (but she had a big ol' Caddy, and I a little Mazda). I thought about hiring someone. But I wouldn't know where to start; contract killers aren't in the Yellow Pages. Killers are legend; killers are unreal; killers aren't everyday souls like Theresa. Like me.

I drove across the border in Fort Erie, bought a handgun, a .22 pistol. Brought it back across the border, sneaking it through customs. Easy. Like the song says: *easy*. I simply bought shoes and blouses too, so that I'd have something to pay duty on. They let me right through. I look so normal. I don't look like a monster.

And so I have a gun. The recipe's contents: opportunity, a weapon…and motive. Motive: something that moves you. Something that makes you take action.

Action. I will take action. I have sat still, too frightened and hurt to move, for entirely too long. Since that last summer: the summer of 1970, the summer after Woodstock, the summer that took the wind from my sails and the breath from my lungs and the desire to ever do anything but hide.

She took everything, by accident or by design. She left me only with the story of my life. And she's not getting that. It's not her life. It's my life. It's mine. Mine.

Mine!

Then

One

So when I was a kid, my Dad used to take us to the lake. Us Canadians, we know from lakes, eh? Right? There's always a lake. We're poxy with them. Millions of lakes. Zillions of 'em. And trillions of asswipes on those little jetrider things. Tell me, what's the point of a jetrider? Do these people think that running over loons is a good way to commune with nature? There should be a reward for folks with 30-30s who can just pick these guys off, like they're skeet. Bdang. Bdang. Got 'im.

Good to have a cottage, though, eh? When I was a kid, everybody had 'em. You had your city place, and you had The Cottage. Ours was in Muskoka. Yeah, okay, like everybody knows Muskoka now, but it didn't used to be fulla celebrities like Goldie Hawn and Martin Short building five-storey cedar palaces and multilevel boathouses with a slip for the fuckin' seaplane in 'em, and then whining that people keep driving by to stare. Of course they're staring, you stupid fuck, you built this big ostentatious Byzantine *castle.* If you didn't want to be stared at you mighta built something that didn't scream LOOK AT ME I'M REALLY FUCKING RICH. Just a tip: if you don't want people to stare at you, don't act like an asshole.

I should talk. Anyway, Barebones. Good name, by Muskoka standards. Muskoka generally has really lame lake names. You go to Haliburton if you want serious names, like Lake Kagashagawiggakoomanish, which is Cree for "fuck off with the jetrider, already." But Muskoka is fulla limpwrist names like Mary Lake and Fairy Lake and Lake Joseph. Except for Barebones. It got its name because when the settlers got there, they found this Indian burial ground, except these Indians didn't bury their dead, they put them up in the trees in little cots. So there's all these mossy, empty skulls staring out from the trees. *Great* place to build a summer resort.

So. Our cottage. Our cottage was a one-room cabin on a fucking *island*, no hydro or toidy, but lotsa water. Water all around. Five of us, in one *room*, man, every summer, all summer. And my mother insisted on cleaning this little one-room shack like there was

an inspector coming or something. She had
nothing better to do, I guess. Meanwhile, my
Dad was waging war on the wildlife, shooting squirrels and catching two-inch-long lake
trout. The only thing for me to do was play
seriously twisted versions of Cowboys &
Indians with this rat-thin little boy I knew,
who was my absolutely *bestest* friend, you
know how kids are, excuse me while I toss
my cookies. Anyway, we were, like, joined at
the hip, except there was a beyond-belief size
difference happening. I literally weighed
twice what he did – like some big ol' bull
dyke ventriloquist and her dummy. We
stopped traffic – I'm serious! People would
slow down their cars to get a better look.
You could hear my thighs slapping together
clear across the lake. That's how my parents
kept track of me, from the distant thunder of
my thighs.

But I still liked the place. Really. I understand the bay that I hung around in as a kid
is now gonna be developed for condos. Soon
the über-yuppies will be sunning themselves
on their poured-concrete common-use areas,
looking across the water to my island and
my cabin. I'm not sure I like that, either –
them all casting their covetous little peepers
on my hunk o' childhood rock, sizing it up
for subdivision and development.

They better watch out. I might sneak up

on 'em, one day, wearing a Brazilian thong, and lower their property values. Hey, don't laugh! I got the right.

After all, it's my lake, ladies and gentlemen, it's mine, mine, *mine*...

In the summertime, when the weather was very high, and very mighty, changing and untrustworthy (a storm on one side of the lake, but hot sun on the Mackenzie Landing beach, so we could watch the storm approach in a wall of black cloud and mist, like the spume from a volcano), we all lived on the island.

Summer began each year on the first weekend of July, when Canada celebrated Dominion Day and the Dad was released from his job as a school janitor. There was a long hot trip on Highway 11, watching the world change from city to country to wilderness pines, stopping only once for a gasoline fillup just north of Lake Kahshe. We'd have the year's first purchase of a Wilson's grape soda, *bottled in Muskoka using water from clear Muskoka springs!* We'd stop in Bracebridge, at the A&P on the main street, and pick up steaks for that night's barbecue: slabs of deep crimson flesh wrapped in brown paper and string, cut while we stood in the sprinkled sawdust that kept the bloodspray from the floor's narrow, warping, planks.

Then we drove on, farther and farther away. The Dad was behind the wheel for the whole trip – my mother did not drive – and Theresa and I shared the back seat, at least until I grew so large that she refused to sit next to me, lest part of me touch her. Whereupon she moved into the wagon's rear, where she could lie down and read her teen mags for the whole trip. David, on the occasions he was with us (home from university; and not working a summer job), sat in the rear of the wagon with her and played "Don't Think Twice" on his six-string. He played "Puff the Magic Dragon," and I always cried when the dragon's scales fell like rain, and he slid sadly into his cave. When I cried, Theresa reached over to pinch me and call me *suck*.

"Theresa, leave your sister alone," said the Dad.

Then, finally, three hours or more after we had crossed Steeles Avenue and left Toronto's outlying, monochrome boroughs, there was the reward: a splash of blue lake, sighted through the trees like a mirage, like Shangri-La. Freshly greened oaks and birches, wielding branches over the road and the Mackenzie Lodge buildings, the volleyball net beside the horseshoe pit, surrounded by a spectating crew of straight-trunked pines and twisted cedars. Blackflies, dozens of them, crawling in the hem of my hairline, and up my sleeves, making me feverish with their venom.

And reunion. Richard arriving with Big Dick and Auntie Alice, by boat from his cottage on Farmer's Bay, meeting me at Mackenzie Landing. He would be poised in the prow of his Dad's bowrider, the *Blue Meany*, skinny arms waving wildly, his mouthful of metal braces flashing in the sun.

"Dee! What snoo!"

"Not much, Richard! What snoo with you!"

Sometimes we had seen each other that very morning, back in the city, where we lived on the same street. We might only have been apart for hours, but we never felt comfortable apart.

Off we go together.

The first weekend of the summer blossoms like a Chinese lantern, plain folded cardboard at first, then full and colourful and brilliant, lit from within. We spend little time on the mainland, at Richard's huge and houselike chalet, preferring Blueberry Island, where we Grahams have our place. By Sunday morning, Richard and I are bug-bitten and sunburned, having spent all Saturday catching toads and putting them into our terrarium, which we start every year and lose interest in by the end of July, because the toads escape or snakes climb in and eat them (even though toads are supposed to be poisonous).

We find a big garter snake curled up and dozing in the bottom of the glass box, and we trap it in there with a sheet of wire screen. It's beautiful, with aligned scales like tiny roofing shingles, and a bright green head and a darting, inquisitive tongue. We feed it grasshoppers. But Theresa says we're cruel to keep the snake, and although we guard the box desperately, as soon as she can, she comes and tips it over, and our pet escapes.

"You guys are so cruel," she says. "The poor thing, trapped in a box."

We cannot understand how she can fly into paroxysms of joy over stuffed plush animals and poodles on leashes and fluffy yellow baby Easter chicks, when she is so consistently and powerfully unkind to us. She's a charged wire of a girl, older than me by more than two years, but still smaller, as is everyone my age (and even those three and four years older). She is, however, much larger than Richard, who is (as his father, "Uncle" Dick, calls him) a runt. Uncle Dick (also known as Big Dick, to the men), is himself a small man but a powerful one, like Popeye: a pugnacious little bantam-weight, six inches shorter than his wife, who finds it funny to whistle "The Baby Elephant Walk" every time he sees me.

When we complain about Theresa, the Dad says that all big sisters are rat finks. "Just say, 'sticks and stones.'"

And Auntie Alice says, "That little prissy-pants will never accomplish anything. You're better than she'll ever be."

And Brother Webster says, "The extraordinary are often ostracized by the ordinary. Pay her no mind, my pets."

And my mother says, "What do you expect *me* to do?"

Theresa is the Dad's pet, but unlike the snake, she enjoys being kept. She paints her fingernails and toenails with pink polish, and the Dad says she is pretty as a picture. He calls her his Darling and his Princess. He calls me his Dumpling.

"You two are soooo out of it," Theresa purrs
to me and Richard, through Love's Baby Soft lips.
"You know, nobody is ever going to like you. Ever.
Not your whole entire lives."

We believe her.

We get to stay up after dark, even though it's
almost ten before dark arrives and settles in. The
bugs drive us inside the cabin at dusk, but we
emerge again once night arrives completely, and
head down to the dock, which the Dad has been
repairing (as he has to repair it every year, for the
winter ice always damages, and often destroys, the
island's dock). The men – the Dad and Uncle Dick
– are often sitting by the firepit, enjoying a pipe or
cigar, watching the flames from the bonfire.

"How ya doing, kids?" the Dad asks.

"Fine."

From the dock, across from us, less than a
hundred yards away, is the rising slope of what
becomes the sheer rock cliff of Bald Face, lying
hunched in the night, with topknots of pine and
hardwood. Bald Face is the home of an Echo. We
can shout at Bald Face and hear it shout back, the
last two syllables of anything we say.

Knock, knock!
Knock, knock!
Who's there!
Who's there!
I asked you first!
You first!

We bring Richard's *How and Why Wonder Book of Stars*, and point things out. The water is ink, the cliff black, the forest dark, the night sky sprayed with stars. Ink, black, dark, stars. We swat mosquitoes and listen to the faint music from up in the cabin, where my mother and Alice play Judy Collins tapes on the battery-operated cassette player: "Both Sides Now," and Leonard Cohen's "Suzanne," with its tea and its oranges and its madwoman heroine. My mother sings a line or two, and Alice's laugh is raucous, appreciative.

We dip our feet in the water, and spread the book out on our knees. Using its maps we locate Ursa Major and Hercules, and then Richard finds Sagitta and tells me it's mine. He points out the three stars in a row and said, "That's your spine. You have a backbone of stars."

We try to find his constellation – Aquarius – but can't, which is strange, for according to the book, it's much bigger than Sagitta.

"I guess that means I don't exist," he says.

"Don't say that, ever."

Beneath the surface of the black water, our bare white feet are touching.

I met Richard in the school library, in the fall of 1963. We were in Grade 1, and he had just moved onto my street, although we had not been formally introduced, mostly because I never went outside except to scuttle back and forth to school. But we had already drawn attention, in those opening days of the year, since I was clearly one of the largest children in the school – already taller than my sister, even approaching the height of my brother, who was ten years older than me, and in the last year of high school already – and Richard was the smallest. He was so thin and tiny that he seemed wizened, like a child with progeria.

That day I was hiding from recess in the library, and I saw Richard there too, nose-down in a book. His glasses were outlandish, they were so thick and heavy; they dragged his face towards the page, where his nose brushed against the paper as he read, his lips moving as a low, soft growl emerged from his larynx. He explained later that the lenses were so thick owing to cataracts. I thought the word meant waterfalls and imagined that somehow, he'd damaged his sight in a near-drowning. I pictured him tumbling over rocks and rapids, his thin-skinned skull striking the exposed and multitudinous rocks.

He read aloud, but he read very fast. And so he sat, hunched into a question mark, grumbling like an asthmatic cat. I was somewhat afraid of him –

even tiny, timid-looking people had said some very cruel things so far – but I had never seen anyone my age who could read as well as I could. So I steeled myself and came to him.

"Hi," I said.

No answer.

"Whatcha reading?"

He lifted the book off the table to show me the cover. It was *The Jungle Book*, and not a kiddie-version re-write either; it was Kipling's original prose. I was impressed, for I myself had read only the *Classics Illustrated* version and a *Golden Junior* edition, but when I had tried to read what Richard was now gobbling up, I had been unable to cope with the language and the dense, insect-like print. Richard's *Jungle Book* had pictures: elaborate coloured plates with slippery onionskin protective sheets, a dozen of them, illustrating Mowgli as a baby, being looked over by the Seonee Pack of Council Rock, or Mowgli as a man, ramming the Red Fire down Sher Khan's gullet. And Hathi the elephant, who was not laughable but the True King of the Jungle.

"I'm Dee," I said.

"I know," he replied. "Dee, Dee, drink a cup of pee."

This was a popular chant – one of many I heard every day. I already knew the songs and calls, as if they were my nursery rhymes.

Which was not to say I was going to hear it from a spindly little half-blind shrimp who spent just as much time running for cover as I did.

"You poophead," I said. "Four-eyed poophead browner."

"You're a browner too," he said, not looking up, and not upset.

He read calmly on.

"How are you doing that!" I cried.

"Doing what!"

"Reading that hard book!"

He sighed the sigh of an adult – of a mother interrupted for cookies or to tie a sneaker – and closed the grown-up book. "I'm concentrating," he said. "Or I'm trying to."

He explained concentrating to me. It meant to take everything else away. "Like orange juice concentrate," he said. "It's got all the water taken away." He leaned forward, as if to impart a great secret. "It's great on vanilla ice cream," he whispered.

"Wow," I breathed. "*Really*?"

In the twenty minutes' recess, we covered a lot from there. Richard lived one house down from the corner, about twenty narrow houses from me. He was a January baby to my November, but those eleven months' seniority meant nothing in terms of size. He was a wasted, fish-pale boy; myopic, chinless, with eyes the colour of over-bleached denim. His lips were barely visible, and he kept them folded over his teeth, pressing them with his incisors. He developed this habit after Auntie Alice – his mother – painted his fingers with No-More-Bite, in an effort to get him to stop gnawing his cuticles into a bloody porridge.

He liked *Archie* comics and DC comics, but not Gold Key, and he particularly liked *Classics Illustrated. Classics Illustrated Juniors* were for babies, but he had some anyway. He did not like peas and he did not believe in God. His parents were agnostics. They did not go to church, but to the Unitarian Fellowship, where he went to Sunday School.

I didn't know there was anything other than church. Even Catholics had a church. But we Pentecostals were the ones who had it right.

"You better believe in God, or you'll go to hell," I warned.

"Hell's made up."

"It is not!"

"People made it up. Did, too! Every religion has a hell. Buddhist people have a hell, and Hindu people, and everybody." He frowned. "I don't know about Jewish people, though."

"What are Puddist and Hintoo and Joosh people?"

He reached to scratch himself between the shoulder blades, his arms so thin he could reach effortlessly. When my back itched I had to rub against a wall or ask the Dad for help. "I said already. Different religions."

"What religions? Where are they, then? How come they're not around?"

"They're all over. They just don't live on our

street, is all. Buddhists live in Tibet. They believe
in Carnation."

"Like for putting on your cereal?" I asked,
thinking of the tinned milk with the flowers on
the label.

"Nah, like getting reborn in a bug. Geez."

He'd found out about the Buddhists from his
Sunday School. At his Sunday School, they did
things like build plasticene dinosaurs and go on
field trips to synagogues. They didn't do Bible
study or colour pictures of Jesus suffering the
children. Instead, they went on field trips: Richard
had gone to a Hindu temple and had a string of
Buddhist prayer beads at home, which were genuine amber. I'd seen amber in the encyclopedia. It
was electric if you rubbed it right, and it held
insects as if they were preserved in museum glass:
golden, transparent, with a bug frozen inside, its
lacey wings spread in peace.

Richard lit up. "You know about amber!"

So he and I pretended to be trapped in amber.
Felt the goo-sap slide over us, trapping our feet,
and rising to our knees, and then our middles. We
pulled at our feet very hard, trying to escape. The
golden lava rose all around, to our armpits and
then our mouths, and it slid into our ears and
down our throats. It closed our eyes like wax.

Miss Whistler, the librarian, came over from
her desk and told us to both get up off the floor
and start acting like a little lady and gentleman,
instead of two ruffian clods.

We had lunch together, sitting on a bench by the wall, still talking about Superman and starfish and Rocky & Bullwinkle and Tootsie Pops and our mothers and his Brownie camera and sleeping in on Saturday and man-eating tigers and the merits of having the crusts cut off your sandwiches and how onions were disgusting. We walked home together, largely ignoring our escort of the other children, which was particularly noisy that day since we were a doubly tempting target. But it was easier to withstand their attention while we leaned together, talking.

He invited me in. And I met his mother, my Auntie Alice. For she said, "None of that 'Mrs.' stuff. Call me Auntie."

She was huge. Even I had to look up to her. But she said nothing of *my* size. I braced myself for the usual line of enquiry (assembled my answers: *Yes, my dad is very tall. No, my mother isn't. No, my brother is normal. So is my sister. It's just me.*) But she never asked.

Auntie Alice wore blue denim dungarees rolled up above her knees and a man's T-shirt, which was covered with brown and red smears of clay, which at first I thought were poop and blood. She wore no shoes around her house, and the bare, scratched, hardwood floors were pockmarked with her multicoloured footprints, like interrogative points leading from room to room.

"I'm an artist," she explained. "That's why this place is such a bedlam."

"Bedlam's like the loony bin, like 999 Queen Street," said Richard.

"Geez, Richie, you sound like your ol' ma. I wish you weren't quite so colloquial, kiddo. Nothing's held me back like the way I talk. And of course biology. I'd've gotten so much farther with some of my projects, lemme tell ya, if I was a guy. No doubt in my mind, sister."

I didn't understand half of what she was saying. Sister? I wasn't her sister. A sister, to me, was a dreadful thing, full of bossiness and pinches and complaints about my appearance.

And what did she mean about the projects? We'd done projects at school and they involved reading about Helen Keller or the Plains Indians and then colouring in some Ditto'd sheets to glue into a duo-tang folder. Nor could she be an artist: an artist was a man at an easel, wearing a French beret, not a great big woman in a dirty shirt. So the word meant nothing.

She wanted to know about my mother. "What's her name?"

"Mum," I said.

"No, her real name."

"Jane. But even the Dad calls her Mum."

"*The* Dad?" she said. "Like, what's with the title?"

I couldn't tell the story I would eventually learn – that "The Dad" was his nickname, acquired from his habit in high school of calling everyone Daddy-O – so I just went quiet.

"He's the Dad," I whispered. "And she's Mum."

Alice mused on this for a moment or two. Then she said, "And what's your mum *like*?"

"She has yellow hair," I said. "She likes to clean up."

"Oh, brother," said Alice, rolling her eyes. "Why don't you kids grab yourselves a Kool-Aid and lemme get back to work?"

I felt as if I'd failed some sort of test, or at least, that my mother had. But what could I tell Alice? That Mum was always home; she wore her hair in a starched flip, like Laura Petrie's; that she showed me how to make my bed and sew doll clothes? After school she served a Satisfying and Nutritious Snack, and she wore a housedress and heeled slippers, even when she was washing the floor.

"I'm sorry about my mother," I said, near tears. "I'm sorry she's not an artist."

Alice practically exploded in her effort to comfort me. She dropped to her knees, throwing her clay-splattered arms around me, kissing me grossly on the cheek. "Aww, baby, I didn't mean anything like that at all! I just have a big dumb way of talking. Hell, your mum should come over for a visit. If she's anything like you, Dee, we'll be buddies for life."

"I'll ask her," I replied, not wanting to tell her that my mother did not visit, or accept visits, not even from church ladies. I had heard them com-

ment among themselves about the way pretty
Sister Jane kept to herself. Our household comprised us, and us alone. Our only visitors, by and
large, were Theresa's friends, but they were infre-
quent. Theresa usually went *out* to visit her many
friends, and had told me it was because it was
embarrassing to have to share a room with her
yucky baby sister.

"C'mon," said Richard. "I'll show you the
house. I have a telescope, you know."

Richard's house had a similar layout to mine,
but where my house smelled of Javex and Ajax
and Pledge and VO5 hairspray, Richard's smelled
of dust and turpentine. Where in my house we
took our shoes off at the door and put them in the
closet, and hung our coats neatly on the child-
level coat rack beneath the adults' in the closet, in
Richard's we threw everything on the sofa, and
kept our shoes on for protection from the dirty
floor. Where my family spoke in "inside voices"
that were lowered, almost reverential, in
Richard's house our voices tangled with the blar-
ing kitchen radio, the din of the black-and-white
TV, the hum of the kiln, and the whirr of Alice's
potter's wheel, over which she muttered salty
complaints in a very loud voice.

Richard grabbed a jug of Kool-Aid from the
fridge and two glasses that had once held Kraft
peanut butter. Mine still had a petrified crust
beneath its lip. "Upstairs," he instructed.

He showed me his mother's room (not his *par-*

ents', his *mother's*) where a double bed – unmade – shared the space with a dressmaker's dummy pierced with thousands of coloured thumbtacks, a multihued coat of mail on a headless and limbless woman.

"That's the Venus Domesticus," said Richard. "Mom worked on that for a week. Dad was furious because he never got fed, so there was one night he didn't even come home. Mom was really mad. You should hear them fight. Do your parents fight?"

I shook my head and ran my hand over the dummy's rubberized mosaic. "How does she use it to sew?" I asked.

"She doesn't. She's an artist. She does things to things. She does *projects.*"

"Is your dad an artist?"

"No way, José! He's an accountant."

"My dad's a janitor. At the *school.*"

"My dad's got an office."

"My dad works really hard."

"So does my dad. He's got *two* offices, one downtown on Richmond Street, and then he's got one here. We're not allowed to go in, but I can show you from the door."

His father's office was very neat. It had vacuumed broadloom in a dull, green, tonsured pile, and a desk with a blotter and a ledger, and a gooseneck lamp that I longed to touch ("Don't!" hissed Richard). The window, a front window, was narrow but had a nicely trimmed pull-down shade, with a small sofa beneath it, and a pair of tartan slippers waiting nose-to-nose on the floor. The wheeled wooden chair, which matched the desk, was tucked neatly in, and on the desk sat an adding machine with a lever to pull, like a carnival game. All his books had the word *tax* on the spine.

"Dad has insomnia," said Richard. "He sleeps in here a lot."

"What's that?"

"What? Insomnia? It's not-sleeping. Ma says that when you're a mess inside, it messes around with your sleeping."

"How is your dad a mess inside?"

Richard shot me a look, as if he was about to defend his father, but then he shrugged and closed the door to the office, rubbing the knob with the cuff of his shirt, to clean off the evidence we'd been there.

"And here's my room," he said.

Richard's room was more or less a bed in a wasteland of books and comics. But by the window was the promised telescope, which Richard informed me had to be sent away for, to the States. He could see Venus, Jupiter and Saturn. He had maps of the constellations on the walls, and paintings he had done himself, and a painting by his mother, of a lake with a dock, at night. She had sunk a moon and a peppering of stars into an indigo sky, and reflected those bodies in the water. I thought they were beautiful, like Merlin's gown might be, but Richard was unimpressed.

"It's not accurate," he said. "She got all the stars wrong. She put them just anywhere she felt like."

"She got the moon right. The man in the moon looks just like that – like he's screaming."

"Hey, did you know, by 1970, we're gonna be able to travel to the moon, by spaceship?"

He showed me a magazine, the size of a *Reader's Digest*, which was the only magazine my father read, and then only in the summer, when he was off work for all of July and August. I loved *Reader's Digest*, particularly the *Life's Like That* column, where people told funny stories of things that had happened.

Richard's magazine – *Incredible Science* – blared the headline, "A TRIP TO THE MOON! Your vacation in 1970!"

"Where do you go on vacation?" Richard asked.

"Vacation?"

"You know. You go away somewhere. Like, to a cottage? Camping?"

I shook my head. "No. The Dad has a vacation, but we stay here for it."

Richard mulled this over. "Then you can come to Barebones," he said.

"What's that?"

"The lake we go to. Barebones Lake."

"But what," I insisted, "*is* it?"

He opened his mouth to say something sim-

ple, even specious, but then his face clouded over
with a worshipful look, like those on the faces of
the few people at church who weren't praying to
show that they were praying, but because they
saw God somewhere. He smiled, revealing baby
teeth that were brown-yellow from neglect; when
his new teeth came in they would grow in askew,
dodging the remnant bad roots.

But it was a glorious smile. He swelled like a
bird about to sing, his fragile little breast rising,
his eyes widening with the effort to put into the
mundane crate of language the feeling of
Barebones Lake.

"It is," he declared reverently, "the best place
on Earth. Maybe you can come up there sometime.
I think Ma will let me have a friend."

The painting with the stars shifted and shimmered, and the ghostly grey face in the moon (just
a few *trompe l'oeil* strokes) stopped screaming
and instead seemed to laugh. This was the word I
had not yet had applied to me. *Friend.* I am going
to Barebones Lake, the best place in the world,
with my friend.

Richard – not understanding how things worked with my mother – thought that getting us to come to Barebones would be a simple matter of asking. After all, it was just autumn now; we wouldn't be going again until next June.

"It'll take a year to get Mum to say okay," I muttered. "If she would say okay ever at all. She doesn't like to go outside. She sure wouldn't like a whole big *bunch* of outside."

Richard and I chewed on this, as we became more and more dependent on one another. We became inseparable. I would phone him the moment before I left the house for school in the mornings, warning him I was on my way; he'd wait by his front window until I scurried up his steps, sometimes and sometimes not tailed by others. We had several faithful followers, who made a habit of waiting for us in the mornings, and although Aunt Alice more than once came barrelling out of her house like she was shot from a cannon, screaming at them *beat it ya little brats or I'll have yer guts for garters*, her objections never had any long-term results.

After school we would hurry back as quickly as possible. I could not run easily, being so large, but Richard could have. Nevertheless, he always waited for me. Often we arrived home with spit in our hair, with scraped knees, or with snowball slush melting in our ears. Alice, while comforting ("have some hot chocolate, ya poor little things," she'd say), her calls to the school and her forays out to find the villains had minimal results. Richard and I knew that putting Joey Steen and Ozzy Meighen into a week's detention would just mean that we'd be *particularly* badly hurt when they were set free. And besides, for every Joey and Ozzy, there was a Billy, a Raymond, a Tim, a Brenda, a Debbie, and on and on and on. Nothing could be done.

"Never mind," Richard would say, as he wiped the goober from my coat with a grimy tea towel. "Summer's coming. You wait'll you see Barebones."

For Alice, it was as if she'd taken on another child. I would arrive after school, phone my mum to say where I was, and then hang around until dinnertime. In Richard's house, I never smelled a dinner cooking; I had to know it was time to go home by the windup clock on his end table, or by the fact that the six o'clock news had started on the TV. In my house, dinner announced itself: not only could it be smelled coming (pot roast, meatloaf, fried chicken, pork chops, veal cutlets), but there were voiced warnings. *Your father will be here any minute. Are you ready for dinner?* We had to be dressed in clean blouses, with our socks pulled up to our knees. When the Dad arrived, we greeted him at the door; when we sat down at the table, we always said a grace. We remembered the absent and the hungry before we plopped Shirriff's mashed potato mix – blessed to our bodies – onto our plates.

Richard's mother didn't make a dinner like that. She would throw together French toast and bacon for Richard, explaining that his dad "ate at the office." His dad usually worked until almost bedtime, and then came home just in time to say goodnight to Richard, so I never met him, although I had seen him arrive home at night. He would screech his tires as he pulled up to a parking spot, always slamming the car door. A man not much taller than my mother, he approached his home with a grim head-down determination, his hat jammed low on his brow, his briefcase clutched tightly in his right hand, moving through the streetlamps' circles as if they were searchlights and he the target.

As summer approached, we grew more desperate: I had heard so much about the lake, and the cottage, that it seemed as if the decision were already made, for our families to summer there together. But we were also practical: we knew that our mothers would have to get together; they'd have to get along. I couldn't see it happening, for my mother was a firm-lipped, if very beautiful, creature, as delicate as a porcelain figurine, but as rigid as one as well. I wasn't sure whether she'd break if struck, or explode into cutting shards.

But Richard took matters into his own hands. My attempts to get my mother to invite Auntie

Alice over had been met with solid, if finely worded, refusals ("What a nice idea, but thank you, no"). In the face of this, Richard simply got sneaky. He told Alice she was invited over for tea the next afternoon, after school.

"Swell!" said Alice. "That sounds peachy."

Later, in his room, I pinched Richard hard. "You're gonna get us in such big trouble," I complained. "Why'd ya do that?"

"Because we gotta do *something*," he said.

"You're something's gonna get me sent to my room for a *month*," I said bitterly, but part of me was actually intrigued. It was as if we were playing with Richard's chemistry set – and now that the chemicals had been poured into the tube, there was nothing to do but wait for the reaction.

At 4:15 p.m. the next day, as designated by the three of us, Alice and Richard knocked on the door. I answered – my mother didn't answer unless she knew who it was – and let them in. Alice had brought Playbox cookies, which were my absolute favourite, thickly iced arrowroot-flour biscuits in colours so bright they seemed magical. She handed those to me, and then she called out loudly.

"Hey, anybody home! It's the Welcome Wagon!"

My mother was in the kitchen, which was no more than twenty feet away, but the swinging saloon-style kitchen doors didn't move. Nor could my mother be seen from where we stood, even though I knew she was at the sink. She must be pressed tightly against it so that the heel of her slipper or the hem of her skirt didn't show beneath the cut-off, louvered doors.

"Where's yer mum, honey?" Alice asked me, as she kicked off her shoes.

"In the kitchen."

Alice started off down the hall, her coat still on. She pulled the pack of Rothman's from her breast pocket as she moved, and stuck one in her mouth. "Hello!" she kept calling, determined to drive my mother from her burrow. "Where the heck are ya?"

Suddenly, in a burst of baby powder and *Evening in Paris*, my mother flung open the doors and stood barring the way to her kitchen.

"May I help you?" she said icily.

"Geez, ya scared me!" said Alice. She put one hand to her breast and mimed fainting against the hallway wallpaper. "Beautiful place you got here. Is the kettle on?"

"I wasn't *expecting* company," said my mother. "Perhaps we could make this some other time."

"Did the kids get the day mixed up? Geez, I knew I shoulda phoned." She glanced back at us, her eyes flashing with amusement. "Kids, you mixed up the day, you little beggars!"

She turned back to my mother, producing from her coat pocket a small curved bottle of golden fluid. "Well, never mind the tea, then. Grab some glasses and an ashtray, *Mum*. We'll close the kitchen doors and have ourselves a little shindig."

I saw on my mother's face a look I'd never seen on her before. She wasn't smiling – my mother was not a smiler – but her nostrils were flared and her eyes were wide open. There was a joke somewhere, a line of thinking that she understood, but I couldn't see what it was.

"All right," said my mother. "Let's do that."

She and Alice disappeared into the kitchen, and the swinging doors slipped shut behind them.

All afternoon Richard and I played upstairs – experimenting with my Midge and his GI Joe, and discussing the merits of various comics. We were enjoying Theresa's absence, for she was off visiting her "bestest friend" Cathy. There was much less to do in my house than in Richard's, for there were few books and the toys tended to be dolls and their clothes and more dolls, but we came up with a scenario where my stuffed Pekingese pyjama holder became Sher Khan and my three baby dolls became villagers' children. We coloured in my colouring books and finished off a whole book of connect-the-dots and drew a series of space monster drawings, and briefly contemplated raiding Theresa's vanity table, then discarded the idea as suicidal.

Our mothers' voices in the kitchen downstairs were oddly engaged. There would be the ominous *rumblerumble* of Alice ("That's her serious voice," Richard explained) and the peeping, almost-inaudible chime of my mother (whose name Alice repeated time and again, as if christening her: *Jane! Jane! Janey! Jane honey!*). In among Alice's roaring and hollering and slapping of knees, I think I heard my mother laugh.

My mother did not start dinner; I never received that warning scent of cooking roast. The Dad arrived home sometime around seven, and at once called for his family. I came bounding down

the stairs with Richard in my wake. I had warned
him about the Dad's size, but assured him he was-
n't scary – the Dad was someone who would cry
over *Lassie* episodes and birthdays and how pretty
my mother was in her Sunday dress. And he could
pick me up and carry me.

"He's big, not mean," I said.

"Big doesn't scare me. Mean I'm used to."

So Richard met my father, and my father met
Richard's mother, and then there was a moment
of name-exchanging, where the Dad introduced
Jane as if Alice hadn't even met her yet ("This is
my wife..."). Jane gave Dad his pipe and his
Telegram, promising that supper would be ready
immediately, and the Dad said not to worry herself, for it was a pleasant surprise to see Jane having a guest.

He retired to the living room, still wearing his
blue board of education coveralls. Instead of
returning to the kitchen, Alice followed him, sitting down in the armchair across from his sofa,
and lighting a cigarette from her tortoiseshell
case.

"So, I'm an artist," she declared.

"You don't say," said the Dad, rattling his
paper. "Jane, how's dinner coming?"

Richard and I hovered in the foyer, sitting on
the bottom riser of the stairs heading to the second floor, watching them at an acute angle. Alice
sat forward in her chair, perched on its edge, legs
spread, elbows on knees.

"So where'd you and Janey meet?"

"High school," said the Dad, putting his paper down with some resignation, and launching into his how-I-met-my-wife story. "She was the prettiest girl in the school. Boys followed her everywhere. But in the end, she chose me. Plain ol' Dad Graham."

"You're not so plain," said Alice, flatly. "You're what, six-five? Didja play football? Captain of the team, were ya?"

"Uh, well, not captain, but I played," he said. "Anyway. She had boys following her everywhere, and…"

"And she quit school to get married," said Alice, in an odd tone. "To the dismay of the hordes of drooling pimply teenagers following her around."

"I don't think we were *drooling*," said the Dad, frowning. "And I'm sure she was used to the attention." He determined to change the subject. "And how did you meet *your* husband?"

Alice lit another cigarette. "Here in Toronto. At U of T."

"There to get your MRS degree, eh?"

"I was a student, Dad. On scholarship. I'm from out West – just outside Calgary."

"What did you study – domestic science?"

"Fine Arts and Drama. Did okay. Won prizes. Thought I'd get someplace, but not yet."

"But you're married, now," said the Dad. "You got someplace indeed!"

"I *had* to get married, Dad, if you catch my drift."

Richard and I glanced at each other, frowning. *What's she mean?* he mouthed at me, and I shrugged in reply. Maybe there was a law about getting married, that we hadn't heard about yet.

Alice had more talk in her. She told of where she'd met Dick and how they'd been hit with a bolt of lightning and how Dick had always gone for the tall ones with the flair, ya know how opposites attract?

"I do indeed," said the Dad, glancing almost reverently at the kitchen.

There was a silence. "I guess we better get going," Alice said at length. "I gotta feed the Lord of the Manor. He gets home eightish or nineish, depending on the workload. Puts in twelve-hour days, six days a week sometimes, but geez does the dough pour in."

"Not to ask a personal question," said the Dad, "but why are you still on *this* street, then?"

"Aw, it's the cottage," said Alice. "He pours all his time and money into that place. Takes the whole summer off. Soon as Richie's outta school, we're outta here. We just head right up to Barebones Lake." An idea seemed to strike her. "You guys oughta come up sometime."

Richard and I, eavesdropping from the bottom stair, grabbed each other's hands in hope.

"Barebones?" said the Dad.

"Yeah," said Alice. "There's a place there,

Mackenzie's. Rents cabins on the shore, has an island for rent too, I think, but that's pretty rustic. We've been going up for years, since before we even had Richie. College friend of mine introduced me to the place – he's installed in his family cabin up there. He's a teacher, so he gets the whole summer off, too."

"Where is it?" said the Dad. We could hear the interest in his voice; by now Richard and I were like contestants on *Let's Make a Deal*, waiting to see what was in Box Number 2.

"Muskoka. You know Muskoka?"

"I love Muskoka. Beautiful. Used to hitch up there, some summer weekends, when I was still in high school. Then I got married, got work – and that was that."

"Well, like I said, you can rent a spot from this Mackenzie fella. You know, it could be fun – if you took the island you could get it so cheap you could stay there all summer."

"All summer…!" The Dad nearly sighed the words. Monty Hall lifted the box from its stand, giving us a peek of the big prize.

"We'll have a blast," said Alice. "Barbecues, water-skiing, that sort of thing. You and Dick oughta get along. He's got no one to play with – my teacher-friend, Bill Webster, well…he's not really a man's man. Dick could use someone to boat with. You like boats, right?"

"Oh, yeah, sure, but I never owned one…"

"Dick's got one he loves more than me," said

Alice. "Which isn't saying much." Suddenly she began an outpouring of information, as if she were a salesman and the buyer had his pen posed above the dotted line. "Janey'll love it up there. Janey'd love my teacher-friend, too; he brings out the best in people, 'specially the quiet ones – Dick calls him Brother Webster because he lives like a monk, never a girlfriend, but Webby doesn't mind being teased like that – he dotes on Richie, brings him books galore – Janey'll get brown as a Butterball turkey, lazing around in the sun, she works too damn hard, Dad – hey, Janey!"

My mother drifted into the room, clutching a dishtowel.

"What you and I were talking about, the cottage thing? Dad thinks it's a great idea. That cabin on the island could do for four people…"

"Five," said the Dad.

"I thought you just had the two girls – Dee and the nine-year-old sister…"

"No, there's also David." The Dad sucked harder on his pipe. "He's got a job after school. Works evening shift at the post office. He's saving for university next year, more than a year ahead of schedule. He skipped Grade 3. Did summer school to get ahead. Don't know where he got his brains from. *I'm* sure nothing special upstairs."

My mother looked at the tea towel she was twisting in her hands.

"Yeah," said Alice, very quietly. "Can't imagine where he got those brains."

At that moment, the door flew open, and in burst Theresa, home from her visit with Cathy. Even at nine years of age, she could command all attention: she cast a basilisk's glare at me, ignored Richard, and pounced on the adults.

"Hi, Daddy!" she squealed, popping her beret onto a clothes' peg as she flung herself at the Dad. He scooped her up and smoothed her slightly staticky hair, kissing her on the forehead and cheek, making big mmmmm-smacky sounds. I looked away, to where Richard sat beside me. He pretended to choke himself.

"Daddy," cooed Theresa, from her perch in her father's arms, "who's that *lady*?"

"This is Mrs. Holmes," said the Dad. "Say 'how do you do,' Princess."

Alice did not say, "Call me Auntie Alice." Instead, she said, "Geez Louise, the kid's nine years old." She said, "Quit mollycoddlin' her or she'll think she deserves it."

"But she *does* deserve it," the Dad protested, snuffling up a big nosegay of Theresa's fine hair, as Theresa giggled and put her arms around his neck. "The prettiest little princess in the whole world. Right, Terry-Bear?"

"Dad, you're overdoing it," said my mother quietly. "Theresa, run upstairs and wash for dinner." Without turning to me, she added, "You too, Dee."

The Dad set Theresa down. As she scampered up the stairs, she hissed at Richard: *four eyes!*

"Theresa!" cried the Dad. "That's rude! Sorry, Alice, that's how big sisters are sometimes."

"I wouldn't know," said Alice. "When mine called *me* four eyes, I killed her and hid the dismembered body in the crawlspace. Okay, gotta run. Richard, you look like you could use a meal. And we don't want to rile your father by being late."

"Can we have chips and egg?" said Richard.

"Eww, gross," said Theresa, from the top of the stairs. "We're having roast beef because it's Thursday."

"Bully for you, kid. 'Bye, now, Dad. Janey, nice talkin' to ya. Next week maybe, like we said?"

"Absolutely," she replied. "I'm looking forward to it."

Alice signalled to Richard, with whom I exchanged secret (and amazed) gestures of delight, poking each other with excitement as he slipped out the door with his mother. I peered through the frosted glass window after them, watching their dim outlines as they headed down our walk, Richard leaning up against his massive mother's thigh. Now, it was just a matter of time: of waiting out the days and weeks and months, until we could go to Barebones, where I could lose myself.

Where I could lose everything.

The Dad often reminded us of how privileged we were, to have the island: to have a cottage to go to, all summer long. Others on our street might have banana-seat bicycles and PF Flyer running shoes, but they were obliged to spend summer downtown, whereas we were allowed to leave the narrow, gritty, overheated street, with its cars parked on both sides and its lawns drying up like parchment, and go up North, where it was cool and clean and you could see the stars at night.

Blueberry Island was shaped like a cat in repose, with its tail extended and slightly curled. The tail was a string of rocks, and it guarded a very small beach only twenty feet long and three feet wide – a narrow bar of granite sand, with a slow underwater slope leading towards the deep channel. The water on three sides of the island concealed rock shoals swarming with fingerling bass; the Dad kept the canoe at the island's far end, so he could get to the fish all the more quickly.

The island's cabin was just four walls and a roof, without even a ceiling, so that the joists and arches showed. Richard said it was living inside the ribs of a dinosaur, making it sound advantageous. Richard's cottage was a white pine palace, with a cathedral ceiling and an indoor flush toilet, which worked by pressing a foot pedal. Richard's cottage even had a TV, which brought in a single, grainy station: Channel 3 from Barrie, eighty miles to the south.

On the island, we all slept in the cabin's one room, with me on the bottom bunk and Theresa on the top, and the Dad and my mother in a three-quarter bed, and David (when he was present) on a narrow divan. In the kitchen-living-dining area, there was a woodstove on which my mother did the cooking in the morning, bacon and eggs every single day, and fish if the Dad produced one, or pancakes if he said that he felt like 'em. We almost always barbecued in the evening, but when it rained, my mother fried chops and heated up tins of Niblets corn and mushy, mould-coloured peas. Everything had to be tinned or kept in the icebox or the Coleman cooler, and every few days there was an ice run over to the main-land, where Mackenzie would haul a block of ice down to the boat, carrying the massive dripping chunk in a set of threatening, iron tongs. At the island, the Dad had to haul it from the boat to the cabin, and then up into the ice compartment, all of which took even a man of his size a great deal of effort.

Where Mackenzie had built the island's dock, the channel – an underwater trench – was sixty feet deep, and across from the dock, slightly angled, was Bald Face. Bald Face was two hundred feet high at its apex, and reportedly descended a further two hundred feet underwater. Brother Webster said there were places they'd dropped a line three hundred feet, and never had it scrape the bottom.

Brother Webster knew everything. He visited the island, from his cottage across the lake, but often stayed with me and Richard, or with the women, more than he did the men. He loved my brother David, and always appeared whenever David was visiting, always with his own guitar, asking David almost shyly if he'd like to jam a little. He was quieter than the Dad and Dick, but not frightened by them; he would sit back in a lawn chair, when he was with the twosome, noticeably apart from them, as if he were watching *The Honeymooners* on TV. Sometimes he said things, sharp things softly delivered, which sounded like both insult and praise.

At summers' beginnings we had to pay the rent to Mr. Mackenzie, who stood as tall as the Dad but who was weasel-thin. Mackenzie smoked a pipe, which smelled, and he cleaned fish, which smelled, and he filled the outboard engines of the boats with gasoline, which smelled, and he sweated, which smelled. The Dad called James Mackenzie *a good egg* and *the salt of the Earth*. Mackenzie called the Dad that big dopey city fella, sometimes to his face.

He said things to my face, too. "She's a healthy little thing, ain't she?"

"Sure is," replied the Dad.

"Any healthier she'd be two people."

"Yep," said the Dad, in the voice of the

which-way-did-he-go sheepdog from the Looney
Tunes.

"Look at the size of her. Big as a sow. Could
use a week of tea an' toast."

"Aw, now, Mackenzie…"

The Dad would follow James Mackenzie into
whatever building the man designated as a place
of business at that point in time. The Dad would
write his cheque, balancing the chequebook on a
tacklebox or a boat hull, and tear it off neatly, ten-
dering it to James Mackenzie, who always made
the same joke. He dropped it on the floor.

"Didn't bounce. Guess it's good."

After that ordeal, the place was ours – but not
"ours" in the way our car and our house and our
clothes were "ours." We had to park in the public
lot at the Mackenzie Landing, and get our key
from Mackenzie. Even Brother Webster, whose
cottage belonged to his mother, could call it his
own, and discuss with passion its family history,
although he did say that the Sword of Damocles
hung over his head in that regard. Any day, he
said, he might be cast out of paradise, for his
mother (who was in a nursing home) had left
instructions in her will that the place was to be
left to Webster's sister, who didn't even want it.

Brother Webster coveted our little island. He
spoke about owning it, and building on it, someday, which would always make the Dad bristle a
little. I asked the Dad about it once – why we
couldn't own our island.

"We can't afford it. I'm just a poor working man. But we will. Just you wait."

Brother Webster said he'd have competition. "That's a tiny Eden, that island. Remarkable geography, good cover, darling little beach. A veritable *sanctum sanctorum*. I'd invest in it myself. My own little retreat won't be mine forever, many thanks to the family matriarch."

"Aw, c'mon, Webby, don't kid around."

"Forewarned is forearmed, Dad. Mackenzie will sell to the man with the money. I don't see how you could manage to accumulate that much *bread*, to use the younger generation's phrasing."

"Aw, Mackenzie'll sell to me," said the Dad testily. "We're pals. Dick, Mackenzie would sell to me, right?"

"Why would you want the place?" said Dick. "Buy on the mainland. Better investment. None of this toodlin' around in a boat, having to go across the water to buy a deck of smokes."

"But if I got the money together, he'd sell to me."

"I dunno," said Dick. "Webby's right. Mackenzie plays with his property like he's playing Monopoly. You shoulda seen how he put the screws to me when I bought my lot, right after he subdivided the bay. My bet is you'd have to be richer than Rockefeller."

I didn't know who Rockefeller was, but I loved the name – he must be a Canadian, from the north, whose name matched the terrain.

Rockefeller was the man who owned all the land, all the beautiful naked stone: the granite and gneiss and feldspar and veins of rose quartz; the sheets of mica that could be peeled off like paper, yet were still stone. Arteries of long-dried lava, memorizing how the rock had once split, and how its crevasses had filled with molten stone, so that eons later, we could trace the path of the extinct river. It was like having a foot in two worlds. Richard and I could liquefy the stone again with a word, and stand astride a bed of bubbling ore, leaping over it when we deemed it dangerous, and sipping from it when we were playing Magmamen. A prop of stone.

Richard and I were not the only ones with games. Brother Webster and Big Dick and Auntie Alice all came to play with the Dad on his island. Theirs were better cottages, of course, but the island itself was for play. There was no better spot for diving (from the dock) or wading (at the small, almost miniature, beach) or sunning (in the clearing by the firepit) or fishing for lakers and smallmouth (at the island's rocky, reefy, far end). Even the constant repairing of the dock and upkeep of the paths and the cabin (which needed whitewashing almost every year) became play, to the Dad and Big Dick at least, who would sing while they worked and sing while they water-skied and sing while they built the bonfire. They would throw remarks back and forth, cracks about

Diefenbaker's jowls or American bomb shelters or
Judy Garland's latest jailbait boyfriend, upping the
ante until someone had been wordlessly acknowledged as having made the wittiest remark. The
women fed them a steady stream of sandwiches:
meat-macaroni-and-cheese loaf, with tomato
slices, on white bread. There was a constant need
for sandwiches and beer.

Occasionally aided by Brother Webster, or
even more rarely by my brother David, who for
our first few summers at the island was a semi-
regular visitor, the men would hammer things
together and organize boulders in a trim for the
pathway. They would gather up the winter's torn
branches and spent leaves and burn them in the
firepit. My mother did laundry by hand and hung
the wash at the far end of the island, only a hundred yards away, but where the tree cover was
thinnest and the breezes fresh. Alice watched her
work, smoking and talking and sometimes handing her a clothespin. They talked, constantly,
without pause, sometimes in low and solemn
voices, and sometimes laughing madly, as if they
might break out dancing from sheer hilarity.

Theresa did not love the island. She lived for the
mainland, home of the Mackenzie Lodge Porch
Gang and Ashleigh's Snack Bar (which had a jukebox!). The Dad would drop her off at the government dock at Mackenzie Landing, taking himself
away from his designated fishing holes, in order to

satisfy her incessantly vocalized need; she would either arrange to stay overnight with a friend or would find her way home by dinnertime, riding in the nose of someone's square-stern rowboat or Seaflea. She learned to paddle our canoe, but the Dad would only let her go ashore on days when the lake was calm, and those days could be rare. Even one full day on the island with us would cause her to bite her nails and twist a lock of her hair around her forefinger, until the flesh turned an inflamed red. She would lie in the sun on the dock, hissing and snapping at anyone who came within range.

"I'm so *bored*," she'd say. "This place is dullsville. Nothing's *happening*."

Once ashore Theresa always left us at once, springing away from us like a dog freed from its leash. "I'm going to a pyjama party at Wanda's!" she'd cry, and the Dad would holler into her wake, "Home for dinner tomorrow night, young lady!" Sometimes she would obey, but there were scares when she did not appear, and searches performed from cottage-to-cottage, dock-to-dock in the nine-horse, *have you seen Theresa?* She was always found, at a beach party or hanging around the landing with the Porch Gang, and although the Dad wasted a lot of worry and perspiration about her, he always found her alive.

The Porch Gang was the biggest reason that I left the island only when the Dad did. In the city, Richard and I traded houses, playing in one and then the other, but at Barebones we stayed entirely on the island, largely because of them: a bevy of exuberant, cultivated cynics, ages almost-thirteen through nearly-eighteen, who had accepted Theresa unreservedly, as soon as she turned twelve. They were mostly the children of lodge guests, but there were imports from all over the lake – ennui-saturated teenagers desperate for anything urbanesque. In trios and octets they sat, splayed across the wide-open, broad-floored wooden porch of the Mackenzie Lodge, feet on the railing, being annoying but not outrageous, so that they never crossed anyone badly enough to be shooed away. They played scratchy music on their transistor radios, catching the last beams of the Huntsville station as it died into the wilderness.

When the boys called out to us, they said the usual things – Richard was *four eyes* and *runt*, and I was *pig* and *dog* and *cow* – but sometimes the girls spoke as if concerned for my future.

"Imagine what she'll look like when she's twenty."

"What a mess."

"Someone should *tell* her. Someone should *do* something."

"Just plug your ears," Richard would say, when my strength would falter. "Keep walking. That's it. Keep going."

On the island they couldn't touch us. On the island I was Wolfgirl, the lycanthrope (a word provided by Brother Webster, who could always pro-

vide a word), and Richard was Silverheels, after
the actor who played Tonto. Silverheels was an
old Indian brave who had discovered Wolfgirl as a
baby, shivering in the bushes. She was a white
baby whose settler parents had been killed by a
rogue bear. Silverheels adopted her, and trained
her in the ways of the wild, but she was rejected
by the other children because of being a paleskin
and all. Then one day a whole bunch of white men
came and killed off all the Indians and all that
were left were Silverheels and Wolfgirl, who fled
in a canoe to the mysterious Blueberry Island,
which was rumoured to be the home of evil spir-
its. It turned out to be true. Every full moon,
Wolfgirl would begin to howl, and Silverheels,
being very wise, realized that she was under the
spell of lycanthropy.

Owwwowoowowowowow, howled Wolfgirl.

Wolfgirl would growl and rub against
Silverheels. "Easy, dreaded beast," he would say.
"Soon the moon will pass from sight, and you will
be human again."

We recorded the tales of Wolfgirl and
Silverheels in various forms: pencil-crayoned
comic strips, songs, neatly printed stories on
Playtime Doodler newsprint, "published" by
being torn from the pad and stapled onto a cardboard backing. Our poems were always in precise,
Kiplingesque meter. Sometimes we showed
Brother Webster, who declared that we were born
writers. He brought us a collection of 10-cent

Pocket editions of Jack London's tales, and an old *Canadian* magazine that reproduced *The Cremation of Sam McGee* (he mistook our delight over the London for an interest in the gold rush, where in fact we were intrigued by the shift in Buck from sane dog to wild wolf). But we still enjoyed Robert Service. His poems were easy to memorize, and we would take turns reciting them to each other, trying to recall every word.

Since I left Plumtree, down in Tennessee, it's the first time I've been warm...

We particularly liked the illustration of the resurrected Sam McGee, which was a reproduction of an oil by some underpaid commercial artist, who'd managed to grace McGee's face with a leer of spectacularly bonkers proportions. The glow of the fire all around him, and the coals on which he sat, generated true heat.

We also were amazed by the narrator's resolve to haul his dead companion so far, in order to fulfill his dying wish that he be cremated.

"Would you do that? Lug a dead person all that way, just to keep a promise?" I asked.

"Depends on who the dead person was."

"Me. Would you lug me?"

"Yeah. I'd lug you."

"I'd lug you too."

Because of being at Barebones all summer, we missed things. We missed Canada's Centennial celebrations in 1967, and Man and His World in

Montreal. We never learned the "Ontario" song or planted a Centennial garden; we never went to the Canadian National Exhibition; we'd never paid a dime-a-ride at the mobile carnivals that set up in plaza parking lots, their creaking roller coasters and merry-go-rounds both rickety and dangerous. We never went to the public pool at Christie Pits, to join a crowd so populous that little water could be seen through the swarm of heads. We did not ride the ferry to Centre Island, or fish in Grenadier Pond, or learn to ride a bike. We were without television and largely without music. We didn't know about what the hippies did to Sharon Tate. So, when we returned to the city each September (still shocked and betrayed by summer's sudden end), we were doubly marked. Not only did we appear strange, we *were* strange. We spoke only each other's language; played each other's games; clung to each other as the winter crept in, cold and hungry and as long as forever.

In the winter, we would sometimes meet at night, in the crunching snow in the back alley behind the garages, and try to see the stars. But Richard's eyes were too weak, and the lights from the city wiped the stars away.

"But look, Wolfgirl," he said, to comfort me. "There's the moon."

Owww, I would say. In the city, the howls were different.

In July of 1969, we went over to the Holmeses'
cottage in midweek, to see the Apollo 11 Moon
Landing on the Barrie station. Richard was already
thirteen; I had not yet had my thirteenth birthday.

The Dad drove us over to Richard's in our
rented cedarstrip boat; Theresa ran away; Big Dick
and Alice served Nuts 'n' Bolts and chilled
Labatt's 50 ale. Brother Webster dropped by
because he wanted to see the landing, but was
tense and clippy all evening, lurking in the
kitchen with the women while the men argued
about the best way to coax a signal out of the sky,
using a straightened coat hanger attached to the
television's rabbit ears.

I was given a cream soda and a box of Pink
Elephant popcorn. Richard, by then, could not
have any, but he had a Tab on ice and gamely pretended it didn't taste crappy. The men continued
to bicker about the TV, and the Dad chased the
irascible signal around the room, waving the wire
extension elliptically about, while Big Dick
barked, "That's it!" and "That's better!" and
"Right there! Good!"

"Got it!" hollered the Dad.

"Oh, huzzah," said Brother Webster, com-
mandeering a space on the floor with us kids.

Bonanza – which we often had driven over to
watch on Sunday nights – always came in fuzzy
and weak, but the moon landing came in doubly

so, for the signal was not only travelling from
Barrie but from the moon itself. I was unimpressed; it looked like white fuzz to me. But
Richard was so excited he couldn't sit on his bum,
crouching instead on the floor directly in front of
the set, earning his father's wrath.

"Get outta the goddamn way, Richie. Jesus in
an ape suit."

"I can't *see*, Dad..."

"Speaking that way to the children will have
repercussions," Brother Webster observed.

"Aw, get lost, Webby. That psychology bullshit bores me silly. Lookit this reception. Jesus,
it's the moon landing, you'd think they'd be able
to come up with better reception."

"The signal has to travel two hundred and
thirty-five thousand miles, Dad," said Richard.

"Arise, fair signal, and bring the evasive
moon..."

"Ya know what?" Big Dick said, rising from
his La-Z-Boy. "Betcha it's fake. Betcha the
Russkies put the fear of God into the Yanks, and
the Yanks knew they had to catch up, but they
couldn't. So they faked it. It's a movie set somewhere. That's why we can't see shit."

"Dick! Language!" called the Dad.

"I'm serious," said Dick, but he sat down
again.

The party went on as I ate my box of pink popcorn and put the Lucky Prize (a green plastic ring)
onto my pinky finger. Richard watched the land-

ing, mesmerized, six inches from the TV ("Christ, Richie, move *back!*"), straining to hear what the astronauts and the newsmen were saying. Uncle Dick yelled, Auntie Alice yelled, and the Dad objected (almost yelling), and Brother Webster straddled the fence, trying to keep peace, pointing out that the kids were trying to listen, and it was good educational TV. My mother sat with her ankles crossed, looking like Queen Elizabeth at a very important but somewhat unpleasant foreign ceremony, perhaps one involving ritual circumcision and the consumption of goat eyeballs.

Outside, beyond our reflections in the blind, black windows, the loons wept. When the landing was over and there were only grey men on the TV, talking, Richard and I crept out into the dark and nosed our way down the path to the lake, and out onto his dock. It was chilly and damp but the night was clear enough to see the moon and the billions upon billions of stars. Some of the stars shot across the sky, leaving visible trails like brushstrokes. Richard squinted at them through his thick-lensed, horn-rimmed glasses.

Back up the hill, behind us, the lights shone from the cottage, and someone put on the hi-fi, Perry Como singing "In the Cool Cool Cool of the Evening."

"Faked!" cried Big Dick from the hilltop.

"Oh, Dick, do shut the fuck up."

"Language!"

Richard and I lay down on the dock, hanging

our heads over the end, where the water was way over your head. We dandled our arms into the black liquid, which felt warm because the air was so cool. The moon was in the water, too. A second moon, accessible it seemed, for we could surely swim to it.

Who could guess what lived in the water? Angler fish with luminescent lures on their prognathous, lumpy jaws; the coelacanth; Nessie herself. Or a trout like the one in the Royal Ontario Museum, bloated and white from its hundred years of life three hundred feet down, weighing sixty pounds, dying only when it was dragged up from its home.

In the summertime, when the weather was high, we could reach up to touch the sky, by lying belly-down and dangling our fingers deep into its inversion.

Two

You think you've suffered? Fuck off, you
have not. You should see real suffering. Try,
uh, bowel cancer. Never mind having to
carry your shit around in a purse for the rest
of your life. Bowel cancer fucking hurts. But
what do we hear about instead? Syndromes.
Like irritable bowel syndrome. Doesn't
sound very fucking serious. Sounds like the
bowel's just a little annoyed. It got up on the
wrong side of the bowel bed. What would an
irritable bowel say, anyway? "Oh, god, today
I just don't *give* a shit."

Then there are the disorders. Post-
traumatic stress disorder. Well, like, fuck off
with the trauma thing. It's amazing what
people consider traumatic. You could call
your bad haircut a trauma. A run in your
ten-dollar pantyhose. Someone farted on the
subway. Someone Looked at Me Sideways
Syndrome.

My favourite is panic disorder. Well,

yeah, d-uh! Can you imagine *ordered* panic? "All right, everyone, line up. Once we're all in order, we'll panic. Move along smartly, please, we're trying to start a panic here."

Then there are the various eating disorders. I mean, *really*. How can you fuck up eating? It's not that tricky a concept. Trust me, you don't even have to use your hands. You can stick your whole face in your cream of wheat, and just suck. But noooo! There are clinics for eating disorders, where they ship teenagers whose biggest problem is they won't stop puking up their lunch. I'll tell you what. Stop paying them so much *attention*, and they'll fucking stop puking.

Yeah, yeah, very funny back there. I'm *fat*. You figure it out all yourself, or did someone help you with the math? But you know what? Being a fat broad of forty-five is great. It's watch out world. I can say anything I want. I can tell good-looking men how stupid they are and not worry because they wouldn't date me anyway. I don't count calories, run laps, wear control-top pantyhose, or own a pair of Nikes. I don't agonize over my multiple chins and I don't buy the low-fat, frozen, coloured water at Baskin Robbins. I go straight for the 90 percent butterfat shit. And this is supposed to mean I have an eating *disorder*? Fuck that. I'm not the one making sacrifices to the great porce-

lain god after every forty-five-calorie meal.
I'm one fuck of a lot less disordered than the
dames at Bally Fitness, who treadmill themselves into apoplexy three times a week. You
know, in Dickens's time people would rather
die than go live on a poorhouse diet and
work on the treadmill. Now we pay for the
privilege.

There was this kid I knew growing up.
This kid was always a skinny rake, but geez
could he sock back the food. It turns out,
eventually, that he's got really bad diabetes.
And I didn't think, when I heard about it,
"Holy fuck, man, he could die!" Hell, no. I
thought, "Poor kid can't go to Mr. Donut
anymore."

Now *that's* suffering.

Eating isn't a fucking *disorder*. Gluttony
is human nature. Eat, drink and be merry,
because tomorrow we're packing up our bad-
tempered bowels and hitting that treadmill.
Life's a fucking workhouse, folks, right out of
Dickens, so eat yourself a Pop Tate's special.
We're gonna die anyway. Might as well do it
chewing...

Sugar, Sugar...

Richard was wasting away. We were like Jack Spratt and his wife. I kept getting bigger and bigger – up and out – yet Richard seemed to be shrinking. He also began to piss a lot, a thick yellow syrup (he reported), and had to excuse himself from class a dozen times a day to get one drink after another. He gulped the water like a horse at a trough; it dribbled from where his lips met the fountain spout, down his neck to the collar of his turtleneck.

"Let me know when it hurts," I kidded him. "'Cause that means ya got hydrophobia."

I had to carry his books home for him, because he was dragging so much he couldn't even keep up with me, and I was a very slow mover.

Richard had always been a good eater, but now he was ravenous, even outeating me. My mother's Satisfying and Nutritious Snack was always ready for us whenever we arrived home at my place, and we'd go through that and then more. She would, on occasion, make for us a Special Treat – banana boats (aerosol whipping cream on peeled bananas sprinkled with chopped walnuts) or chocolate Jell-O pudding with maraschino cherries in it (Richard called it Tumour Soup). He would eat three and four servings. And yet he just got thinner.

Auntie Alice had enrolled, part-time, at night

school, to take English composition classes. She said she hadn't explored that side of her artistic being. Which meant, Richard said, that she had brought home a lot more books and now not only said, "Kiddo, please, I'm working," but "Kiddo, please, I'm studying" as well.

So perhaps it's no surprise she didn't notice the state Richard was in, and that he very nearly died while in her care.

It was a long time coming, and yet it came all at once.

Richard and I were in the library at recess, immediately following an assembly to announce the winners of the Spring Athletic Games Badges. Richard and I didn't even receive Participation Awards, for he had given up trying after having twice had his pants pulled down in line for the Sit-Up Derby. I just hid in the bathroom and refused to come out. We had been friends for more than two years now, and this year – Grade 3 – we had the joy of being in the same class, where we sat together at the back of the room, drawing pictures of the island and caricatures of the other kids, among whom we could not count one other friend.

That morning, throughout the assembly, Richard had been speaking very strangely, and complaining that he couldn't see. He said there was a jelly on his eyes, but then he claimed to be walking underwater, like Aquaman, and I went along with the game. He seemed fine when he sat down at our table in the library, although he took a long time to read one page, and he was breathing through his mouth like a panting dog. His breath was sweet as syrup. He turned a page, looked at me, and said he needed some more water.

"Yeah, okay," I said, or something equally noncommittal, and then he stood up and then he fell down.

People falling down really do crumble. Someone who is tripped or pushed is prone to flailing, and I had certainly seen Richard be tripped and pushed. I myself had been shoved off my feet more times than I could count, and knew that the arms fly out, groping for purchase where there is none, and then striking the ground before the rest of the body. But Richard folded elegantly from the knees and at the waist and at the shoulders and the neck. At the time I had a toy, a simple articulated puppet that stood on a cylindrical stand, supported by the tautness of elastic strings which ran through its plastic body. When I depressed the base of the stand, the strings relaxed and down went the puppet. Richard went down like that, and he stayed down.

The librarian ran over and chafed Richard's hands and told me to go get the nurse, which I did, and the nurse came in and took one look at Richard and at his eyes and his gums and muttered, "I thought so, I knew it," and ordered the librarian to the office to phone for an ambulance.

As if there were a schoolyard fight, kids were gathering, and teachers from the teachers' lounge, crowding around and leaning over the long reading tables, displacing piles of books, and the nurse kept snarling at them. *Keep back, give him air.* I stood at his feet, watching his chest rise and fall, never thinking for one second that it might stop doing that. Even when the ambulance arrived, and they began thrusting needles into him and looping his arm with a blood pressure cuff, and talking in hushed tones as if they were in church, I wasn't worried. I got worried when the school secretary put her arm around my shoulders (something which she had to reach up to do), and spoke to me kindly.

"I'm sure he's going to be fine, Deirdre, don't you worry one bit."

I tried to follow the ambulance workers and the stretcher, but I was stopped. I can see now the looks on the faces of the people who stopped me, and can remember their names: Miss Whistler, the librarian, whose nickname was of course Miss Whisper; Miss Crawford, the secretary, who was a tubular woman of the same girth from collarbone to midcalf helm; Mr. Curtis, the principal, who looked exactly like Mr. Weatherbee from *Archie*; Mr. Harrington, the only man teacher in the school, who coached baseball for the Grade 6's. They blocked my way, and I looked into their faces, except for Mr. Harrington, who was probably six feet tall.

"Be a good girl now, Dee, and go back to your book."

"That's a good girl. My, your hair looks pretty today, with that red hairband."

"Dee, sit like a lady. That's a good girl."

"Bell in fifteen minutes, Dee. Good girl."

I went back to my book, and sat like a lady, preparing to read my book. It was still, and again, *The Jungle Book*, which by now I had virtually memorized (*they called her Raksha, the demon, and trembled!*). Many games Richard and I had created were based on the denizens of Mowgli's jungle, and we had scoured the libraries at school and on Bloor Street, pestering the librarians for similar tales of children who went to live in the woods. We had gobbled up the *Tarzan*s, but they hadn't stayed with us, because without wolves, the jungle was too foreign. Mowgli's wolves connected his life to our own forests. We had often talked about someday escaping into the woods to live with wolves. We'd be there, alone, together, and it would be so cool. We wouldn't come back to the city ever, not after Labour Day, nope. We'd keep adding on to our house, like in *Swiss Family Robinson* and *Robinson Crusoe* and *The New People* on TV.

I tried to read, but found that I had jelly on my eyes, and could not go on.

That Saturday – two days later – we got a visit from Alice, who was dressed in a cotton blouse and dark skirt, and a raincoat and rubbers. She carried a clutch bag from which the corners of Kleenexes peeked, like tiny escape artists. She gave me a hug as she passed, but said nothing until she reached Mum, who stood in the kitchen behind the swinging doors, waiting.

They talked, and I heard much loud crying from Alice, and much quiet soothing from Mum. "It's my fault, I should have paid more attention!" Alice roared, snapping her clutch open and shut. "He was pissing like a racehorse! I'm an educated woman! I should have known!"

Alice was going to the hospital to visit Richard, and since visitors were restricted to those twelve and over, I decided to produce a Care Package for Richard, like those advertised on television for the starving children in China. I retrieved from my room a dozen comics and a Playtime Doodler with some of our most recent notes and stories in it, and two ballpoint pens and a package of Laurentian pencil crayons (neatly sharpened), and the prized *Classics Illustrated Jungle Book* (which only reproduced a few of the stories, but was otherwise very satisfactory indeed). I also threw in the paperbacks of *Call of the Wild* and *White Fang*. I wrote him a letter, very quickly, telling him to get completely better because we can't live in the woods together if he's sick. Something might kill and eat him. I signed it *Wolfgirl*.

"Why, you little angel," said Auntie Alice,

when I produced the pile of comics and scribbler and pencils. "But he won't be able to use it yet."

"Why not?"

"He can't see very well and he's very sick." Her voice grew loud when she said this, trumpeting the news. "I'm going to lose my son!" Alice cried.

Mum took Alice's hand and squeezed it. "We lose them anyway, Alice," she said. "They grow up, go to school, never look back."

This took Alice aback, and shorted out her crying. "Humph," she said, blowing her nose into a smushed handful of tissues.

"I didn't mean to sound unkind," said my mother.

"You weren't unkind, Janey." She gathered a quivering breath, and took from me rather roughly the Care Package, which I'd deposited in a paper grocery bag. Her eyes were red, and her cheeks were flushed, but she was no longer actively crying. In fact, when she spoke, she was as calm as an Old Bailey lawyer.

"I think you're right. You got an excellent point there. But I'm not losing him yet, Janey, and maybe not ever. Dee, thank you for the books and stuff. I will read them to him until he's up to reading them himself."

I showed her to the door. As I let Alice out, she leaned over and whispered to me.

"I could sneak you in to see him," she said. "You could pass for forty, let alone twelve."

I shook my head. "That would be lying. God doesn't like lying."

Alice snorted. "Aw, c'mon, Dee, sweetie – you don't fall for that God stuff and I know it. I've heard you and Richie talking. You're smart as whips, the pair of you. It's almost creepy how bright you guys are. So if you're gonna say no, say no for a real reason."

"I don't wanna see him sick, I guess."

That seemed to satisfy her, but the truth was that I didn't want to go anywhere near doctors. Our family doctor was getting more and more agitated about me, giving my mother firm and fatherly lectures at my annual checkup (I was never sick, otherwise) about how she was failing to control my eating. I felt sorry for her, as she stood there looking right back in the doctor's face, her eyes blinking in metered recognition of the admonition. I wished I could help, but the fact was, she couldn't be expected to control my eating. I couldn't control it, either. It had, by then, a mind of its own.

Alice phoned later that evening. Theresa answered, as always. She thrust the receiver at my mother with a barely tolerant sigh. "*Please* don't be long," she said. "I'm expecting a call."

Richard was improving. He was out of danger. But he had juvenile diabetes. Auntie Alice was going to have to look after him carefully from now on. He was going to need to have needles every day, and not eat anything with sugar in it except at special times.

"How long is that going to go on?" I asked.

"His whole life," said my mum. "Or until God sees fit to send a cure."

"When's that?"

"No one knows but God, Dee."

"Auntie Alice says that God stuff isn't true," I announced.

"I know she does," said my mother. "She says a lot of things that get one to thinking. But now is not the time to question. Now is the time for faith. Have faith that He will never give us more than we can bear."

I said nothing more, and neither did she. But I suspected there were many things that would be more than I could bear. Like not having Richard, or the island. If it wasn't for summers at the lake, I would shatter like old china slipping from damp hands. Without those reliefs, how could I continue walking to school, weighed down by my own body and by the hovering pack of children? Without the calm of Richard, and the calm of the lake on an August morning, I might fall down and never get up.

Tomorrow was Sunday. I would ask God about it then. God would give me strength.

The next day my mother was in high gear, very bustling and organized, like the killdeer that ran about in the playground at school. We were all to go to church, even Theresa, who (in keeping with her Grade 6 status as almost-teenager) had lately been refusing to go.

"I'm not going," she avowed, from beneath her frilly blankets. "Why's it so important *I* go?"

"Because we are all going to say special prayers for Richard," Mum said.

"I thought women were supposed to keep silent in churches. Like, if God wants us to keep silent, then what makes you think He listens to us praying? Huh?"

"You can ask the Minister that," said Mum.

"Yeah, like, I would if I *cared.*"

"Perhaps you would like to spend a week without your record player?"

Theresa stiffened; pondered this. Then, at last, she rose morosely from her chenille crypt, and began to dress.

My mother outdid herself at breakfast. The prospect of praying for the Holmeses warranted toast, pancakes, raspberries, cream, bacon, cream of wheat and fresh-squeezed orange juice – a bribe for God's ear. The berries were frozen, but she had whipped the cream by hand. I realized she must have gone out on Saturday afternoon, outside of the scheduled weekly "shopping," to the corner store, especially to purchase cream.

I was in love with my pancakes. They were Silver Dollar Pancakes, from the *Betty Crocker Cookbook*, with each family member's names baked into the floury flesh. My pancakes spelled out D-E-I-R-D-R-E, because D-E-E would have meant I didn't get as much as THERESA or FATHER.

I had a boiled egg, my name's worth of pancakes, berries, cream, more berries, more cream, three glasses of orange juice, tea with enough sugar to form a syrup in the bottom of the cup, a bowl of cream of wheat with cream and sugar, three pieces of toast with cinnamon sugar, a banana and a half-a-grapefruit. I felt none of it. At one point, I glanced up from my bowl of cream of wheat, and saw Theresa staring at me.

"Mum, look what she's eating!" said Theresa.

"Leave your sister alone," said the Dad.

"She's a freak," said Theresa.

"Dee," sighed the Dad, "try to control yourself, honey."

"God loves all His children," said my mother, finishing the last few siplike spoonfuls of her cream of wheat.

I finished my own bowl of cream of wheat and started in on the toast.

Later that morning, we stood in the pews in church, we Graham women. The Dad was beside us, puffing his lungs in preparation for singing. He enjoyed the hymns; the first thing he did when he walked into the building was check the hymn board.

"Hot dog! 'Old Rugged Cross'!" he'd crow.

He had an impressive baritone, audible above everyone else, amplified by his height. He sounded as if he were barking orders, albeit musically. A drill sergeant, singing God's praises: *Are you washed in the blood of the lamb?*

The Dad had religion in his background, but not as seriously as my mother's. Mum had been raised a devout Pentecostal, and she only missed church if she were very ill or up north at Barebones, when the nearest church was a boat ride and a forty-minute drive away. She didn't show any passion for the faith, however, but moved precisely through the service, stiff-spined and stiff-skirted, hands in lap. But the Dad was in his element. He'd been raised Catholic – a very strict and solemn faith, by his description – and he much preferred the Pentecostals' shouting and singing and laying on of hands. He had even discharged popery from his heart and had himself baptized in the big aluminum tank beyond the chancel.

My brother David (whom I had not seen in so long I had forgotten when the last time was) used to sing in the choir, until the church organized a rock 'n' roll burning. It was years before he'd step inside a church again.

Today, Mum had dressed splendidly for church. Her plain turquoise cotton dress, with its pinched-tight bodice and square neckline, matched her Jackie Onassis–style pillbox with mesh veil. The men tried not to watch as she made her way to our pew, and she tried not to watch them not watching.

My own dress and Theresa's were catalogue purchases. Mum spent a morning each month shopping from the Simpsons' and Eaton's catalogues, although recently Theresa had been given a "clothing allowance" from which she had been making her own purchases at the Dufferin Plaza and even the new Yorkdale Mall, which had both an Eaton's and a Simpsons, and two beautiful wishing-well fountains. Theresa had been there twice now, with her friend Cathy's parents, who even treated them to a movie at the cinemas that were *right inside the building!*

Theresa had dressed for church as only Theresa could. My mother's promise that she would confiscate Theresa's record player had shaken her; she knew that on matters such as church attendance and household cleanliness, Mum was a determined opponent. The prospect of losing her makeup for a week, or the seizing of her transistor radio (Mum would carry it in her apron pocket in Theresa's presence, playing not the hits of 1050 CHUM, but the Andy Williams pap of CKEY), ensured compliance. So Theresa came to church; but dressed like the Whore of Babylon.

She wore a lime-green mini-dress that she had shortened to just below buttock-level (she had once been sent home from school for wearing it – the rule was that skirts had to be knee length, and the test was that when the girl kneeled on the floor, her skirt should brush the tiles). Over the mini-dress, she wore a hip-length crochet vest in bright yellow wool, and had pulled back her long hair with a yellow plastic headband. Her naked toes protruded from her slingback sandals like tongues, with a splash of glitter-pink polish on each tiny half-shell nail.

As for my outfit, I was draped in one of my mother's creations, an Eaton's "Stout Shop" dress altered with ribbons and ricrac. Mum bought clothes for me in whatever size would manage my measurements, and then tried to alter them into something a ten-going-on-eleven-year-old might wear. They were clothes designed for women who were seen to have given up on life – geriatrics, and victims of elephantiasis – and here I was, clad in a bag, singing of blood and garments and trying to be filled with the fire of faith.

We had prayers for the sick (Richard's name was held up like a sacrificial baby), and then the minister cleared his throat for the sermon. This one I had heard before, many times, because every now and then, the pastor felt that we had to be reminded of why we were at church. We were there because if we didn't accept Jesus as our personal saviour, we would end up in hell.

"The lamb of God, transfixed to the wooden tree of Golgotha, hung there to die! Brothers, sisters, see him suffering, and rejoice! For in his suffering he takes upon himself all the pain that we, as the driven creatures of the dark, are born to endure! Man that is born of woman is of few days, and full of trouble! Job 14:1! But in Jesus' holy sacrifice, we are saved! Saved!"

Okay, I thought, addressing God: so Richard's not saved, he hasn't done the right thing and accepted Jesus and stuff, and therefore you decided to make him sick with die-a-beaties. He has to take needles every single day. I want to tell you, God, that I think this is really unfair, because you make us all and you must have known when you made Richard that – first of all – he has a mum and dad who don't go to church so he's not gonna learn about accepting Jesus, just like the heathens and stuff who never hear the word of God, and – second of all – you knew when you made him that you were gonna give him die-a-beaties so it was like you planned the whole thing. And while we're on the subject, what you did to me really stinks too. Why did you make me so big? And why am I always so *hungry?*

I awaited the answer, while holding my hands beneath my chin, fingers threaded together in the talking-to-God posture. The minister, I had always been taught, would have the answer in his sermon, if I was open to it.

"For all have sinned and fall short of the glory

of God, brothers and sisters! We are soiled with sin, and only through the loving Grace of our brother Jesus Christ, god-made-man, can we move above the pain and suffering of this world and ascend to the holy, bright love of our Father!"

"Spare me," murmured Theresa, and a woman with a face like the butt end of a green pepper turned around to glare. My mother's gloved hands tightened on her clasp-closure handbag.

"And for those who will not repent – who deny God's glory – there is a lake waiting!"

A lake! My eyes flew open as I awaited Word From God.

"Yes children, a lake of fire is waiting! For those who deny God's grace, who move through their lives sinning and falling, sinning and falling, there is a golden slough of steam and fire! Around the pond of amber agony falls a rain of stones, through the howls and torment of the other sinners who failed to turn to Jesus! We are all granted everlasting life, children – the holy promise of everlasting life! Do we spend that life in the glorious sight of our Father, or do we join Satan and the other unbelievers, those who lived their temporal lives in sin and denial, not believing that one day, they would be bathed in the lake of fire?"

"Boooooring," said Theresa.

"For shame," said the pepper-faced woman, not turning around.

"Shhh," I said, to my own surprise.

Theresa pinched me as punishment for back-talk, but I barely noticed, for I could feel my faith boiling away in my outrage at the injustice of this. Richard was going to hell. Not only was he being punished on Earth for being an infidel, but if he had been *killed* by the die-a-beaties, he'd now be wallowing – burning forever! – in a lake of fire which God had built, to punish people *He* had made, when He *knew all the time* that they were going to fall short.

God has a plan, the minister said. But I could see that God's Plan had no variables: whatever was God's Will For Us was not a bendable thing. It wasn't negotiable. If God wanted us to suffer, then suffer we would. If He wanted us to be crip-pled, then we had to bear that as well. He never gave us more than we could bear, the story went, but He could make the load as heavy as He liked, having designed us to suffer under it.

It wasn't that God couldn't hear us. It was just he'd already made up his mind.

I looked at my mother, and my sister, and my father, who sat in an upright row, although I could see the Dad's thumbs twiddling, and Theresa had formed the fingers on both hands into the "bull-shit" sign.

And then, I heard what I needed to hear.

"Remember how our own Lord Jesus fought the devil! Remember how he struggled with him, refusing the temptation to show his powers! He lived in the wilderness, and he would not give in!

He would not give in! Out there he stayed, in the wilderness, alone..."

Driven out into the wilderness. The wilderness. It was a word that Richard and I used to describe our summer weeks, at the lake. We were not just *up north* or *at the cottage*, which is what the adults said. We were *in the woods* and *in the wilderness*. Suddenly, some of the things that Richard and I had been playing at began to take the shape of possibility. We had imagined much, and never taken it straight to heart, but if Jesus – a fictional character, according to Auntie Alice – could wander out into the desert and quarrel with the devil, surely we could figure out a way to build a house in the woods and live there together?

I imagined what it would be like, this house we'd build – this little fort. I wished I had my Playtime Doodler so I could take notes and draw pictures. Every year, Richard and I built a playfort; could that not be expanded into a house? Could we not live in the woods, like Mowgli? What about the cold? Well, the men in the Jack London tales managed, so could we. We could learn about fire and what wild foods to eat – there were lots of books on the subject of wilderness survival. God might have a plan, and so could I have one. And one summer (maybe not this one, but one summer soon), when our families came back to the city on Labour Day, they would be short two members.

But when? When to do it? It would have to be before high school. I couldn't bear the idea of high

school, imagining teenage demons with pitch-
forks pursuing me through the cafeteria, and
health teachers weighing me in public, and
Theresa prancing around at the apex of her popularity, pointing me out as the *monster who is my
baby sister*. But to do it right, to *survive* in the
wilderness, we would have to prepare, Richard
and I. We would have to plan.

I counted on my fingers. My deadline was the
summer before I'd turn fourteen. 1970. It seemed
such a magical number, 1970. A transitional hex
of a number, right up there with the mystic Age
Thirteen, which was the age at which children are
no longer children, but entering into being adults.

I itched with the freshness of inspiration, and
the desire to tell Richard right away. I would do
sketches for him, and lists of what to bring and
what to do. Here, I would say, this is what our
house will look like, and here is the ice cave
where we will store food that might spoil. Here is
the wild horse we will tame (it had escaped from
a farm, where it had been beaten daily and over-
worked almost to death, and we caught it and
tamed it and now we ride it all over the woods). I
could draw for him the site of our heaven, seizing
it in firm blue lines on the pages of my Playtime
Doodler, where it would grow and become as real
as anything in the Bible.

We could make this happen. Okay, so we'd
have to wait, and it would take a lot of planning,
but we could start this very summer. Richard

would be out of the hospital by then. The needles thing would be a problem, but we'd figure that out. Maybe he could find a friendly doctor who would keep the Wilderness Children's secret, who would heal Richard and deliver food to us in the cold months...

"Quit wiggling around," Theresa commanded, backing it up with an elbow to my side.

It took forever to get home. The Dad kept us waiting after service, outside beneath the neon *Jesus Saves* sign. He had to stay behind and say goodbye to everyone, shaking the men's hands, tipping his grey felt hat, with its ground pepper–coloured feather in the brim-ribbon, to the women. My mother stood at his elbow, her eyes shifting from side to side as the people pushed in close, laughing quietly at the Dad's excellent good nature, his kind and almost-flirtatious remarks, his encouragements. The Reverend Wiles came out onto the steps overlooking the lot and looked at the exuberant blue sky, which was gusty with clouds and wind. They discussed Richard with solemn shakes of their heads.

"Well, we're on our way. You keep praying for that boy, eh, Rev!" the Dad called.

"I will, Dad! Never fear! He's safe in the arms of Jesus!"

In the car, on the way home, the Dad started singing.

Shall we gather up the liver?
Tear the onions from the sod?

Shall we fry on up the liver?
Sizzle it with peas in the pod?

"Please don't," said my mother. "Remember that a boy is sick."

So new was Richard's illness that for a moment I wondered, *which boy?* But then I remembered, and out of habit I nearly prayed for him. Instead, I stopped myself, and merely confirmed to myself: he had to hurry up and get better, so we could get on with what I had already named the Plan.

Dear Richard

I am dying here. It's so awful and it's so lonely. I went to the corner store today and some girls called me Bigass. I wanted to go tell on them but what's to tell? It's not like they can unsay it. So I went back inside and watched Commander Tom. *Promo the Robot is just a man in a cardboard suit and his arms are vacuum cleaner hoses. That show is getting very stupid. Are you watching it in the hospital? We should watch it at the same time and pretend we're watching it together. Love Dee*

And

Dear Richard

Come back soon, Richard, please. Library was closed because Miss Whisper was away, so I had to go outside for recess. I went to put my coat on to go outside and someone had horked snot in the sleeve. I put my hand right in it. I would do anything to get you back home and sit in your room with you. I would spend the rest of my life locked in a dungeon as long as I had a flashlight I could shine around and see you there. Love Dee

And

Dear Richard

Hurry up Christmas is coming. If I have to hear Theresa's Christmas Wish List read over at the table one more time I will have a BARF-IN. Please come home all well because I have been working on something and you're going to love it a lot. I wanted to send you cookies but mum said you can't have cookies. How long is that going to go on for? Love Dee

Alice came over almost daily. She said that without Richard around, she had no human contact at all – and Janey was the only one on the street she cared to talk to. Her college friends were long gone. "They got *jobs*," she said, bitterly. And the composition classes were a bust: she'd got an F for saying "damn" in one of her papers, and then fought with the teacher who'd said ladies never made good writers. She told my mum that sometimes she'd think she was going nuts, alone in that house. If it wasn't for the art, she'd have done herself an injury.

"Yes, keeping a house is very tiring," said my mother.

"I don't keep the house," said Alice, exhaling through her nose. "The house keeps *me*."

Richard was getting better, slowly but surely, but he'd almost died and they wanted him to start putting on weight, and to make sure Alice knew how to tend to his blood-sugar levels and his diet, before turning him loose. They must have suspected her as the cause of Richard's collapse, for she did not look like a mother at all. She no longer dressed up to go to the hospital, but wore the same paint-splattered clothes she wore in her house.

Big Dick and the Dad visited each other on Saturday, heading up to the beer hall at the Royal Canadian Legion for an afternoon's escape-from-the-women, as they put it, and then they would go to the hospital to visit Richard. They sometimes met Brother Webster there. Brother Webster was a big fan of Richard's; he took him games he could play by himself, like Instant Insanity and Pick Up Sticks.

Eventually Alice said Richard was responding well to the insulin. He was down to three shots a day, and when he was down to two he could come home.

"I have spent the last two days going to a god-damn diabetes *school*, I swear to God. I said, gimme the literature and lemme read it; never mind this school shit. Sorry, Janey, when I get going I just can't watch the language. Anyway, we spent a whole day yesterday injecting water into oranges. Tomorrow I have to shoot one into poor Richard's bony little back end. These syringe things cost a mint, too. Good thing Dick's got a company plan, because I tell you, this would be taking some bite outta the moolah."

The days dragged on, and I worked harder and harder on the Plan, and Richard was allowed to come home just before Christmas holidays. He wasn't allowed to go back to school until after the holidays, but the school was not concerned about his marks – the principal said he was sure to pass, even with another few weeks' absence, so not to worry. Our class worked on a huge get-well-soon card made of two desk blotter–sized pieces of bristol board covered with tissue paper flowers. It was a class effort, where all thirty-one of us were assigned a group (I was in the cut-out letters group), and each group would have forty minutes to complete its part of the card. But when my group's turn came, and I brought my cut-out construction paper letters which were to contribute to the message GET BETTER SOON RICHARD HOLMES WE MISS YOU A LOT PEACE AND LOVE YOUR FRIENDS IN ROOM 6, I found that the other group members had worked extra hard to make sure that my allotted letter load was already covered, so that my letters would not be needed. I protested to the teacher, saying they wouldn't use my letters, and she came to the back of the class to face their solid concerted denial of my claim. Of course they would use my letters. *Here, go ahead, Dee*. But they had worked so hard that only two or three spaces were left. I got mucilage all over my fingers and did a terrible job of pasting.

"She's *ruined* it," hissed one of the friends in Room 6.

Richard came home on December 20th, so he had missed my tenth birthday, but the first thing he did when he came home was phone me and serenade me with the birthday song.

Happy Birthday to you
You belong in the zoo
You look like a monkey
And you smell like one too!

"So we're the same age now for a whole month," he said.

"Ooo, Mr. Big Shot Grown Up!" I replied. I could hardly speak, I was smiling so broadly; my lips wouldn't work and I couldn't stand still. "Can I come over, can I?" I begged, and of course it was allowed. I could hear Auntie Alice in the background saying hell, I'm surprised she wasn't camped on our goddamn porch.

Richard couldn't come out to visit me yet, being in convalescence, so we spent all our time at his place, scouring books for information regarding the Plan. Richard examined each page of the Plan carefully, a chewed pencil clenched like a bit between his teeth, nodding as he absorbed every word and every drawing.

"This is fabulous, Dee," he said, when he turned the last minty-coloured page. "Great drawings, too. You are a really good artist."

"I am not," I said. "You're better than me."

"No, you're better. You're really good."

"Not as good as you."

We dropped the flattery game, and Richard said, "Bring me my *Popular Mechanics*." We started looking up how to build a shortwave radio. Richard assured me we would need one.

"Why?"

"To contact the outside world."

"Why would we want to do that?"

Richard laughed. "Good point."

Our research was in earnest. Our material included the *Book of Knowledge* and the several sets of supermarket encyclopedias that Alice had bought, one book at a time, from the A&P. There were no encyclopedias in my house, and hardly any books, except for the ones I had in my room, many of which had been donated by Brother Webster (all the Edward Lears, for instance), and some library books that I'd neglected to return. Theresa liked to raid my books and write on them. I'd turn a page of *The Just So Stories* and find YOU THINK YOU'RE SMART BUT YOU'RE REALLY FAT written in green Bic pen, very neatly, above the words *How the Camel Got His Hump.*

Richard embraced the Plan with the same passion and devotion as my own, but without him to lend me support on the long walk there, it was hard to get to the Gladstone Library for books. We had already stripped the school. I dreaded the walk, knowing what I would face, but I braced myself, carrying all my overdues and a dollar for the fine.

I made it to Dufferin Street safely, but while I was waiting to cross the street a group of boys from St. Anne's Catholic School spotted me from the park, and hurried to attack, dodging traffic in their zeal to reach me. *Hey pig, hey pig, wanna suck me off? Hey monster-chick...*

The last one across, struggling to keep up with his friends, barely made it ahead of a big red sedan which had passed a bus on the inside, and not seen him; the sedan driver screeched to a rubber-burning halt. I gasped and stepped back, but the boy made the curb safely, and recovered within a second. Then he too joined the chorus.

Sooeeeey, hey fatso, hey, how'd you get so ugly?

Eventually they gave up, but not for a while; they danced around me all the way up to Bloor Street and the junior high, where a group of their friends saw them from the play courts and for one brief, hideous moment I thought I would have ten of them on my tail. But they were distracted by a basketball game that some teenagers were starting, and that they wanted into; I made my escape by sliding into a cluster of pudgy, black-clad, Italian women on their way to afternoon Mass, who stomped across Dufferin inside the crosswalk, but against the lights, defying anyone to hit them.

I returned to Richard bearing a worldful of books.

"Ehhhxcellent," he wheedled, rubbing his hands together in his Demented Mad Scientist persona. "You have done well, my faithful lycanthropic servant. You may feed on a single villager tonight as your reward. But do not let them see you, for if they suspect that the gentle soul who serves me is in fact the very demon who tears their throats when the moon is full, they may storm my laboratory."

I returned this salute with a slobbery, growling, bent-back routine.

During Richard's three-month lay-up, we developed more characters, many based on comic readings, and expanded others drawn from Kipling and other material involving children stranded in the wilderness with animals. Richard, by necessity, had to stay recumbent or at least in his room, so I got to perform the more active roles. He would be the evil scientist, or the merman in a wheelchair whose tail had to be disguised by a blanket, or he would be the enormous-brained alien who kept me as a study object. At one point he was Alex, and I was the Black Stallion, and from that game I invented the Whicked Whinny, a sound which was sure to make Alice come to the bottom of the stairs and shriek that we were making her *nuts*.

"I can hardly wait," said Richard, "until we can get away."

Richard did not return to school until after March break. His diabetes was volatile and hard to control. Auntie Alice was nightmarishly disorganized at keeping track of dosages, feeding, and sleeping schedules; she was supposed to keep a binder but that was not the sort of project she could maintain. Richard was always having dizzy spells and even fainting. As time went on, I learned to check his blood sugar levels with him, and to keep track of his mealtimes, because we would get involved in things and forget to feed him. I learned to recognize the slurred speech and odd behaviour that meant he was about to seizure. I learned that the roll of orange Life Savers he kept in his pocket were not treats, but medicine.

His eyesight, too, was terrible. Whenever he went off his eating schedule, it would blur and fuzz, but even when that would clear he still couldn't see.

"You really oughta tell your ma," I said.

But Richard refused. With his history of cataracts, he knew that all that could be done was an operation. "And I'm not going back in that stupid hospital. They'll just give me needles and more needles. I hear they put needles in your eyes, Dee. Needles in your *eyes*."

The needles truly horrified Richard. He faced each injection with a sort of wide-eyed trembling resignation, like a dog at the vet's. The needles horrified me, too, and I watched through my fingers as he shot insulin into the soft innards of his own thigh.

But neither of us grasped the permanence of what was happening. We did not understand the prospect of *this can never stop*. We treated it as something assigned to us by doctors and parents, another burden to bear until we could get away.

By spring, when the tulips were all erect and waving in the flowerbeds, we had the Plan in excellent order. We kept it in three-ring binders, watching it grow as we added illustrations and recorded notes from our research books – whole-earth catalogues that gave tips on returning to the land, and of course the *Farmer's Almanac*. We took inspiration from Stevenson, Burroughs, Kipling, Verne, London and Defoe, craving the tales of those who enjoyed exile, and who could shapeshift into animals.

We continued, too, with our stories about our prospective adventures: *Richard and Dee and the Rabid Fox. Richard and Dee and the Electrical Storm.* And Richard's personal favourite, *FLOOD!* We had a pet pack of wolves, befriended as puppies, and moose to ride like horses (we rescued them as calves when their parents were killed by hunters – we had no concept of hunting being restricted to a season). Our homestead was on the mainland (we had rejected the island because we would be easily found there – it would be the first place they'd look). We would have a deep stream of fresh water, full of trout, and our house would be a treehouse nestled in a tri-pronged fork of oak branches, and we would make a fireplace from stones and adhere the stones to each other and to the wall with clay from the riverbanks. Our mattresses were of long dried grass from the clearing (where we let the moose graze), and our roof was thatched grass too. We grew oats, wheat, corn and green beans, and had an orchard of wild apple trees, and we boiled the blueberries and raspberries for jam. We had a cave that served as an ice house, and in the winter we cut big blocks of ice from the river and dragged them into the cave. We milked our moose and made moose cheese.

We wrote it all down in our Playtime Doodlers, then punched holes in the paper and transferred it to the binders, under headings such as THINGS WE WILL EAT, THINGS WE WILL NEED, and HOW TO GET AWAY. It was all delicious with portent and possibility; it was only a couple of summers off. We two timorous beasties sat together and planned and planned, certain that we had it all beaten. We had our instruction book, we had our Plan. And of course, we had each other.

What could possibly go wrong?

No matter how many back-to-nature books we had read, no matter how many playforts we'd built from scrap wood, and no matter how many plans we made, we would never learn how to make insulin.

Richard told me this, in late August, 1969, after men had walked on the moon, when the summer perched on the lip of fall. Autumn was coming; we could smell it. Summer life was folding around us like a collapsing tent in a high wind. The heat strained unnaturally, loaded with warning of cold storms of hard rain, and the waves on the open side of Blueberry Island were high enough to swamp small boats. Boys from the landing slapped across the crests in their flat-bottomed, one-man Seafleas, their whoops drowned by the wind and the roar of the water charging against the rocks.

We were to start Grade 8 on the day after Labour Day. We had already spent a year in a "new" school – Kemp Junior High – and had hoped Grade 7 would be easier than the elementary school, but it had turned out to be even worse (no recesses, and rotation between classes that drew us out into the halls where we were mobile, obvious targets). Richard's eyes were so bad that to open his locker, he had to press his face to the dial and turn very carefully, feeling the clicks like a safecracker. But he never let on to Alice. He said he didn't want any more *interference*.

The stink of school lay on the other side of Labour Day. Barebones Lake, the island, summer: all would be gone. The Dad was planning his annual Labour Day Weekend barbecue, his close-of-season party. The day after that, the holiday Monday, we would close up the cabin – pack up the sleeping bags, the cooler, the lantern, the board games, the blankets, the swimsuits – and go home.

But for now Richard and I were together. It was still warm, and we were sitting on the dock the Dad had built with Big Dick. David had not dropped by once all summer, although he did send a postcard, which the Dad brought back from an overnight trip to the city, and which he tacked to one of the struts of the cabin, beneath last year's calendar and the plastic-framed print of a man fishing for trout. He took it down to read it to Big Dick, who expressed no interest at all, but when Brother Webster came over (his visits had been very few that summer), he could barely contain his urge to read it.

"Don't read it to me, Dad, give it to me so I can read it myself."

"Geez, Webby, what's the difference?" said the Dad, handing it over nonetheless.

"If I read it myself," said Brother Webster evenly, "I can hear the writer's voice."

The summer seemed weak and incomplete, as if it should extend itself to make up for the events that had not occurred. The best thing that had hap-

pened, we decided, was the building of our fort –
our *house*. We had always built some sort of playhouse every summer, but this year's had been an
obsession. It was to be practice for the next year's
house, which we would be living in by that summer's end, so we took construction seriously. We
had good lumber scraps from the dock building
projects, and on one occasion Brother Webster had
helped us with the nails, showing us that Ardox
nails with their twisty shafts would be more likely
to hold, particularly if we drove them in on an
angle, like this. We lay shingles from the cabin's
roof-patching job on top of leftover plywood, and
although there wasn't quite enough to cover the
entire roof of our fort, we reinforced the gaps with
Glad garbage bags ripped out into sheets and stapled to the frame. We covered the one window with
a piece of wire screen, and hung a sheet over the
door. Richard could just about stand up inside,
although of course I could not. But it was a house:
a prototype; a promise.

That was finished now. The Dad had burned
the rest of the lumber scraps, in the firepit overlooking the lake. The new dock was done; the
tools put away. The dock's wood still bled sap
where the nails pierced it, and the Dad's little
rented nine-horse lay tethered to its side, nodding
gently.

I spoke to Richard of how soon it would be
before we had our own dock, on our own private lake
somewhere, that we'd find up in the wilderness

behind his cottage or behind the lodge. We'd build a proper cabin, better than the one we'd just made. Just one more year to hang in there, to grow a little more, learn a little more, and then we could leave.

"That was the best fort ever, eh?" I said.

He nodded but didn't reply.

"Don'tcha think, Richard? That it's the best we ever made?"

"Yeah," he agreed at last. "It's pretty good."

"Next year, we'll check out the woods on the mainland and find the perfect spot."

"Sure."

"I wish we could stay on the island. But they'd find us right away."

"For sure."

"So we'll have to figure out how to get all the lumber and nails and stuff. And next summer spend more time on the mainland to find the perfect place to build. That's one thing we didn't do enough this year, eh? We didn't get to shore enough. Eh, Richard?"

"That's a big problem, all right."

"So, like, next year – no more practice sessions! Next year, it's for real, baby."

He said nothing to that.

"Richard, it'll be so great."

He turned to me, exhaled a sharp blast through his nostrils, and said, "Dee, it isn't gonna happen."

"What?" I went cold, as if I'd dived into the water. "Why not?"

"I'm a diabetic, dozo. We can't make insulin."

"So?" I said. "By the time we leave, they'll have a cure."

"They can't make a cure. They tried already." He smiled, with sad pride. "Canadians found insulin, though. It was us Canadians."

"And they're still trying, aren't they?"

"Yeah, but, like, so far no chance."

"So we'll sneak into town and buy it."

"With what money?"

"Okay, we'll steal it."

"It's in a pharmacy, Dee. On those shelves behind the drug counter. Like, how are you gonna steal past the guy? It's not like lifting a Dubble Bubble, ya know."

"So we'll take enough with us and can store it up."

"It won't keep. It'll go bad."

"We can put it in the ice cave."

"Yeah, right. As *if*. Geez, Dee."

It was the first time I'd ever heard Richard truly sneer at me, and it was both startling and painful, like a darning needle concealed in a wad of cotton wool.

I sat, running my finger around a gout of sap that had oozed up around a nailhead. Given time, this would harden to rock.

"I guess there's going to have to be a change in plans," I said, after a while.

Richard nodded. "Sorry," he said.

"I'll go by myself."

"Okay. Yeah. I can help you find the place, and build everything, and you can go on your own."

"You can come visit. And then when they do come up with a cure, you can come live there."

"Yeah, sure. I'll visit."

"But how will you find me?"

"We'll figure that out."

So the Plan went on, with the amendment: I was going to leave on my own, but Richard would be my last link with civilization. Next summer, once I had settled by that perfect private lake I knew was out there, somewhere in the bush, I'd creep back to Richard's cottage, and leave a sign. Three acorns on a certain stump, or a thong of deerhide around a particular tree. Richard would understand, and he would follow the clues to where I was. He would bring me things I needed and couldn't make myself, like thread and cough drops and socks and frying pans. Richard said he would always be there for me.

I saw myself at sixteen, as I had written myself into the Plan. I was tall (maybe just a little taller than I was at that point, which still approached six feet), and my skin was tanned, and my hair was waist-length and kept tangle-free through daily, ritual combings with a bone comb. Legends sprang up around me, because sometimes I was seen, when I came close to a farmhouse or cottage, and my howl could be heard for miles as I spoke with my brethren, the wolves. When people tried to catch me, I melted into the bush. Melted, like butter into the softness of a pancake.

My family would give up the search for me. The Dad, with sadness, would tell the police that it was no use; I was too clever. I had too much experience in the bush. My mother would return sorrowfully to her kitchen, weeping every time she mixed cake batter, remembering how I used to beg to lick the spoon. Every spring, a mysterious letter would arrive for her in the mail, saying *your daughter is well* or *don't be sad for Wolfgirl survives!*

David would write a song called "Wild Baby Sister," and Lightfoot would record it.

Theresa would get married to a really mean fat man and have thirty-two children, and she'd get fat too, like the mothers were in *Archie* comics, who were drawn with thick waists and double chins.

Richard would visit.

"You'll visit, right Richard?"

"I said right. I said I'd visit."

I took up my Playtime Doodler, which was almost always with me.

At the very summit of the mountain that Wolfgirl had called Woodwind, she stood poised and alert, waiting for the signal from Silverheels.

Richard stood up and brushed off his shorts, then pointed to his watch. "Time to eat," he said. "Let's go."

And summer drifted away.

Three

Seventeen searches into the future – as far as the mind can comprehend – and envisions the wonders of a dramatic new decade. In the air, under the sea, at home, in our schools, in the arts, in the sciences, here are some of the miracles of the stirring, Soaring Seventies that will alter your life: there'll be floating airports on the seas and you'll speed, often faster than sound, to sun and surf for mini vacations and "stretch weekends" and there will be movie theatre–sized planes equipped with discotheques and you'll be tuning in to more than eighty TV channels and telephones with pictures – and no lines – will also be used for teaching and "fashion mirrors" reflecting through slides, will let you see yourself modelling clothes without trying them on & windows will control the direction, colour and intensity of light and what you wear will be temperature controlled, sweaters will close up when breezes blow, dresses will change colour when the sun shines and chairs will turn on with

music and lights when you sit down and
"self destruct packaging" will keep you from
drowning in waste and liberal arts will be
emphasized again over the scientific and
technical fields and electronic libraries will
bring you the greatest experts in the world
on any subject and eighteen year olds will be
pulling levers in voting booths and typewrit-
ers will automatically correct mistakes and
produce carbons though secretaries will still
be in great demand and motor vehicles will
be eliminated as a prime source of air pollu-
tion and space age art will turn to three
dimensional painting and sculpture with
sound and motion programmed to run by
electricity for three thousand hours with
never a repeat impression and hot soup,
warm buns and freezing ice cream will be
served from the same pre pack and cancer
will no longer be the number two killer and
artificial hearts operating with internal
power sources will be implanted with fre-
quency. But the dazzling new inventions that
make living easier and travel swifter may
also make more precious those quiet
moments of joy that the human spirit has
cherished throughout history: a walk in the
rain, a dip in the briny sea, a sight of a glowing sunrise, a peaceful hour of reflection.

Having reached the moon in the sixties, perhaps in the Soaring Seventies we shall rediscover the earth!

Seventeen Magazine
January 1970

The young girl talks to her little notebook as she formerly talked to her dolls; it is a friend and confidante...In its pages is inscribed a truth hidden from relatives, comrades, teachers, a truth with which the author is enraptured in solitude...

Simone de Beauvoir
The Second Sex

It's amazing how much you can remember about a particular year, when you settle down to the work of it. You remember your Midge doll, and your Chatty Cathy, who only chatted for a while before the ring-on-a-string which activated her broke away, and she never spoke again. There were daisy-print curtains on your mother's window. The men smoked, then discovered they couldn't stop when it was proven cigarettes caused lung cancer, so they denied that cigarettes were bad for them. You made asbestos-clay ashtrays in art class for presents and then they took away the asbestos clay because it was making people sick. You didn't care if it made you sick; asbestos clay is fun.

The kitchen is changing, for cakes are mixed from mixes with a portable beater, and not beaten by hand with a wooden spoon, from scratch. Shirts are permanent press, but your mother still irons them. She doesn't seem to be working any less. She washes the floor before using the Mop-

and-Glo. She dusts and *then* she sprays with Pledge and dusts again. She uses plastic roast-in-bags for the Sunday roast. There are still Sunday roasts, and your mother's best friend comes over with a book, saying it had changed her life and it will change your mother's. The friend reads aloud from it, saying, listen, it says that institutions for the *retarded* did a study and they found that *housework* was best done by feeble-minded girls – *feeble-minded*, Jane! And this – that the time we spend on housework varies inversely with whether we've got something better to do!

Surely we have something better to do…

Your mother thanks her. She puts the book in a drawer the moment her friend leaves. Your mother says she's too busy to read.

You're not. Your box of comics now contains Marvel *Love* Comics as well as *Archie*s and DCs and *Classics Illustrated*s. *My Love, Our Love Story, Teen Romance.* You can get a whole world through the comics; you can *sell greeting cards and earn big money.* You can *gain up to 50 powerful pounds of muscle* or *lose up to 50 pounds of ugly fat.* You can order Joe Weider's book which is *chock full with PHOTOS of STRONG MEN and DYNAMOS once WEAKER than you* and *see their PATHETIC before photos. In MINUTES A DAY you in the privacy of YOUR OWN ROOM you can mold 16-inch arms and a big 45-inch chest.*

You already have 16" arms and a 45" chest, but that's not good on a girl.

A cartoon boy named Cap gives you Hobby Hints, some about carpentry, which you clip and put in your binder. You can MAKE MONEY GET PRIZES with the American Seed Company. You cut out the pictures of the prizes and paste them in your scribbler. The sleeping bag, the fishing outfit, the archery outfit and the mountain tent and the walkie-talkie and the knapsack and the Daisy Air Rifle. You could buy for your friend, too, the Gemini Rocket and the Chemistry Set and the 600-power microscope and the 40X telescope. Your brother could use the guitar. Your sister would get things like the pink vinyl wallet and locked diary and the transistor radio and the silver-plate brush and comb set, although she already has these things and you wouldn't buy her anything anyway, not in a million years. So maybe you would get the diary for yourself. You could use a lock on your writing.

Your sister sees what you've cut out from the comics and glued into your notebooks among the stories and lists and poems and half-finished letters. She too cuts out a message from one of your comics, and pastes it into the pages:

MONSTER! S-I-Z-E MONSTER!

That's you, freak! She pencils in.

Your sister abandons her garter belt and stockings for pantyhose, and then for a baby blue pantsuit. She joins a protest march at the high school to force the authorities to let girls wear pants to school. She babysits and with the power of money, she dresses as she wants. She buys LP albums, one of which is plain white and has two records in it. It's the Beatles' last album, she claims, her expression solemn and pious. It is a 33-1/3, and too big for her portable record player, so she tries to play it on the living room hi-fi, but is chased away, in tears, by your father. Your father says he's sorry, but he can't listen to that junk. In ten years, that music'll be forgotten, he says.

Penthouse magazine features models who display their pubic hair – your friend brings you a copy; he got it from his father's office, for in among the tax books, close to the wall, there is always a *Penthouse* or a *Playboy*. The smiling, sleek, women with their tiny neat triangles, blonde and black and red, are so beautiful that you could have looked for hours, even with your friend calling you a perv and poking you with his elbows, and besides his father is so organized, he has *all his ducks in a row*, that he knows such a thing will be quickly missed. So you spend only minutes looking at the gleaming, happy women, with their buffed skin and controlled smiles, before your nervous friend insists on returning the magazine to his father's office.

You learn about sex in health class. It's sex education, but they don't call it that. It's just health. You learn things you knew nothing at all about, although your best friend says he knew all this stuff and hadn't mentioned it because, well, it's kinda sick. So in private, naked from the waist down, you press in your stomach and thrust out your hips and try to see if you have hair growing, but you can't see over your belly, so you get your sister's hand mirror and look at yourself. And you thought your *face* was ugly.

You start to read Tolkien. Your friend's eyes are bad so you read to him about the hairy-toed being that lives in a hole in the ground, and the Gollum that loses its precious. Poor Gollum, in his little boat, deformed by the dark and by craving.

Your father appears in the evenings for dinner, reads the paper, watches TV, goes to bed. On Saturdays he goes to the Legion to have a beer. Your father wears his overalls when he works. He is no longer ashamed to be a high school dropout, because inflation has raised his income, he says, and he's been paying for his house for fifteen years so he's way ahead of the game. He has a grown man for a son and a paid-for house – that's what you get for starting young, he tells his friend.

Sometimes his other friend, Brother Webster, comes over, but only rarely, to bring a postcard or letter he received from David, with whom he is in touch. Brother Webster gets arrested at the bust of *Oh! Calcutta;* he now has a frizzy Afro haircut. You show him a poem you've written. He says your poem is *mind-blowing*. He folds it up and says he'll keep it forever.

Your mother serves the men coffee as they sit

in the living room, smoking. You help; you carry the cups carefully, one at a time, and bring in the cream-and-sugar service. They say you're a good girl. You glow.

Your friend's mother joins a women's consciousness-raising group and discovers she's too old for it because it's at the university downtown and all the other women are just girls wearing fun fur vests and floppy-brimmed hats and granny glasses with lavender-tinted lenses, and when she showed up in her good skirt and red lipstick she felt so old that she turned around and came home. But she says she's not giving up yet, not yet, dammit.

Men your father's age wear narrow ties and the same old suits, but other men – young men, and some teachers – are wearing striped bellbottoms and broad flowery ties and long scarves over their calf-length Victorian-style coats. There are lots of male teachers at your school. The science teacher is a lot like Brother Webster, but not so old. He might not even be thirty (you are not to trust anyone over thirty). He has longish hair and sideburns and huge brown eyes, and he's not too tall and he smiles a lot. The other girls follow him around the schoolyard at lunch hour, and join his after-school Science Dimension Club even though they are afraid of lighting the Bunsen burner and nauseated by the fetal pigs in jars of formaldehyde. You want to join, too, but of course you don't. One day you see that someone has stuck a label on one of the jars of dead pig. BABY DEE GRAHAM, it says. The smiling brown-eyed teacher does not smile. He takes down the jar and the next day it's back, without the label. Nothing more is said.

There's a war on that nobody wants, but we're not involved because we're Canada. People are shot in the United States at something called Kent State, and your Uncle Big Dick tells your Auntie Alice that they deserved it, the dirty hippies who should learn some rules about life. They argue so loudly and so hard that neither one can really be heard, and your father takes your Uncle Big Dick out for a beer. Your Auntie Alice rages around the kitchen, smoking compulsively and smashing the butts in the onyx ashtray and saying she doesn't know how she stands him.

There is an earthquake in Peru, and thousands of students flood Washington to protest that unwanted war. Your teacher explains the Domino Theory and you realize the Americans are keeping you safe. But Brother Webster tells you your teacher is wrong, even though he himself is a teacher. Brother Webster knows a family that's hiding a *conscientious objector*.

People are not supposed to buy green grapes. Your mother still buys green grapes.

For Christmas, you have just turned thirteen, so there are no more dolls. Instead, you get a transistor radio, just like your sister's, which pleases you (which surprises you), and she gets a proper, portable, multiple-speed turntable with detachable speakers. She is so amazed she bursts into tears and hugs your father until he cries, too. The day after Boxing Day she uses all her saved-up babysitting money to buy "Inna Gadda Da Vida" and a Big Brother and the Holding Company album. She makes you crazy singing to a close-minded God to deliver unto her a Mercedes-Benz and a colour TV. She plays the stereo so loud the booming shakes the glass in the windows. You roll yourself in blankets and try, try, try to read.

She decorates. She hangs a black-felt psychedelic poster on her wall, and has a pink fuzzy footprint rug on her floor. She crochets a bedspread all by herself. It's pink and orange and it's so invitingly colourful that you often sneak onto her bed to lie on it.

On New Year's Eve your brother, amazingly, appears. You cannot remember the last time you've seen him. He is as strange and foreign as any man on the street. But your sister squeals when she sees him, then giggles and purrs, as if he were her boyfriend. Your father cries again, in his father-crying way, just misting up a little, and says, "The whole family's here. The whole family."

Your brother is wonderful. He's full of stories, which he tells you on demand. You show him your stories, which he praises, but you know that your stories aren't real. Real things happened to David. He has been in the United States, and Europe, and he almost went to India but then the whole maharishi thing turned out to be a fraud so he turned around and came back. He earned a Master of Arts and paid for it himself, he says, and your father says that he did not pay for it all himself is he out of his mind? And does he think he can just disappear and why didn't he write and your brother says he did write, he wrote all the time. Postcards. And a letter, from Marrakesh. One letter, your father says. One lousy letter. *You sent more letters to Webby, for gosh sakes! What does that go to show?*

Your brother gives you a present – a pottery horse from Mexico – and for your sister he brings a macramé belt to wear with her hiphuggers. She likes it so much she wears it every day for a week. For your father he brings another onyx ashtray and for mother a set of turquoise-and-silver earrings made by the Navajo. They are very big and dangly, made for pierced ears. They are nothing like the single pearls your mother wears, but she thanks him and tells him she loves them.

He says he's giving up on his doctorate, and concentrating on music. He says he played session backup in a recording studio with The Stampeders. He says he's got a chance to appear at The Riverboat.

For New Year's you and he Scotch-tape balloons to the living room ceiling and you think he's going to stay and so does your father and sister and mother. But at eight-thirty that night, your brother comes down the stairs, wearing low-slung velveteen pants and a hip-length sheepskin jacket, carrying his guitar; even though your father had loaded a whole case of Labatt's 50 into the fridge, and invited over your friend's father and Brother Webster, your brother still goes out. Brother Webster leaves early, saying he's not much one for late nights, even at the turn of the decade.

Your mother serves canapés and wears a silver tinsel corsage, and your father sits in his chair with his fingers to his forehead and listens to the Guy Lombardo broadcast, while his friend talks about hockey games. Your sister says that never ever ever again will she ever spend a New Year's Eve with this family. "Thanks for ruining my life, Dad," she says, and steals a big gulp of his beer, right in front of him. At 12:05 a.m., your mother goes to bed, guests or no guests.

In mid-January, your father buys a new station wagon. He is doing all right, he tells your mother, not as well as a professional man, but well enough. He tells her to buy new furniture, and gives her a strict budget. She gets the Eaton's catalogue and she and your sister go over the pages, clipping out photos of modular chairs and swag lamps and harvest-gold refrigerators. Men come and install a green shag-pile rug in the living room, and a new cushioned-linoleum floor in the kitchen, and your sister hangs green-and-purple paisley-print wallpaper on the walls of her half of your room. You don't care. You're waiting for summer. After summer, she can have the whole room.

School is full of noise and new things, but the work is a little more interesting, and they put you in a special group of talented readers who get to study advanced works like Poe's *Cask of Amontillado* and Ovid's *Metamorphoses*. You suggest they read some Kipling but to your surprise everybody's already read Kipling. *Read it to bits*, someone says, and for a second you have something in common with someone else other than your solitary friend.

They have gotten used to you somewhat. They have better things to do than chase you. They are beginning to chase each other. It is Grade 8; some of them are fourteen and fifteen years old already. One boy in Miss Tyler's home-room – who failed Grade 5 twice – even has his driver's licence. Some of them have part-time jobs. There is kissing in the hallway. There are mini-skirts; breasts and brassieres in gym class. You don't have breasts yet, or do you? You have fat boobies, but you always had fat boobies. You wear an undershirt, not a bra. Your sister wears a bra. She has several; she bought them from the catalogue. They are a 32B. You looked.

Your sister's boyfriend picks her up in a purple Dodge Barracuda, and your father complains that the boy didn't come to the door to meet them, but your mother is obviously relieved that he did no such thing. She had been hiding in the basement, doing laundry. Your sister comes home at 2 a.m. and there is an argument, to which you listen from your bedroom, awake because you couldn't sleep from wondering what she might be doing. Your sister comes running into your room, and she has cried all her eyeshadow and mascara into a set of smeared shiners. You can smell her Yardley cologne as she climbs into her babydolls and into bed, beneath her candy-coloured comforter, peeping like a wounded bird.

Strange things are pulling at you. You check your ugly crotch every week or so, and sure enough, there is a fuzz of hair there. You are having trouble with the Plan. It doesn't seem so likely that you can do it; the problems are more complicated than you'd thought. In all your three-ring binders full of work, you have not addressed every problem. How far could you walk? How much could you take along? How will you carry it all? What will you do if they find you? What if you get sick?

What will you do, when you get your period?

You find yourself thumbing through your sister's *Glamour* and *Seventeen* magazines. You look at the makeovers. They take thin, pretty girls and paint them, and put them into modern, hip, happening clothes. The girls are usually college girls. They are going to be *career* girls. Susan MacPherson wants to be a doctor, and she "digs the new women's liberation movement – it's happening!" She needs a makeup routine that can be completed in less than forty-five minutes. Sherie Lowe wants to be a scientist, and to "serve man as best I can, to help man understand what he can do." *Seventeen* says that Sherie is a Phi Beta Kappa, but until *Seventeen's* makeup crew showed her how to do it, she had never even plucked her eyebrows!

You start looking at the advertisements in the back of the magazines, which talk about your future and your career and colleges to go to. There are advertisements for Fun Fun Fun and Good Health Too weight loss camps, all of them in the States. You could join the army. The Women's Army Corps *needs girls as well as generals*, because *girls make things go*. Girls keep things moving in the office, handling personnel and figuring the payroll. If You Love Animals You Can Become a Veterinary Assistant. *F u cn rd ths msj u cn bcm a scrtry & gt a gd jb.*

You can read the message. Maybe you and your friend can use speedwriting as a code, when you have to leave each other top-secret messages in the woods.

In guidance class at school, the guidance counsellor tells you that you should be a newspaper reporter. A journalist. Like Brenda Starr. You look at a picture of Brenda Starr and try to pluck your eyebrows, using your mum's tweezers from her makeup kit. It hurts too much and you give up. You don't know the trick of putting Vaseline on your brows first. You don't know that you should be using deodorant. There are no clothes to fit you. Your mother orders half-sizes for you from the cat-

alogue, which are for short fat women. You are a
tall fat woman, but she buys the half-sizes because
they're bigger around, and short is in fashion.

You are a size 24 1/2. But you are no longer the
tallest in the school. One of the boys in school is
actually taller. His nickname is Ichabod. He is
half an inch taller than you.

You have so many names that you sometimes
forget who you are.

Just after Christmas, when you're listening to
the Archies on your transistor, your friend comes
over. He just lets himself in and comes right up
the stairs, because by now your houses are inter-
changeable. He comes in the room and you're on
your bed, surrounded by a spread of comics. He
sits down on your sister's bed – sacrilege! – and
you're about to warn him (for she knows when
her bed has been sat on) when you see the look on
his face.

"What is it?" you ask. "What's going on?"

And Richard said, "We're moving away."

I didn't understand. I thought at first that he meant we as in he and I, and I almost brushed him off and said, well, yeah, but it's just because we're in separate classrooms and separate gyms and not seeing each other so much. What he had said was as impossible an announcement as *we're turning into fish* or *my diabetes is cured*. But the split-moment of confusion passed and I sat staring at him, and he sat staring at me, his eyes cloaked in the morass of lensed glass which he required to see.

"Moving away where?" I said.

"Bolton."

I knew Bolton. It was a town out-of-town, miles away, not reachable by bus or subway. It was surrounded by farms and fields, old stone houses and greying windblasted barns. Cows. Haybales. We had been there on our way by schoolbus to the Albion Hills Conservation Area, where we went on a class outing, and I sat at a picnic table all day because for some reason, I hadn't brought a swimsuit.

But Bolton was *north* of Toronto – closer to Barebones – and it had a lot of countryside around it. Maybe we could move there too, for after all, the Dad and Big Dick were friends, and Jane and Auntie Alice were friends. It made sense that we would go, too.

"If you guys are moving," I said, "then we'll be moving too."

"Ya think?"

"I bet. I bet any money."

We settled on this, and he came over to my bed and read comics with me, or at least I read them to him while he lay back with his arm thrown over his forehead. He was long and thin and his feet were huge, like a German shepherd puppy's. A few years earlier, his father had insisted he get braces (*kid looks like a moron, with those big rabbit teeth*), and the metalwork pushed his lips into perpetual semi-openness.

Not long into our reading the front door burst open – a sound we heard from upstairs – and we listened carefully to Auntie Alice breaking the news. Alice was crying hard, coughing on her cigarettes, but soon we heard the whistle of the kettle and the cookie cupboard opening. We heard Alice's voice muffle as she ate shortbreads and smoked at the same time.

"I'll kill him, Janey, I can't believe he's done this. Well, I'll beat him. I won't sign the deed. Jesus, unless the bastard put the house in his name. They can do that. They can get around your dower rights."

Murmur-murmur from my mother. Something about a nice new house in a nice new town.

"Pffft!" spat Alice. "Janey, it's not even suburbia. There are no lawns yet, or sidewalks. All the houses are like that song, about the little boxes made out of ticky-tacky that all look just the same. I'm not going to go live in the goddamn sticks. No way. No fucking way. There. I said it. No fucking way he's doing this."

"She doesn't want to go," I said to Richard.

"No guff. Shhh."

Alice did quiet down, and there was a lot of quiet conspiratorial muttering. We heard my mum say, loudly for her, "You don't want a broken home, Alice, you don't want that." We were dying to hear Alice's strategy: what she had up her sleeve, to prevent the move. Would she fight it head-on with refusal and threats, or would she try to sneak her way into the problem, with begging and bribes, like Mum did when she needed the washing machine fixed or spring bulbs from the nursery or new sheers for the front window. I couldn't imagine Alice creeping around that way, making Uncle Dick's favourite dessert and plying him with compliments.

We crept to the top of the stairs and then halfway down, and heard Alice say, "Marriage! What a crock. I tell ya, Janey, if he didn't let me do my work, I'd be out the door. I would. I'd be right out that door."

"And where would you go?" said Jane.

"I have a degree. I could teach."

"Don't you need a certificate for that? Bill Webster has a certificate. Can you type?"

"Janey," said Alice firmly, "you're not listening. I tell you I'd leave."

"I don't think so," she replied.

There was some silence after that, during which silence I mis-placed my foot and caused the riser to squeak revealingly. Instantly Alice was on to us.

"Mind your own beeswax, you nosy parkers!" she called out.

"We're not doing anything," Richard called back. "As if you own the world."

"I own *your* world, you mouthy little sasspile. Get your backside out of hearing range this minute."

Grudgingly, we retreated to the bedroom and started up with our comics again, straining unsuccessfully to hear what was going on. I showed Richard an ad for Mattel's Agent Zero secret message set with crypto pen and spy scope and blow gun target game.

"So what?" he said.

"We could spy...we could...I dunno, write secret messages. So when you live in Bolton, I can send you secret messages and coded stuff about the Plan and all."

He turned a page laconically, lazily, without looking up at me. "Okay, sure, good idea," he replied, in an absent tone. I watched him, waiting for him to come back, but he kept on thumbing through the comic, sitting up with it in his lap. I realized he wasn't really reading, because his nose was not brushing the paper, and suddenly remembered that first meeting of ours, and how he had read with his face against the print, sucking in the words that I craved.

When his mother called for him, and instead of saying he'd like to stay, he got up at once. "I'll see you," I said, and he tossed me the comic and said, "Yeah, see you."

Yes, I thought. But for how much longer?

I am to imagine you
the trust, the wisdom, the turn of your phrase
to phase you into my mind's eyes, and follow
to place you beside me in the safest of spots.
You, who do not exist. I am to make you real
So that when the pain comes
I can turn to you for comfort...

"Kindred Spirit"
from The Kitchen Counter by J.E. Graham

"I miss them," my mother said.

"Me too."

Richard and Uncle Big Dick and Auntie Alice left our street on a Sunday morning when we were all at church. There was no goodbye party. Uncle Dick and the Dad went out to the Legion on a Thursday night, and Alice came over for tea on Saturday. Nothing more was said about how Alice was going to fight. Whatever fight there had been, Uncle Dick had won.

My mother tried to return Alice's book to her, saying she hadn't had a chance to read it, but Alice would not take it. "Please read it. Please. It's important. Okay?"

I offered Richard a pile of selected comics, but he said he was already packed and they'd just get torn. "Bring 'em to Barebones this summer," he said. "We'll keep our collection there."

With the Holmeses gone, my mother and I

found we had huge stretches of time where we were both in the house at once, with no Richard and no Alice. When I came through the door after school, I came through alone. There were no thrice-weekly afternoon invasions from Auntie Alice and her deck of smokes and full-blown complaints about the consistency of her latest batch of clay.

New people moved into Richard's old house, and within days knocked down the old garage. From my bedroom window I watched the men swinging crowbars and hammers, ripping the old boards away from the rickety frame. They tore away the front porch, which Alice had painted purple, and the broken purple lumber lay on the front lawn for three days, waiting for the trashmen to come for it.

My room seemed vacant, even though it still had the same contents: the same dolls, the same comics. I still read and re-read my texts, reading out loud (from memory, more or less). But standing on the bed and shouting, "Chil the Kite brings home the night that Mang the bat sets free!" felt foolish, without Richard there to reply, "Good hunting all that keep the Jungle Law!" Without him, I was less content to stay exclusively in my room. My plain, beige-walled, brown-bedspread, pine-desked half-a-room rubbed shoulders with Theresa's Carnaby Street wallpaper, fuzzy-footprint throw rug, and dressing table with its Polaroid photos of the Barracuda Boyfriend taped to the triple mirror. Her re-decoration of her half of the room made me feel as if I were looking into one of the glass-walled dioramas in the museum, or perhaps one of the perfect rooms in the Eaton's catalogue – a room any girl should want.

Theresa campaigned constantly to have David's room. But neither the Dad nor my mother would consider this request. David comes home all the time, she was told. Why, he was here just last Christmas. How would he feel if he found his room were gone?

"Why would I care what he feels? He's not even *here*," she said to me. "And meanwhile, I gotta split everything with *you*."

Theresa was nearly sixteen. And she was beautiful. She had skin that never blistered into acne, and lips that glistened beneath their peach-tone gloss, and huge wide blue eyes with lush thick lashes. Her hair, naturally straight (although it easily *held a curl*) billowed around her shoulders, falling halfway to her buttocks. She had a forty-five-minute beauty routine, just like Susan MacPherson in the *Seventeen* magazine, and she let me watch her as long as I didn't ask too many stupid questions or eat something (she could not stand to watch me eat). Every now and then she acknowledged my presence: once she said I had strong fingernails and good eyes.

We looked up my eyes on the Andrea False Eyelashes Eye Chart. False eyelashes were *outsville*, Theresa explained, but the eye chart was a handy guide. Your eyes could be almond-shaped, round, narrow, half-moon, shallow-set, turned down, big, small, deep-set or turned up, and since mine were deep-set I might want to wear false lashes despite their being outsville, because my own lashes were so sparse. I could choose natural medium flutters or standard heavies, natural triples, standard shaggies, natural sunburst or standard featherys. I should also consider getting an Avon's Maxim-Eyes Eye Kit.

One time, as she sat at her vanity table and I sat (with permission) on her bed, she touched me on the chin and tilted my head up and examined my face. It was as if a blessing were being conveyed, for except to slap or pinch me, she had never touched me that I could recall. I held so still that I began to wonder if I could hold the pose much longer, but was terrified to move and break the spell of her examination.

She nodded and withdrew her lovely hand.

"You can use my Phisohex," she said. "It degerms your face."

"Degerms my – you bum! My face doesn't have any germs!"

Her expression told me that for once, for just once, she was not trying to hurt me. This had been a kindly gesture: she degermed *her* face. Now I could degerm mine. I scrambled to apologize, stammering that sure-that'd-be-great, but she had turned her back on me.

"Screw you," she said. "I was trying to help. Go ahead. Be a big fat freak forever."

I recoiled into shame and distress at my mistake. Longing for Richard, I picked up the *Seventeen*, and turned to the eye chart, to see if I could see Richard's eyes anywhere.

"Put that down," said Theresa. "Don't touch my stuff. Go write to your boyfriend or something. At least somebody on this Earth can stand the sight of you. And he's half-fucking blind. The only person on this whole planet who can stand you is a four-eyed browner spazz. What a joke."

What a joke indeed. For Richard was not writing back. Mum got letters from Alice, one every other day, and the ritual visit from Alice was replaced by the ritual of getting the mail. The mailman came at lunchtime, when I was home for the break, and when the mailbox on the front wall of the house rattled, Mum would instruct me to go fetch the mail. She would set the bills aside for the Dad, and then slip Alice's letter into her apron pocket. She would not read it in front of me, but would often be reading it when I got home from school. As soon as I came in, she would fold it and replace it in her pocket. It was, she explained, *private correspondence*.

But she did report what Alice said about Richard. He had settled in nicely at high school. In his new town, the Grade 8 classes were held in the high school building, so he was in with older children (as she called them). They were helping him adjust. He had joined the astronomy club, which was called Stargazers, which used high-power telescopes. Richard, by benefit of his knowledge of the subject, had been made president already, the first time a Grade 8 had received such an honour.

"I miss him, I miss him," I said. "Mum, ask Auntie Alice to get him to write me?"

"It sounds as if he's very busy, Dee. Now. Let's do the vacuuming, and when we're done, we'll bake."

Helping Mum – helping each other – became part of filling up the absence. I was also learning to cook – to properly cook, not just lick spoons. I was learning verbs like *sauté* and *fold* and *dice* and *simmer*, and how to handle a knife, and the difference between a hot oven and a moderate one. I was also learning to clean – not just standard, dismissive, run-of-the-mill clean, but hands-and-knees, over-and-over scouring. We cleaned the oven twice a week. We did the inside of the windows every day. It filled the time. I could only write so many unrequited letters, or record his presence in so many stories, which I would then have to carefully hide, in case Theresa might stumble upon them.

So I went about my business, working with my mother through our thoroughly thorough activity, me singing "A Spoonful of Sugar" from Disney's *Mary Poppins*. The work was soothing in its never-endingness. Perhaps this was what I would do when I grew up: checking the corners for dustballs; pulling the sheets tight over the mattresses; wiping down every surface of every kind. I could even see it happening – that I would have my own house, where I would do what Mum did – but then I would remember that I was supposed to be leaving in September, to live in the woods alone.

As I took over, Theresa's contribution to the domestic upkeep waned away. Relieved of any sort of chore (for I had either already done it or was about to do it), she launched herself out of the house as often as she could, visiting Cathy and Karen and Sharon and Debbie, and going to practices and parties and movies and shopping malls and once, a Trousseau Tea for a girlfriend's older sister, who had "earned her MRS" her *very first year* of university. Except for ironing her own clothes (which she did because she didn't want anyone touching her stuff), Theresa no longer helped at all. She did no dishes, no dusting, no emptying of the laundry hamper; she did not sweep or mop or wipe down counters. Mum and I had already done it all.

"Auntie Alice is not the only artist," said my mother once, out of the blue (for she rarely spoke, except to give instructions).

I could see what she meant, for the amount of work we put in was as great as Alice's labour on her projects, but in the end I had to disagree. We were not artists. As much as we cleaned, the dirt came right back. If we cooked, it was consumed. There was no sculpture or painting to show off at day's end; nothing anyone would buy and put in a gallery, or hang on a wall. Our ham roast with pineapple glaze was stripped to the bone in less than an hour, the scraps relegated to lunchboxes throughout the week. After a day's use, the toilet bowl had another ring around its water level. The projects were never complete.

I was reminded of how Alice devoted herself to her projects. I wondered how she was doing, out there in the *sticks*, and if she'd made that new little box into a messy museum as well.

"It's not a little box of a house," said the Dad. "It's twenty-four hundred square feet."

This meant nothing to me, so the Dad explained that our house was only twelve hundred square feet. I wanted to see this big house that Richard lived in, that was twice the size of our own. Only the Dad had seen it, for only the Dad could drive. He had driven up to Bolton one Sunday after church, an act I counted as a betrayal. But the Dad said, "Aw, Dee, we men just wanted a little time away from you girls. Next time I go, it'll be a family thing."

"How was Richard?"

"I don't know. He wasn't there."

"Where was he!" I wailed.

"He was around somewhere, Dee. He had a friend over or something."

A friend!

And so it went, with me shifting slowly into

my mother's ways. She was not a talker, so I did all the talking, and she was not affectionate, so I did all the hugging and patting, and of course I was much bigger than she was so she always winced or jumped when I moved too quickly. This was not an unkind thing; I had stepped on her feet more than once, and once knocked her flat when I came around the corner from the dining room and collided with her head-on. She was a nervous, fine-boned mare trotting around her paddock, and I was the lumbering draft beast.

"Try to move a little more gracefully," she said. "Statuesque women need to be graceful."

Every Sunday I still went to church, although I was a complete infidel who sat smugly in her pew, holding silently over the others' heads my knowledge that God was a schoolyard bully, from whom I had a plan for escape, albeit one to which I had not paid a great deal of recent attention. Nevertheless, that I had thought things through – tackled God as I never once tackled a single human tormentor – gave me a feeling of superiority. I knew what God *really* was.

Besides, church was not an uncomfortable place. There were a lot of fat women there, who often greeted me as "sister." And since my own sister often had her friends over on Sunday, church was a true sanctuary, despite the presence of God.

"Where's your other girl, Dad?" the parishioners sometimes asked my father, and he'd say,

"Well, you know teenagers!" This would cause much clucking of tongues and censure of Theresa's lack of piety, and I was often praised for my devotion. I was a good girl, strong in the spirit, honouring my mother and my father.

So despite Richard's absence, and the dreadful, mysterious lack of correspondence, I slid into a bland, vanilla-pudding period of contentment, waiting for the first weekend in July, when I would be back at Barebones. At least my longing for the lake had not changed. At times I wondered what was becoming of me, that I did not play Jungle Book with my Barbie and a GI Joe; that I now listened faithfully and with pleasure to pop music on my transistor (as Theresa had done for years); that I did not spend hours lying on my bed, travelling to the lake almost as effectively as a physical attendance. Such flights of pretending were now hard to create. Whenever I opened the Plan's binders of schematics and illustrations and stories, it took an effort to make the rapture come – the being-there feeling, where I was surrounded by my delightful inevitables. To conjure the wolves' cold noses snuffling my cupped palm, to imagine the ice cave and the treehouse...it was work. I no longer believed fully that I could milk a moose.

So as spring approached, I swept myself up in the domestic, soldiering on, refusing to change, but unable not to. If I could only continue, just a little longer, to stay the doubt that was clouding the Plan, I would soon be back at the lake, and with Richard. I had only a few weeks to go.

Surely, if I held my course, nothing too much would happen, until I could lay my eyes on him once more.

Easter arrived. Being thirteen, I was considered no-longer-a-child, and was therefore excluded from the Easter Egg Hunt at church. And because the church said thirteen was too old for Easter Egg Hunts, the Graham household Easter Egg Hunt also ended. There was no scramble through the living room, up the stairs, into the basement, and along the kitchen baseboards, collecting pastel sugar-booty in a ribbon-festooned basket. There was no *Giant Hoppy in Hollow Milk Chocolate* waiting on my bedtable when I woke up. I would not bite off Hoppy's head like Saturn devouring his children. All that occurred at Easter Sunday was that we said a special Jesus Christ Is Risen Today grace and then we went to church.

Richard, however, finally wrote. On the Tuesday after May long weekend, I received an envelope from him, with a letter in a next-to-impossible-to-decipher hand. The bottom loops were missing from his p's and f's and q's, written on every other line of broad-gauge foolscap, like the primary grades use, with huge margins around the edge.

Dear Dee

How are you doing! I don't have much to write about. School is okay (believe it or not!!!!). It is a brand-new building with a very cool gym. The PE teacher for boys is diabetic too. He is teaching me weightlifting. It's for the football guys in Grade 10 and up but he lets me do it. We have to change for gym all in the same room and they tell us to shower but there are no curtains on the showers!!! NO WAY JOSÉ!!! But I am going through a GROWTH SPURT Mom calls it. Sounds like I'm spitting or something PTUI PTUI. Anyway I get sore legs at night. So too I also met this guy who used to have a cottage on Lake Muskoka and he knows where Barebones Lake is. He went there once to go fishing. He remembers James Mackenzie and says yes he is a REAL SHITBURGER. The guys in my astronomy club are also cool. We hang out after school. My eyesight STINKS. Mom took me to an eye doctor and he FREAKED OUT. He says I have burst blood vessels as well as cataracts. I'll have to have an operation but the doctor says not yet. And my mother has gone WEIRD. She says boohoohoo I'm a bad mother my kid can't see boohoo. I am not used to her being after me like that. She is smoking a lot of cigarettes and the house just STINKS. Dad made her put all her art and things in the basement, which isn't as bad as it sounds. The basements here are not like our basements. They are big and a lot of people have Wreck Rooms in them. Some of the kids have pool tables and ping-pong tables and this guy Peter has an INGROUND POOL! They are opening it up next weekend (Victoria Day weekend!) so yahoo I'm going swimming!!!! CANNONBALL!!! That is if I can talk Dad into

*letting me stay home with Mom when he goes
to open up the cottage. He always drags us up
there for May weekend when the bugs are so
bad it's not like you can go outside, and the lake
is too cold to swim. And we always miss FIRE-
CRACKERS! This is the first year I am staying
in the City (haha some city) to see the fireworks.
So haha on buggy Barebones! BOOORRRING
as they say on* Laugh-In. *Anyway I better go. See
you at the lake in July!!!*

I read the letter a dozen times. I could have
slapped him for saying Barebones was boring, but
perhaps he didn't mean it that way; perhaps he
meant it was boring without me. He still said,
after all, that he would see me there in July.

I had never received a letter before. This one
was electric with information as foreign to me as
the photos in a *National Geographic*. Inground
swimming pools? Wreck rooms? I wrote back at
once, and again a day later, and then the next day
too. On my way to school, head down and arms
crossed over my books, I stopped at the corner
postbox with its heavy red drawer and the coat-of-
arms of Her Majesty's Postal Service, and slipped
the letters into the slot.

But the mailman brought nothing more.

The Dad tried to comfort me, as I sat beside
him during *Get Smart*, trying to find Maxwell
Smart funny. I found him pathetic. I wanted to
shake him and tell not to act that way; people were

laughing at him.

"What's wrong, Dumpling?" said the Dad.

"Richard hasn't written me any letters."

"Sweetie, he's only been gone a few weeks. Besides, men don't write letters."

"Richard's not a man."

Maxwell Smart began to talk into his shoe. An idea struck me.

"Can I phone Richard?" I begged.

"It's long distance, Dee. Expensive."

"But you said we had money. You let Mum and Theresa decorate."

"I'm not made of money. In fact, I'm saving for something. Shhh. It's a secret."

I didn't care about his secrets, although I should have. "Please, Daddy?" I said. "I'll pay for it out of my allowance."

"Oh, all right. If you really can't wait."

So one Saturday I learned how to dial long distance direct. I paid a dollar for the privilege. The Dad set an egg timer by the phone so that I would not go beyond three minutes. But when I called, Auntie Alice answered. She babbled on for an entire precious minute, asking me how school was and had I drawn any good pictures lately, before telling me that Richard wasn't home. He was out with friends, she said.

The Dad still made me give him the dollar for the phone call. He was, he explained apologetically, really watching his money now.

"Dee, stop bawling, sweetheart. It's only a

dollar. It'll teach you responsibility…"

"It's not the dollar!" I wept. "It's Richard! He's got *friends*!"

In early June, the Holmeses paid a visit one week-day evening. There were, for now, no more Saturday Legion trips for Big Dick, who started his Barebones season the minute the ice left the lake. I recognized the car and flew out the front door, shoeless, and was halfway down the front walk before I saw that Richard had not come.

"Hiya, honey," said Auntie Alice. "You're lookin' great!"

Uncle Dick walked briskly by, lighting a ciga-rette as he walked. "How's the baby elephant?" he said.

"Dick, you're a jerk," said Alice. "Ignore him, Dee."

They had dropped by to bring the Dad his income tax papers, which Dick was supposed to have submitted in April, but hadn't; the Dad was frantic because he said he wanted the refund. "I gotta get the moolah before I see Mackenzie," he said.

"Take it easy. You're getting money back. You can file as late as you want."

"But I need the money!"

The Dad and Dick sat in the dining room going over Dick's figures. My pestering queries as to Richard's whereabouts were met with a "Beat it, Dee," from Dick and a "Scoot, honey," from

Dad. I went after Alice and was met with even more unsatisfying replies.

"Where's Richard? How is he?"

"Richard's fine, sweetie, growing like a weed, loving school, doing great," Alice said.

"But where is he!"

"Home. He had stuff to do."

Mum said, "Give us our privacy, dear. That's a good girl."

She and Alice retreated to the back porch and sat on the step there, and when I came to the screen door and lurked behind it, Alice stood up and closed the wooden door. "People who listen at keyholes seldom hear anything good," she said, as she shut it firmly in my face. Through the closed door, I heard her say, "This is why women never accomplish the same stuff men do. They got no room of their own…"

I retreated to the living room and kneeled on the sofa by the front window, head on folded arms on the sofa-back, imagining Richard was still in the Holmeses' car, and would be emerging any moment. I produced him, and he came trotting up the walk and through the front door. He leaned in the entryway to the living room, his spindly arms crossed and his eyes watering from strain.

Hi, he said.

Hi. How are ya?

'Kay.

Got any comics?

Yeah. Got an Archie giant.

They're a quarter now.
Yeah. Tell me about it.
Inflation.
Yeah. Inflation.
What a gyp.
Very un-cool.
Very un-cola un-cool.

Richard said he was there to take me to the lake. So we went. Summer dropped in, and it was like all the other summers. There were motorboats, water skiing, dock building, hotdog burning, card playing, late nights, early mornings, mist on the water when it was calm, whitecaps when it wasn't. There were mothballs in the sleeping bags, corn on the cob at dinner, cool forests, dusty roads, trips to the dump, sightings of whitetails, visits to Brother Webster's, ice cream at the Mackenzie store. We fled into the woods behind Mackenzie Landing, out deep as we could go, and we kept going deeper and deeper and then we found a clearing, and we went across the clearing and found a clear, rocky stream with sheer sandy banks, and we followed that stream and found a small lake with overhanging oaks and birches and maples, and a beautiful granite-sand beach.

This place is perfect, Richard said.

Someone in the kitchen laughed very loudly. My imagination failed; the dreamscape disappeared.

I never saw the place again.

Four

VAGINA DENTATA'S "SISTERS" ROUTINE
HARDY HARHAR'S COMEDY SPOT, NEWMARKET

Any of you people have sisters? Big sisters? Big sisters are different from little sisters. Big sisters are the rottweilers of siblings. Big sisters are the narcs. They're the speedtraps on the road through adolescence. Just when you've got a good head of steam up, and you think you're doin' okay, they pop out from the side of the highway and aim their radar gun at you. Okay, pull over, you! You're not actually thinking of *wearing* that, are you?

Big sisters have absolute power, and boy, it corrupts absolutely. They're the always-thinner, always-smarter, always-favoured, good-marks, good-looking, good grief. Big sisters run your life and won't let you wear their makeup. If you happen to be smarter than them they'll be more cunning. Everything you do, they did first. By the time you come along, your parents have seen it all. So you learned to walk? It's been done. And it was done better, by a much cuter kid.

There are three hundred photos in the family album of your big sister's first step. They got a professional photographer in and had the kid's hair done. There's a framed 8 x 10 glossy of her over the fireplace. You get a Polaroid, tacked to the back cover of the family album...

Big sisters have the street-smart advantage, too. They know all the fads first. They've got three, four, five years on you. They know the best swear words, but they're savvy enough not to say them in front of your dad. They'll get you to say them and then they'll tell on you. *Mom! Suzie said a bad word!* Whack. And you end up grounded, in the room you share with her, trying desperately not to touch her stuff – which, by the way, comes with a kind of homing device thing. All big sisters' stuff gives off this signal, this pheromone or something, that summons little sisters. You can't fight it. It'll drag you clear across town to where it's been hidden in a drawer, under forty pairs of very pretty, neat, folded, ironed, Downy'd, big sister underpanties. Her diary. Her copy of *The Sensuous Woman*. A letter from a boyfriend. A really nice silky shirt that disintegrates into shreds the minute you follow the signal to its source. Big sisters' stuff is made to break the minute you find it. And of course, she always knows you did it. *Mom!*

She was the pioneer, you were at the end
of the wagon train, cleaning up after the
horses. When you're older, grown-up, okay,
there'll be an advantage to it. She'll be forty-
one when you're only thirty-six. She'll hit
fifty before you do. But you'll never forget:
she was kissed first, fucked first, married
first. She went to the prom before you even
graduated from Grade 8. She got her driver's
licence when you were still falling off your
two-wheeler, or God help us, your tricycle.
She knew about cigarettes; the names of lead
singers; how to hold a lungful of pot smoke;
how to roller skate; how to French; what a
blow job was (you thought it meant people
blew on each other). Yes, you did. Admit it.
She was at the best parties when you were
still brushing the hair on your Baby First
Step. She knew what penises were *really* for.
She was the coolest, the hottest, the thin
one, the one that was best dressed, and you
never even got her hand-me-downs because
your ass was too big for her hiphuggers.

Ya know, I'm feminist, right, I'm into the
sisterhood, but lemme tell you, I wish we
had another name for it. Because brother,
there ain't nothing more scary than certain
sisters. Absolute power, man. Absolute
power...

*Amoral or suspect gatherings and dances you
should avoid entirely, no matter what your
friends might say, and no matter what is the
style or your own personal desire...*

A Guide for Young Christian Women, 1950

Theresa came home with the news that she was
going to the Senior Prom with Colin. She pinned
on the fridge the notice of the time and date and
dress and behaviour codes, and my mother
marked the appropriate Thursday in late June on
the calendar, by lining its square in red felt pen.
The Dad saw the date and took his handkerchief
out of his overalls pocket, removing his glasses to
wipe his eyes and blow his nose.

"Ah, Jane, do you remember my senior
prom?"

"Yes."

"You were so beautiful. You wore a green
dress with a big skirt. Great big skirt with lots of
poof to it. What a beauty. Just like your daughter."

Theresa giggled and shimmered with pleasure.
It was her first Prom, and she had parental sanc-
tion. The Dad began to lay down rules – Colin, for
once, would get out of his car; Colin would bring a
corsage; Colin's parents were to give the Dad a call
– and Mum began to make dress patterns and dress
plans. I was left alone, vacuuming and dusting and
applying Javex to the countertops, while Mum and

Theresa sat at the dining room table with the Simpsons' and Eaton's catalogues, and all of Theresa's magazines, speculating on the best look.

Cathy came over, several times in fact, for she too was going to the Prom, with a boy named Noel. "Noel, Like Noel Harrison in Man From UNCLE," she said, virtually every time she mentioned his name. "My boyfriend Noel, you know, like Mark Slate..."

"Yeah, but Colin's cuter," said Theresa, and it must have been true because Cathy went all quiet.

Mum dedicated herself to both girls' outfits, quietly but faithfully, and even accompanied them to the Fabricland to choose material. This so pleased Theresa – that her mother would walk all that way, and move among all those people, when she could have ordered the fabric from the catalogue – that she hugged her and said, "I love you, Mum."

I was lost in my own house. Now my mother had abandoned me too.

The dress was taking shape on the dress form in the corner of the kitchen, the expandable headless woman whose body was cut into panels which could be drawn inward or pressed outward. Right now, the woman was Theresa's size. At other times, it had been inflated to represent me, losing its hourglass shape as it grew in the middle and retreated at the bust. The rest of the time, it lived in the basement with the laundry and the cottage gear and the boxes of Christmas decorations.

The giggling of Cathy and Theresa as they sneered at some of the fashions they saw in the magazines (*look at this hood thing! and that skirt! they don't really expect us to wear something like that!*) called me down from scrubbing the upstairs bath, and I would lurk in the kitchen and listen. Sometimes I'd come around the corner and say, "Can I see, too?"

The laughing would simmer down, and they would show me the picture that had caused so much amusement: a woman with white lipstick wearing a pink bridesmaid's gown with a head-dress "inspired by the Apollo missions." A see-through plastic midi-dress. A tiger-stripe fake-fur micro-mini with a fringe. The three of them would wait patiently until I said something like, "Yes, ha-ha, that's awful," and then they'd pull the magazine back and I'd return to what I'd been doing.

If my mother wasn't with the girls – if she was doing laundry, or if they were up in our room doing their nails and toes – they were a lot less tolerant of my presence. Theresa, depending on some random mood-regulator that was beyond anyone's ability to read, would either ignore me or tell me to get lost. But Cathy, who came from a big family of seven, was magnanimous. She'd say, "Let her stay, Theresa. She's your little sister, and she's got to learn."

"She'll never learn," said Theresa. "She'll never change."

The Monday of the week of Theresa's prom, we Grade 8's received notice, on a Ditto'd sheet still damp and smelling of purple ink, of the GRADE EIGHT GRAD DANCE. Immediately the squawking and chatter began among them, for they had not expected the principal to permit a dance, and this was a joyous surprise to them. It took the teacher several minutes to settle them all down. I sat very still, and read the notice again and again. It was the last thing I'd been expecting.

HEY EVERYBODY!!!!!

THE GRADE 8 GRADS ARE BLASTING OFF
INTO THE FUTURE!
COME BE HIP WITH THE IN CROWD
AT THE GRADE EIGHT GRAD DANCE
DISC JOCKEY WILL PLAY ALL THE HITS
FROM STATION 1050 CHUM!
THURSDAY, JUNE 17
6:30 P.M. TO 9:30 P.M.
BOYS' GYMNASIUM
IT'S A HAPPENING THING!

I felt the paper all over, and picked it up to smell the ink. I had never received an invitation before, of any kind.

I could go to this dance. Thanks to my Christmas radio, and years of second-hand music from Theresa, I knew all the hits from 1050 CHUM – the words, the music, everything. I could sing along. My mother could make me a dress. My hair could have a cloth daisy headband in it, and I could wear blue eyeshadow and paint on my fingernails, and wear windowpane pantyhose beneath my floor-length daisy-print halter dress, which Mum would make me. We would go through the catalogue for ideas, and the headless woman would wear my dress for a change.

Craig McIlroy, who sat next to me, suddenly snaked out his hand and snatched the invitation from my grasp. He crumpled it up and threw it in his desk. It was too fast a gesture to see; the teacher was speaking with someone else, and the class was busy nattering, one kid to another, about the prospects and plans for the event.

What Craig did, however, was a revocation. I was no longer invited: that was clear. He sat, his hands folded in front of him on his desk, full of pleasure at having ended the chance that I might come, too. The two or three kids around him had seen him tear the paper from me, and they were all smothering snickers of delight, while keeping their eyes on the blackboard. Their shoulders and lips quivered and their fingers were clenched. I could see the smashed ball of my invitation inside Craig's desk, within reach if I pushed past his stomach and simply took it away.

My hand flew out as his had done, but I wasn't agile and I caught him in the belly. I missed the paper completely and struck Craig hard enough to knock him sideways, right off his chair, and because of my inexperience at lunging I overbalanced and fell out of my chair, too. But I took my chair with me, which meant I took my desk with me, since they were one-piece units. The desk landed on my leg and I howled, but Craig was howling too, shrilly and with real fear because I was on top of him, my head on his stomach. His legs were around my waist, because he was struggling to push himself away. I saw that fear in his eyes and something in me loved it. My hands went up to his head and I sank them into his soft hair; my face found his belly just above the buckle of his wide mod belt. He was pinned beneath me, and I was pinned beneath my overturned desk. But before the teacher could sail in and disentangle us (for the kids around us had formed a wall of interest), I did the only thing that I could, face-to-face with something so sweet and soft and dangerous. I bit him.

Craig's howls amplified. "She's biting me! Help!" he screamed, and at this point the teacher – Miss Petrie, a diminutive lady – cried *my God!* and sent one of the girls to the office for help. "And *run!*" she yelled, as she struggled with the desk. I was now snuffling into Craig's stomach, and Craig was actually crying as he kicked at me and tore at my hair with his fingers. When he landed a good blow to my ear I reacted by sticking my tongue through the gap in his shirt and into his inny belly button.

Then I was off and upright. Mr. Cohen next

door had heard the screaming, and he was a big man capable of pulling me to my feet. Craig crawled away, down the aisle half-a-dozen desks before it occurred to him to stand up. On his feet, he stood trembling all over, a badly frightened boy with tears on his cheeks and his hair messed and his shirttails pulled from his pants.

Mr. Cohen was shaking me, and Miss Petrie was squealing. "What's wrong with you!" they demanded. The principal burst in, asking what was going on. He, too, wanted to know what was wrong with me. "What's happened to you!" Miss Petrie cried. "You were never any trouble!"

Wheels turned quickly that afternoon. After they calmed me down, for I continued to fight and writhe as they walked me down to the office (I heard the principal tell my mother on the phone that I was acting like a wild animal), they made me come back to the class and apologize to everyone. They wrote out the apology and I read it aloud: I am sorry that I hurt you, Craig. It will never happen again. I am sorry for disrupting the class. I know that I was wrong to behave this way. As I read, I began to stammer, as I often did when made to read aloud, and the hiccupping sound of it made the teacher think I was laughing.

"Nothing is funny, Dee," said the teacher. "There is nothing to be laughing at here."

But I almost did laugh when I was sent home with a suspension for the balance of the year – a blue slip of paper shame in my schoolbag. I cleaned out my desk and my locker, and left the Junior High forever, a little sooner than I'd expected. And I was banned, of course, from the dance.

Not until I was almost home did I take out the slip to read it. There, on the paper, was a line of text I'd never seen before respecting me: words relating to each other, which could not relate to me. *Dee has been fighting.*

I read the whole thing again – from the preamble, where my name and classroom and the date of the infraction were listed – to the section called REASON FOR SUSPENSION. Reason for suspension: Dee has been fighting.

I walked slowly along, reading the blue note, my head bowed over it. *I have been fighting.*

I fought. I fight. Dee fights.

I walked on, thinking it was possible, just possible, that I could fight. The only thing they could do to me, when I fought, was push me away. Not want to see me. That was not a problem, for I did not want to see them. If I was attacked, I could hit. I could hit hard. I could even bite.

I ascended the steps to my home, still with my head erect on my weak and wobbly neck.

"Heyheyhey," someone, somewhere, sang out. "Look at that dog!"

What a cow, what a pig, what a hog, look at her. Look at that.

I turned quickly, before my nerve collapsed under fear and shame, to shout at them: *you shut up, you bums!* But the car was already gone. There was nothing in the street, and nothing at the stop sign at street's end. They moved too fast to be struck back, and I was left standing there, coated with their cobra-spit venom.

I remembered the Bandar-log: the monkey-people who tormented Mowgli and his noble animal friends, Baloo and Bagheera. Even Baloo, the wise teacher, had nothing to offer Mowgli respecting the monkeys' torments except the weak statement, *ignore them*. "We do not notice them," Baloo had said, "even when they throw filth on our heads."

With filth on my head – filth I still noticed, weakling that I was – I went in to face my mother.

I expected my mother to be standing there waiting for me, hands pressing the front of her skirt against her thighs, face trim with the preparation for a scolding. But she was not there.

"Mum?" I called, as I hung my bookbag on the peg and took off my shoes.

"In here," she said, from behind the swinging doors in the kitchen.

I walked slowly down the hall towards the closed saloon doors. I could see over their tops, that she was sitting at the kitchen table, reading a book. Not a *Family Circle*, or a scrapbook, or a cookbook. But a paperback book, and she was about halfway through it.

"Mummy, I had an awful day," I said.

"I heard about it," she said, looking up, at the

same time inverting the book on the table, so I could almost see its title. The word *feminine*, and a French word. *Mystery? Mystique.* That sounded sexy. A French sexbook, and my mother was reading it.

"What are you reading?" I asked.

"A book Alice gave to me. And David said I should...but never mind all that. The school called. I am not pleased, Dee."

"I had to do it, Mum. I had to fight."

"Humph," she said, like Kipling's camel. "Fighting will get you nothing."

"But, Mum. I have to do something. If I fight, they might stop the teasing..."

"There will always be teasing. People will always say things. You have to stay away from what they say. They can't be stopped; that's the way they are. Keep your mind on your duty and never mind all this fighting nonsense."

"Fine, great. So they can just call me whatever they like and I'm not supposed to do anything to stop them."

"I told you, you can't stop them. If they weren't bothering you about your...*size*...they'd find something else. You could be physically perfect and they would still interfere. They'd follow you around, slathering. There is nothing to do but avoid them."

"As if you'd know what it's like!" I cried. "You're pretty! You never had a person hurt your feelings!"

"Well, I see you know everything about me," she said, with a smile as bitter as alum.

"You don't even have any feelings! You're a – a robot! A lady in a cardboard costume with – with – vacuum cleaner arms! See if I ever, ever, ever help you in this house again!"

"I am perfectly capable of keeping a house on my own. Now, respecting the hurtful remark you just made, perhaps you had better go to your room."

"What if I don't want to?"

She ran her fingers over the book, and her line of vision slid longingly towards it. "Suit yourself," she said. "There isn't anything I can do to force you."

"But don't you even want to know what happened?"

"You hit somebody is what happened. What do you want, a prize of some sort? Hitting people just makes things worse. Dee, *move around them*."

"I've been moving around them for my whole life!" I cried. "You don't have any idea what it's like out there!"

"Of course I do. That's why I'm in here. Now, please, Dee," she sighed, drawing the book towards her, "I would like to finish my chapter before I have to start dinner."

"Go to hell!" I screamed, before I could remember that from her perspective, these curses were true curses; they were magic summonses and viable maledictions. I had never attempted that before – that slap of severity – and my mother's eyes widened and then closed.

"There is no need to attack me," she said. "I am doing the best I can with the lot I've been given."

"Your best stinks!" I yelled.

I charged through the swinging doors; forcing them back on their hinges until they cracked against the plaster walls of the hall. I expected to be called back, even as I ascended the stairs at a foot-stomping, foundation-shaking run, but there was no response from the kitchen. I stood listening for the sound of her chair being drawn back from the table, but she had not even stood up to follow. She remained in her chair, reading that dangerous book. I screeched at her, a single syllable that was no par-ticular word, but it didn't move her.

I had to fight harder. I leaned over the banis-ter, from the crest of the stairs, and with every cubic inch of air in my forty-five-inch-chest, I flung the worst thing at her that I could.

"THERE IS NO SUCH THING AS GOD!"

Suddenly, to my left, from the dimness at the crest of the stairs, came the whack of an opening door, and a pale white figure appeared, furious of face, thin of frame, with ribs sticking out and arms outthrust in shock. It was a man, alive and bug-eyed, with a dark beard and dirty blond hair falling past his shoulders. He wore light cotton trousers – pyjama bottoms – and they were nearly falling off.

"Jesus H. Fucking Christ in a handcar, Dee," he said. "What are you fucking *doing?*"

My brother, David, was home.

I flew at him, forgetting (as always) how big I was. David made a pretence of fear, and threw his arm over his eyes, thrusting his other arm out in front of him.

"No! Back! Back! It's my little sister! She's gonna kiss me! Help!"

I wrapped my arms around him and hugged his thin body, burying my nose in the damp locks that lay strewn over his shoulders. His hair was nearly waist-length, and I could feel it beneath my hands as my arms encircled him almost completely. He had been much more solid the last time he was home – had that been only Christmas?

"The Dad's gonna hate the beard," I said.

"I couldn't care less what the Dad thinks about my beard. Mum likes it. She said I look like the Blessed Saviour. It was weird when she said that. Almost as if she was making a joke." He gave a pretend shudder, like a horse shaking off flies. "Eww, Mum making a joke. It's like she might be getting real or something."

"Are you staying long?"

"'Til the spirit moves me."

He went back into his room and retrieved a shirt with long, belled sleeves and an African-style geometric print along its V-neck. He told me it was a Dashiki.

"Did you go to Africa again?" I said. "Did you see the animals…"

"Geez, Dee, I'm not made of money," he replied, sounding frighteningly like the Dad. He slipped into the shirt and sat down on the top riser, patting it to indicate I should sit too. There was no room for both of us on the one, so I sat on the next riser down. From there, I could look up at him as he spoke.

"So where have you been?" I asked.

"All over, States mostly, on the power of my own two feet. Look! No shoes!"

He held out his filthy, red-rimmed feet. The skin on their soles was black and shot through with pink cracks, and the metatarsals stuck out like cello strings.

"You certainly are a hippie," I said.

"Yeah, but that's not why I'm barefoot. Someone stole my shoes."

"Stole them!" I cried.

He explained that the previous night, he'd been in Flesherton and had found a place to curl up in an alley, behind someone's shed – very neat, clean, alley, no rats or anything, very safe – but in the morning he found his shoes had been carefully removed from his feet. His backpack and guitar were still with him, but the things he needed most for comfort in travel were gone. Someone had played a very dirty trick, he observed, and after that he decided just to take the train into Toronto and see how we all were doing.

"Where'd you get the money for that?"

"I called Webby – uh, Mr. Webster – and he

wired me some."

"Did you go to that bird thing?"

"What?"

"Like the bird in the Snoopy...Woodstock!"

"Oh, yeah, that. Wow, it was far out. There was no place to camp and it stank like you wouldn't believe. I was supposed to meet Webby but it took two days and then when we did meet up it was just a fluke. A wonderful fluke..." His face smoothed over with pleasure at the recollection, as if he could see the moment happening all over again.

"David?" I said.

"Oh, yeah, sorry. Anyway, we met up, and of course the first thing we did was head for the lake, but man! Some lake! It was a pond. Nothing like Muskoka, man. And the music, holy cow, I know I coulda done better than some of the acts. But it was good to see Webby. He's been really generous with, like, helping me out with bread sometimes. Don't tell the Dad, though, okay?"

"You shoulda called the Dad – he'd have given you bread."

David spat out a bitter laugh and said, "I'd rather have come back to Toronto, walking on my knees in a hairshirt, than ask the Dad for another penny. Every penny, Dee, it's got a string attached to it."

"What's a hairshirt?" I said.

"A really scratchy thing they used to make sinners wear. How is the Dad, anyway?"

"What do you mean, how is he? He's the Dad."

"He treats you girls okay, right?"

"Yeah. Sure. Whaddya mean, okay?"

"Never mind. Is he still pinching pennies 'til they scream?"

I hadn't noticed the Dad or any screaming other than my own, but then I remembered the dollar for the phone call, and the Dad's statement that he was saving up for something.

"He's pinching, all right. He's saving up for something," I said.

"What?"

"He hasn't said yet."

"Is Theresa still acting like she owns the world?"

I laughed. *That* I had noticed. "Yeah."

He put his hand on my shoulder and squeezed. I looked away.

"And how are you, Dee?"

"Okay."

"Really. What's going on? Why are you home from school? What was all the yelling about? Did you do something wrong? You never..."

"Yeah, I know, I never do anything wrong. I got in a fight with a boy at school."

"Man, that's heavy. Too much. What happened?"

I thought about the invitation, and how it had been snatched away. How could I explain, that I had bitten a boy because he took a piece of paper off my desk?

"Dee? Did he hit you? What happened?"

"He took something."

"Aw, Dee. That's no reason to fight. We're all brothers, you know. We gotta get along or we're never gonna have peace. You shoulda talked to the dude. Got his side of things. Maybe he didn't know what he was doing."

"Okay," I said, after biting my lip to hold myself in. Nobody, so far, had been happy that I'd been fighting. "So where you been? What you been doing?"

"Let's see. Where've I been? What'd I do? Well, last year I put in some time on the dissertation, right? But the teaching fellowship fell through, something about me always taking off on them, imagine that, ha-ha, so I was really low on money. It was far too establishment anyway. So me and three other guys and these chicks from down east – one of them was a Newfie but she was smarter than any of us, so don't believe what Uncle Dick says about Newfoundlanders – we decide to go look at things, you know..."

David had taken the train from Montreal to Windsor, and after that they'd all crossed the border into Detroit, which they all wanted to see because of the Black Day in July. But it was just a big ugly city; the worst thing was how small-town Windsor was, how dullsville but still not bad all-in-all, and then just across the river there's a huge corrupt American city. One side of the river, you're a free man, and on the other, the government can take you and send you off to war.

"We were all really glad to be Canadian and not have to live there," David said solemnly.

From Detroit they went everywhere, man, straight down to Miami Beach again, because they'd been there in February and liked it so much, and now it was early April and sure to be a total experience. But they didn't like it; it was full of old American men smoking cigars and telling them they couldn't come onto the private beaches unless they shaved. Very bad scene. So they had hooked up with a dude from Tuscon and his chick, and he had a VW van; he had been kicked out by his parents when he got the chick pregnant. So he figured it was no sin to take the van, which his parents had given him for his high school graduation present.

"Dude was rich, but he'd given it all up for his woman," said David. "It was so cool."

In Las Vegas they stayed in a motel and went to the casinos, getting thrown out of each one in turn, because they weren't wearing shirts or shoes and they still hadn't shaved. When they went back to the motel, hoping to put together enough clothes to get them admitted to a lower-class casino ("We didn't want to gamble, just have the experience"), they discovered that someone had broken in and gone through all their stuff. They didn't have anything of value, except their guitars and Bruce's flute, and these were missing.

"It brought us right down," he said.

But the next day, they scoured the pawnshops and found three of the four guitars, although they never did find the flute.

"What's a pawnshop?" I asked.

"It's a place where thieves take the stuff they sell, and the pawnshop gives them a little bit of what it's worth. Then they sell them to other people."

"Do you mean that whoever stole your things sold them at a store and you had to buy them back?"

"Yep. That's capitalism for you. Property is crime, Dee. I don't really mind. It was karma. I don't sweat things like that. It wastes energy."

"It isn't fair, though," I said. "They took something of yours and you had to buy it back."

David shrugged. "They can't take my soul, man. Nothing can do that."

"But they took your guitar!"

"It's material, Dee, just material."

To me, material was what you made dresses out of. I shook my head, indicating I did not understand, and David's lips tightened in thought.

"Okay, it's like this. It's why you shouldn't get upset enough to, like, physically punch somebody. What they do is just material-world. You'll never stop them, so just rise above it. Material stuff isn't real. Or, at least, not important. You can't get enlightenment out of material things. And then there's the classical idea – that it's the *idea* of the thing that's the real thing..."

"Coca-Cola!" I burst out, before I could stop myself.

"Aw, geez, never mind." He laughed. "I keep forgetting you're just a little kid, because you look so – mature. Hey, I'm sorry, that wasn't meant as an insult."

"It's okay," I said. How had he known I was hurt?

David ruffled my tangly hair and stood up, so that his bony shins and knees were right in my face. "I'm gonna take a bath," he said. "I got in about an hour ago, I guess, and thought I'd be sleeping all day. But then you and Mum decided to have a theological debate right outside my door – holy shit, Dee, you got some bellow on you."

He slipped into the bathroom, closing the door behind him. There was the sound of running bathwater, and above that, David's longed-for, always-missed tenor, as good as anything I ever heard on Theresa's radio or the Dad's hi-fi or *Singalong Jubilee. That's what you get for loving me...*

I went into my room, pulled out my Doodler, and started to write, while I still had the guts.

The suburban house is not a concentration camp, nor are housewives on their way to the gas chamber. But they are in a trap, and to escape they must, like the dancer, finally exercise their human freedom...

Betty Friedan
The Feminine Mystique

I sat on the carpet, my spine pressed against the sofa, watching *Saturday Morning Cartoons*, while Mum hemmed Theresa's dress in the dining room. I was on Day 3 of being grounded by the Dad, which was a most unsatisfactory repercussion, because I had hoped to see what he would say about my decision to fight back. But he had been typically overgentle. He said he knew I was a good kid, that he didn't want to come down too hard on me. David, I suspected, may have spoken to him privately on my behalf.

So the Dad sentenced me to stay inside, which of course was where I always was anyway. Punishment – suffering – would have been to lock me outside, where I would have had to fight to the death.

David had been sent to the Beaver Lumber store in the Dad's car to purchase a gallon of wood stain for the backyard fence, so that when the Dad returned from Saturday overtime (the four-hour Saturday shift in June was up for grabs), they could work in the backyard. This, Mum said, meant the men were out of her hair, and she could get Theresa's dress finished.

Theresa pirouetted slowly on a kitchen chair, and my mother measured the distance from the floor to the hem with a special stand-up yardstick. The dress was taking shape: a nautical-themed floor-length gown of polyester blend, halter-style in the bodice, with a square sailor-style collar that draped down her bare back. Brass buttons ascended the front of the skirt, to the seam of the bodice, and bold golden piping trimmed the seams and the armholes. Theresa complained that it was itchy.

"Itchy, but pretty," said Mum. "Put up with it."

I had said nothing about the Grade Eight Grad Dance. My desire to go had dissolved, more or less, and of course I was no longer welcome. I had, however, written a story, based on the myths I'd been reading in the Advanced Reading Group, where a giant came and ripped the roof off the school on the night of the dance, reaching in and picking up kids in their party dresses, and biting their heads off, crunch crunch. When they all ran out into the schoolyard, the giant stepped on them, one by one, and ground his heel into them like Uncle Dick putting out a cigarette. No one escaped. And when the blood soaked into the ground, thornbushes grew, and each thorn had a kid's face impaled on it, and the thorn pressed into the kid's brain, and the pain never stopped. Every day, grackles came from the hydro wires to peck at the bushes and eat the kids' faces. Next day, though, the kid would grow back, and hang there, in permanent pain.

Cathy knocked at the door just as the calliope music rose to end *The Bugs Bunny Hour.* Theresa ran to the door and let her in.

"Hi, Dee," Cathy said.

I didn't reply and she slipped into the living room, carrying the bag of cloth which was her own dress-in-progress. "What's with Dee?" she asked Theresa.

"Didn't you hear?" said Theresa. "She bit a kid. I am so embarrassed. It's like, I always knew she wasn't right in the head. But now, boy, it's so awful. She's going to be at our school next year too, my God, I can't stand it Cathy, what should I do?"

"You should drop dead," I responded, crawling over to the TV to change the station.

"I don't think you have to do anything," said Cathy. "Geez, my sister bit me when she was eight. I was bugging her and she bit me. It got infected, it went all blue and stuff. Lookit the scar I got on my..."

"She's crazy and she belongs in 999 Queen," pronounced Theresa. "I keep telling Mum to take her to the doctor so she can get rabies shots."

My mother entered the room from the kitchen, and I heard her set the portable sewing machine down on the dining room table. "I expect that it's some sort of phase," she said. "Theresa, mind your own business about your sister."

"It is my business!" cried Theresa.

But Mum went on as if Theresa hadn't spoken. "Here, Cathy, let me see your dress," she said. "How did you make out with the darts?"

Theresa gave up and the three of them returned to work, to their intense, quiet discussion over the chugging rumble of the Singer. I went into the kitchen for a box of graham crackers. Eating in the living room was strictly forbidden, but I carried the box proudly before me as I strode through the dining room, hardly glancing at the pattern they were pinning to Cathy's laid-out dress.

"Dee! Not in the living room," said Mum.

"Try and stop me."

She did not. I sat back down before the TV and debated crumbling some wafers into the carpet, but I had vacuumed the carpet that morning, in defiance of Mum's statement that she could manage fine without me. So I ate my crackers carefully, shoving each square entirely into my mouth, ensuring no crumbs fell from the fracture of a broken biscuit.

Suddenly, above the chatter of the sewing circle, I heard Cathy calling out to speak to me.

"Dee, are you going to the Grade 8 dance?"

"Nooo," I sneered. "Dances are for drips."

"Then you should fit right in," Theresa sang out. "Oww! Cathy! That hurt!"

"Stop being so mean to your sister," said

Cathy. She came the few feet into the living room, but the effect was one of her crossing a broad and busy road. "Dee, you gonna go?"

My Mum spoke up. "Dee, you have a dance to go to?"

"No, I do not have a stupid dance to go to."

"There's a dance on Thursday," said Cathy. "My sister in Grade 7 was complaining she didn't get to go. Dee, why aren't you gonna go?"

I glared at her, trying to get her to shut up.

"I am not allowed to go," I said. "Okay already? I'm being punished. Like, as if it's a punishment not to go to a stupid dance."

"Oh," said Cathy. "Gee, I'm sorry, Dee. I shoulda known, eh? Kept my big mouth shut."

Who was she to poke at me, as if I were a zoo animal in a cage, who could be stuck with a stick and made to move? I would *not* move, and instead shrugged and crammed a double-decker of crackers into my mouth. The TV started playing a Casper the Friendly Ghost cartoon, which I hated: Casper's ongoing misery, his irreparable condition, were too close to my own.

"Go away," I said to Cathy. I crawled back over to the TV to change the channel, but not before I saw Casper trying – and failing – to make friends with some children.

Behind me, the ghostly trio laughed.

From my knees I threw the cracker box clear across the room, through the dining room portal, and hit Theresa right plonk in the head. Theresa leaped to her feet and moved to attack, but Cathy intervened bodily. Mum stood up and said, "Dee, that is enough."

"You big crazy mental case cow!" Theresa screamed at me.

"Fuck fuck fuck you!" I sang back.

Theresa made a convincing plunge towards me, one which was only interrupted by the larger Cathy's quick grab of her arms. She held her hard by both elbows, cooing as she struggled to hold on: *your nails, don't mess up your nails, we just did your nails yesterday!*

"Dee, please, just go to your room," said Mum.

"I'll go," I said, "but because I want to. Not because you said so."

"Just GO!"

I had won. My mother had raised her voice. I turned, prepared to float majestically up the stairs, when in through the front door came David, carrying the paint stain.

"I can hear you guys all the way down on the street," he said. "Even you, Mum. What's happening, man?"

"Dee's out of her mind," Theresa began.

"I think I better go home," said Cathy.

"No, stay, okay!" said Theresa, but Cathy shook her head and slipped out the door, taking her dress with her.

Theresa began to wail. "David, make Dee go to her room. She's like throwing things and stuff.

She scared off my friend!"

David sighed and shrugged. "Maybe you oughta go upstairs, Dee," he said. "And like, later, we'll rap."

"I was going anyway," I said.

In my room, I began at once to write: I wrote about dresses that were possessed by dead girls' tortured souls, and I burned those dresses and I ripped them and I impaled them on spikes. I ground them into the mud and tore their sleeves away. It was a massacre of the bodies of cloth, and they flailed in the wind, flapping in their torment. It never ended for them, and the sewing machine needle crunched through the folds of their flesh.

I did not go down for dinner. Instead, I ate a box of Pop Tarts which I had stored under the bed for emergencies. I ate them slowly, licking off the frosting with a languorous tongue. The house was quiet, although I heard David raise his voice once, but could not make out the words. I heard the Dad come home. The tones of the voices were deep, portentous.

Soon came the clatter of plates, and supper. Then there was silence for a time, and the evening TV shows. Theresa showed them her dress: I heard the wheels of the dressmaker's dummy as it was pushed into the living room.

"Beautiful, Theresa!" cried the Dad. And from David, "Theresa, just beautiful!"

Beautiful Theresa, Theresa-just-beautiful. Not-there Dee, Dee is not-there. I ran my finger around the inside of the Pop Tarts box. I was not spoken of, and later I heard David go out again, and then Theresa went out too. She was escorted out the door by the voice of the Dad cheerfully yelling, "Ten-thirty, young lady! Ten-thirty at the latest!"

"Okay, Daddy, no sweat," she called back, her voice outside already, and coming in my window instead of up the stairs.

The day sank into evening. My room grew dark. I did not move from my bed. I had crumbs on my chest from the Pop Tarts. Downstairs, I heard my name spoken, in a conversation too low to decipher. *Dee...*

Like a birdsong, like a little winter bird, my name came up the stairs, a piping misnomer: *Dee, dee, dee.*

What are we going to do, they said, about Dee?

"Prom night!"

David walked around the house like a trouba-
dour, guitar slung around his neck, composing ad
lib. He was working towards a three-chord wonder called Theresa's All Grown Up. Theresa
claimed she hated him for this, but as she sat on a
dining room chair with my Mum behind her,
wrapping Theresa's long hair in hot rollers, she
called out suggestions for rhymes.

"City rhymes with pretty!"

"You could say best little girl in the whole
wide world!"

David came up with something a little more
cynical – "so many boys have already kissed her,
her lips are just one enormous blister" – but
Theresa was too pleased by all the attention and
grooming and flash-photograph-taking with the
Dad's Instamatic to take offence. There were
phone calls: Cathy, and half-a-dozen other girls,
phoned half-a-dozen times each to confer with
Theresa on the subject of hairspray brands and
nail polish colour. Brother Webster telephoned to
wish her a magical evening, although we were
unsure as to how he knew (David suggested that
since Brother Webster was a high school teacher,
he probably had a prom night at his own school,
and had put two and two together). We also finally heard from Colin's father, who assured the Dad
that there would be no hanky-panky. Colin had

been instructed to come to the door like a gentleman, not some hippie-dippie bum. The Dad's thanks to Colin's father were effusive. He knew, he said, how hard it was to get any respect out of kids today, so he especially appreciated Colin's father's efforts.

Theresa, hair still in rollers, ate a Spartan dinner of two sliced beets and a nibble of fried chicken. She then pronounced herself stuffed and sprinted up the stairs to dress. Mum calmly finished her own dinner and set down her napkin, then rose to follow.

"Dee, do you mind clearing things up?" she asked me.

I shrugged. I didn't mind, because clearing things up meant finishing off the leftovers. There were three more big pieces of chicken, and probably half-a-pound of homemade, thick-cut french fries, Niblets corn with lots of real butter, and ice cream in the freezer. I would be alone with all that food.

Suddenly, David said, "How come Dee gets shafted?"

"What?" I said.

"What?" said the Dad and Jane.

"All this Theresa-this, Theresa-that shit. It's The Theresa Show. How come Dee doesn't get a new dress? How come all Dee gets is the dishes?"

"It's okay, David," I said, longing for everyone to leave, so I could get to the food.

Then Mum said, "But David. She didn't want to go to her dance."

David's jaw dropped. "Are you saying Dee has a *dance*? Dee? You have a dance, too?"

"Yeah," I said, wishing he'd just shut up. "It's okay, though, I'm not allowed to go."

That made it worse. David leaned back in his chair, pushing his upper body back from the table, and rolled his eyes. "She's not allowed to go. Jesus Christ. Theresa gets a dance, and Dee gets to stay home and scrub pots. Lucky Dee. No wonder she's so unhappy."

Mum said nothing, but she looked at me. It was my turn to respond, but I couldn't think of what to say. Saying I didn't want to go was actually, somehow, a lie. I had not been *allowed*. I put a handful of fries in my mouth, and contemplated what else would go in.

"This is a bummer." David was on his feet, puffed with indignation. "What are you trying to do to her, Mum? Turn her into a little housewifey? Don't you think maybe there might be something better for someone as smart as Dee?"

The Dad cleared his throat. The time had come for him to speak. "Yes, Jane, it isn't fair. How come Dee has to be Cinderella? Get our little princess down here and make her chip in."

I tried to catch Mum's eye, to assure her that I was perfectly happy to be left alone in the kitchen. Theresa would no doubt blame the having-to-do-dishes-on-prom-night fiasco on me. Mum, though, seemed to be looking at nothing, standing very still, avoiding everyone's eyes. She stood there, doing nothing, until the Dad finally tossed his napkin onto the table and stomped off to the base of the stairs.

"Theresa!" he bellowed.

"Yes, Dad!"

"Get down here and help your sister with the dishes!"

There followed an astounding silence, like the deafened moment after the firing of a gun. Theresa emerged slowly from her room, and from the top of the stairs looked down at the Dad. His hand tightened on the newel post. He took his pipe from his shirt pocket and stuck it, unlit, between his teeth.

"That's my girl, come on now and help," he said.

An icy fog descended the stairs, like the plague-mist in Cecil B. DeMille's *The Ten Commandments*. "You have *got* to be *kidding*," she purred.

"Don't let her cop out, Dad!" said David. "She rules this house!"

"She does not," replied the Dad nervously. "Do you hear, Theresa? You do not rule this house."

"Daddy, knock it off! It's my prom night!" said Theresa, alarmed now at his persistence. "Mum, I need help with my dress! I could even be late! Mum, get up here, *please!*"

"I'm coming, dear," said my mother.

"Jane, don't you move!" bellowed the Dad,

pointing at her with his pipestem.

"Don't you tell her what to do, you old *fart!*" screeched Theresa.

At once, like a cloudburst, there was a squall of discord: David charged up the stairs to shout at Theresa, then shouted back down at the Dad, calling him a spineless old fool, which brought the Dad halfway up the stairs, yelling in self-defence, while Theresa screamed tearfully a string of largely unintelligible syllables, most of which were "prom." Then the three of them surged into the kitchen in an arguing lump, Theresa in a slip and bunny slippers, David's ponytail sparked with static, and the Dad's big arms waving dangerously as he tried to make points over the din. My mother stayed completely out of it, her back to them all, the only sound she made the snapping of rubber as she put her hands into her Playtex Living Gloves, in preparation to do the disputed dishes.

And then, David said, "Hey," in an awestruck voice. "Dig Dee."

They all turned to me. Only then did I realize that I had so much food in my mouth that I couldn't chew. My jaws were stretched open. Niblets of corn dribbled from the aperture of my face, striking the plate in front of me, like beads from a broken necklace.

"God," said David.

"Ewww," said Theresa. "See, Dad. I *told* you."

But the Dad's reaction was the worst. It was

the pity of a man faced with the pain of a hurt animal: the helpless need to lend aid, or the obliga-
tion to put the beast out of its misery. His urge to
communicate with me, to draw me to him, was
almost palpable, but so was his revulsion at the
picture of that much abnormality, as if I were a
baby born with some terrible deformity. He wanted to help me, but he also wanted to put me from
his sight.

I tried to swallow a little of the food, but it
wouldn't move. I realized I was going to have to
spit it out or choke, because my throat was react-
ing with a gag reflex. I could explain, I supposed,
but not entirely. I didn't understand it myself. All
I knew was that once I started eating, I could not
stop. Nothing could fill me. Nothing brought the
message, *enough.*

"Now do you see!" David said to the Dad.
"You have to get her some help!"

"Like what?" The Dad's voice broke. "What
do I do?"

"She's ruining my prom," said Theresa evenly, but for once no one listened. The Dad and
David were beside me, with a hand on each of my
shoulders, as if to press me into my seat.

"She needs a psychiatrist," said David.

The Dad was shaking so hard I could feel it.
"A headshrinker! You're out of your mind!"

"No, she's out of her mind," said David calmly.

"I ab dod!" I protested, spitting out the rest of
my food.

Theresa cried out in distress. "Oh, God, no, Daddy, David, no! If the kids find out I've got a sister at 999 Queen, oh my God, no!"

I began to cry, earnestly, because 999 Queen was the insane asylum. "Please Daddy, not 999 Queen!" I said, slumping beneath their kingly hands.

"Aww, Dee," said David. "Poor Dee, poor Dee. Of course it's not 999 Queen. Theresa, go away, for Chrissake, just go away. Dee, it's gonna be okay. I promise. Don't worry."

He dropped to his knees beside me and put his long arms around me. The Dad, standing on my other side, patted my head and said the same thing. *Poor Dee, it's okay, we're here. It's okay now.*

My mother turned, water dripping from her hands, which were armed against the steaming, soapy brew by a pair of pink Living Gloves. "Is Dee finished eating?" she asked.

"What?" The Dad's fingers tightened in my hair.

"If she's done eating, I'd like to wash her plate."

"Jesus Christ!" David picked up my plate and frisbee'd it at her. To everyone's shock, she caught it niftily and slipped it into the sink.

"Thank you," she said. "Dee, be a dear and pick up that spilled food?"

"Has everyone in this house lost their mind?" said David. "This is the sickest, saddest family on the entire planet. I got Plasticwoman for a mother, and some kind of Sparkle Cindy doll for a sister, and Mr. Spine of Jell-O for a Dad."

"Oh, and you're perfect, I suppose," said Theresa. "By the way, thanks for ruining my prom. Thanks a whole bunch. You too, Fatty."

The Dad had to move quickly to restrain David, who sprang at her panther-quick, seething with intent to harm, all of it directed at Theresa. The Dad caught David around the waist and held him, but Theresa, lithe and slippery as a salmon, had already vanished up the stairs, and slammed shut the door to our room. There, we could all hear her banging doors and drawers, and swearing a sing-song litany of hate.

"Big fat pig spoils everything! Who cares about the big fat pig!"

See me dress Theresa for the ball.

Theresa is in a book. She is made of glossy, cardboard-thick paper, and I punch her free of her frame of cardboard, applying the half-moon cardboard stand so she can be on her feet. She wears a demure bra – a Junior Missy Starter Bra With Magic Gro-Cups – and waist-high white panties. Her feet are bare. Her hair is perfect, the product of a thousand strokes of a commercial artist's brush. No liner or shadow paints her face. Her look is the natural look.

Theresa has a wardrobe full of paper dresses. Not paper dresses that people really wore, which were briefly in fashion but then died away. No, these are dresses which I cut from the pages of a book, with scissors. I cut out dresses for day wear, for shopping, for school, and for a party. The party dress is orange and yellow and brown zig-zags, with an empire waistline. The school wear is a tunic. To go shopping, Theresa wears culottes and a pretty sailor blouse.

I want a dress. I want a dress. I want a beautiful dress, and I want to be little, and I want to look up to the boys and feel them close to me, their hands on my shoulders. I want a boy in a Purple Barracuda to come and collect me, calling from the sidewalk, come on now I'm waiting. I want to be embraced. Nobody touches me; I want to be touched. Not with rocks and spittle, not with savagery and bites. I want my little feet, in their little white shoes, to peek out like two little mice from beneath the hem of my long gown. When the Deejay comes from See Aitch You Em Ten-Fifty Toronto, to play the hits that keep us hopping, I want to have a space on the floor, and to dance like anyone else.

Why can't you dance, Dee?

Because nothing fits.

My breath is as thick as gum. It fills my lungs with golden fluid, as it pours down my throat like honey, like lake water. I am drowning, I think, but then I realize: I'm just waking up.

The storm has blown over for now. Everyone has apologized to everyone, in formal tones. I'm sorry I said that. I didn't mean it. That's okay. No harm done.

It's ten minutes before Colin. I sit at the dining room table, reading the newspaper. I read all of it, even the sports section. The Dad, my Mum and David sit together in the living room. The Dad is on the couch, smoking his pipe and rubbing his forehead, straining at thoughts; David is seated on the edge of the recliner, tapping his heels against the carpet, his hands clasped before him. The Instamatic camera is at his feet. Mum is on the couch with the Dad. She has her Bible in her lap, but it's closed. I wonder what happened to the sexbook.

"Well, well," says the Dad. He clears his throat. We all look up, and the Dad and David stand. Theresa is on the landing, her eyes lowered, her dress flowing around her. She has one hand on the newel post, and the other wrapped in the folds of her gown. Shyly, coyly, she peers up and semi-smiles, chewing her lower lip gently with her straight little teeth.

"I'm sorry, Daddy," she says.

"It's okay, Angel."

"Dave, I'm sorry."

"Yeah, okay. We're cool."

"David, the camera," says the Dad.

The camera flashes, and "Oh, Daddy," says Theresa.

"You are pretty as a picture," he replies. "Dave, get one of us together."

Colin arrives. He shakes hands with David and the Dad, who greet him in a phalanx at the door. He is wearing a brown tuxedo with wide satin lapels and a huge brown-satin bow tie. He hands Theresa her corsage and she gives him the same downcast smile and thanks him. My mother, summoned, helps her pin it on her dress. It is a good match for the dress: a yellow camellia. Theresa coos at it like a baby.

"Oh, it's so cuuuute."

The Dad blows his nose and slaps Colin on the back. David takes more pictures; more flashes of lightning and the smell of the blown cube. The Dad says we need a picture of the princess, her prince, the King, and the Queen Mum – that's you, Jane – and he herds everyone together and hands the camera to David. Theresa grins, Colin grins, my mother stares. The Dad's lips quiver with pride. He and Mum flank the young debutantes, and the Dad puts his arm out and encircles them both.

"Smile," says David.

At that moment, as they stand framed and smirking, I step into the picture, and ruin it.

Five

Hands up if you've been to a shrink. Liars.
Oh, there's an honest man. Or is he the liar?
C'mon, don't be shy. There we go, there's
some honesty. Look at all those hands! Good
to know I'm in a roomful of whackos. You,
buddy? You with the teeth...yes, you. You
didn't know that about your teeth, did you?
Your friends did. Okay, never mind the teeth
thing; don't get all obsessed. Tell me, why'd
you go to the shrink? Aw, c'mon. We're all
friends here. Sure we are. Tell me. Tell me,
asshole, or I'll ask you girlfriend. Or I'll
make something up. You're a compulsive
ear-wax eater. Of other people's ear wax.

    Okay, okay. Enough of that.
Psychiatrists. Lemme at 'em.

    Psychiatrists are the sickest bunch of
power-tripping head cases ever to stroll the
antiseptic halls of our various medical institutions, and there are quite a few ordinary
M-D head cases out there. You pay three

hundred bucks an hour and they all have the
same line: tell me about your mother. I want
to hear about your mother. What do they do
when people don't have mothers? How come
mother gets such attention? She's not paying
the three hundred bucks, I am!

Psychiatrists, when they were children,
not only pulled the wings off flies, but took
notes while they did it. Psychiatrists were
the guys – and girls – in high school whom
nobody wanted to sit beside in cafeteria
because they always stole your french fries,
then couldn't understand why you were
angry. They were the ones who couldn't
throw a ball or tell a joke, but somehow
managed to feel superior. They all looked
like Woody Allen, even the girls. The teachers loved them. They didn't hit puberty until
they were nineteen and a half. They had a
solitary pulsing vein at the temple, and the
ability to communicate telepathically with
all the other telepathetics. They were the
oddest balls in any given spot in the time-
space continuum, they couldn't make a
friend, and they thought they were God. Why
have we forgotten this, and can no longer
recognize them? Is it the upscale brownstone
in Rosedale and the matching BMWs in the
circular drive that's making us think they're
saner than us?

Anybody who goes to a psychiatrist

should have their heads examined, preferably post-mortem. The followers of Dr. Sigmund Freud. Did you know Freud said that all women are masochists because we suppress our natural urges? Yeah, but if you ever display any urges – natural or otherwise – in front of a shrink, he'll ship you off to 999. They ask you why you're so angry. You say it's because you have busfare to last you until Sunday, are on a first-name basis with the food bank volunteers, and here they are up to their armpits in brocade and polished oak, without a single readable magazine in their waiting rooms. They nod and write that down. *Patient displays irrational resentment.*

I've had shrinks tell me I've chosen my misery – that's the Jungian guys – and others tell me I wanted to fuck my father and steal his penis – that would be the Freudians, obviously – and then there are the Adlerians who blame everything on the flawed environment I was nurtured in, which the Jungians say I chose. As for fucking father, if you'd seen my father, you'd understand how ridiculous that is. Dad was a highly unfuckable individual. He had three kids but I figure he musta anaesthetized my mother. Here, honey, here's your special drink.

Any shrinks in the audience? Well, whaddya know. You writing this down, then? Good. Write away. None of it's true. This is a complete lie. I stole this. No, assholes, not the jokes. Nobody would steal these jokes. I stole the *life*. So whaddya say, shrinks? Whaddya say about this life?

Lemme guess. You wanna know more about the mother...

It was 2 a.m. I was eating.

I started with a tin of tapioca pudding, using the hand-operated can opener because the electric one made a sound. I shook the tapioca into a bowl. It retained the shape of the can, a glutinous cylinder of wobbly white. I could smell its creamy aura. I searched the fridge for the can of Top Whip, found it inside the door rack, and popped the lid. I inverted the spigot over my open mouth, filling my hole with squirting cream, my head thrown back, my gullet open. The air in the cream relaxed, and all down my throat I felt sweet, sweet, sweet.

But hurry! Someone might wake up. Someone might hear and creep down the stairs. David was out, scouting gigs he said, but he could arrive back home at any time. I swallowed the cream and licked my lips and the backs of my hands, then sliced two bananas into the semi-solid tapioca, slabs of sticky fruit everywhere.

I started searching for more. Lately, Mum had been hiding things: the desiccated coconut, the Philadelphia cream cheese, the Baker's semi-sweetened chocolate. Her subterfuge slowed me down. The baking products – the canister of icing sugar, the cello-bag of semi-sweet chips, the jar of chopped walnuts – were all moved from the cupboard over the stove. I went through the spices and the cups-and-saucers and the electric blender and the mixing bowls. Where was it all? I did not have enough yet. Never enough. Never enough. Needles of panic ran up my arms; my hair was standing on end. Where was all the food?

I came across a tin of presweetened Kool-Aid – flavoured powder and sugar. I peeled off the lid and shook red sand over my meal. Enough, it seemed, for now. The Kool-Aid powder bled lava into the melting tapioca.

I slipped out-of-doors, through the back door, and into the balmy, early-summer night. The maples rustled in their dark yards, and the cedars stood like menhirs in rows between the gardens. Beyond their shadowy mass the night sky seethed with stars. Standing in the damp cool grass in the middle of my safely fenced yard, I shovelled in my feed and stared at Richard's stars and moon. The moon was two hundred and thirty-five thousand miles away.

And so, while I ate, was I.

Sunday morning came a tiny tap on the door. My mother's voice: "Dee?"

She was coming to make me go to church, I knew. I hurled my Playtime Doodler into the closet and plopped cross-legged on the bed, before saying, "What?"

"May I come in?"

"No, I hate you," I replied, but she came in anyway, and pulled up my desk chair. She sat there, as formal as a girl about to make a speech at school.

"Dee, we've all been talking."

"Gotohell."

"I don't think my Blessed Saviour will allow that," she said, and I had to resist the temptation to look up, because it almost sounded as if she had made a joke. She went right on, though, and I lay on my back with my arm over my eyes, singing la-la-la to cover the sound of her voice, but not loud enough to really drown it out.

"That's very amusing, Dee, that noise. Well, I will say my piece anyway. David says you are upset about losing your friend, and about the way the other children bother you. I know they bother you a lot. I know something of what it's like to be bothered."

Here I would have broken in and denied her claim, but argument means attention and I was not about to let on to that. So I stayed there, motionless, la-la-la-ing and listening too.

"We also thought perhaps you were upset about missing your dance. That Theresa had a nice dress and you didn't."

"Ha!" I spat.

"All right. I didn't think so. It didn't seem much like you to want a dress."

I sat up, like Dracula in his coffin, except that I had to use my arms to raise myself because I couldn't do a sit up. "It has nothing to do with the stupid dress. You are all so wrong it isn't even funny. Nothing is bugging me except you people. If people left me alone, I'd be happy. Okay?"

"Fine," said my mother, as if I had made an entirely satisfactory reply. She rose and returned the chair to its place. "By the way, David is coming to church, if you'd like to come too. He's going to perform in a folk service."

As she left the room, she closed the door behind.

I did go to church. I did not want to miss the chance to hear David sing, even in a folk service. I'd rather hear "Puff the Magic Dragon," but "Shall We Gather at the River" was almost as good if David was singing it. Folk services were fun – often a singalong was involved, with the duo or trio of guitar-playing "young people" urging the still-somewhat-suspicious congregation on. Many in the flock were terrified that singing along to a guitar might offend God, where singing along to a plastic Simpsons-Sears four-octave electric organ wouldn't.

David had never done a folk service before, but he knew all the songs and he was known to the church. When Mum asked him to sing and he consented without too much protest, although he did remind her about the record burning.

"They thought it was a good idea at the time," said Mum.

"It's as bad as book burning," David replied.

"Books can cause a lot of trouble."

"It's not the books, Mum. It's *thinking*. Trouble's a good thing sometimes, Mum. It's how we change and learn and get things done."

"Get things done in Jesus' name," she corrected, but the correction sounded half-hearted.

"Mum, not everything is done in Jesus' name."

"No," she said, musingly. "I suppose not."

At the folk service, David sang with two other men. The men were not much more than teenagers, but David was a man, a slender but large-framed man, with a big beard and long hair, who wore a long-sleeved tie-dyed shirt and frayed trousers and flimsy sandals of tooled Indonesian cowhide. The Altar Guild elders grumbled, loud enough to be heard, when the trio sat on the steps of the vestry with their bongo, their guitar, their flute – hippies, they muttered, should get a haircut.

But when David and the others began "I Hear My Saviour Calling," with three-part harmony, tenor/baritone/bass, even the elders were won over. David caught my eye as he sang, and he winked at me. People turned to look and they smiled beneficently. I had to hold tight to my own arms, wrapped around my body, to keep this brief happiness from showing.

After service, the Dad and Mum stood in the parking lot with the other parishioners, the Dad talking interminably, while David and I waited by the car. Theresa had not come, and for once, no one argued with her, possibly because they had David instead. The return of the prodigal had certainly affected us all.

"What the hell can they be talking about so long?" said David.

"Shh, don't say 'hell' on Sunday."

David looked at me, realized I was kidding, and laughed. "Yeah, no hell on Sunday. Even the Lord of Darkness needs a day off."

I was about to say something else, when suddenly a car drove by the parking lot – a convertible with four people in it, young people, but not Young People – and I didn't have a chance to hide or look away. In fact, I made eye contact with one of them, out of sheer negligence. Standing there beside my beautiful brother, I had forgotten who I was.

After they'd struck, silence hung between me and David like a thick velvet curtain. I wanted to believe he hadn't heard what they'd said, but that was not possible. They had even honked their horn, heralding their attack.

At length, he said, "Don't listen to them, Dee."

I was looking at my feet. I wiggled my toes. Yep, those were my toes all right, hanging out the front of my "nurse's duty sandals," which were the only women's shoes in the catalogue that came in a size wide enough to fit me.

He went on. "I guess that's like saying, 'don't think of a white horse.'"

"What?"

"It's a koan – kind of a riddle, Dee. Life is a big riddle, and koans are little riddles to help us figure out...oh, Dee, sweetie, don't cry. They're just a carful of assholes, don't cry. Don't think of a carful of assholes."

He put his arm around me and gave me a quick hug. "You know, maybe you oughta think about going on a diet."

I went cold. "What?" I whispered.

"Well, it would...make things easier...you know, if you didn't look – I mean, Dee, if this is happening all the time, why don't you try to do something about it?"

"Why don't they just learn to keep their mouths shut?" I said. "How come it's *my* fault?"

"I didn't say it was your fault."

"Yes you did. You're saying it's my job to stop them. I have to change to stop them. Until I stop being a big fat pig, they can say anything they want to me. I'm not allowed to be what I am. *I am what I must not be.* There's a riddle for you.

A fucking *cone*."

"Koan," he said gently. "Dee, I'm so sorry. Please forgive me."

I settled back against the car upon which we were leaning. The Dad was still talking to people, and I realized that this was the last Sunday we'd be coming here, for next Sunday we'd be packing up the house and things, for the trip the following Saturday morning. It was such a production to move the whole house up north for a summer, and to arrange lawn mowing and to cancel newspapers and milk deliveries and arrange for a neighbour to keep a key and to take in the mail. The Dad always asked the Giovanettis, who were friendly, he said; he'd even been over to visit. They had red-and-black wallpaper in their living room, and a pigeon coop in their yard.

He finally finished talking, and came to us with his arms widespread and his face grinning. "Time to go," he announced.

I took a long last look at the church, with its neon sign of salvation, and climbed into my father's car. The brothers and sisters waved good-bye from the sidewalk.

"We'll be back in the fall!" the Dad called out to them, through the open window.

But not me, I thought. *Oh, please, please – not me!*

The car moved into traffic, and we all headed home from church, for the last time.

And so it became officially summer. Hot weather arrived, filling the house with oven-warm, heat-sticky air; the Dad went to work in a lightweight shirt with no undershirt beneath, and Theresa wore her hair tied up in high pigtails, to keep her neck from sweating. David wore cut-off shorts and a leather vest and an ecology symbol on a leather thong, and talked about the FLQ as if we knew what it was. The Dad's standard greeting to him was, "David, get a haircut."

When cleaning our room, sometimes I would sit at Theresa's dressing table, with its triptych of mirrors, and hold up her hand mirror to examine the back of my head. I had dandruff, I saw, and a mat of hair where my head struck the pillow. I could not untangle it on my own, and would not allow Mum to approach me with a comb (not that she offered more than once or twice). I found myself cultivating the mat, and the dandruff: they said I was ugly, and ugly I was.

I had stopped writing about Richard, concentrating instead on my ever-growing collection of myths, all of them as perversely violent as anything Ovid had produced. I threw onto the paper the bloodiest and most extended tortures I could conceive. Every now and then, I thought perhaps I was – as the Dad and David had said – sick in the head. But then I told myself that God had created hell, and the Lake of Fire, and if thinking like this made you a crazy person, then God was a crazy person. And if God was a crazy person, then there was nothing wrong with me.

My report card arrived in the mail, and with it came a form to be completed by a doctor, for the board of education's records, certifying that my vaccinations were up-to-date, and I could attend high school in September without infecting everyone with polio or diphtheria. I thought about what would happen if I got sick in the wilderness, and realized that I would simply have to not get sick.

My mum had been told by the Dad and David to make a doctor's appointment for me, but she had not yet done so. I thought I might escape this – that there would be no vaccinations and no trip to a "shrink" – until I came downstairs one morning and found Mum at her kitchen table, her mop and pail beside her, and the ironing board set up by the back door. She had some lavender-coloured stationery in front of her, and a pen in her hand. There were a few lines on the pale purplish paper, lines of dark blue. No more than half-a-page, but she had been writing.

"Letter to Auntie Alice?" I asked. "We're gonna see her like next week, so why bother."

"It's not a letter," she murmured, folding the pages. She put them into her apron pocket and took up her mop and pail.

"What is it?"

She ignored this and said, "You have a doctor's appointment Friday afternoon."

Shit, I thought. "Oh," I said.

"Your father will take you. I don't want to go."

Well, neither do I.

She sloshed the hot water into the corners of the kitchen, and dragged the mop listlessly along the baseboards.

"Can I help you do something? I'm kinda bored." I was, too. I was tired and bored and hot and sweaty. There were six rooms and a cellar in my world, and a fenced backyard. But she said nothing, as if she hadn't even heard.

"Mum," I repeated, "I'm bored."

She dipped her mop and drew it clear of the pail, watching the water drip. "Me, too," she said. "Bored beyond all belief."

She pushed the mop again against the floor tiles, push and drag, push and drag. "Bored mindless, bored mindless, bored out of my mind," she said.

Not knowing what else to say – Mum had never used such a word as *boring* to describe her life – I lowered myself into my chair and sighed mightily. "I know how you feel," I said.

"Oh, you do. You know how I feel. Clever thing, aren't you, to know how I feel. Yet when I suggested I knew how *you* felt, you said it wasn't possible."

"But you just said, you were bored."

"I did say that. I did say that indeed. But that doesn't mean you know how I feel."

"Mum," said, as if talking to a growling dog, "are you okay?"

She snatched at her apron front, pulling out the paperback book she'd been reading for weeks. A slow reader who absorbed every word with a cautious appraisal (I knew this from when she helped me with my homework), she should nevertheless have finished it long ago.

"This," she intoned, as she held the book up like the preacher speaking of the Lake of Fire, "is a dreadful book."

"Don't read it then."

"'Don't read it!'" she shrilled, taking an alarmingly aggressive step my way. "I have to read it! It's exactly how I feel! You say you know how I feel. Well, this is how I feel!" She ripped through the pages, looking for something, and I could see that she had underlined the words in places – I could see striae of ink across the paper. "Here," she said, and thumped a page with one finger. "It says that sometimes housewives go berserk and go running into the street – shrieking – *without any clothes on!*"

"You're not going to run around with no clothes on!" I said, thunderstruck.

"Don't you tell me what I'm going to do! Don't you tell me you know how I feel! Do I ask you how you feel? Do I pry into your life? Do I? Well? Do I?"

With the book raised like that I honestly thought she was going to hit me with it, like one would a puppy with a rolled-up paper. I had certainly been hit before, by my schoolmates and my sister, and knew the posture of someone about to strike a blow. Gun-shy, I cowered, but from my cringing, averted pose I heard once again the slosh of the water in the mop pail. She was back at work.

The threat had passed, and in its wake I couldn't believe who had threatened me. She had returned to washing the floor as if nothing had happened, although now that I looked at her closely I saw that she had not ironed her housedress very well. It had a distinctly rumpled patch on its back. The flip in her hair, too, was sagging.

"And David thinks I need a psychiatrist," I pronounced. "You're the crazy one. He better make an appointment for you, too."

She did not dignify the remark with so much as a hesitation. I waited to see if Expression Woman would come back, but the mopping seemed to have absorbed whatever was left of her outburst. That she would ever burst out about anything amazed me.

Friday afternoon, the Dad came home early, to take me to the doctor.

The doctor was our family doctor, not a shrink. He had sometimes come to our house for house calls, mostly for Theresa, for I was rarely sick. Social Theresa picked up every infection and virus going, but I was both resilient and impermeable. However, when I had needed a vaccination or a check-up, Jane would take me to his office. It meant a subway ride, to Islington station, and then a transfer to one of the buses that sat, snorting and steaming like horses, in their futuristic concrete bays.

But the Dad was home early, especially to escort me.

"I'm not going to any stupid doctor," I said.

"Dee, I had to get off early. It wasn't easy."

"It was your last day of work, Dad. Don't give me that."

"Watch your mouth," he said. Then he tried cajoling. "Dee, on the way back, we'll stop at Country Style Donuts and get eclairs. The ones with the chocolate. I love them, don't you?"

"Your tricks won't work," I said. I knew the Dad was reluctant to physically fight me into the car. I had the advantage of immovability.

He had practice, however, with intractable girls. "Get in the car and behave yourself or you will not be allowed to have Richard over to the island this summer."

"You wouldn't do that," I gasped.

"Just watch me."

I got up at once and stomped out the door, straight down the walk to our car. During the fifteen seconds it took me to reach the car from the front of the house, a boy on a bike, who'd been playing some sort of tag with his friends, sailed past me and let me have it with the pig call. *Soooeey pigpigpig.*

I whirled and lashed out with my fist, but he

was quick as a gnat. He circled back and swooped in, this time followed by a couple of friends, evil Snoopies in their Sopwith Camels. I stood with my back to the car and swiped at them, hollering as they whirled by, carousel horses with darts and daggers. "Fuck off!" I yelled. "Fuck off and die you fuckfaced bums!"

"Dee, what on earth?" said the Dad, coming down the steps. "Are you out of your mind? Watch your language."

"Hi, Mr. Graham!" called one of the boys as he leaped his banana-seat bike onto the sidewalk, and cruised amiably by my father. "How are you today?"

"I'm fine, Tim, how are you?" He unlocked the car and motioned for me to get in, as he waved to the kids, who waved back, baring big smiles. They seemed to know him; my big friendly father.

"See you later, sir!" they chorused, speeding away.

I got in the rear seat. "You're not gonna sit up here and keep me company?" he said.

"I'd rather eat maggots."

The doctor's office was on Dundas Street, way out past the Etobicoke creek, along Dundas and beyond the downtown district where we lived. We drove along, out of my cramped neighbourhood with its small, wire-fenced rose gardens, its narrow storefronts, and its ancient, dusty maples struggling for the juice offered in twenty square feet of front yard. We kept on and on, over the railway switching yards and through the Junction, where I once went to Woolworth's with Richard and Auntie Alice, where she took us to buy fabric for a collage she was attempting. The Woolworth's had not changed; its red-and-gold sign and the windows of goods and flyers advertising sales were the same as that day, when I'd been fed a lunch at the luncheonette, a grilled cheese sandwich and a chocolate shake. Alice bought me a paper bag of marshmallow bananas from the bins of candies. I had been still young enough and small enough to look up into people's faces. The floor beneath my feet (in orthopedic shoes, not patents with buckles and bows, for my feet had never been small enough for such dainties) was stained chocolate-brown; it was hardwood and someone had spread sawdust on it, dusting it like icing sugar. At the back of the store there was a cage full of mint-coloured budgerigars who fluttered around in their pen, seizing the bars laterally, hanging upside-down from the roof. There was Hartz Mountain brand bird seed and hamster food. I had thought Hartz Mountain was a place I could visit, where they had lots of parakeets and hamsters, and the earth was covered with seeds.

We drove on, into the suburb of Etobicoke, where the houses had broad frontages, remnants of the farms they once surveyed. I saw, on one of them, a room-for-rent sign. I remembered the waitress at the lunch counter in Woolworth's, and how she made milkshakes and sandwiches, and I thought of career day at school, when representatives of different companies had come to explain what careers the boys (and yes, even the girls, in some cases!) could have. I thought now: I could be a waitress and rent a room-for-rent. I would have a bed, and a desk, and a table lamp with a gooseneck and a red plastic shade. I would buy a ribcord bedspread from the Eaton's catalogue, and matching ribcord curtains, in a sunshine shade like orange or lemony yellow. It would be very mod. I would stand on my fire escape and watch the traffic. Sometimes, my father's car would go by. David would come to play his guitar; he would bring Brother Webster, who would admire my stories. I would have a chocolate shake at lunch every day.

I had not, except for reading the ads in *Seventeen*, really thought about leaving home before. Now it seemed both likely, and impossible. Sure I could do it; of course I could not. I had never had a job; not a paper route; not babysitting. I had not gone door-to-door, asking to wash cars, or worked night shift at the post office, like David had; I hadn't minded the Riveras' kids after school for two full years, like Theresa. I had never planned for anything except finding a secret lake and building a secret cabin.

What was I capable of? I could write a little, and I could read. I could thread scrap lumber together into a ramshackle shed, and sit inside it and pretend I could live there. I could stay in the water all day without getting cold. What earthly good was I?

I longed for the taste of marshmallow bananas, and for Richard beside me at the Woolworth's lunch counter.

"Dee, sweetheart?" the Dad asked. "Would you like a Kleenex?"

"Why don't you just go jump in the lake," I replied.

The Dad pulled the wagon into the parking lot, newly paved with gleaming asphalt. He parked expertly between two of the new compact cars that he called deathtraps. He claimed that in an accident, these cars would crumble like so much Alcan foil. You need some bulk around you, he said, if you want to stand up to a big crash.

"I'm not going in," I said, as he got out of the car.

"Oh, Dee, not again."

He sighed and came over to the back-seat door. Immediately, I pressed down the lock button, but he calmly applied the key to the passenger door and opened it. His huge arm reached in and grabbed me by the collar, resignedly; he held me tight by the twisted fabric while he popped up the lock button. I remembered how he'd pressed me into the kitchen chair; there wasn't much point in struggling right now. But I knew what to do: as soon as he loosened his grip, I would bolt. I would find the train tracks and hop a northbound freight, like in the Gordon Lightfoot songs. Or I would run upstream, through the still-clear water of Etobicoke creek, stumbling over the mossy stones. If I kept in the water, the bloodhounds wouldn't be able to find my scent. I would keep going as the city and the suburbs died away, leaving me trodding the smooth stones of the river-bank, surrounded by steep cliffs peppered with swallows' holes. Somewhere north of Woodbridge, I would hitch a ride in the back of a pickup, or catch a different train, one that would take me straight into the rarest hills of Muskoka, where no one would ever know to look. I would hop off the boxcar as it rounded a turn, and I would make my way through the neck-high goldenrod to a deserted barn, where I would bed down in the hayrack, covering myself completely in the prickly stalks, glorying in the scent of cut grass stems. In the morning, I would slip into the farmhouse and raid the pantry, wrapping just a minimum of necessities in a sheet or tablecloth, so that I'd have a swag to carry, and I'd take a knife too...

The Dad steered me through the automatic doors of the building, which was a glass-and-steel low-rise, with an open staircase in artificial marble and twists of wrought iron. The doctor was three floors up; I had to rest on the second landing, to catch my breath. As I stood panting, my father, still with his hand on my arm, stared in disbelief.

"What are you gawping at?" I gasped.

"Nothing, sweetheart."

I would not be jumping off any boxcars. I would not be raiding any farmhouses. I couldn't even walk up two flights of stairs.

At the door of the doctor's suite, my knees collapsed and I went down onto them, grabbing upward at my father's belt and his shirttail.

"Daddy, please, please don't make me. Please,

let's just go to the lake. I wanna go to the island. There's nothing wrong with me. I'll stop eating, Daddy. Daddy, please let's just go to the cottage, okay, c'mon Daddy, please..."

He crouched down, squatting and putting his big arms around me, folding me against him to lift me to my feet. My spine wouldn't work, and I bent boneless as he lifted, looking down because my head would not look up. There were my feet, in men's sneakers; white running shoes with ankle supports and heavy rubber soles. There were my black polyester pants, size 24 1/2, from Eaton's. Where were my tooled leather sandals? Where were the corduroy hiphugger bellbottoms?

"Come on now," he whispered. "The doctor's gonna help you."

He kept murmuring at me, about how much he knew how I felt: that he hated to get needles, and so he was afraid of doctors too. But I didn't care about needles; I was afraid of the examination and the censure and the scales. The chart he would show me, with the dot on it, way above the line of normalcy, that would show what I was. Too big. Much too big.

And yet my father was bigger than me. He was big enough to pick me up from the floor and pull my sodden body through the doctor's office door. He was big enough to speak calmly to the receptionist, while I hung there like a carcass, and to sit me down and hand me a copy of *Humpty Dumpty* magazine, which I threw across the room. It was a good thing he didn't hand me the *Big Book of Bible Stories*; it would have dented the plaster.

My father was big. Why did no one, no teenager, yell things at him in passing? Why didn't he cringe when a car slowed, waiting for the inevitable sooey-call? He didn't slouch when he walked into a room. He took up space as if it belonged to him; he had no shame. He had played football. He was a big man. A big man.

The receptionist, who wore a white uniform and duty shoes, called my name from across the room. "Deirdre Graham!"

The Dad moved to help me up, but I struck him away. "Don't you touch me, you bumwipe," I said, and he tsk-tsk'd helplessly at me. He and the nurse exchanged glances of understanding and unhappiness, in my favour.

"I will never ever forgive you," I told him. "Never ever, even if I live to be a thousand."

I stood, on my own power, and walked into the examination room.

It was the same doctor – an Englishman who said he hadn't seen me in three-and-a-half years, according to my file. He had muttonchop sideburns, but not to be fashionable. He had always worn them, together with a curled and luxuriant mustache that the Dad envied. The doctor even waxed its ends into little scimitars, like Salvador Dali.

He gestured at the scale, and I stepped up after

only a moment's hesitation, calculating how much of a fuss would be made if I refused. But I was tired, and I complied. Up I went.

It was an upright scale, a black-and-silver monster with sliding weights. The doctor set it at 150, then 200, then 250, and his lips made a little vibrating sound as the balance teetered and came to rest.

"Two hundred and fifty-three pounds. You know, Cassius Clay only weighs two-twenty."

"His name," I said, "is Muhammad Ali."

"That's hardly the point. He's a heavyweight boxer."

"So how come it's okay for him to weigh two-twenty, but not for me? What's the diff?"

"You weigh 253," said the doctor, ignoring my question. "If you pass 300, we weigh you on a meat scale. For sides of beef. How do you feel about that, young lady?"

I shrugged. "I've had worse things happen."

"I'm serious." He held out his clipboard and showed me how much weight I'd gained since I was eight years old. "You weighed 107 pounds when you were only eight. Most girls weigh no more than 50 or 60 at that age. We have to start looking at a weight control program. Something sensible."

"I'll go on the Special K diet," I said, trying to distract him, or mollify him. "I saw it on TV. You have cereal with skim milk in the morning, with a grapefruit."

"It's a little more complicated than that. I can give you a complete diet plan for you to follow. Your mother can help you with it. It will keep you away from fried foods, peanut butter, butter itself, and so on and so forth. Fats and starches, young lady. That's what they feed to swine, to fatten them for market. And that's what's put you in the condition you're in now. That, and a sheer lack of self-control."

"I have a lot of self-control," I said.

"It's hardly evident," he said. "Now, hop up on here, there's a good girl." He patted his padded examination bench. I wormed my way up onto it, and sat mortified while he pressed a Popsicle stick into my mouth, uhm-humming and that's-gooding until I thought I'd be obliged to bite him. He pressed his fingers into my abdomen while looking off into space; his whole hand sank into me, into the layers of my seated body. His eyes met mine, and he shook his head sadly.

"What a pity. The things a person your size misses out on."

"Just leave me alone about it," I said.

"I can't. I can't see a person in such pain and leave them alone. Do you know why you're here, Dee?"

"Because my mother made an appointment to fill out a form. I have to get vaccinations."

He nodded. "That, and also…Dee, your parents are worried about you."

"She's a stinker of a mother. She's a bad housekeeper and she reads dirty books."

It was the only thing I could levy at my mother, as a criticism, because she'd never been enough of a solid entity in my life for me to have cause to complain. She'd fed me and taught me to wash, and to knead, and to fold whipped egg whites into batter, and to sort colours from stripes and whites, but she'd never met my eye and told me she had an opinion on something. Least of all on me.

"Dee, I have been to your home. Your mother is an immaculate housekeeper. I've never seen such an antiseptic home."

"Fine, don't believe me." I crossed my arms over my chest and examined the ceiling tiles dramatically. "My mother's acting weird, not me. This is the way I've always been. So you all are wasting your time."

"Your mother doesn't think so. She says your father is very concerned about you. I saw him out in the waiting room. He seems distraught."

"Who cares what he seems."

The doctor turned his back and retrieved my caramel-coloured file from his desk. From it he withdrew the health form that the board of education required before it would admit me to high school. He clipped the form onto a board and began to check items off.

"Periods started yet?"

I shook my head miserably, anticipating criticism for that as well. *If you weren't so fat, you'd be a woman by now.* But he just kept checking things off.

"Well," he said at last. "You're in very good external health, Dee. Except that you're morbidly and chronically obese."

I exhaled in relief, but too soon. He set down the chart. "Off with your shirt then, and let's take a good look at you."

"No way," I said.

"Now, come along," he cajoled, moving towards me. His hands went into his labcoat pocket, pulling downward, and pulled out a pair of rubber gloves.

"Get stuffed."

"Dee, I have to listen to your heart."

"Listen to this." I showed him the two-horned bullshit sign, which I confused with the single-digit up-yours symbol. It didn't matter; he wasn't driven back. Instead, both his hands landed on my bruised shoulders, and he tsk'd at me.

"You're a very angry young lady."

"So?"

"Your family is worried about you. Your mother says you eat massive quantities of food. She has to shop twice a week."

"Bullroar," I said. "She goes shopping on Mondays and only on Mondays. She never told you that."

"She says you cost as much to feed as the entire family."

"She never said it. You're lying."

He backed away from me and looked at me from a few feet away, as if I were an abstract painting he couldn't for the life of him understand. "Don't you care about your family?"

"Not any more."

"I see." His fingers stroked his sideburns. "Dee, do you know what a psychiatrist is?"

Boy, was he pushing it. I was thirteen years old, going on fourteen, and of course I knew what a shrink was. They lay you on a couch; they had billy-goat beards and spoke with German accents, like Harvey Korman on the *Carol Burnett Show*.

"Of course I know," I grumbled. "*So?*"

"So," he pressed, "have you ever thought of seeing a psychiatrist?"

"Have you?"

"Yes, I have, actually," he said, which threw me a little.

He waited for me to ask: why would you go to a shrink? He could wait until hell froze solid before I'd care about him.

He was quiet for so long that I grew curious and looked his way, from the corners of my eyes. Quickly, I snatched my glance away, for he was regarding me with a bizarre sympathy.

"Poor little blighter," he said, almost too quietly for me to hear.

That did it; I didn't need his pious mercy. I hopped down from the examination table and regally strode to the door, aware that I was still being watched, if not stopped.

When my hand fell on the knob, I heard the snap of the clipboard's metal jaw. "Here's the form for the school, Dee," he said. The tendered paper fluttered behind me.

"Keep it. I'm not going."

"All right, then. I'll mail it. Here, let me get the door for you."

He stepped forward and pushed the door open, and in doing so his hand fell on mine and gave it a very soft squeeze, like an encouragement but even more useless. As I stepped into the living room, the Dad rose from one of the orange vinyl waiting-room benches, his summer hat in his hands.

"Hi, there," he said. "Everything okay?"

The doctor gathered my father over with a gesture, while I slopped myself down onto one of the benches, and put my fingers in my ears so I wouldn't hear, and closed my eyes so I wouldn't see. Only when the Dad touched me on the shoulder did I open one eye and peek up at him. He was leaning over me, one hand on the wall, and the other where my neck met my shoulder, rubbing gently with his massive mitt of a hand. He smiled weakly through tightly closed lips. The doctor was gone; the nurse sat behind her high-walled counter, thumbing through nameless, countless papers.

My father's touch, under ordinary circumstances, would have been soothing. I refused to be comforted. I would not be approached. With my fingers still in my ears, I glared up at him, imagining a comic-book ray of anger and betrayal shooting up at him, and braced myself for whatever news he would have to deliver.

But all he said was, "Ready, honey?"

Cautiously, I slipped my fingers from my ears. "For what?"

"To go home."

I stood up. God, I was tall. I could almost look him in the eye. Was it the extra inch of my sneaker soles, or was it that my father had shrunk?

"Can we stop at Country Style for eclairs?"

He flinched, closing his eyes as if he'd just seen something tragic, but unstoppable: an animal hit by a car, dragging itself off the road, its back end useless, but its jaws still working in self-defence.

"Okay," he said.

"What about the shrink?" I said suspiciously.

"We'll deal with that in September."

I rejoiced all the way down the stairs; I even ran a little, playing with him as a reward for giving in. Coming up the risers was a mother and her little boy. He was dressed in a smart and snappy going-out suit, short pants and a pea coat, and a hat much like David used to wear. The boy's mother held his hand to hold him back, for he was only a little kindergartner, and might have fallen down all these stairs.

"Wow, Mummy!" he cried, when he saw me coming. "That's a really fat lady!"

The mother snatched him away, shooting me a look that was not quite apology, for her own horror got in the way. Obviously, she was thinking the same thing: she simply hadn't said it.

My father took my hand and tugged, for I had somehow stopped moving; all my energy for moving forward, for fighting on ahead, had drained away, dribbling off the stair risers in a yellow stream. At that moment, with the sun pouring in the long glass windows of this contemporary building, and my guts streaming away from me, I wondered how I'd ever go on. How I'd even got this far.

"Dee, c'mon, don't cry," the Dad said, slipping his arm around my shoulders and pulling me along. "We'll find you some help. You know what they say in church, Dee. The shepherd seeks out the lost sheep."

But I've been lost for years, I thought. Why are you looking for me now, when I'm long, long gone?

It was Saturday, June 27th, 1970, and I was packed, ready, primed and alert, before the sun had risen. I had my suitcase at the end of my bed, and my sleeping bag rolled up like a caterpillar and tied with its ribbon drawstring, and my book-bag full of books and the notebooks that comprised the Plan, and my pencil crayons, and the best comics, my favourites and also the most recent ones, bought from the corner store at the usual price of pain.

Among my papers was a booklet, which the Dad had given me, quietly and sadly: a glossy-covered, 5 x 8-inch, PHYSICIAN'S WEIGHT CONTROL PLAN. He said he wouldn't "put me on a diet," as long as from now on, I tried to control my eating.

"We'll help you," he said. "All of us will do anything we can to help you."

Theresa lay curled beneath her bedspread, one slender leg exposed to the cool air. It was not even 6 a.m., but I resented her sleep. Already the Dad was out at the front of the house, slamming the tailgate of the station wagon as he loaded boxes of tinned food, and the cooler, and the Coleman stove, and the Coleman lantern, and the lawn chairs, and life preservers, and toolbox, and fishing gear. I hadn't come down to help him, which I had always done in the past, and it was hard not to do so, for loading the car was part of the anticipation, like standing in line for an ice cream. But I was still angry at the Dad.

I made plenty of noise getting dressed, but Theresa didn't react except to mutter *fuck off fatso I'm trying to sleep.*

Foiled, I unzipped my tartan fabric suitcase and checked its contents. Swimsuit; long crimpelene pants in black and brown and dark green, other long pants in flannel and cotton (Mum's creations), sleeveless shirts, underpants, undershirts, pyjamas, socks, my bulky sweater that Mum had hand-knit for me, with a howling wolf on its back.

"Would you please fuck *off* and let me sleep?" said Theresa, as I zipped it up again.

So downstairs I went. Mum was in the kitchen, cooking breakfast. She was fully dressed in her cottage gear – casual cotton trousers in salmon pink, belted with a narrow white patent leather belt, and a white-and-salmon twin set that she'd always owned, probably since high school.

In her apron was her book, and a little coil notepad, and a pen.

I came over and pinched a piece of bacon out of the pan, to see what would happen. She did not look up when my hand shot forth and snatched at the food, but she did stare – almost glare – at the vacancy in the pan, before adjusting all the other pieces to cover the absence.

I sat down and waited, listening to the Dad's voice carry from out in the street. It was Saturday morning, early, and people were surely still asleep, but the Dad had found someone to talk to and they were calling out their conversation from their front lawns.

Yep, at least a three-hour drive.

Lucky dog to have a place to go.

Always thought so myself. Couldn't live without the lake.

Well, we'll watch the place for you, while you're up there lying around in the sun...

Mum continued preparing eggs. Each of us had an egg cup and a saucer with two slices of toast; the Dad had two egg cups and four slices of toast. I took up my toast and bit into it.

"Hey," I said. "It's not buttered."

"The doctor says no butter. I have to buy some margarine for you."

The Dad came in, and immediately attempted to kiss me. I leaned away and put up an intervening hand.

"Oh, come on, now," he said, not particularly distressed.

Upstairs he went at a happy trot, to rouse his other children. "Up and at 'em!" he yelled, pounding on the doors and blowing reveille through his lips, kazoo-style. He started to sing. "It's time to get up, it's time to get up, it's time to get up in the morning!"

"Dad, Jesus Christ!" came David's voice, murky with exhaustion.

The doors shook on their frames. It sounded like the Dad was kicking them.

"Take it easy, dear," called my mother. "Children, the Dad says up and at 'em."

The Dad came downstairs again, shedding nervous energy. His smile was an inch too broad, and his tone an octave too high, when he plopped himself down at the table and leaned over to pinch my cereal-plumped cheek. I slapped his hand away.

"There's no sugar for my cereal!" I complained.

"They're Alpha-Bits, Dee, they already have sugar on them," he said. Then he clapped his hands together and spread them immediately out, as if to welcome me, or to take in the sight of me with pleasure. "Good old Dee, ready to go right on time. At least someone's on the ball." He slammed his hand on the table and yelled into the air. "C'mon, you two! Jeez Louise! Let's get this show on the road!"

Theresa staggered downstairs, still in her babydolls with the pinprint roses and the matching frilly-bottomed panties. She slapped me across the back of the head in passing.

"Oww!" I said. "What was that for?"

"For making all that noise and waking me up."

"Daaaaad," I protested.

But the Dad wasn't in the mood to intervene. "Why aren't you dressed yet?" he asked Theresa.

"Because it's the middle of the gee-dee night."

My mother brought Theresa her egg.

"Yecch," said Theresa. "Egg. I'm not eating egg."

Mum picked it up again at once and turned away. "Hey!" said Theresa, in surprise. "It's okay – put it back."

She set the plate back down so hard the egg toppled over in its cup. Then, neat with self-control, she slid into her designated seat.

"Where's your brother?" the Dad asked Theresa.

"How should I know? Do we have any grapefruit?"

"I'll see," said Mum. Then, without moving at all: "No, we don't."

"What are you so jumpy about, Dad? It's just a trip to the cottage. We'll get there eventually." Theresa pulled her unbroken egg out of its cup and rolled it unevenly around her plate.

We roll his skull here at midday, Mowgli said to me, speaking up from *The Jungle Book*. I smiled and thought of Richard, and ate faster.

"I have an announcement to make," the Dad said.

The Dad took my mother's hand, swallowing it in his own. She sat very still, as if waiting for a balloon to pop.

"What announcement?" she said. "You know I don't like surprises, Dad."

"You'll like this one."

David rounded the corner and pulled up a chair. He was dressed in a rust-coloured long-sleeved undershirt and clean bellbottoms, and he had tied his hair back with a bright yellow bandanna.

"Man, you people are something else," he said. "It's Saturday morning, man. You must be out of your heads."

"Early to bed, early to rise, makes a man healthy, wealthy and wise," said the Dad. "You got in at two-twenty, David Graham. So I have no sympathy."

Mum presented David with an egg. David looked at it as if it were the head of John the Baptist, but then he sighed.

"Thanks, Mum." He lopped off its summit and dug into the viscous soup, his face screwed into a Popeye grimace.

"Your Dad has been waiting," said my mother. "He has a surprise for us."

"No guff," said David. "Hey, where's the sugar? I like sugar in my coffee..."

"They took it away so I wouldn't eat it," I said sullenly.

"The Dad has an announcement," said Mum again.

But even the Dad seemed to have forgotten his big surprise, for at that moment a lock of David's hair tumbled free from its bandanna, and the tip fell into his egg, curling up in the yellow matter.

"You are a mess," he said. "Why are you so tired? Where were you last night?"

"Out."

"Out where? You know, you're completely irresponsible. You never used to be this way."

"What way?"

"Disrespectful. Shabby. Look at you. You look like a hippie. A long-haired bum."

David smiled munificently. "That's me. Glad you noticed, man."

"Why don't you get a job? Nearly twenty-five years I've worked, and I can count on one hand my sick days. And you don't work at all. You wouldn't even know when there are weekends. I tell you, I even work on my weekends."

"Give the man a hero cookie," said David. "Dad, I'm not interested in twenty years in a smelly old school, pouring flavoured sawdust on kindergartner puke. I'm not into sweeping compound and revving up the boiler every October 10th. No way, man." He paused and swallowed a lump of egg. "I'm gonna sing and write and shake the trees a little."

"Wow," said Theresa. "You got gigs, David?"

"Gigs don't pay the rent," said the Dad.

"Consider the lilies of the field," Mum put in quietly, but nobody noticed.

"I don't have rent to pay," David continued.

"Okay, fine. In September, I'm charging you rent. You wanna stay here, you pay rent."

"I don't wanna stay here. I'm only here because it's handy."

The Dad frowned and changed tack. "You're coming to the lake, aren't you? I'll need help with the dock."

"Yeah, I'll come."

"And you'll help."

"If I've got time. I was gonna check out some of the summer places up there, you know, that have dances. I was gonna head into Huntsville and Bracebridge and over to Bala, too."

"You're not coming to the lake and not working!" said the Dad. He spread his hands and grasped upward at the air, as if pleading or praying. "I was counting on you, son. I was looking forward to it. Do you know how long it's been since you spent a summer with your family?"

David shifted uncomfortably. "I never said a whole summer," he muttered. "But sure, I'll help out."

"That's my boy," said the Dad.

David dropped his egg spoon, emphatically, so that it rattled on his dish. "I am not your boy. I am twenty-three, and I am a man. I am a man, and I'm not your kind of man."

"Did you go to that Yorkville last night? Did you take some kind of pot drug?"

David shook his head miserably. Theresa and I caught each other's eye. Her eyebrows were raised in appreciation, as if she were watching something hatch. "Wow," she whispered to me, soundlessly.

"Well, did you?" repeated the Dad.

"Take a pot drug? Oh, Dad…you're so establishment it's sad. 'Pot drug.'"

"Pot drug," Theresa snickered.

"Oh, please," whispered Mum. "I would like to hear the Dad's announcement. Please, Dad, what's your announcement?"

"I told you," said the Dad, "I don't approve of Yorkville. It has hippies."

"Dad," sighed David. "Just give us your news..."

"Do you know how much it cost to send you to school? Do you know how much overtime I had to put in?"

"Hey, I worked every Saturday during Grade 13, and after school, and I've looked after myself just fine with my degrees – I tended bar, I did tutoring, I typed up people's really bad term papers. I did anything and everything. I've even worm-picked. I can't just fold up and go back to your petit-bourgeois capitalist lifestyle, that sick and dishonest system..."

"Sick and dishonest!" said the Dad.

"David, David, please," said Mum. "Dad, your announcement. What have you done?"

"I paid most of my tuition myself, Dad. I earned that money..."

"Everybody please stop fighting," said Mum.

"Nobody's fighting," said the Dad. "David, son, you misunderstand me. I know you're a grown man, but you're young. I'm still in charge of you. When I was your age, I was married already."

"I don't want to be married this young," said David.

"You could at least date," said the Dad.

"Haven't you noticed? I'm the artist type. I'm

the quiet loner type. Not the dating type."

"I'm the dating type," chimed Theresa.

"When I was your age, I was married already," the Dad said.

"You were *not* married at sixteen," said Theresa.

"Princess, I'm talking to David. I was married at eighteen. Responsible. Earning a wage, learning a trade. At eighteen years old!"

"And a father, too," said Mum.

"What?" said David.

"The Dad was a father at eighteen," my mother said.

The Dad's face blazed red. David's eyebrows raised and he leaned back in his chair. "Well, well," he said. "Shall I count on my fingers, Dad?"

The Dad turned red and dived into his egg. "Don't you speak to me in that disrespectful tone. We'll discuss this later."

"I just find the lecture on responsibility rather out-of-place, considering this latest revelation…"

The Dad leaped up from his chair and leaned directly into David's face, speaking in a level bass growl, almost without inflection. "That's enough." He glanced at my mother, who continued eating her egg, lifting tiny teaspoon-tips of mucous to her lips.

"Okay, okay," said David. "Just don't talk to me ever again about being responsible."

"I am more goddamned responsible than you'll ever be. You think you know what you're talking about. You think you're so smart. You know nothing, son. You have no idea at all what really goes on."

David raised his chin, his lips tight with smothered smugness. "And neither do you."

"Well," said my mother, putting down her spoon. "What a delicious egg. Isn't it funny what you can make out of an egg."

She started to laugh, an unearthly sound because of its rarity. Surprisingly, she had a pretty laugh, not a giggle, but a rise-and-fall hahahahaha, which ascended a scale and then came down again. All the notes were major. It was not a laughing-with amusement, though. It was a laughing-at. My mother was laughing at the men.

"Jane, that's quite enough," said the Dad, and she stopped.

"Dad," said David. "What's your announcement, man?"

The Dad grimaced at him, indicating disapproval at being called *man*. Then he placed his huge hands palms-down on the table, and leaned back, taking a moment to construct his speech.

"Young people today, they're all freedom-this and groovy-that, all Daydream Believer and drugs and hanging out." Theresa and David shook their heads disparagingly, but they said nothing. "They don't have any idea how to work towards a dream. A dream without a plan is nothing. I had a plan. I've budgeted, I've been careful, and now my plan has come to its logical end. This summer, I get to fulfill my dream. I'm buying the island."

He smiled at my mother as if he'd just asked her to marry him, then sprang up and tore her from her chair. He seized her by the back and the wrist and began to tango her down the hall, singing all the while.

"'Leave the dishes in the sink, Ma!'" he chortled, squiring her back to the table, and dropping her on a chair. David and Theresa sat, their faces set in a *so?* expression.

"Well?" he demanded.

"Cool, I guess," said David. "*You're* gonna buy it?"

His tone held some sort of untraceable worry, and the Dad picked up on it. "What's your problem?" he said.

"Nothing. Geez, Dad. I never woulda thought you'd have that much bread."

"Well, that's because you're a hippie-dippie, and I'm a working man. I'm sorry you don't think it's a big deal."

"Oh, no, it's not that," said David. "It's nothing. Congrats, Dad. Far out. Cool."

"Yes, Dad, it's very cool!" I cried, forgetting that I hated him. Now Mackenzie would never say no to us. The Dad had bought the island.

The Dad herded us all to our feet, trying to get us to hug, but I was the only one responding. Theresa mouthed *so who cares?* to David, who still seemed distracted, even as he acknowledged Theresa by moving his finger around his temple in the universal symbol for crazy.

Mum extricated herself and returned to her egg.

"Janey, what do you think of your old man now?" the Dad asked her.

"I'm happy for you," she said, not looking up.

"Janey, aren't you happy..."

"*I'm* happy!" I burst out, for out of everyone I was the only one who seemed to be as pleased as the Dad. As Theresa and David returned to their seats, David still oddly subdued, Theresa indifferent, I hung onto the Dad, pressing my entire length against his side.

"Daddy, thank you so much!" I said.

"Dumpling," he replied, choking up, "you're welcome."

I was over the moon. Now that we were going to own the island, I had an inspiration. I could live *there* all winter – surely by winter they'd have stopped looking for me – which meant all I had to do to run away would be to build a little shelter on the mainland somewhere, just for the fall, until snow fell. I had always wondered how I would handle the cold, and now I had a solution to that problem. Falls and springs and summers I could cope with in the woods, and then when the freeze came, I'd retreat to the island. It was perfect. It had a woodstove and everything.

Summer in the forest, winter in the cabin, and Richard this very afternoon. I could hardly wait to start.

"Almost there, Jane dear," said the Dad.

In response Mum closed her eyes, as if to hold something in, or down, and her hands tensed on the upholstery. The Dad was driving fast, and the Vistacruiser shimmied as the speedometer passed sixty-five.

"Hear that, kids," she said. "The Dad says we're almost there."

Theresa and David, stretched with practised abandon in the rear of the station wagon, looked briefly at one another.

"Big horse-fucking deal," said David quietly, and Theresa giggled.

"I heard that, young man," said the Dad.

"Sorry."

David was propped on his elbow, flipping through a *Contemporary Guitar*, and Theresa lay on her back, her perfect breasts aimed ceiling-ward.

"I'm carsick!" she wailed.

"Not too much farther," said the Dad pleasantly.

"You might try sitting up, in the back seat, with your sister," offered my mother.

"Like, really. I'd rather sit with Gentle Ben. He smells better."

"Theresa, stop it," said the Dad.

For the entire three-hour trip to Barebones Lake, Theresa and her sprawl had consumed the free space in the back of the wagon. David tuned his guitar, jammed into a corner of the wagon's rear, and I read comics, and Mum stared out the window. My notepads, books and I had the use of the entire back seat, although we shared it with some of the luggage and the Coleman cooler. The presence of the cooler at first pleased me, but when I reached in to take a sandwich, I was shocked to have my hand slapped by the Dad, who twisted around from the driver's seat and struck at me aimlessly.

"They're for lunch," he said.

"I made some without butter," added Mum.

Soon we were long from the city, and after Bracebridge, the world opened itself; there were no more towns and only one or two gas stations. The highway dwindled to a narrow, two-lane, unevenly paved blacktop, which twisted around to avoid swamps, lakes and massive outcroppings of Canadian Shield. Every mile or so we passed a familiar lake, a cousin of Barebones which broke through the woods and approached right to the rim of the road. We saw trees laddered with hand-painted signs, their ends notched into arrows. BALMER, FLOYD, ROBERTS, LEDBETTER.

I watched for my personal milestones. The places I had selected, over the years, as having potential for living quarters, when I put the Plan into effect. The abandoned log houses, pioneer sheds of dovetailed beams, their roofs collapsing and their chinking gone. *I could live there*, I'd think. The chicken coops, eaves-deep in lilac bushes, and of course the dilapidated houses, so ownerless they weren't even boarded up. I had always longed for the Dad to stop, so I could stroll up the neglected driveways to these frequent, passed-by mansions, with their dead barns in the back acreage, and their porches sagging. Each year that we passed, these houses were worse-off; one place I watched decay, like a dead mouse eaten by worms in stop-action photography, trip after trip. Each time we passed, it was more decrepit; finally, it was just a pile of lumber.

"Almost there," said the Dad again.

We turned left, leaving behind the civilized blacktop of the secondary highway, onto the rutted Mackenzie Landing Road. It had a strip of grass growing up its centre, like a Mohawk Indian's hairdo.

"I wish to heck that Mackenzie would throw a load of chopped stone down on this thing."

The sugar maples crept up to the car, as if begging for food, lush from the lateness of northern spring. Theresa opened her suitcase, which was a Samsonite with a mirror in the quilted interior of its top. She began putting her hair in pigtails, Elly May Clampett–style, adjusting their heights carefully.

"Mum, does this look okay?"

"Fine," she replied, without turning around.

"Mum!"

She turned briefly away from her book and

gave Theresa a once-over. "*Fine,*" she said.

We rounded the second-last washboarded turn before the lodge, and the Dad made a sound, a throat-clearing hum, like the whine of an anxious dog. He leaned forward over the wheel and peered through the windscreen, his lips parted.

"Thar she blows," he whispered.

Another dog-leg turn, and the sun, which had been playing coy games with the cover of clouds, suddenly ripped free and poured across the road in splashes. The Dad stiffened like a racehorse in the gate. Help was on the horizon; the future looks bright; there is peace in our time. We're at Barebones Lake.

The road dipped a little, turned and forded a stone bridge; through the plush, green, leaf-laden trees, we saw that first sparkle of blue. Gaps opened, and the lake lay in full display, a peacock spreading its tail. There was nothing like that blue, deeper than its twin, the sky; the sun was out, and the wind chopped the surface into the manes of white horses. My throat closed, and my eyes did too. I couldn't stand to look for too long, while I was still enclosed in the car.

We crept along the road as it slipped between the Mackenzie Lodge buildings – the ice house, the bait house, the main lodge itself – and the beach. The Dad whistled between his teeth, a tuneless mash of every song he'd sung along to on the way there. My mum kept her eyes on her book.

"Isn't that something, kids?" said the Dad.

"What is?" said Theresa. "It's the lake. Big whoop. Oh, look, there's Linda! Linda! Linda! Hi! Oh, Daddy, hurry up and park!"

The lake was to my right, a smash of blue. The beach dwindled after we passed the boathouse, and became a boulder-strewn embankment. The road was so close to the lake that its flank was eroded, chewed by the lake's waters.

I could see Blueberry, just its far end, the reef side, and a large section of this side of Bald Face. Then the road jogged and Blueberry disappeared behind the cliff and the larger islands.

The Dad pulled off the road, up to the tree-lined dust-and-gravel lane that led to Mackenzie's second-class parking lot, into our parking space, No. 32. Regulars had their names on signs on the main lot, but we were not considered regulars, even after seven years.

"That's gonna end," said the Dad. "Soon as I talk business to Mackenzie."

Theresa was already gone, bounding down the driveway after the Dad, on her way to meet her friends. They were all charging over to meet her, too, shrilling and squealing. I got out of the car, but did no shrilling. This was a moment of reverence for me – the meeting of the lake, for the first time in the year. For these moments, I could forget it all: the horror-show of my life, and the sideshow I was. The long forced walks to school. The playground. Cars. People.

"C'mon, Dee, honey, let's go down to the lake," said the Dad.

We did, my hand in one of his, and a suitcase in the other. As we descended, the song of a slow boat, with a small outboard, sounded from the islands. We crossed the road and picked our way down the rock shore to the lake, then stood there at the water's edge, small waves rippling around our shoes. He slipped his arm over my shoulders and I leaned confidently against him. Together, we watched the little boat dock among the other boats, and saw an old man climb out, hoisting from the boat bottom a pair of ten-pound lakers, strung together by their gills.

"Trout on the menu at the lodge tonight," said the Dad. "Ahoy, Mackenzie."

Mackenzie glanced up, and immediately looked back to his fish. "'Lo," he said, to the fish.

"I'll speak to him when he's done," said the Dad to me. "These country men have a way about them. C'mon, we'll walk out to the dock's end, then go unload the wagon."

So we walked to dock's end, and sought out Blueberry together. It could be seen, almost entirely, from that point, peeking from behind the larger Marble Island, hanging off its end like an afterthought. It had pine and cedar cover, with very few maples, and even the conifers were thinly spread. Blueberry's cabin was fully visible, right down to the red shutters and window boxes, that Mum would soon be filling with pansies.

The Dad leaned over to me, as if I were a friend, and not his little girl. "We're this close to

owning her, Dee," he said. "I've got the down pay-
ment, and the bank'll put a second on the Lindsey
place."

I didn't understand, and I said so. "A second
what?"

"Never mind. I'm just bubbling over." He
stretched his massive arms out, his wrestler's
build casting a heavy shadow along the scuffed
boards, and I sat down on the end of the dock,
where the wood was guarded by a heavy iron cow-
catcher device, which served to fracture the spring
ice before the ice fractured the dock.

Behind us came the sound of Mum's and
David's shoes – her canvas runners, his Dr.
Scholl's wooden clogs – as they approached with
armloads of cardboard box and grocery bag.

"There she still is," David said, and I thought
he meant me, but he was speaking of Blueberry.
Then he was beside me, crouching, with his hand
on my back. One finger tickled the cleft where my
spine cowered beneath my flesh.

"Good to see her, eh?" he said.

"She's not a ship, you dope-o."

"Sure she is. A big rock boat. A floating
island. Like Gilligan's."

"Gilligan's Island," I pronounced haughtily,
"does not *float*."

"Guess not." He sat down on the icebreaker
apron with me, clanging his wooden shoes against
the steel.

"Metal's still warm from the sun," he remarked.

"Yeah, yeah, sure, sure."

David leaned in and spoke sideways, from the corner of his mouth. "Don't trip out," he whispered. "Richard'll be here any sec. Any money."

How did he know? Was I so obvious? But he was right – now that I had seen the island, all I awaited was the arrival of Richard. I didn't want to move from my spot, in case his boat arrived while I was in the parking lot, unpacking cardboard crates and sleeping bags, so that someone else, someone who wasn't me, got to see Richard first.

Theresa, having carried her makeup case and Flower Power sleeping bag to the dock's end, dumped it with a liberal application of wounded sigh as close as possible to where I was sitting. The Dad arrived again with a huge armful of gear, for his theory of moving items was to take as many as possible each trip, and therefore make fewer trips. I wondered if it was possible that we might get the boat loaded and launched before Richard appeared? If so, could I stay behind, and walk over to Richard's cottage, which was more than a mile down the road? I didn't want to walk a mile, but I would, for Richard.

The fear of not seeing Richard began to inflate and take over. What if Big Dick and Auntie Alice were doing something else, and didn't bring Richard over to the island until tomorrow? It had never happened before, but it might. It suddenly seemed very possible that I wouldn't see Richard

today after all, but would have to wait all afternoon and all night and all day again, depending
entirely on what the adults decided. I had already
been scheming what we would do today: we
would have a sleepover, we would check out last
year's fort and see if it survived the snow, we
would swim, we would snorkel, we would dig
clay. We could convince the parents to let us pitch
a tent and stay outside in the clearing by the small
rock face. We could launch the canoe; we could
dive for quartz and maybe GI Joe, who always
sank beautifully.

The equipment built up behind me. Opening-
cottage things, which would stay all summer: my
box of toys (Theresa: *Oh, Mum, not the dolls!
She's going in to high school in September! Please,
make her stop playing with Barbies!*) and my tea
set and tin cooktop stove, which I hadn't played
with since last summer, but it had been a lot of fun
then and would be fun again now, I was sure.

The last box arrived (a small one, in my mother's arms) just as David gave up on me and moved
away, brushing rust flecks from the butt of his
Levi's cut-offs, where the embroidered patches
read UP THE ESTABLISHMENT and KISS THIS
PATCH. The Dad dropped *his* last box as loudly as
Theresa had dropped any of hers, and I swivelled
slowly to accept my scolding for not having
helped.

But the Dad just waved his arm across the box
he'd brought. It was full of fireworks – long paper

tubes with bright stars and sunburst patterns, in primary colours.

"Labour Day's Show-in-a-box!" he cried happily, fishing into the cardboard carton for the prepackaged rockets, sad descendants of true Chinese spectacle. Hands Brand Fireworks, which he would set off after the long-away, closing-weekend barbecue: fizzlers and sparklers and promising-looking paper volcanoes, which spewed feeble magnesium instead of lava. I wanted lava; I wanted destruction. I wanted the whole mess to explode and take everyone with it, leaving only the rocks and the water and me and Richard.

"Dad, it's only June," I said.

"Can't buy fireworks on Labour Day – only Victoria Day is it legal to sell 'em." He winked at me. "So I'm keeping these in the shed, and on Labour Day weekend – Saturday night party! – we'll have a real blast!"

"Hardeeharhar," said Theresa.

The Dad ignored her. He pulled a panel of cherrybomb firecrackers – pencil-thin and pencil-length, red paper rockets, strung together in a sheet like an Indian's bone breastplate – and held it before him. "Bang, bang," he warbled, aping the Sonny & Cher tune. "I shot you down."

"Sonny and Cher have nothing to worry about," said Theresa, chewing thoughtfully on a licorice whip.

"Hey," I said. "Where'd you get that?"

"Store, bonebrain. Where'd ya think?"

"Dad," I whined, "Theresa's eating candy!"

"Theresa's not trying to cut down, sweet-heart."

Theresa stuck her tongue out, and it was black from the licorice. I turned away quickly, so as not to see her eat. But I could imagine savouring it as she threaded it between her lips. I ached for it.

"Dad, I'm finished helping load. I wanna go hang out," she said, through the licorice.

"No, you come over with us. You can see your friends tomorrow."

"Dad, that stinks!" She stomped her foot and snapped her whip. "I'm sixteen years old! I can even drive!"

"Across the water?" I put in.

"No," she said. "But I could put you in the water and use you as a *barge*."

"Dad!" I wailed.

"Girls!" cried the Dad. "Let's all make an effort!"

Theresa whirled on her heels, yarn-wrapped pony-tails brushing against her shoulders.

"Where are you going?" the Dad called.

"To see my friends! To get away from this stupid family!"

"Theresa," said Mum warningly. She was standing aside, with her finger holding her place in her book.

"What?" challenged Theresa.

"Theresa," said the Dad darkly, "Sit *down* and stay *put*."

So Theresa sat down, with a thud and a scowl, stuck. David was now standing in the boat, silently loading gear handed down to him by the Dad; I returned my attention to the open water. A ravening mass of black flies had found me and were supping on the flesh below my hairline, and buzzing around my eyes in a darting, annoying cloud. The burning schoolhouse firework tumbled from the Box of Fun as the Dad picked it up – it was my favourite. I could hear the tiny screams, see the tiny melting bodies. I would watch the small flames leap in the windows, and see the hands clutching helplessly at the disappearing air.

A boat, a big boat, appeared at the mouth of the bay, its bow slapping the whitecaps. It approached Mackenzie's harbour at high speed, having swerved in from Farmer's Bay, which held not a single farmer – only huge, cathedral-crested homes, complete with septic systems that leaked into the sand-bottomed water, leaving the beach sands slightly gummy. Farmer's Bay beaches had nothing on the sifted-sugar sand of Blueberry Island's tiny strip of beach.

The boat came close enough to recognize as Big Dick's fibreglass bowrider, *The Blue Meany*. I resisted the urge to leap up, waving my arms and jumping around, as I always would have done: the Hihowarya Salute, we called it, which involved pointing first to one's ass and then to one's friend's face, making the equation. Your face, my ass.

Hihowarya hihowarya hihowarya, dancing in small circles on the dock, or in the dirt, or in the roadway, wherever it was we met, oblivious. Big Dick saying, "Richie, knock it off. Ya look like a prancing fag."

Big Dick made a swipe at the dock with the boat, swooping close like a raptor, turning the boat's underside our way. The wake sprayed up and the Dad responded with a blast of whistle, through his fingers. He was as happy to see Dick as I was to see Richard.

"They coulda *walked* over from Farmer's Bay," said Theresa, who was sitting on a suitcase, picking at the polish on her toenails. "Always Uncle Dick with his big show-off boat." Her shorts were lavender denim hiphugger short-shorts, and as she spread her legs to stretch, a few tendrils of blonde pubies curled around their hem.

"Take a picture, pervert," she snarled at me, slapping her legs together. "You are one sick pig."

"Theresa," said the Dad. His biggest punishment: saying her name.

"What? She's a lesbian."

"Theresa. You don't even know what that means."

"Oh, for – never mind." She rose and brushed her bottom clean of nonexistent dust, and stomped off, unstopped, to join her friends on shore just as Big Dick's second approach ended in the engine's cut-off wail, and the splash of disturbed water against the pylons. The Dad let her go, because he was busy greeting his friend. I, too, jumped up and came to greet the boat, although the Dad was largely in the way.

Big Dick stood poised behind the wheel, a cigar crunched between his terrier teeth, his horn-rimmed sunglasses an utterly opaque beetle-black/green. I imagined he had stuck his straw hat to his bald head with two-sided carpet tape.

Now, as Dick bobbled his boat towards a mooring spot, I stood stiff and rooted behind the Dad, moving only to swipe the blackflies from my neck. I could see part of Richard, who was lying, absorbing the sun, on the floor of the bowrider's prow, his one leg bent. That was how he would read – flat on his back on the boat – with a book three inches from his painfully myopic eyes. All that was exposed to me now, though, was the point of his knee, which was glittering somehow, with spun gold. The hair on Richard's leg was catching the waning sun.

"Richard," I called, but the engine was too loud and the wind was up. That, beyond a doubt, was the reason for his not sitting up at the sound of my call, waving and grinning, pulling a rictus-face.

From the shore, at the dock's root, I heard a young man's voice crooning. He was talking to other young men, loud enough to be heard. Mocking me.

"Rich-aaaard," he mimicked, to his friends' applause. "Kiss meeee, Richard. Kiss my big fat ass, I'm a hunka-hunka burning *lunch*..."

The Porch Gang. I did not look their way, for it would be too much, of course: all that bright grasshopper behaviour, as Theresa met them and they all dipped and cuddled, four girls, five boys, wearing Levi's, the girls in halter tops made of string and daisy-print scarves, cunningly knotted. Flip-flops on their slim feet; hair straightened and touched up with Sun-In spray. The smoothness of the boys; the girls' peach or baby-pink lipstick, their mascara and blue shadow, even here where it was the least of necessary things. Hair clutched back in fat cords of neon-green yarn designed for only that. Hugging, popping up and down like corks, heading straight for the porch of the lodge, where they would settle in, pert bums perched on the railing, or sprawled in the inclined white-washed deck chairs. How their voices carried, whenever I snuck past. How they carried now, to me – the object of their sight.

"Bigger than ever! Jesus Murphy!"

"How do you *stand* her, Theresa?"

Richard, hurry, they've seen me, and I'll never get off this dock alive.

My mother touched my arm. I realized that I was so afraid, that I had actually stopped seeing.

"Dee," she said quietly, "here's Richard."

I turned, and there he was. And there he was not.

Six

...Fuck friends, man. Fuck that kindred spirit stuff. You know what friends do? They make you behave weird. Right from square one, from the very beginning, Grade 1 like, you're doing stuff to please your friends. You might...oh, I dunno...like classical music, say. And all your friends are into say, something dreadfully urbane and witty, like say, gangsta rap, but you don't dare fucking say a word. Why? Because if you don't toe the Official Friends Party Line, they won't be your friends. And you gotta have friends, man. If you don't have friends, there's something wrong with you. Ask anybody whose next door neighbour turned out to have pulled a John Wayne Gacy, hiding a dozen rotting corpses in his crawlspace, freshened up with just a sprinkle of lime. The first thing they're asked about is the guy's popularity. "Did your murderous, axe-wielding, psycho killer neighbour have any *friends*?"

Like they're a barometer for normalcy or something.

The fact is – Gacy had lotsa friends. And look what he did to 'em. Man, don't trust nobody...

And yet the metamorphosis does take place.
The little girl does not grasp its meaning…

Simone de Beauvoir
The Second Sex

Stretched out, an Odalisque of a man, reclining in the bow seats of the boat, one knee, frosted with spun gold, pointed to the sky, the other earthward, or rather waterward, so that his long, muscled – *muscled!* – legs bowed into a diamond, his shorts, fashionably denim, fashionably short, cut high above his quadriceps. His leg muscles bulging like any man's might, and his shorts bulging too, like a father's, an uncle's, oh woe!

He was shirtless, and his bare chest shone with oil and bugspray. He already had a tan. How? How much time had the burrowing, molelike Richard spent outdoors? Doing what? Tennis lessons, perhaps? What was going on in Bolton, anyway?

"My goodness, it's nice to see you all," my mother was saying. There was some indecorous scrambling on the part of Big Dick and Auntie Alice, who were too short and too tall, respectively, to climb out of the boat efficiently. The Dad interfered with Big Dick's disembarkment, grabbing him around the shoulders and shaking him like a rabbit, picking him up, and causing him to suffer other small-man indignities. As my mother inclined herself towards Alice (who was already lighting a cigarette), the Dad put Big Dick in a headlock. Big Dick punched the Dad in the stomach.

"Hit me again!" the Dad cried. "Hard as a rock! Hit me again!"

Hit me again, too, my eyes. I'd give anything not to see this, give up my comics, my books, my scribblers; I'd spend an extra two weeks in school, if only this weren't true, if only there wasn't such damage. Where was Richard, not here, not here...

"Dee, what on earth's got into you?" said Auntie Alice. "C'mere and gimme a big ol' Dee hug."

I stepped back and away, not looking at her, unable to take my eyes off Richard. The godling was moving, taking his arms down from their casual disarray behind his head. He yawned a leonine yawn. The braces were gone from his teeth. What white teeth you have, the better to show disdain!

All the air went dry and still, although the wind still whipped me; it was like the moment in the movies when the mummy walked. I trembled, he sat up, and tapped his dark sunglasses closer to his face, and his fingers were a man's, and his hands had golden hair on their backs, as did his arms and calves and thighs. His chest, though, was bare, except for a brass ecology symbol – a segmented oval – which he wore on a rainbow-coloured cord. He did not so much as look at me.

The Dad stopped tussling with Big Dick and the two of them signalled to David to accompany them, to seek out Mackenzie and pay the rent (and to do the manly, gas-buying, money-exchanging, fish-measuring things that men do). I started to follow them, but the Dad saw me move and frowned, shaking his head; I was not to come along.

Porch Gang on the shore, Richard coming out of the boat. There was nowhere to go.

Dickweed, I said to myself, and that opened the gates for all the insults to fly behind closed lips and closed eyes. My litany gave me power, looping and raging. *Bastard son of a bitch jerk dickweed bumhead fucker asshole bastard son of a bitch...*

Snob!

I widened my eyes to face the snob, who still hadn't had the guts to look at me, or to say a word. His glasses-cloaked gaze swept over me as if I wasn't even there, something to which I was accustomed, for when people weren't striking me they were pretending I wasn't there. Now Richard was *people*. One of them, one of the normals. The snob. The bastard. The bumfucker.

Still, he should be looking at me, for I was fixing him with a really creepy full-force killer-beam stare, so that he'd know he was a bumfucker and a snob, and that I knew who he really was under all that lionish hair and behind those freshly released teeth. But no, he would not. Not a moment's steady fix on my face, from behind those octagonal wire-frame glasses, tinted deeply – regally – blue. How cool. How cold. How insect-like, this walking-stick man, who had hatched from the wriggler of my Richard.

"Richard, get out of the boat, dear."

Something strained in Alice's voice. Mercy, worry, pity? She said, "get out of the boat," but the phrase rang with inference. Careful, poor thing, my baby, caution: this was her subtext. I glanced at her, and she saw the movement in my stiff neck and caught my eye in return. She frowned at me. Apparently, I was breaching some sort of protocol – doing something wrong. But what?

My mother clutched at her elbow, like a ten-year-old girl. I saw she was angry with me, as well. Well, to hell with them both, then. I don't care what they think. Typical. Now that he's good-looking, he's the one who's right.

I folded my arms even tighter, as Richard put his hands on the dock, oddly unbalanced as he did so. He had to lift himself up, but he was hesitating, sizing up the distance. Someone with that much power should be bounding from the prow to dock level, as I had seen the Porch Gang boys do many times, exercising simian talents.

But not Richard. Aha! Not accustomed to your stolen skin, eh? Not quite up to your costume. Another Richard, I would have helped. But this one was on its own.

Richard leaned unsteadily forward, as if he were seasick or dizzy, and ran his hands at the edge of the dock, which was at chest-level to him.

I watched as he lifted one leg and placed the side of his foot on the planks, awkward and sloppy.

But then he drew a breath and straightened his arms and he was upright, on the dock, having virtually bounced out of the boat, which swayed gently in his wake.

"There," he said, adjusting the hem of his shorts, which were actually nearly knee-length. I must have imagined they were shorter. Like a pony shaking off the rain, he shook his skin and hair, and smacked a couple of blackflies from his neck. He was as tall as I was. Six feet tall. Richard was six feet tall, and he was smiling, and he looked better than Bobby Sherman, he looked better than a Beach Boy, he was golden as a summer evening, he was crisp as a Granny Smith apple, he was the best thing I'd ever seen, and he wasn't mine.

"You're out of the boat," said Alice. It was such a stupid thing to say that it startled me, for Alice was not likely to say stupid things. Insensitive, brutal, unkind, and inept, yes; fight-starting political statements about women's liber-ation and the Chicago Seven and the Black Panther Movement and Judy LaMarsh, sure. But a bland plop of a remark like that, was not an Alice thing to say.

"Yeah, I'm outta the boat. Ya happy?"

He was still smiling. Pleased with himself. Sharing an in-joke with his mother.

"I'm ecstatic," she said, recovering herself. "And now, what's next? Harvard Law, the NHL, your first concert at Carnegie Hall?"

"Violin or piano?"

"Oh, how mundane. What about guitar?"

"Of course. Like Feliciano."

Alice smiled, somewhat grimly, nodding. My little mother clung to her elbow, digging her painted nails into Alice's sleeve, while her other hand covered her mouth – a cloaking and crushing of an expression.

Alice, reeking too of self-control and forced gaiety, stepped closer to Richard and gave him a bundle of five slim white batons, each about a foot long and a little thicker around than a cigarette. I had not seen her carrying them earlier; perhaps she had held them behind her back. They were cuddled together, a cartridge of sticks, and Richard reached for them without looking at them. He took them from her hand, and held them before him, running his one hand along their length.

Then he snapped them, with his wrist, and they unfolded, clicking like a carapace, shooting out like a tongue, forming a white cane.

His mother and mine stood back. "There are boxes all over," my mother whispered. "We'll clear you a path."

"Don't, Auntie Jane." His voice was deep, deeper than his father's, and infinitely more kind. "Nobody's gonna edit the world for me, 'kay?"

Alice's breath caught and she spoke without thinking. "Oh, Richard!"

"Maaaah," he chastised her, gently, nosing the boxes with the tip of his cane. His steps were small but not completely tentative. I had seen him more cautious when walking from his desk to the pencil sharpener at the front of the class.

He only took a couple of steps, to orient himself, and to give Alice a chance to suck herself back into shape. He cast his cane around, holding his one hand slightly extended from his side, as if expecting a broadside from something large and overfriendly.

"Okay, I'm off," he said.

"Tell me where you're going." Alice was not letting go too soon.

"Just up to the general store, I guess. I think I can find it okay." He stood, the returning wind threading through his hair, tangling it with the earpieces of his granny glasses. "I wanna find Dee. I thought she'd be here. Auntie Jane? You seen Dee?"

My mother's face was still mashed behind her home-manicured hand, her eyes all pupils. She shot me a glance which was unmistakably an order. *Speak to him*, she commanded.

Bullroar! Fat chance! I thrust my tongue at her, and she glared at me, as did Auntie Alice. I spun around and flounced to the end of the dock, dropping myself onto the apron of steel, shaking from toes to scalp.

Richard asked again. "You got any idea where she is? I mean, like, can you narrow it down a little?"

"No," my mother said. "I'm sorry, Richard.

But I have no idea what's happened to Dee."

The tapping of the cane: the first time I heard it. Moving away. Moving away more quickly than I ever would have thought.

By Sunday morning I was not sure myself what had happened to Dee. The shock of Richard's beauty had left me prickling and embittered, unable to think through the blasting heat of my rage. His blindness was nothing – it was temporary; it was a mistake; it was a game he was playing. But that *beauty*. How dare my Richard change like that?

I refused to help with breakfast; was unable to concentrate on reading; found *Superman* stupid, and burst into tears over the music the Dad played on his battery-operated cassette player. For the Dad, whose excitements he always imagined were contagious, had started the day at 7:30 a.m. (sleeping in for him), with his party-song tape, in anticipation of the arrival of Big Dick and Auntie Alice, and probably Brother Webster too, who often came over on Sunday of the opening-season weekend, to have a barbecue, chat with the wives, and get the summer rolling.

The Dad had not managed, on Saturday, to discuss with Mackenzie his "proposition," and had succeeded only in paying the rent before Mackenzie waved him away, telling him it was too busy a day to be jabbering on. So the Dad, all Saturday, had muttered discontentedly about his frustration on the subject.

"He wouldn't even listen, Jane, even when I said I had cash on the barrelhead. Said he was a busy man. A busy man, Jane!"

Frustrated, but not entirely thwarted, the Dad warbled a version of "No Man Is An Island" which he improvised to his own comfort:

This man's bought his island
This man's bought his home
This man's rock and trees are his
This man's cabin's his own!

"Not bad for an old fart," said David graciously, and the Dad was so pleased by the compliment that he didn't object to the impolite epithet in his wife's presence.

I draped a blanket over the top bunk and let it hang in a curtain, cutting me off and holding me in. I had smuggled into my bunk, during the unpacking rush, a box of Honey Grahams and another of Malomars, which I now consumed in a panic lest someone notice their absence. I didn't even bother separating the marshmallow domes from the Malomars' jelly-and-cookie platforms. I discovered that five Malomars fit in my mouth at once, and that morning I reached a new low, eating the whole bag in less than ten minutes, letting the sodden semi-chewed mallow blobs slide into me like brains, like goldfish.

I finished the grahams more slowly, for they

were dry and I was running low on spit. My gums and teeth ached from the sugar. Beyond the curtain, the small cabin buzzed with action and motion, like paper wasps pouring in and out of their nest. Mum cooked: a sizzling, snapping, panful of eggs, while the Dad proclaimed about things "we" were going to do today. Theresa tried to engage Mum in a conversation about her friends; David compulsively tuned his guitar.

The little tape deck played Joan Baez, and the Dad danced, by himself at first, and then with Theresa, who complained he looked like a goof waltzing around all by himself. "So dance with me, Princess," he said, and she did, first the waltz, and then the Twist, the only "modern" dance the Dad knew. I could see their shadows outside the wall of my cloth house, gyrating in the faint tones of an Andy Williams cassette.

"Shake it, Daddy-O!" cried Theresa, laughing as he clowned.

Then David played his guitar. Some Dylan, and then to lure me out, "Puff the Magic Dragon." "Shut up!" I yelled at him, and he played another bar or two then switched to a rhythm version of "Yellow Submarine," which got the Dad singing, although he only knew the opening verse and would sing it over and over. Then, for our mother, "I Say a Little Prayer for You," which sounded a little odd on guitar, but David could play anything. Mum would not sing, for it wasn't really a hymn, but I heard her pull a chair away from the dining table and knew she had seated herself, to give David her attention. The Dad and Theresa sat, too. I peeked out from the bottom hem of my refuge and saw eight feet settled, relaxed, on the floor, together.

"That was lovely, dear," Mum said, at the song's end. "Breakfast, everyone."

The morning dribbled on. They ate. No one came for me. Mum and Theresa did the dishes, heating the water in a metal scrub-pot, then scraping away at the caked-on egg. When they were done, David hauled away the dirty water, and brought fresh water, for the hand-pump had cracked over the winter and would have to be repaired. The Dad had a pipe and then went out fishing; Theresa went to sunbathe; David to dig up the garden for Mum; Mum filled a pail of water, got several J-Cloths and a broom, and began the annual fight with the squirrels and mice.

Just before lunch the Dad returned with Theresa bouncing in his wake, squealing and gurgling, for he had caught a big trout, right off the shelf of granite on the far side of the channel. He slapped its wet body down onto the counter.

"The man of the house has caught dinner!" cried the Dad.

Much admiring of the fish from David and Theresa. How big, how beautiful, how horrible, eeewww. What a beauty, what a monster.

"Hey, Dee, wanna see the fish?" David, making an attempt.

"Not in a million years," I barked.

"Poor thing, put it out of its misery," said Theresa.

She meant the fish, of course, but for a moment I thought she meant me. I realized that the fish must still be alive. I could picture it, quicksilver-skinned, its gills rising and falling in pain, exposing the heartfelt red of its gill fringe. David would loop a single cruel finger into those delicate organs and lift the wet brute from the tabletop, leaving it to dangle half-dead. Stuck in the wrong world, and suffocating.

I heard a footstep approach, and braced myself in case he drew back the curtain. Thinking quickly, I pushed the Malomar bag down between the mattress and the wall. But David only touched my blanket wall, bulging it inwards for a moment.

"Leave her alone," Theresa said. "She's a sulk. What kind of fish is it?"

"Trout," came David's voice, from right outside my wall.

I should come out and look, since I would be catching fish in my new life, in the wilderness. But I didn't feel like seeing it gasping away on the counter. So instead I sat back, and in time the activity started up again in the cabin. Conversation, ordinary talk: Mum was upset about all the squirrel poo.

"There was a nest, Dad, in the linen drawer. The oven mitts are ruined. There's...you know...*mess* everywhere."

"You're right, they're really bad this year. There must be a dozen of them; they sound like monkeys, hollering from the trees. Poison might do it. I'll talk to Mackenzie and see what he says. Theresa, when I go ashore, you want to come?"

"Yes!"

"Dee, you wanna come to the mainland?"

"Leave me alone," I said.

"What is *with* her?" said the Dad.

"She's upset about that Richard kid," said David.

"What about him?" said Theresa.

"He went blind."

That's not it, you dummies, I thought. *He went beautiful.*

"Like, completely?" Theresa breathed. "When?"

The Dad said, "Ask your mother. She knows all about it."

Mum had known? How could Mum have known? Ah, the letters...

Theresa prodded my mother, who spoke, but in a voice that I'd heard before only when she spoke about the importance of ironing open a seam allowance or levelling off the measuring cup full of flour. "The cataracts in his eyes have spread. There are also problems with burst blood vessels. But he said nothing to his mother, so the condition was exacerbated by neglect."

"It was *what!?*" said David, almost gleefully. "'Exacerbated!'"

"Yes. It means to make it worse."

"I know what it means," said David, incredulous.

"Go on, honey," said the Dad.

"The deterioration has left him with limited vision. He can see shadows and shapes, and can detect movement, and he can discern bright colours. But he has multiple problems with his vision. The combination of conditions is pure bad luck."

I heard the Dad going tsk, tsk, and David murmuring *bad trip*, and Theresa said it was *too much*.

"Well," said the Dad at last. "I'm heading over to the mainland. David, Theresa? You coming?"

Hiding in my cave, the troglodyte princess, I listened to the fols-de-rols of departure and organization. David complaining to Theresa as she organized her hair and beach bag (*you're beautiful, now can we go?*), and the Dad reciting his itinerary of the day to his wife. Other than to get talking to Mackenzie, and pick up a block of ice, he was going to put a phone call in to the lumberyard to deliver the wood and cement for the dock repair. It looked pretty bad this year; it would need a new crib again. The last one had been ripped up, and the rocks spilled out.

"Gonna build a deck too, I decided. If this is gonna be my place, I don't mind putting in the money."

"As long as you look after the squirrel business," said my mother.

She took out her broom again and began to
sweep, remarking bitterly that look, she'd found
more squirrel matter. The Dad said he'd block off
the squirrel holes. It wasn't easy to find the holes
every year, because this old cabin was sagging
more and more every winter, with new gaps opening between boards, and shingles getting torn
away in the wind. One spring, he said, we'll come
up and it'd just be a big pile of timber, squashed by
the snow and the wind.

"Well," said the Dad, "off we go."

And off they went. I waited until their voices
had faded completely, and I was alone in the cabin
with my mum, whose broom banged woodenly
against the legs of the dining table.

"You can come out now," she said, still banging.

"Wait until I hear the boat."

After a bit the motor started up down at the
lake, and I heard it pass alongside the island, heading for the open water outside of Mackenzie Bay.
When it was far enough gone, I came out.

Mum said nothing to me. She kept her back to
me as she accumulated piles of pine needles, dust,
wood shavings, squirrel poo.

"I'm gonna go check out my fort," I said.

She did not reply. She simply let me go.

Mirabile dictu. It was standing. Not only was it standing, but the roof was intact; the walls had not caved in; the screen on the window was only torn at one corner, and the only thing missing was the bedsheet door, which was wrapped around a nearby birch like a filthy shroud. I retrieved it and shook it out, then folded it neatly and lay it on a rock, amazed, delighted.

I crouched and entered, and the floor was more or less dry. Around the bases of the walls the dampness lay dark on the soil and pine needles, but no pebbles or stones had wandered in or popped up, and in fact there was a ball of kapok-like fluff in the corner, indicating that mice had found the fort solid enough to choose it over the cabin. I touched the mouse nest carefully, for often they housed mice or pink, hairless, wiggly mice-babies, but it was empty except for a few cylindrical poops. I smushed up the ball and threw it out the door, then settled down to think.

So much better, to be here in my nest. I stretched my legs out, clad in their cotton draw-string pants, and observed the geography of my thighs. My stomach crested like Buddha's to about halfway down to my knees, draped in the trousers' matching top, made of a bedsheet's worth of material. The earth, not totally dry, dampened my spreading buttocks, particularly between their cleft. The sight of myself, and the feel of me, was exhausting: too much to deal with. I longed for there to be less of me. Less history. Less landscape. Less and less and less, until nobody could see me at all.

Except Richard. *My* Richard.

Richard, at ten years old, wore a flannel blanket pinned around his shoulders and pretended to be Superman and tied a skipping rope around my neck and pretended he was Wolfgirl's master. He was due any minute for a swim and he'd be staying for a sleepover and we'd make Quaker oatmeal cookies even though he couldn't have any until dinner. We'd catch leopard frogs and lumpy toads and the frogs would wriggle free and the toads would pee on us. Richard would say cool that our playhouse had survived; he'd have ideas about building a door. We'd canoe over to the mainland and we'd sneak past the lodge and the Porch Gang and up into the woods all the way to the beaver pond and we'd find the perfect spot in the woods for where we would live when we ran away.

When we ran...

Richard, eating a bowl of fruit, one piece at a time. The fruit is made of cut glass. When I touch one it dissolves into yellow sugar. "Those are amber sands from the hourglass," Richard says. He has a voice like a baby's and three eyes lined up in a row on his forehead. I ask him how he sees with that many eyes. He shakes his head and won't tell me, but instead offers me the bowl. "Go ahead," he says. "It's safe. It won't make you fat."

I'm angry at him for saying fat *and ask him again. How does he see! Now the bowl is full of toads and they catch on fire.* "Save them!" *Richard says.* "Do something! Dee, you have to do something!"

Something grabbed me by the ankle and pulled.

Richard. In the hut with me, sitting by my side, shaking me awake by the ankle, as if the rest of me was untouchable.

"What are you doing here?" I demanded. My neck was stiff from my sleep, for my head had been dangling on my chest. It had been a long nap, full of so many dreams that they'd tired me out. I rubbed my nape with one hand, while trying to avoid touching Richard with the other. "How'd you find me?"

"Mah led me here. Boy, you were out like a light. It was so funny. You were snoring."

For one dreadful second I thought he was going to imitate a snore, and make a pig noise. But he didn't. "Did it ever occur to you I wanted to be alone?" I said.

"No, not really," he said guilelessly. "Not alone like completely alone, anyway. Where were you yesterday? I looked all over."

"I was right there. You couldn't have looked very hard."

"Geez Louise, Dee. I'm blind, ya know." He tapped his sunglasses. "Looking isn't something I get A's at. Anyway – hey, where ya going?"

"Away from you."

I crawled forward, out of the hut, and as I moved I realized my bottom, and my trouser crotch, were wet. The hut hadn't been watertight after all. I stood up, straining and twisting to see the wet damage, but couldn't see around my buttocks or the shelf of my belly. Then Richard emerged on all fours, and I stopped my contortions at once, even though he couldn't see me.

"Wait a goddamn sec," Richard said. His hands groped in the dead leaves and pine needles, trying to reach my feet. I waited until he was an inch from touching me, and then stepped back a foot.

"I saw *that!*" said Richard. "What the hell's wrong with you, anyway? Boy, have you ever changed."

"Me! *Me! I've* changed!" I kicked leaves at him as he stood up, once again flaunting his remarkable butterfly self. He would not have been out-of-place on the cover of *Sixteen* or *Tiger Beat*. I whirled, intending to march off, but he grabbed my arm with his man-hand.

"Hey, I'm sorry I didn't write letters, but it wasn't exactly easy to write, ya know. First I was busy in the new school and stuff and then this eye stuff happened and I had to go get training for the cane. They're fucking teaching me Braille. I don't wanna do it! I don't wanna learn fucking Braille!"

"Yeah, but blind people use Braille," I said, startled because his hand on my arm was pinching hard. "Hey, owww."

"I don't wanna be a fucking blind people."

"Ow, ow, ow!"

"Sorry." He released me. "There was even talk of getting me a dog, but I'm not blind enough and I might get better."

"You might see again?" I said, temporarily mollified by the thought of Richard with a big, lupine German Shepherd. "Would that mean you couldn't keep the dog?"

Richard laughed, and it was uncanny to hear. His laugh had the same cadence of his trademark adenoidal, donkeyish, giggle, but now it was deep as a bell.

"Don't you laugh at me!" I yelled. "You think because you're some big Beauty Queen Superhero Guy now with your tennis clubs and your friends coming over you can laugh at me? Thanks a bunch! You backstabber! Traitor!"

"Tennis clubs...what the hell are you going on about? Geez, Dee, I can't help growing up. You should maybe think about it yourself." He switched to a mocking imitation of the Alka Seltzer commercial voice: "Trryyyyyy it, you'll liiiike it..."

"Oh, such a big shot grownup! Such an adult! Did they send you to babysit me? I knew you'd turned into a big snob the second I saw you."

"*I'm* a snob? I'm the one tracking you down, chasing you all over the island, and you're calling *me* a snob?"

"Yeah. Snob." I said it, but I had to acknowledge that he had indeed made an effort to find me, which no one else had done that day, or was doing anymore. I could have stayed in that stupid fort, or my curtained-off cell, all day, and no one would have come to get me. I dug my toe into the earth and chiselled a furrow.

"Thanks a bunch," said Richard quietly.

Neither of us spoke, and neither of us left. A squirrel screeched from a nearby pine, declaring its territory with a cry that was part sewing-machine whirr and part scream of pain. We both looked up towards the sound.

"Do you see it?" I asked, without thinking.

"Aw, fuck, Dee, all I see is a big fuzzy grey wavery foggy happening. It's so weird, only seeing light and dark."

"What's that like, only seeing that?"

So he told me, as we walked down to the lake, and along the path to the beach. He had his cane, folded in his pocket, but instead of using it he asked if he could hold my arm. His hand circled my bicep, just above the elbow, in the same place where he had grabbed me to stop me running away. His fingers could not surround the girth of my arm completely.

I looked at his hand, with its hairy back, sinking into the bulbous flesh above the bend in my arm, and then at his face, which held in it the remnants of Richard, as if he'd been added on to, or inflated. We walked slowly, like a bride and groom descending the aisle, me and this unrecognizable pin-up of a boy, who had kidnapped and consumed my Richard.

We followed the footpath to the beach. The beach was a peninsula, a long spit of rocks and sandbar. We sat on a pair of boulders that we had once named the Boobsey Twins, tossed our shoes up onto shore, and sunk our feet in and out of the heavy, wet, sand. He told me what had become of him, more or less, and every word he spoke pulled him farther away from me. Left him less and less my friend Richard.

"The new house is much better than we thought it would be. Even Mah got used to it, and to the cleaning lady. Dad got her a cleaning lady, twice a week already! She's Yugoslavian or something and boy does she hate me. I like leave stuff lying around on purpose just to piss her off. And Mah has her own bedroom now which she has like completely full of books and papers, because she's been at school. No guff, yes, school again. She's getting another degree or something. Social studies. No, wait a sec – social *work*. She goes to that university in Downsview and it's so embarrassing because she brings home like these people who are like maybe, I dunno, Theresa's age or something, and has rap sessions and they plan stuff. Committees, she says. Dad says she's going to Hippie-Dippie U. Hey, Dee, remember Wattsamatta U in Bullwinkle? Saturday morning cartoons?"

"Eenie Meenie Chili Beenie," I said. Boy, the sand sure was cold when you stuck your feet far down in it.

"Anyway, so like Mah's got a car now, because you have to drive everywhere. There's no like corner store. Even for milk and bread you have to drive. Hey, next year, I get my licence."

I didn't remind him that he couldn't get his licence if he was blind. Instead, I tried to get to something we had in common. "What about getting comics?"

"Pfft," he said. "I'm not reading comics that much anymore because of my eyes. All I can see is blobs of colour with comics. I'm doing real reading now, from the CNIB's large-print library. They've got books on cassette tapes and stuff..."

"CNIB?"

"Canadian National Institute for the Blind. They're the ones teaching me Braille and blind-guy things. Bleah. Anyway, I'm reading Dumas, like, and this guy Conrad? Mr. Webster recommended him this one time he came over to see my Dad about taxes. He talks and talks..."

"Yeah, Mr. Webster can talk a blue streak, but I still like him."

"Not Mr. Webster, dope, *Conrad*. He goes on and on but then he suddenly creeps you out. There's this scene in this book where the natives are eating this purple-coloured meat and suddenly you realize they're cannibals and they're eating people meat. At least, you think that's what they're eating. It is so cool. And oh, yeah, I read *Moby Dick*. All that seafaring and boat stuff is dynamite. I really hope this eyes thing clears up because some day I could get into sailing, and the ocean, and stuff. I mean, I always liked boats and water. Dad's been letting me drive the bowrider when we're on the open water, even though I can't see fuck-all. So what? It's kind of a charge, ya know, buzzing around when you know you can't hit anything, because there's nothing near for like miles."

"Since when are you getting along with your Dad?"

Richard shrugged. "Aw, he's okay. You can't take stuff people say too seriously, even old people like my Dad. I mean, he hardly ever says anything anymore, you know, about me not being able to catch a ball or being skinny. I don't really think he meant any harm, anyway. I think I was being too touchy."

"Oh, really?" What was that supposed to mean?

But Richard went on, ignoring my tone of voice. "So where was I? Oh, yeah, the house and Mah and stuff. So we got a three-car garage and only two cars so the third space Dad had all dry-walled off and now Mah's studio is out there. She's concentrating on pottery, so lots of her paintings are in the attic, but some of them she hung up. Oh, yeah, she had a show! Seriously! At a gallery in the Caledon Hills. I wish I could fucking see the Caledon Hills. They smell great. Anyway, she sold some paintings. She sold two of Barebones Lake. The ones I always thought had the stars in the wrong place? She sold 'em. No guff."

"No guff."

Richard's new house had five bedrooms, three

bathrooms and a powder room, and Big Dick had two rooms to himself. Big Dick had also installed a billiards room in the basement, and a weight room.

"What's a wait room?" I asked.

"A place where you work out with weights, whaddya think?"

"Oh. A weight room." That wasn't nearly as interesting as a room where you did nothing but wait.

Richard's wait room had a walkout to the garden, which backed onto a greenbelt. He was using a lot of language that I had to ask him to define. A garden was a backyard, but Richard's grandmother, who had come in from out West for a two-week visit, had called it the garden and the name had stuck. I barely had time to absorb that Richard had met his grandmother (for I had never known either of mine), when he moved on to explain a greenbelt, which was a place where the trees and land were protected, usually around a river, in this case a creek that was a branch of the Humber, the very same Humber that ran all the way down to Etobicoke where the doctor had said I needed a shrink.

"See, we're connected by water," he said solemnly.

"Yeah, sure."

Undaunted, Richard went on. The greenbelt had a really good biking path, very dangerous, lots of rocks, and people even rode their horses along it, because Bolton was surrounded by farmland. Several of the kids in Richard's class had horses. All of them had bikes.

"How can you bike when you're blind? You didn't used to know even how to ride."

"Some guys taught me. It's okay, I just don't go too fast and…"

"What guys? What guys taught you?"

The guys were Nigel and Rick One, who had befriended him when he joined their astronomy club. They taught him how to use a bike, even though he was like, stone blind! – using one of theirs, and running alongside it as if Richard were a toddler on training wheels. Then Auntie Alice had bought Richard his own bike, from the Canadian Tire. It was a ten-speed. All the guys in Bolton rode ten-speeds, none of this banana-seat-monkey-bar shit, which was for kids. Nigel and Rick One were both also in Richard's class, and since there were two Richards in the class, they were labelled Rick One and Rick Two, Richard being Rick Two. They had briefly discussed calling Richard "Dick," but Richard wouldn't go for that since his father was Dick. He had not tried to keep being Richard.

When his eyesight got so bad that he couldn't see the stars anymore, Nigel and Rick One quit the astronomy club too, because it wasn't any fun if the Three Musketeers couldn't be in it together.

"So you're the Three Musketeers, you guys?"

"Yeah. So anyway, they read to me, too. And

when we go biking, Rick One leads, with – get this! – a bell on a string around his neck. It's a riot. Dee, it's a big Christmas bell from the Christmas decorations, a big jingle bell bell. He sounds like a budgie playing with a cage toy, dingdingding. So I follow him and the bell, and Nigel – he's from India, or at least his parents are – anyway, Nigel follows me yelling go-left-go-right, that sort of thing. It works out pretty good. We've had some cool wipeouts."

"I'll bet. So, like, you're Mr. Popular now, I guess."

"*No*, I am not," he said, replying in kind to my sneering tone. "But things are different, that's true."

"You realize they only like you because you're good-looking now."

Richard bared his teeth, taken completely aback. "What!" he said.

"You're good-looking now. If you were still ugly, they'd never have made friends with you."

"Oh, give me a fucking break. You are so paranoid."

"What the hell's paranoid?"

"You think everybody hates you."

"Everybody does hate me!"

"Well, maybe they got a reason to! Geez, Dee, look at yourself! You were always the biggest fucking crybaby! I mean, I always liked hanging around with you, because you have like the best imagination! But you're a big sulk, and you're not getting any better! I come up here all happy because I'm gonna see you, and okay, so like some stuff has changed, but I was gonna tell you about Alexandre Dumas – he's an author, before you ask…"

"I know Alexandre Dumas, you big snobbag know-it-all. He wrote *The Count of Monte Crisco*. Don't you remember we had the *Classics Illustrated*?"

"*Cristo*, for fuck's sake. I can't remember everything we did. But yeah, I remember the *Classics Illustrated*s. Of course I do. I still like 'em. Fuck, man. I had like this whole idea about how we were gonna be the same, even though like this whole last few months I've been kind of thinking like, what were we gonna talk about, because we're not grooving on the same things, like you don't even own a bike and I'm not into Barbies and GI Joe anymore, but I still thought we'd be okay. But fuck, Dee, you haven't even cracked a smile or said one single fun thing. Not one thing. Like, fuck! What's wrong with you?"

Everything is wrong with me.

"Nothing is wrong with me!" I yelled. My feet were mired to the ankles in the gripping, cold, sand. "It's you people! 'Dee has to go to a shrink, Dee's too fat, Dee's supposed to want to go to a stupid dance in a stupid evening gown with her stupid hair done up in little curls. Dee's supposed to be just like her pretty little mother, so Dee better change.' I am so sick of everyone telling me there's something *wrong* with me! No fucking wonder I'm gonna run away!"

"Oh, brother," Richard said, rolling his eyes. "See? I can't believe you're still into that run-away-from-home scene. What, you think you're Huckleberry Finn or something? That's what I mean, Dee, exactly. You gotta get real. I was trying to tell you this last year, when you kept going on and on and on about the Plan. The Plan was a game, Dee, a really fun game, and that's all. You can't really live in the woods, all alone, without like starving or freezing or something."

"Why the hell not?"

"Because you're just a kid."

"Oh, I'm supposed to be grown up, but I'm just a kid? Make up your mind."

"Dee," he said, "I gotta go eat something. Lead me back?"

But I wasn't finished. "I can too run away!" I said. "People have done it. Mowgli did it. Robinson Crusoe…"

"They're made up, Dee. God. Just because me and Rick One and Nigel call ourselves Athos and Porthos and Aramis and yell *yaaah!* at our bikes doesn't mean we think we're Frenchmen or that our bikes are horses."

"That's not the same thing. That's pretending. This was a plan."

"It was a *pretend* plan. Do you know what it would be like, to really live in the fucking woods? Do you know how cold it gets? We went to

Claireville Conservation Area late in the winter with the class, and we learned about winter survival. Fuck, Dee, these grown trained men spent days putting up this shelter, and it was sooo far beyond anything you and me ever made. It was really solid and it had a firepit inside. It was based on an Indian thing. But even with the fire and everything, man, was it cold inside! You woulda froze. And that was in, like, fucking *March!* Imagine January, Dee. Never mind stuff like there being no bathroom or anything to eat. You'd fucking freeze."

"I would not. And I'd find stuff to eat. I know where to do it."

"You haven't ever been in the woods in the winter, not even tobogganing in High Park, Dee, because you wouldn't go because you were afraid people would tease you. So you wouldn't go."

"*You* didn't go either!" I said, not remembering any particular discussion on the subject, although perhaps it had come up from time to time.

"I didn't go because you didn't go. I was your friend, so I didn't go. It was enough to do stuff with you, so I didn't need toboggans. Now I'm doing other stuff and you still wanna do this play thing. I bet you even brought your Barbies up."

"No," I lied, defiantly.

"Okay, so maybe not your Barbies. But you still think you're gonna run away and be Wolfgirl. And they call *me* blind."

"You deserve to be blind, you big snotbag snob."

His face went red, or maybe it was just the glow of the setting sun.

"Man, Dee," he said. "You are so out of it."

The sun hung, a boil about to burst, half-an-inch from the surface of the lake, the water smooth and motionless as a sheet of ice. Already, the day was gone. My first whole day of summer, and yes I was sitting with Richard, watching the sun go down, but we were poisoned and the lake was a yellow-red broth, carbuncle-coloured and very unclean. Richard and I should be swimming right now, with diving masks and snorkels, swimming from the point where the dock lay in tatters, to the tip of the peninsula where the island faced open water, or to the rock wall of Bald Face to touch it and tell it we were back. We should have snuck through the bushes to spy on the Dad and Big Dick, and we should have picked blueberries, and we should have worked on the house and we should have summoned Wolfgirl. We should have read comics and perhaps made GI Joe and Barbie hump. We should have ended up, at the close of this day, friends.

From the cove beyond the point, where the Dad had the firepit, came the sound of logs striking one another, as the men hurled them from the shed into the pit itself. The Dad had come back from the mainland, and Brother Webster had arrived; his "carrying voice," with its slightly

British elocution, carrying above all others. I did not hear David. Likely, he had not returned from shore with the Dad.

My body ached, starting somewhere above my belly button, and the pain crept over me in a fever. I stood up and took one last look at Richard, who sat with his blinkered eyes to the sun. The blue lenses of his glasses went black in the fading light.

I couldn't breathe, so I walked, not breathing, back along the footpath. Eventually, with great effort, I found I could take a breath, and let it go, without the feeling that a sob or a sound would twist it.

Richard would have to make his own way back. It didn't matter if he was off his schedule. It didn't matter either that it was getting dark. He had his walking stick, and his memory of the terrain. We had walked that footpath – overhung with blueberry bushes, wintergreen, ginberries, ferns – hundreds and hundreds of times. All he needed to come back was to walk this way, with the sound of the lake to the left, and the forest to the right, and familiar voices in the distance ahead.

I sat in the woods, in the dark at the edge of the forest, letting the mosquitoes bite me. Their shrill whines strafed my ears, and their feathery feet brushed my arms and face. Whenever their wheedling call paused, the moment's tense silence signalled that they were about to bite. I knew that pause well: the silence before the stab.

Normally the bugs would have sent me inside. The Dad had often summoned me in when the bugs came out, calling *Dee Richard c'mon in kids before you're eaten alive.* Not on a barbecue night, though – a good soaking in Off, and liberal spray-bombings of Raid (as well as the infernal blast from the firepit), kept the bugs away from those close to the fire. I was not close to the fire, though. I was watching from a distance. Surely they could see my animal eyes, reflecting in the light like Bagheera the panther's.

I listened carefully to see if anyone had noticed that I wasn't back yet, but all that was said was an enquiry by Alice, regarding Richard's whereabouts. "Where's my kid?" she said, through a haze of cigarette smoke.

"He's off with my kid," said the Dad.

"Okay. She'll look after him. Good that they're friends again."

Brother Webster spoke up from his lawn chair. "They had a bit of derring-do, did they?"

"Aw, Dee got bent out of shape over something. But she's over it, obviously. They've been gone for hours. But he oughta come back soon. I don't wanna mess around. Gotta check his level."

"These are times sent to try us," said Brother Webster.

That was the end of their concern. I sat, concentrating on ignoring the bugs' biting, then made one mosquito explode by pinching the flesh around its impaled proboscis, trapping it and forcing it to eat. Its abdomen swelled, an almost-invisible dark spot against my whitish arm, and then it popped. I brushed away the carcass, causing the bug's survivors to rise up in protest at my movement – me, their meal. They chorused their whine, and I settled down again to watch the barbecue unfold. Still, there was no Richard.

Theresa was back, having arrived special delivery by a boy in a putt-putt, square-stern, wooden punt. David's whereabouts were unknown, although Brother Webster mentioned almost dismissively that he'd seen him earlier at the landing. The Dad and Auntie Alice and Big Dick and my mother were seated in web-mesh lawn chairs, drinking OV and Red Cap Ale and smoking one cigarette after another (at least, they all were except Mum, who had a plastic BP giveaway tumbler of iced tea and was dressed for company in black cigarette pants and a pale blue twin set). The Dad had the fire going strongly, so that everybody was glowing and shadowy, like Sam McGee in the furnace. The men had set up a pair of portable barbecue grills, ready for the charcoal to be lit, just as soon as the Lost Lamb (David) decided to show up.

In David's absence, Theresa held sway. The adults all listened with semi-feigned amusement to Theresa's account of her day. She'd been water-skiing, slalom, and there was a new guy, Scott, who was American, his family drove all the way from Rochester, and he talked so funny. He kept talking about the *sacker* game and it took everyone forever to realize he meant *soccer*. Scott had his own car – a Corvair – and they were all going into Bracebridge tomorrow, all of them.

"That's what you think," said the Dad pleasantly, and Aunt Alice sprayed her beer in an explosive laugh.

"But, Daddy!" Theresa protested. "Everyone *else* is going!"

The Dad said they'd discuss it later, which seemed to satisfy Theresa, who must have thought that she'd have a better chance tackling the Dad on the subject were he not obliged to win the argument because of the presence of Big Dick and Auntie Alice and Brother Webster. Or more likely she decided that she didn't have to argue, because she'd go to Bracebridge in the Corvair no matter what the Dad said.

The party continued, the women talking quietly with heads leaned in towards each other, like a priest and a penitent, and the Dad and Big Dick discussed money and docks and last season's hockey, while Brother Webster sat and listened, occasionally offering a comment, which comment was often waved aside by the others.

"Ya talked to Mackenzie yet?" asked Big Dick. "Said you were gonna when you went to pick up the ice."

"Nope," said the Dad. "He was busy with guests, renting boats and chasing those damn kids off his porch, and then I headed back here. Wanted to get started tearing up the busted-up bits on the dock. But David didn't come back with me – he disappeared like a thief the minute we hit shore, for Pete's sake – so I didn't get much done."

"By the way, Dad," said Brother Webster, "let me not forget to speak with you about something of some consequence."

"Yeah, sure Webby. Dick, you want another beer?"

"Ya ever known me to say no?"

The Dad rose, but on his way past my mother he paused to pat her; to stroke and massage her shoulders mindlessly, as if he were kneading hamburger mix. While he was there the two women stopped talking and sat quietly, looking at nothing in particular, until he went away. They then began to talk once more.

He returned to Dick and Brother Webster, handing Dick his beer. "I want Mackenzie's full attention when I talk to him. And in case he changes his mind, I want things in writing."

"You betcher," said Big Dick. "Ya thought

about that ya might have to pay land speculation tax?"

"Noo…" said the Dad, edgily.

"You won't," said Brother Webster quietly. "I know. I checked it out. Listen, Dad, about this purchase plan of yours, there's something I was going to…"

"Oh, yeah – always listen to high school teachers for tax advice," said Big Dick snidely. "Stick to the Shakespeare, bookboy."

"All right, fine, I'll do that," said Brother Webster primly, crossing his arms in a sulk.

Theresa sat on a rock, staring into the fire, her hair and face shining in the glow, her mind obviously two miles away, back on the shore with her friends. She had a half-smile on her face, and her eyes were soft with recollection. At one point, she pitched a huge, self-satisfied sigh, and the smile parted into a grin. I heard Auntie Alice say, "That kid is up to something," and my mother replied, "Yes. She's always up to something."

"Since when have you noticed *that*," I muttered to myself, but no one heard even when I repeated it loudly.

It was fully nighttime now, and the bugs were beginning to dwindle, for mosquitoes always surged into activity in early evening, and then drifted away again, perhaps sated. Richard was not back yet. He couldn't possibly have got lost, because the track back from the beach was only a hundred yards, if that, and there was no way to lose the trail. It did not fork and it did not narrow. I peered away from the fire down towards the lake and the mouth of the trail, which was black shadow among black shadow, and at that moment out came Richard, lurching a little, his white face most visible, but his eyes gone behind the blackened lenses of the wire-frame glasses. In the odd night, and the fire-born blast of glow, he looked as if he had no eyes at all.

He stumbled into the fireside clearing midst, zeroing in on the heat and glow, sweeping his cane before him erratically. With melodramatic timing, he tripped over one of the hundreds of roots that threaded the thin soil like varicose veins, and fell full-forward onto the hard ground. Auntie Alice screamed, and the men swore mildly – *goddamn! Holy God!* – and Theresa squealed *ohmygodisheokay!* My mother, however, was by his side in a few practical strides. She helped him to his feet, and he swayed groggily, and said something incoherent about honey being very much like the sun. Did we have any?

"Get him some sugar right now," she said. "Alice, where's his sugar?"

"In his pockets."

She patted Richard down, as Big Dick and the Dad stood nearby, serious-faced, like surgeons or supervisors. "Richard, why didn't you take your sugar with you?" Alice demanded, not entirely gently, and Richard replied with a big lummoxy shrug.

"There's no candy in his pockets," announced my mother, finishing her search. "Theresa, get up to the cabin and get the Tupperware of Tang."

"Why don't I just get him a bowl of sugar?" said Theresa, poised to run.

"A suspension's better," said Alice. "Go on, get!"

"Wait," said Jane. "Get his insulin kit, too. It's on the washstand, a zippered black pouch, like the Dad's shaving kit only black."

"I'll never remember all this!" Theresa cried, panicked.

"Yes, you will," said my mum.

"But I need the flashlight!"

There was scrambling and motion until the flashlight was located under one of the barbecue grills, at which point Theresa seized it and took off up the hill to the cabin, disappearing into the dark, the tube of white light bobbing ahead of her, tapping the soil and the trees, very much like Richard's cane.

Richard was becoming incoherent. He'd spent a long time with me, and then longer still after that off by himself, maybe struggling to find his way back. He had mentioned on the beach that he was hungry; at that point, he should have checked his sugar, and maybe had a meal and a shot. Upset, and exercise, and change of routine – I remembered that all these things were to be avoided by Richard, with the Threat of Death as punishment for transgression. We had never taken it too seriously, but then again, we had never done anything serious, or gone beyond the span of our two houses. Richard was transgressing most thoroughly.

But I did not get up and investigate. I continued to sit in the blueberry bushes, watching like Sher Khan or Tabaqui watched the villagers' campfire, uncaring, unconnected, perhaps even a threat myself.

"Okay, Richard, you're doing fine." Alice had found her back-up roll of Life Savers and had stuffed a few in Richard's mouth, rubbing his throat to get him to salivate and swallow. Big Dick, who had got Richard settled into a wooden chaise longue, and thrown his windbreaker over him, now stood back smoking a cigarette with vicious, clockwork precision. He sucked and blew, sucked and blew, while glaring at his wife and son.

"Bloody kid, he knows better. What got into him?"

"Don't get like that, Dick, he's *sick*, for Chrissakes."

"I know he's sick, I'm just going on a little. Jesus, Alice."

"Really, though, Dick," said Brother Webster. "Many a true word is spoken in jest. How is the boy to know you're joshing?"

Alice took the pitcher of Tang from Theresa, who arrived breathless and pink cheeked.

"Is he okay?" she panted.

"I'm fine," said Richard, who was coming around a little after the Life Savers. I couldn't see him, but he sounded irritated. "I was just out of breath."

"You're not out of breath, you're heading into insulin shock, you irresponsible dope." Alice held the pitcher for Richard as he slurped back the astronauts' drink. "Where the hell is Dee? I thought she was looking after you."

"She went to the outhouse," Richard said.

"Why didn't you wait for her to come back?" said the Dad. "Theresa, go find your sister."

"No way, not me," said Theresa. She kneeled beside Richard and put her hand on his knee, where it was covered with Big Dick's coat. "Oh, look at you, you're all covered with bug bites."

"Yeah, well, that would be because of the *bugs*," said Richard scornfully. "So Dee's not here?"

"Kid sounds okay now," said Big Dick, and he returned to his chair. "C'mon, everybody, the kid's fine."

"Oh, Dick, go take a long walk off a short pier," said Auntie Alice.

The women continued to fuss over Richard, with Alice straightening the jacket and rolling up her sweater to make him a pillow. Mum offered to get him some calamine for his bug bites. Theresa marvelled at how awful he'd looked, just like a guy with a skull for a head. I couldn't see Richard's reaction to this, which vexed me. I had to get a better look at things.

I moved as quietly as I could through the bushes, to get to a spot where I could see him in his long throne. My ass was still wet from sitting on the ground, and then on the damp rock, and then wet ground again – it felt positively syrupy and I waggled my bottom, trying to make the moisture less uncomfortable. The bushes rustled, almost betraying me, and I remembered how Wolfgirl had always been able to move with stealth. Where was she now, when I needed her?

I managed to ring the clearing, and arrived at a better vantage only somewhat scratched by the brambles and pricklebushes. Settling in, however, resulted in the cracking of twigs and branches beneath me. Everybody heard, and everybody looked up.

"I'm fine, I just got dizzy," Richard announced, loudly and suddenly.

"Dizzy, and a little freaked out," said Theresa, in an intimate way that she had no business using. "Boy, it must be hard to get around when…"

"Yeah, yeah, it's a pain," said Richard, cutting her short. He seemed to be looking right at me, with his blacked-out eyes. Sitting with his legs extended, ankles crossed, and golden skin gleaming in the firelight, he seemed to be soaked in flame. The black lenses of his glasses shimmered with the reflection from the firepit, and when the Dad stood up and threw another log on, a fountain of sparks spewed into the sky, in a column of floating, golden dust.

I stared defiantly back at him, daring him to point me out. To tell them the truth – that I'd left him sitting on the beach, after keeping him out and getting him excited, and then he'd had to make his own way back, in the dark, although of course the dark shouldn't matter to a blind boy, hahaha!

The villainy of being me!

That was not the end of the night, at least, not for me.

Shortly afterwards, David pulled up in Brother Webster's fibreglass canoe (which, Brother Webster quickly explained, had been at Ashleigh's Marina being grouted, when David graciously offered to deliver it, when they'd met at the landing). David, at this, theatrically complained that he had paddled all the way over to the north side, where he'd gone to look up Ray Best, but Ray's parents said Ray wasn't welcome to darken their door anymore, so David had headed over to Brother Webster's, only to find that Webby wasn't there.

"You been at Webby's all day?" said the Dad.

"Uh, no, went to Ray's first, was on the mainland some…"

"I coulda used help today is all," said the Dad.

David said nothing, but took a beer out of the cooler. My mother stood up, and so did Alice, and took the flashlight to head up to the cabin for the steaks and trout and corn. "Come along, Theresa, you can lend a hand," Mum said, and Theresa rose slowly and arthritically, moaning about slavery being abolished in the States but never here. But she had begun to follow the women up the path when David spoke.

"Hey, Richard, where's Dee?" David asked. Richard was still cuddled beneath the coat, silent to the point of being sullen.

"She took off, I guess."

"You guys hang out all day, as usual?"

"Yeah. As usual."

"Actually," said Theresa, who had stopped, "we haven't seen her for like an hour. She went to the outhouse and left Richard all alone. Richard got sick. He went into insulin block."

"Shock," said Richard sharply. "And I did not. I just got dizzy."

But Theresa was into her tale. "Dee ditched him. She left him all alone. He had to come back all by himself, and I swear to God he looked like a dead guy. He came outta the woods and he's all white and the woods are all black, but his eyes are black because of the sunglasses, it was really scary. We all screamed!"

Alice and my mother chorused, "All right, that's enough!"

David rose from his rock to go look closely at Richard, and feel his forehead. He clucked his tongue and shook his head, as if he were a doctor. "Feel better now?" he asked.

"Yeah, yeah."

"So has anybody bothered to look for Dee?" he continued, good-naturedly. He had returned to his guitar and was strumming "Eve of Destruction," with no particular dedication to craft.

There was no answer. David looked up from his strings, eyebrows raised to cajole an answer, and someone cleared their throat. I heard the click of a cigarette lighter; Big Dick had lit another Player's and settled defiantly back into his chair.

"Hmmm?" said David, with the flat, bored hum of a hornet before it hits you. "Dad, did you bother looking for your daughter?"

"Oh, she's just having a big sulky baby pout," said Theresa. "She's doing that hiding thing again. C'mon, David, she's been like doing it all week."

The Dad leaped in, with agreement. "Dee doesn't want to be found."

And my mother. "She does need her privacy, dear."

"I see." David set his guitar down and clasped his hands together before him, on his bent knees. He nodded, head lowered, mulling this information over. "Dee wants to be ignored and abandoned."

Even Richard spoke up. "She wants to be left alone," he said.

"Okay, okay. I just wanna get this straight, that's all," said David. "Richard comes back sick enough to look like a dead guy, because Dee had left to go to the john and not come back. And that was what? An hour ago, and she's still not back. Has anybody even done so much as call her name?"

"What the hell dya expect?" put in Big Dick from the other side of the pit of flames. I couldn't quite see him, but he was there, leaning back in his web-chair, hand poised over his lips as he dragged on his cigarette. "Why the hell should we

chase her? About time she learned some consequences. Some ability to get along with a group.
Christ, as soon as Richard's out of her range, his
life just takes off. He's got friends, he's getting
exercise, he can ride a goddamned bike even
though he's goddamned blind. And look at the
muscles on the kid. I can't believe how much of a
difference it's made for him to get away from Dee.
So if she goes running off on him, it's not damned
likely I'm gonna be chasing her down."

The silence that followed was full of the crack
and boom of the firelogs, as they split in the heat.
Finally, Alice spoke.

"You are *such* a goddamn jerk, Dick Holmes."

"Language," said my mother, very, very softly. Alice's arm was around her shoulders. The
Dad, too, had hung his head, and Brother Webster
was biting his lip so hard that the skin on his chin
had been drawn upward, thrusting his beard out
into a point.

David stood up slowly, magnificently. "Well,
that was totally unnecessary and irrelevant, but
what else could we expect from you, Uncle Dick?
Richard, did anything happen before she left for
the outhouse? Did you guys fight?"

"Why would we fight?" said Richard testily.
"We're friends."

"Pah!" said Big Dick.

"Dick, would you please go to hell!" said
Alice.

"Everybody shut up and let's get looking for

Dee," said David. "We'll check the cabin first, because she's probably just gone back into her nest to read her comics or something. She wouldn't be sitting out in the woods, in the bugs. That would be nuts."

Slowly, reluctantly, everybody stood up, even Big Dick, once Alice had hissed *get up before I kick you all the way to Christendom*. Nobody wanted to be the one to find me.

I crouched very low, forced to eavesdrop as they organized themselves, and closed my eyes, breathing *I don't care I don't care I don't care* in and out of my mouth. Brother Webster and David paired off, and Theresa volunteered to stay and sit with Richard, and my mother and Alice were another team, and the Dad and Big Dick a third. Brother Webster got a flashlight from his boat and David had a penlight on his keychain. Big Dick muttered an apology to the Dad for saying that stuff about Dee. "Aw, it's okay, Dick," said the Dad. "You're right. Dee's always held Richard back some. He's been a good friend to her."

"Hey, Richard," said Theresa. "You should come to Bracebridge with us tomorrow. A whole bunch of us are going."

"I do hope you realize that a Corvair's only got room for five," said the Dad.

"What the hell is this!" cried David. "Can we please concentrate on Dee!"

That was enough. I stood up harshly and all-at-once, rising out of the knee-deep bushes with a shout as my greeting. "All right, all right, already!" I yelled.

They all started and gasped a little, for I had literally been only a few feet away, but invisible in the cavernous dark. It would have taken them a while to find me, but how much more would I have had to hear while they looked?

"Jesus, Dee," said David.

"Told ya so," said Theresa, to no one in particular.

"Come here, young lady," said the Dad. "Right now."

By reflex I moved, but it took some effort. As soon as I'd stood up, I realized that it had taken work to crouch and creep for so long, and I was sore, scratched, and bitten. I stepped over the bushes, carefully raising my feet so as not to trip like Richard had (such a fall on my part would not have elicited sympathy). Arriving to stand before the Dad, I determined to keep my head up. But it would not stay. It kept dragging down, and I kept willing it up, and it kept sinking low again.

"Look at me," said the Dad, "when I'm talking to you."

"Never mind looking at you, look at Richard," said Alice. "Dee, I'm surprised at you. Is this how you treat a friend? You know how dangerous his condition is."

Richard folded his arms heavily over his chest and clenched his jaw. "You people," he growled.

"Yeah, Auntie Alice, he's not like a cripple or

something," said Theresa. "Right, Richard?" She smiled at him dazzlingly, granting him her most wonderful gift, but it was the gesture of an idiot, for he couldn't see it.

"Right," said Richard anyway. "I'm not a cripple. Dee, are you okay?"

"Fuck you!" I cried to the Earth and to my shoes, which I could not see beyond the shelf of my stomach. I could only see my shoes if I stood on one leg and held one foot off the ground. The enormousness of this suddenly struck me: I could not see my body. Not without mirrors and contortions and information from others could I grasp what my body was.

"She's really lost her mind," Big Dick said, and Brother Webster observed very softly that he hoped someone was getting me some help. The Dad, however, seized me by the shoulders and gave me a shaking. My head snapped back and forth three, then four times, as he rattled my body. Up went my face, then down again, a fast-action version of my trying to look him in the eyes.

"What the hell's got into you, Dee!" he said.

"Dad!" cried David. "C'mon, don't freak out!"

Ah, there was Wolfgirl! I could feel her coming. It had been so long since she'd come, I hardly recognized her approach. She was right behind me, about to leap into my form, and then I would sprout hair and my eyes would narrow and turn to amber lights with pupils closed to pinpricks in this shocking firelight. Wolfgirl had never attacked Dee's family, but she could now: she had my permission. She would spare David, but everyone else must die. The throats would bleed gore; hell's bells would ring. I opened my mouth to loose her snarl, but as my lips parted over Wolfgirl's fangs, I heard Theresa's voice instead.

"Eww, ooh, that's so sick, lookit! Mum, Auntie Alice, lookit!"

Even I looked, around myself, up and down. I could see nothing that would summon that disgusted tone in Theresa, a pitch reserved for a sighting of a squashed raccoon on the highway, or someone's cystic acne. And now, Theresa was looking at me, or rather, at that part of my body which was eye-level to her kneeled posture beside Richard's chaise. Richard, even, twisted around to look with his shielded eyes, saying "What? Look at what? Theresa, look at what!"

Theresa leaned over to him and whispered something in his ear.

What? What's wrong? What's happened?

"Oh, dear," said my mother.

"Oh, shit," said Alice.

The men suddenly seemed to lose interest in me, or to find it very necessary to leave me alone. They broke ranks and wandered off to their lawn chairs and rocks, and settled down with their backs or shoulders to us. Jane and Alice swept over to me and put their arms around my waist and shoulders, whatever they could reach. The flashlight clicked on, and with gentle pressure and herding murmurs they ushered me emphatically away from the circle.

Later, in the cabin, I had a quick look at my pants before they spirited them into the washtub of cold water and dish soap (handy tip: wash bloodstains in cold water, so the stain does not set). The amount of blood I'd produced was phenomenal. The stain spread over my loins and down the inseam of the trousers. My panties were ruined. I had to sit on a towel, with another towel covering me, as my mother brought me a washcloth and the water basin, and then found me a sanitary belt (hers). It was, of course, one-size-fits-all, and of course it did not fit *me*.

"We'll pin it," said Alice.

So they pinned the thick pad into another pair of my panties, and stood with their backs to me as I put on the improvised diaper, and then Mum handed me another pair of panties ("in case you spot") and a clean pair of cotton drawstring trousers. I put on the pants and drew the cord tight around my middle.

"Poor kid," said Alice, patting my head when she turned back to me. "No wonder you took off on Richard, and hid."

"Yes, Dee, we're very sorry we didn't look for you earlier. We thought you'd been bad."

Alice frowned and shot Jane a glance. "Not bad, Dee, you're not bad."

"No, no, of course you're not bad," agreed Jane.

"This is a perfectly natural thing that's happening to you," said Alice. "In many cultures it's celebrated. They have a big party. A big period party!"

"Alice!" said Mum. I thought she was shocked, but I saw she was smiling, behind her fingers. She looked at Alice the way Theresa had looked at Richard.

"Yeah, we should be like that. We could throw a period party," said Alice, charging ahead. "We could play music, like 'Red Sails in the Sunset' and – and – 'Red River Valley' –"

"'Red River Valley'!" gasped Jane. "Oh, and...'Fountain of Blood'!"

"Janey, that's disgusting!" squealed Alice. "But it's perfect! And we could have a big cherry cake shaped like a big sanitary pad, and we could decorate with red streamers and hang sanitary pads all over and we'd all wear red dresses so that if we spotted, nobody would know. We'd fill the candy dishes with Midol!"

"And we wouldn't invite any men!" cried my mother. "Just us, no men, and we'd drink cranberry juice." She paused, and thought. "It would be a BYOHWB party."

"Okay, I'll bite. A what?"

"Bring Your Own Hot Water Bottle."

Alice's laugh rose to bellow; she grabbed my little mother and hugged her. My mother barely came up to Alice's breasts, but she hugged back, her eyes closed in comfort. I sat there, bleeding on to my little paper shield, revolted beyond belief. For one weird moment it seemed they might even kiss, as they rocked each other, laughing. I wasn't even in the room anymore.

"Hey!" I said. "You guys are making me wanna puke!"

They separated, laughing still, but stayed linked by their arms. My mother's makeup was damp and beginning to run. She smiled at me. "Oh, poor old Dee, it's not much fun, is it? Never mind. You'll get used to it."

"I don't want to get used to it. I don't like it. I can't believe this is going to happen to me, every month, for like forever!" My voice sounded waily-and-whiny, but I couldn't make it sound angry; it simply wouldn't behave.

"Not forever. It stops when you're old," said Alice.

"Has yours stopped?"

"Dee!" said my mother. "Personal question."

"No, mine hasn't stopped. Not yet." She laughed. "All the changes, eh, girls? In one door and out the other. Anyway, Dee, listen, you have questions, you just ask me."

"Or Mum," I said firmly.

"Yeah, sure. Or your mum. We're the experts."

They stood there, above and before me, the Indomitable Alice (as Brother Webster often called her), and my mouse-mother, who was smiling that rare and strange smile. They were shoulder-to-shoulder in the glow of the Coleman lantern. I had always found the Coleman lantern miraculous, with its tiny cloth mantle of flammable fabric that, when touched with a match, would burst into active, burning life. A pocket of fire. A little tiny thing like that, just a silken bag, and yet with the right fuel and the right ignition, it lit the whole room.

So on I went, into the summer onto which I'd pinned everything. And now it was crippled and dying, a ghost with missing parts. Wolfgirl, her back broken, crawled through the underbrush, dragging her body with her forearms, moaning piteously.

There were practical things, too. The pad against my genitals drove me crazy, as did the seeping blood, and the cramps that hit me the next morning and made my lip quiver with nausea. My mother gave me a Midol, and I thought, what would I do for Midol in the woods? And for pads? I tried to write a story, but as soon as my pen touched the foolscap I remembered that I'd left the myths I'd written back in the city, and realized that someone would read them after I'd gone. It gave me the same feeling, to think of people reading those stories, as I'd had hiding in the bushes and watching them discuss whether it was worthwhile searching for me. Exposed yet unfound; examined yet dismissed. The urge to write another tale dried up, in the fantasy images of unknown people, laughing at my poor, unguarded, unjustifiable stories.

On Tuesday I went to the mainland with the Dad, who was determined to pin down Mackenzie. My first reaction was delight – oh, good, Richard and I can explore in the backwoods! – but then I remembered Richard was gone, and I would be doing all my searching alone. I remembered, too, the dreadful words he'd levied at me; at how he'd told me my ideas were impossible. He had to be wrong, but it seemed he was right. Sure, I had finally built a house – a playhouse – that had lasted a winter, but on an island where anyone could find me, even a blind boy.

A blind boy who looked like a blond Bobby Sherman. Who'd gone to Bracebridge in a Corvair. When the Dad and I arrived at the mainland, the Corvair was parked outside the lodge, and a small swarm of teenagers (those who had not returned to their respective urban homes the night before) was orbiting around it. The Corvair itself, which was a convertible, had six teenagers in it: three in the front, three in the back. The driver – Scott-who-played-sacker – had sideburns and a mustache and a yellow-and-purple long-sleeved see-through shirt and a skinny neck with a huge Adam's apple, and the two teenagers in the passenger bucket seat were Theresa (who had canoed over earlier that day) and Richard. Theresa was sitting on Richard's lap. They all drove off, without even noticing us, leaving not a single teen behind. I would have peace.

While the Dad was chasing down Mackenzie ("He's in the bloody ice house, mister, didja bother to look before interrupting my work?" said Mackenzie's sister Maureen from the lodge's kitchen door), I dropped into the general store and spent some allowance on a twenty-five-cent box

of Smarties. Ensconced on the porch, in command
of one of the sloping wooden chairs, I relaxed: put
my feet on the rail, and bled, and ate.

Seep, seep, seep, went the blood, and pop, pop,
pop, went the Smarties. I bit each one open, then
swallowed the halves, without chewing. Within a
minute, the whole box was gone.

I thought about getting another box. I had
another quarter. But the chair was very comfortable, and low-to-the-ground; I didn't want to drag
myself out of it just yet. Broad-slatted, white-
painted wood, low-slung and wide-berthed, with
armrests large enough to rest a drink on. I did not
have a drink. I could get a Coca-Cola, too. In a
minute, when I was rested.

Here on the teenagers' territory, I could see
what they saw when they looked out onto the bay.
The railing of the porch was within reach of my
raised feet, and I moved the chair away from the
barn swallows' poo, for the swallows had built a
dozen grey-brown nests around the inside of the
porch eaves, and the droppings showered down
and stained the floor beneath. Every nest had a
squadron of tiny heads peeking over its brim – little, black, sharp-eyed baby swallows, who would
throw open their mouths in desperation as soon as
a parent arrived with a beakful of bugs. They
screamed to be fed, and the parents did nothing all
day but feed them.

It was still well before noon, and there was
not a bug in the air or a cloud in the sky. The

water was very calm and very blue – a pale, morning-textured blue, ruffled by silver where the wind breathed across it. The swallows veered in and away, in and away, like fighter jets or fairies, and from Seagull Rock beyond the bend the gulls all began to scream at once, perhaps at the approach of a boat. For the boats had started up – big boats, from Ashleigh's Marina – and were scudding or swooping across the bay, depending on their horsepower; they were either off to bounce across the open water beyond the archipelago, or to visit friends on one of the undeveloped Crown land beaches. In deference to their noise and interference, and to the rising sun, the old-timer fishermen were coming in, the high point of their day already over. They docked and cut their engines, and tossed their strings of lakers up onto the dock.

Mothers – lodge guests – brought their toddlers to the water's edge, armed with beach umbrellas and bags full of toys and suntan oil and headscarves. They paddled into the water, wearing swimsuits or shorts and sleeveless cotton blouses, and dangled their babies – held by the armpits – over the surface. The babies kicked and hollered. The mothers did this for a while and then set the babies down in the water, then retreated to the sand to open lawn chairs, to organize pails and shovels, and to supervise. They settled in a row, four women in straw hats or headscarves, and started to chat and watch their children.

A bubble of blood passed out of me. It was an outrageous feeling, invasive somehow. I looked at the mothers again, and how they bent over their children, bending from the waists in their old-fashioned swimsuits. They were so very, very much older than the teenage girls, who wore fringed or crocheted bikinis. They were a completely different creature.

Another burp of blood. I would have done anything to stop it, and could not believe that I would have this happen to me, every month, forever. Until I got old. Until I got...*pregnant*.

Pregnant! My hands tightened on the wooden arms of my chair. The mechanics of getting pregnant I had of course learned in Health, but the physical minutiae of the process itself were beyond me. *I could get pregnant.* I knew how it was done. The penis enters the vagina. I certainly had a vagina. Right now, I was more aware of my vagina than any other part of me. It was the loudest, most annoying thing I had, and I would have done away with it if I could.

But surely nobody would ever want to put their penis in my vagina. It was ridiculous to imagine such a moment, where someone would come so close to me. It was something I had never understood about "sex ed": we had all been warned very firmly that no matter how much we might *want* to have sex, we must not do it. We could not give in. Because if we did, the sperm would travel through the cervix and the uterus and into the fal-

lopian tubes where it would meet the egg and fer-
tilize it and then the blastocyst would become a
zygote and the growth of the fertilized ovum
would begin. But no one ever explained *why*: I
never understood why anyone would *want* to
have sex. It sounded horrible.

And as for babies, over which the bathing
mothers now cooed and fussed, and sometimes
shrilly scolded: I had no longing in that regard,
either. I had played with dolls, bathing them and
dressing them, but I had also played with toy cars.
I had not longed to own a car and had not longed
to have a baby. My dolls I had used, often, as props
and equipment for amusement, and my amuse-
ments were eclectic, particularly whenever
Richard was involved. We drew pimples on their
plastic bums with magic marker, or ripped out the
stuffing of a soft-bodied doll, playing "surgery";
we hanged them as rustlers; we served them up to
Sher Khan as the man-eater's victims. We pulled
off their arms and legs and then jammed the legs
into the arms' holes and the arms into the legs'.
We had launched them out the back window in a
cardboard box with glued-on cardboard wings, and
were gravely disappointed when the box didn't fly.

But now, I could have a baby. What a curse;
what a dreadful, unfair thing. I'd never held a
baby, or changed a baby, or considered looking
after a baby. Babies? Who cares about babies? I did
not want a baby, and I did not want a lawn chair
on the beach. I didn't want to chat to the Other

Mothers. I just wanted to feel like I'd felt every summer forever, when I'd been working on something artistic and ripe and possible, with someone who was a like-minded soul, who could believe that cardboard could fly.

Here I was, baby-ripe and bleeding. I couldn't even go in swimming. The limitations were endless.

Maureen Mackenzie came out of the front door of the lodge, carrying a broom. She looked this way and that, down the length of the porch, then harrumphed to herself with satisfaction when she saw that there was only me. She may have been frightened of the Porch Gang, but she certainly wasn't frightened of me. "Don't you go hanging around here all day," she said.

"I won't."

"You're not a lodge guest."

"I know. My Dad has business with Mr. Mackenzie."

She harrumphed again, this time with disdain, and then raised the head of the broom above her, as if to mop away cobwebs, but instead she began to whack away at the nests of the barn swallows. The babies fell, screaming terribly, and instantly the parents returned, all of them (it seemed) all at once. They swooped in at Maureen, screaming too. Maureen did not even look at the parents, whose cries of distress were one long, sustained, squeaking, shrill. They sounded like tiny lost souls, fluttering at Maureen's grey-brown head, trying to peck, trying to stop her with their ineffective beaks and pleas.

She had heavy galoshes on, big black-and-red Wellingtons, and she stomped on each baby bird, popping the little heads and bodies. The parents wailed. Whistling through her teeth, she swept the carcasses together, from one nest after another, swarmed by the agonized little swallow-parents, which never once managed to land a blow on her. Swipe and stomp and sweep and whistle, she moved down along the length of the porch, until all the nests were gone, and the deck was stained with bits of blood and infinitely tiny, downy-black feathers. She scooped up the carcasses into the garbage drum, still whistling with bored tune-lessness, and went back into the lodge, carrying her broom.

The unbelieving, wretched swallows searched the eaves for their nests, calling and calling, landing in the rafters and looking this way and that, back and forth, before taking off to swoop again.

Maureen came out with her big tin bucket with the built-in mop wringer, and the mop itself. "Get yourself outta here," she said to me, not looking my way. "I gotta clean up all this junk. Been waiting weeks to do it, but there's always a big crew of riff-raff here. So you get now."

I stood up, wishing I could stop her, but of course it was over already, and I had not said a thing, nor taken any action, to save the birds. She prodded me with another few words – *get yourself gone* – and I tried to move a little more quickly. The adult birds were already beginning to fly away, back over the lake. Just a few forlorn forms sat up in the ceiling beams, their yellow beaks parted in a bewildered summons: *I'm here. Where are you?*

Right then, descending the steps of the Porch Gang's world, with the beach-women chattering before me and the bereaved birds behind, all I could think of was the possibility of falling asleep and never, ever, ever having to wake up. The alternative – living among these people, growing into baby-making and baby-keeping, living so long that you become a heartless crone – weakened my mind; I could not think of how to escape. I could not even begin to plan, or to hope. Life ahead of me seemed like a nearly endless, miserable trip, a thankless walk-a-thon, with no reward at its end and no purpose propelling me in between. Never seeing another human being, except Richard, was what I had worked towards, for years. And all that work had just been the flotsam and fairy tale of my imagination. The reality was: I was stuck with the broom-wielders, the bleeders, the Corvair-driving devils. Life by Hieronymus Bosch.

I walked, exhausted even though it was only morning, up the flagstone steps to the woods beyond the lodge hall, and slipped into the forest, which here on the mainland was less tangled underfoot than on the rocky, thin-skinned island. I went a hundred yards into the forest's perimeter and lay down on the leaves, smelling them so deeply that I could almost taste them. I had no idea what I was going to do. I had always had a plan. My purpose had kept me going. There was nothing I wanted to be when I grew up. But something I would have to become. What on Earth else could I do with me?

Thirteen was to have been the lucky year. At thirteen, I was going to be capable. At thirteen, I was going to leave. But thirteen had not made me brave; it had not left me competent. Instead, it had given me breasts and blood and bulk. It had given me awareness. I had been forced to eat from my own tree of knowledge, and all the fighting I could muster hadn't removed this bright and blinding realization, that had overtaken all my desperate creativity, and twisted it into impotence.

I was not going to be Wolfgirl. I was going to be a woman.

And too, through my semi-adult eyes, I saw what everyone else had been seeing. What was going to become of me. I would always be a freak show; the one-in-a-million. The tallest woman, and the fattest, in any group. And yes, sadly, the ugliest. That tore me open, knowing how ugly I was, with my small eyes and single dark slash of eyebrow crossing my orbital ridge like a scar, and my frizzy black hair and my puffy cheeks and throat. Maureen was ugly, and what a monster she was, hiding in the lodge until the teenagers left, and then coming out only to kill things. She was fat and ugly, but not as fat and ugly as I was. At thirteen years old I was already more monstrous than her.

The prospect of living my adult, female, life, fifty or sixty years of it, in this body, and with this face, sank me like a stone. How could God have made me so ugly? Wasn't it enough that He had made me impossible?

Eventually, ants crawling on my skin disturbed me enough to move me. I rose up from the leaves and headed, automatically, down to the landing and then to the foot of the dock. There now seemed to be dozens of people around, all the lodge guests lying on beach towels on the dock, their bathing suits blooming like flowers; the children with their kiddie-geared fishing tackle trying to catch the little perch that swarmed around the pylons. The yahoo-like young men in their twenties or thirties, setting up for water-skiing, and the old men who came in from Utterson to visit Mackenzie, solely on the strength of him being their age, and remembering what he remembered. And the rare teenagers who weren't part of the Porch Gang, and the children, and the three-year-old girl who cried out when I passed:

Look, mommy, a fat lady!

I had to find the Dad. I had to get back to the island, or what was left of it.

The Dad was nowhere to be seen, not waiting there by the footbridge, outside the general store as we'd agreed. Then I heard his voice, loud and stressed, from back by the ice house and carports.

"No, I understand completely, my friend. Don't you worry."

Mackenzie's voice replied. "Didn't say I was worried."

"I understand, I understand. I wouldn't just give it away myself, it's a beautiful..."

"You understand nothin'. It's got nothing to do with beautiful. It's an investment. I own the whole shootin' match, every island in the string. It's like breaking up a set. You wanna break up a set, I gotta be paid for hurtin' the rest of the set."

"Like I said, I understand."

"Yeah, sure you do. So you still want all that lumber delivered?"

"Yes, yes...I'll still fix the dock...don't mind at all, my friend."

"Don't call me 'friend,' Graham, you're a customer, is all. I'll bring the wood over when it arrives. And the twenty-two. Just gotta dig it out from somewheres."

I had crept over to the footbridge, listening, but not straining to, for the men's voices were loud and echoed between the buildings. I heard the ice-house door creak closed and knew the Dad would be coming, so I hurried out of the way, for he would not like for me to have been listening in on business.

He marched past me, eyes straight ahead, his hands scrabbling blindly in his shirt pocket, trying to get a grip on his sunglasses, which seemed to be evading his grasp. He had his straw fedora-style hat on low and tight, as if he'd jammed it on, and when he finally negotiated his glasses clear of the fabric of his shirt, he thrust them onto his face as if he were trying to hurt himself.

"Daddy," I said, "wait for me."

He said nothing, but walked on hard and fast; a big man who could cover ground quickly. I ran, ten steps, walked, ran again, walked, dodging the sunbathers. By the time I got to him, he had already jumped into the boat and was trying to start it, ripping the starting cord so hard the engine banged against the transom. It was flooded; it wouldn't catch. He had already untied, and there were eighteen inches between the dock and the boat. I knew I couldn't bridge that gap.

"Daddy, wait, please!"

He tore once more at the engine. The gasoline-smell was as strong as at the marina's workbay. A shimmering slick of mother-of-pearl glistened on the water.

"You're so slow," he said to me, not looking my way. "Why are you always so slow?"

I could barely summon a voice, but something came out, a little half-dead (or dying) peep. "I can't help it, Daddy. Please, Daddy."

The rage seemed to flow out of him, and he sagged over the unco-operative engine, supporting himself by one hand pressed against the cowling. "Aw, shit," he said. "C'mon, kiddo." And he held up his arms for me, as if I were about to pass something down to him.

I put my hand in one of his, and climbed into the boat, clumsy as always, unbalanced as could be.

He'd cried when David appeared on *Tiny Talent Time*, and he'd cried when I'd won the golden ribbon for first prize in Bible studies class, and he'd cried when Theresa wore her prom gown, only a few weeks and several hundred thousand years ago. He was crying now too. Those crying faces were always embarrassing, but this one was also frightening.

"What happened, Daddy?"

"Never mind, Dee."

"Was it the poor little birds?"

"What?" he said, snappishly, not really listening and not wanting anything further in the way of discussion. With mouth clenched shut, he brandished a paddle, to propel us out into deeper water, and away from the bathers who were splashing about, close to the boat and its prop. I took up the other paddle and tried to help, but my pad shifted. I had to tug at my trouser crotch to get it back into place, and my father winced in embarrassment.

"Don't do that, Dee, it's not ladylike."

"Sorry."

Away from the dock by a dozen yards, where the green sand bottom had disappeared and the water was now rich cobalt blue, the Dad returned to the motor and started it at the first pull. We puttered carefully out of Mackenzie Bay, away from the hubbub and traffic. As soon as we were clear, he twisted the throttle-handle fully open. The prow of the boat reared up in surprise, and we took off.

The Dad said nothing the entire trip. When we pulled up to the dock, which was untrustworthy and leaning, he told me to climb out onto the rocks along the shore, so as not to do any more damage to it. Then he did the same.

The wind had picked up, for it was now at least noon and the day was wide open. "Jane!" he hollered, standing on the rocks, "Jane!"

My mother, summoned by the sound of the boat, came mincing down the path. She was hurrying a little, for normally she would have met the Dad at the shore, and helped hold the boat while he disembarked. Her steps were quick and somewhat guilty – small, measured strides across the firepit clearing.

"Hello, Dad," she said pleasantly. "How did it go?"

"You didn't clean up yet," he said, gesturing with a sweep of his hand to the firepit area. Indeed, she hadn't cleaned up yet. The barbecue ash had not been emptied, and the beer bottles lay uncollected around the rock circle. She had not put away the lawn chairs, and the plates (with their tinfoil balls from the corn and potatoes) lay speckled with blown earth and pine needles.

She regarded the clearing, absorbing the spread of leftovers and trash and appliances. "Yes," she said mildly, and brushed a strand of hair out of her face. It occurred to me that heavily sprayed hair doesn't drift in the wind like that. My mother had not done her hair; it was flowing in the current of the wind from the lake.

"Any particular reason why not?" said the Dad.

"Yes." She had to hold her hair now, because the wind gusted strong and warm, pulling it into unruliness.

"Oh," said the Dad, impatiently. "What reason, Jane?"

"I was busy."

"Busy."

"Busy. Reading."

"Okay. Busy. Up in the cabin?"

"Yes. Busy in the cabin."

"What's for lunch?"

She looked at him blankly. "Anything you like, I suppose."

He sighed. "Aw, Jane, sweetie, life really stinks."

"Yes," she said, not enquiring further, but instead turning – pivoting on her toes – and heading straight back up the path, deliberate but delicate in her ascension. The Dad watched her go, then turned to me just as I made another attempt to ease the discomfort of the sanitary pad.

He rolled his red-rimmed eyes.

"Women," he said. "God, I'm glad I'm not one."

It was several days before I found out exactly what had happened. He had not been upset by the birds, but by Mackenzie, who had told him flat out that the Dad could not buy the island.

"Those were his exact words?" asked Big Dick, who came over almost every day with Auntie Alice.

"He wouldn't even entertain the discussion," the Dad replied.

"What sort of terms did you offer?"

"I offered a pretty penny. A very pretty penny. But I'll keep working on him. Next year, even, I can…"

And so he went on and on, conniving regarding his dream.

Mackenzie delivered the lumber for the dock, and my father and Big Dick and Brother Webster made a party of the unloading work. Mackenzie's big pontoon barge bobbed in the little cove by the beach, anchored by a long rope and a heavy iron block, while Dick and the Dad and Brother Webster steered the planks over to shore by floating them, one by one, wading alongside in the hip-deep water, and singing an ersatz-Russian version of "The Volga Boatman."

"He-eyy, ho! MEN!" sang the Dad.

"Hey, l'chaaaii-im!" sang Brother Webster.

"Iy-yi've got PHLEGM!" sang Big Dick.

Mackenzie stayed on his barge the whole time, sitting in a folding lawn chair, watching the others work.

"We coulda used a fourth hand," said the Dad pointedly. "Like David. But he took a powder. Kid's harder to keep track of than a ping-pong ball in a hurricane."

"When'd he go?" asked Big Dick. "I coulda sworn I saw him last week at the landing, buying smokes."

"That's possible. He comes and goes. Kid thinks the world revolves around him, eh?"

"He's hardly a *kid*, Dad," said Webster quietly.

The Dad and Uncle Dick didn't seem to hear him. "They all do," said Dick. "Even Richie. Ya know, he mighta been some help today, even with his eyes and all," said Big Dick. "Not that I can get him to come over here anymore."

"He hangs around a lot with that crew at Mackenzie's porch," said the Dad. "Hey, Mackenzie, you planning on putting a 'no loitering' sign up this year, like you said you might?"

Mackenzie was talking to Brother Webster, who had waded over to the barge; Mackenzie was bending over so he could listen as Webster stood beside him in the water.

"Mackenzie!" called the Dad.

"What!" Mackenzie snapped, irritated by the interruption.

"You gonna do something about those kids on your porch?"

"Dunno," he said, and returned to his conversation with Brother Webster.

I could have helped drag all the two-by-fours and one-by-eights out of the water and onto shore, and to cover them with a tarp, but instead I sat on the beach while the men finished the unloading. My period had ended and I could swim again, which I did, although this year, the water seemed much colder.

Along with the pile of timber and the bags of unmixed cement, Mackenzie also delivered a .22 rifle for the Dad. For this, I came off the beach and walked along the path to the dock, to see the gun for myself. I had never seen a gun.

"What's it for, Dad?" I asked, stroking the blue-black neck and the wooden stock.

"Well, I thought I might try to scare off the squirrels," said the Dad.

"By shooting at them!" I said.

"Yes..."

"Just to scare them, right? Not kill them?" The memory of the swallow babies was still fresh in my mind.

The Dad didn't answer right away, and in the meantime, Big Dick took the gun and practised aiming here and there, in the trees and into the undergrowth, making explosive noises with this cheeks. *Pkowpkow.*

"Angels and ministers of grace, defend us,"

said Brother Webster, shaking his woolly head. "Dick, put the toy down."

The gun passed from hand to hand, and even Brother Webster examined it, declaring it a relic of another time. "It's not as if we have to defend our homes, that we should be bearing arms, like the Yanks," he said.

"It's a fucking .22, Webby, not a bazooka. And they're squirrels. Squirrels," he intoned, "are dangerous."

Theresa arrived home, delivered by a pimpled and hopeful swain, who had obviously borrowed his daddy's boat. He came in far too fast to the dock, and kicked up a huge backwash that caused the Dad's precarious, still-makeshift dock repairs to tremble. Then he took off in a similar gush.

"What's that?" said Theresa. "Oh my God, it's a gun!"

She came over and stood back, behind the Dad, while Big Dick showed off by breaking the gun open and inserting shells into the magazine, then unloading it and trying to show her the rifling on the inside of the barrel. She wouldn't look, though.

"It might go off," she said.

"It's not loaded!" chortled Big Dick indulgently. "It's perfectly safe."

"What's it for?"

"The squirrels," said all three men.

Theresa's spine stiffened visibly. The temperature dropped several degrees, and she said, in a voice as different from her *what's it for* squeak as Janis Joplin's was from Doris Day's, "You're *not* shooting the squirrels."

"Oho!" said Big Dick. "Looks like you got bigger problems than just squirrels, Dad."

The Dad explained to Theresa that this year, we had serious squirrel problems. We had at least a dozen of them – it was only humane that we trim them down, because they'd starve to death. Eat themselves out of house and home, he claimed. They'd been left on the island when the ice receded, and they had cleaned all the pines of all their tender sprouts and cones; they had destroyed the song sparrows' nests and eaten the eggs, and that gorgeous fulsome blueberry crop had been gnawed into nothingness before Jane had managed to make a single pie.

"Mum hasn't made any kind of pies this year," I observed.

"Never mind that," said the Dad, and went on, blaming the squirrels for everything. They had scared away the chipmunks that we fed from the porch, the Dad said, because squirrels and chipmunks are enemies.

"I see them together in High Park," said Theresa.

"Those are *grey* squirrels," said the Dad. "Chipmunks, when they hear that chirr of a *red* squirrel from a tree, they just pop right back in their hole."

It was true that these squirrels were not like

city squirrels, who were plump as pet rabbits with long, curving, voluptuous tails. Red squirrels were ratlike, weasel-thin and unfriendly. They would not take peanuts from our hands, like the chipmunks, which in years past had sat in our palms while they shelled nuts and sunflower seeds, their four ounces' weight as amazing to hold as it would be an angel, or a tiny unicorn.

But Theresa wasn't buying it. "Chipmunks and squirrels might be natural enemies, but that doesn't mean we have the right to shoot the squirrels," said Theresa.

"Good reasoning, Theresa," said Brother Webster. "Well put."

"Oh, here come da judge!" Big Dick slapped his forehead with the palm of his hand. "It's not the chipmunks, it's your Mum and Dad, sweetie-pie! They are knee deep in shit!"

"Dick," cautioned the Dad.

"Well, you know what I mean. Not knee deep, but they're doing a lot of...*mess*."

That, too, was true. Shit sometimes fell in our hair as the squirrels ran through the naked rafters, although of course that might have been mice. Droppings, which were distributed up on the beams, actually *dropped*. Once, the Dad got a flashlight and stood on the dining room table, so that his head was up in the rafters and cross-beams. He reported that there was a ton of it up there.

Dick proceeded to tell a story about a boy at

his summer camp, when he was a kid, who had been bitten in the face by a squirrel, which had leaped out of a tree and attacked, cutting the kid's face very badly.

"Oh, come on," said Brother Webster. "Killer squirrels?"

"I was there," said Dick defiantly.

"Oh what a tangled web we weave, when first we practise to deceive!" said Brother Webster, and Dick pointed the empty gun at him and said, in an Elmer Fudd voice, "It's windbag season! I'm hunting windbags!"

"Dick, stop it," said the Dad.

"I don't believe that story," said Theresa haughtily.

"You don't have to believe me for it to have happened," said Dick. He turned to the Dad. "Believe me, Dad, they're vicious. Get rid of 'em. You gotta be practical about these things."

"Why do we have to shoot them!" I cried.

"We've tried everything else, Sweetheart," said the Dad. "They're too big for mousetraps, and too smart for poison – not that your Mum much likes me putting poison inside the cabin. And they keep chewing through the patches I put on the holes. If I have to go up that ladder one more time, I'll pitch a fit."

"I don't know why we're even discussing this," said Big Dick. "The Dad's gonna deal with the issue. The case is closed. Okay, girls?"

He swept his eyes over us, including Brother

Webster in with the *girls*.

The Dad retook possession of the gun. As it passed to his hands from Dick's, Theresa took a swipe at it, as if to spank it.

"I'll stop you," she said. "I will."

"No, you won't."

"That's telling her," said Big Dick.

But weeks went by, and though the Dad dismantled the gun, and reassembled it, and even loaded it and aimed it a few times, he didn't shoot a thing, not for the longest time. Big Dick offered to do it for him, particularly when Dick found the Dad up the ladder again, re-nailing the shingle that the squirrels had been treating like a trap door. "Don't pitch that fit while you're up the ladder," he said. "When are you gonna get some balls and just blast them?"

"But they're clever beggars," said the Dad sheepishly. "I swear they know I've got the gun. We used to see them running along the rafters. They practically flipped us the finger. Now all I know is that they're getting in, because I hear 'em. And there's shit in the bed."

"Yeah," said Uncle Dick, "but it's *your* shit."

"Hardeeharhar, Dick. Hardeehar."

The Dad didn't shoot, the squirrels kept up their assault, and summer moved in on us, golden, syrupy and miresome, full of the dangerous calls of the cute little creatures which, at any time at all, might leap down upon you, and tear your face right off.

Seven

You know what slays me? The way people get about squirrels. You know, fuckin' city rats. They are the stupidest, vilest, scruffiest little brutes – the winos of the rodent world, and that's saying something, being that rodents aren't exactly celestial beings. I'm in the park, I see a big bruiser of a pit bull bombing along after one of those things, I'm rooting for the pit bull. Let's see some entrails, boy! Atta boy! Get 'im!

No, seriously, those little fuckers are dangerous. The red ones will attack you. Yes, they will. They're like muggers. They're carnivores. They're cannibals. Yes, cannibalistic, carnivorous rodents are lurking in the treetops. They have teeth like a buzzsaw, and that noise they make – that whiirrrr thing – that's not the squirrel itself. That's them sharpening the sawblades. They have little red-squirrel toolshops where they hone their little squirrel bandsaws and their little squirrel chisels and their little squirrel red-handled Robertsons. At night there are whole work crews of red squirrel workers whose job it is to pry the boards off the fascia of your cottage so they can get into your attic and shit in the insulation. The fact that these fuckers can chew blown-glass insulation batting oughta tell you what you're really dealing with...

Country squirrel, city squirrel, red, black, grey or flying. They're pretty but they're deadly. Don't be fooled by that cute helpless gimme-a-peanut-I-got-a-wife-and-six-young crappola. They're assassins, man. They know you're stupid enough to get fooled by a pretty little pink nose going wriggle-wriggle. Awww, ain't that cute. Fuck cute, man. Cute's deadly. Don't let 'em fool you...

Now the serpent was more subtil than any beast of the field which the Lord God had made...

Genesis

Sharp.

The word was a weapon, an elephant-goad of meaning, crowned with a red jewel that looked wonderful but in fact carried a curse. Theresa had used it, and in the strangest context: she had applied it to Richard.

Theresa continually issued bulletins on how her summer was proceeding. She was bored, she was happy, it was a blast, it was a bad trip. But in sum, the case was: as long as she was away from the island, she was content.

The island was *nowheresville*. It was a *bummer* and a *bad trip*. The mainland was *happening*. On the mainland there were boys who could drive and there were boats pulling skiers and there were pyjama-party overnights at the fancier cottages in Farmer's Bay. They had dances at Ashleigh's Marina, and seances and cookouts, and they sunbathed their bodies into tones of Kraft caramel.

The trip to Bracebridge in the sacker-player's Corvair had been *too much*, and during that trip, Richard had gone from *persona non grata* to someone much desired by all. Richard was cool, he knew about stars and stuff, and lots of jokes no one had heard; all the girls were watching out for him and making sure he didn't get, you know, sick. And he was a *hunk*.

I pointed out that he was only fourteen, and that Theresa was sixteen and far too old for him, but she said that he was a very mature fourteen – fourteen-and-a-half in fact – and mature enough to go out with.

"What!" I couldn't believe what I heard.

She shook back her hair defiantly. "Sure I'd go out with him. Any of us would. He is sharp."

There was that word. Richard was *sharp*.

A few times I had gone to the mainland, shadowing the Dad, and seen Richard sitting with the Porch Gang on the Mackenzie Lodge porch, his feet on the railing. He did look cool; he did look sharp: very in and with-it, behind his opaque, shaded, lenses. Under his influence, the Porch Gang's taunting of me had slowed, even stopped. Richard (surrounded by cooing girls offering him Popsicles or asking him if he'd like to go for a walk up the road – I'll hold your hand to guide you) had power, and he had wielded it to earn mercy for me. The treachery of the fiend, to extract lenience from *them!*

Alice and Big Dick were distressed about Richard, who rarely came home for supper, and wouldn't come to the island. All of it frightened Alice – she who had once so neglected his diet and care that he'd almost died; who had failed to notice as his eyes clouded over and he walked into walls. Now, she wanted to monitor him, but he would not stay still long enough.

"Yeah, sure, yeah, sure," he'd say, from his perch on the porch, and all the girls would snicker, and Auntie Alice would redden from the chin to the hairline.

"Fine, you little creep," she said once. "Get yourself killed."

He insisted he was capable of checking his own levels and giving himself his own shots, and he watched his eating times and how much sleep he got. He assured her that his friends were looking out for him, too. The friends agreed in a chittering chorus, the girls all cooing, "Oh, Mrs. Holmes, don't worry, he'll be fine, my mum will make sure he eats!" Alice had to give in, although her reluctance and hand-wringing tended to cease the moment she got to the island and slunk off with my mother to their private promontory.

My friendship with Richard, and what it had been, was like the wake of a boat that had passed far away and a long time ago, but was only hitting shore now. I went on, about my business, rocked by the force of its rolling blows. I spent days rambling the island, striking the trees and rocks with sticks that I tried to say were swords, swimming in water I strained to believe was bottomless, catching frogs and wishing that I cared about their jewel-like brilliant green skin. In the evenings playing two-handed crib with the Dad, while my mother sat and read or wrote, right in front of us. Alice had brought her another book – another sexbook – this one with its nature declared right in the title: *The Second Sex*.

The things I had loved before had not stayed with me. And I kept coming back to *sharp*. I kept imagining what it was like to be on shore, going to a pyjama party, having a weenie roast at the Farmer's Bay beach, seeing Richard in his dark glasses and denim shorts. Going, not to the wilderness, but to human events: even to the Ashleigh's dances, to which Theresa went every Saturday night, wearing short-short denim hot pants and midriff-baring T-shirts with a leaf of marijuana stencilled on the back. LOVE, her shirts declared; LIKE WOW, read a patch she'd sewn onto her pants. She would be picked up by a boatload of similar souls, the girls all wearing sunglasses and halter tops and hiphuggers, with pretty scarves tied around their pretty throats. Sometimes they waved. "Hi, Mr. Graham!" they'd say. "Hi, Dee!" they'd cry.

The Dad asked why I didn't go over to the mainland, too – after all, my friend Richard was part of that crowd now. The Dad had always objected to Theresa's association with those juvenile delinquents, but Richard's presence had given them legitimacy. Or perhaps, he thought I'd be safe from whatever Theresa might fall into.

"I don't wanna," I said.

"Dee, you can't just hang around the island all summer, all by yourself."

"Why can't she?" my mother put in. "Leave her alone, Dad."

She certainly left me very alone. There was only the one room of the cabin to clean, which she tended to quickly and without asking me to help. When I attempted to help, we collided with each other and she would pick up a book and go outside to read, in the patch of rocky soil that in previous years had been a small, carefully cultivated garden.

When Alice came over, the two of them retreated at once, cantering away to the end of the island with a tartan blanket and a Thermos flask of coffee, insisting they not be bothered. "Don't come looking for us unless someone's bleeding from a major artery," Alice said.

David returned, went back to the city, returned, then went away again. We never knew where he was, and whenever he appeared – dropped off by the Ashleigh's Marina water taxi, or by Brother Webster, who seemed to often run into him on the mainland – he arrived sunken-eyed and grey-complected. By late July, his appearance was so haggard (his beard, which I'd always kind of liked, was now thick and intimidating) that my mother insisted he bathe in the big metal tub before he got into bed. And so he did, once she heated water on the stove. He looked like an Andy Capp cartoon, but miserable.

David would sleep for ten hours straight and then do two hours of manic labour – painting the outhouse, digging a run-off trench beside the foot-path, staining the deck the Dad had built to complement the still-not-completed dock – and then he'd hop in the canoe and disappear again, often without saying goodbye. On rainy days he would pace the cabin, his guitar hanging from his neck, like a minstrel with a mandolin. Even in the hottest weather, he wore a long-sleeved tie-dyed shirt that was so old its collar had frayed clean away, and his elbows protruded from the cloth. His fingernails, once hard as diamonds, split to the quick, and he mourned having to learn to use a pick.

He refused to discuss his plans. He was finished with school, he said. And no, he didn't want to teach. He wanted to sing and record. Why couldn't people understand that?

"Webby's the only one who understands what it's like to be an artist," he said. "To need a place of your own, to escape, to be alone. He's behind me, man, and my own family – none of them gets it. None of them."

"I'm trying to get it," said the Dad weakly, "but how does an artist pay for that place of his own? You gotta be practical, son. Life isn't art. It's work."

"Art's *work*. Artists should be paid, man, more than janitors and boring little run-of-the-mill broompushers."

"That's enough, bucko. Remember who you're talking to."

He was no kinder to Mum, who served him a plate of eggs one morning, only to have him tell her she was a slave to antique notions of patriarchal chauvinism. She looked at him and at the eggs, tight-lipped, not as if she were about to cry, but as if she had an answer.

It passed, though, and she said, "You're welcome, dear."

In late July David got a gig playing in a small folk-rock festival near Gravenhurst, and said he'd be back the next day. We were all excited to hear how it went, this paid engagement for which his name even appeared in a poster (the Dad took one down from the telephone pole in Bracebridge and brought it back to us to crow over). David had forbidden us to come, of course, so we all wanted to know what songs he'd played, and whether the crowd had liked him, for he was a headliner (DAVID GRAHAM FROM TORONTO). We wanted to know if there'd been a big audience that had applauded and cheered and called for an encore.

He didn't come back for lunch, and dinner passed without anyone coming over, not even the Holmeses. After dinner the Dad and my mother and I went for a canoe ride until dark, and then we played Hearts and cribbage and pinochle until nearly midnight. Theresa gave herself an elaborate manicure and pedicure, humming under her breath a series of David's regular songs. He never appeared.

Somewhere after midnight we all went to bed, by mutual decision. It was mid-August before David came home again. By then, it was a whole different world.

The gun, which had no case, stood like a broom or any other ordinary household implement, leaning in the corner beside the icebox. It was cool and smooth, and it smelled of steel and oil and fireworks. I thought, I could take this with me, and use it to hunt for food, and at the same time, thought, *as if.*

I aimed it at the rafters, and at the windows, and then at the mirror over the washstand. I pointed its sight right between my eyes. I put the barrel in my mouth and let it rest there, with the sight scraping my palate, watching myself from the corner of my eye. With the gun held up, its stock elevated, I seemed to be drinking from it, from the black pipe that tasted no different to me than any other thing I'd eaten lately.

I put it back in its corner, and for the moment, let the matter rest.

In the absence of anything else to do, I begged to visit Brother Webster. I had not ever before needed to go to Brother Webster's; I had always had Richard, and therefore better things to do. But now that I longed to go to his quiet, reclusive little log cabin, he was scampering away from the idea, offering adult-sounding, falsity-laden excuses such as *I'm not up for company* and *it's not really convenient* and even *the place is a mess,* Dee. I thought he was mad at me, but he was also stiff and uncomfortable around the Dad, like a dog that has wet the floor and not yet had the deed discovered.

But, one day, out of the blue, he turned up in his slow-leaking cedarstrip, asking if someone named Dee lived on this island. I grabbed my pencil crayons and Doodler and swimsuit and jumped into his boat before he could rescind the offer.

All the long way across the lake, I sat in the front of the boat like a figurehead, forcing the wind out of our way. Brother Webster's was a rare treat: an eccentric and crowded place, made of hewn pine logs complete with peeling bark. It had an outdoor privy but hot-and-cold running water, with the hot water heated by a small electric furnace. Brother Webster had paid a fortune, he said, to bring hydro in from the main road, for he needed a good strong light to read and study by. Coleman lanterns were romantic, but eventually they just drove you batty.

"It's money thrown away, though – investing in this place," he said.

"Why?"

"It's my mother's, Dee. You know that. One day, she'll join the choir eternal, and that will be the end of my adverse possession of her cottage. She turns a blind eye to my using the place, I suppose because she can't *really* stop me. So she'll strike at me from the grave, Dee. Poor old woman. It must be a hard thing, to live that long and still be angry."

"Why is she angry?" I said.

"Oh, well, sometimes people get that way," he said. "Nothing to be done. And I've made other arrangements for summer housing – awhile ago now, which – oh, dear – have unfortunate repercussions. Nevertheless, Dee, nevertheless! We must soldier on, we minions of the mighty!"

I didn't care for the idea of Brother Webster's dead mother taking away his cabin. It was such a remarkable spot. The walls were festooned with paper: poems and clippings and cartoons, torn from *The New Yorker* and *Canadian Magazine*, as well as many pictures of English bull terriers. Hook-nosed, squinty-eyed dogs, their stocky little bodies pugnacious and appealing. Along the upper logs of the cottage he had installed a plate rail, which wore dusty china figurines of women in swirling ballgowns, fishing boys, matching spaniels, rearing stallions, and also the occasional plate. Every wall housed a bookshelf, and the coffee table lay drowning in ratty *Look*s and *Life*s and mimeographed, hand-stapled "litmags" in which he was always showing me his published poetry. Stand-up photos of Brother Webster's foster children in Biafra and Mexico, in cardboard frames, fought for purchase among the reading material.

Framed on his wall was a story he'd written for *The Bracebridge Banner*, back before we Grahams had ever come to the lake.

"See, Dee," he said. "I do understand what it's like to be a writer, and to love this lake." But he wasn't really saying it to me.

When I asked him about the bull terriers, he told me about his dog, Oscar, who was named after Oscar Wilde, but whose nickname was Mel. I didn't know who Oscar Wilde was, so Brother Webster told me. He was a famous man, a writer, who had fallen in love with the wrong person, and then not kept it a secret, so they sent him to jail.

"You can go to jail for that?" I demanded, incredulous.

"Yes, in some cases."

I snorted. "Well, better watch out who you fall in love with, I guess."

"It's not like you can help it."

The dog, whom Brother Webster had loved, died when I was very small, again before Brother Webster became a friend of the family. Brother Webster told me the story of its death: it got tetanus, somehow, up here at the lake – Brother Webster thought it had perhaps stepped on a nail or ripped its claw – and the vet just outside of Bracebridge had not diagnosed it properly. Brother Webster kept feeding it the useless pills the vet had prescribed (some sort of antibiotic, Brother Webster said bitterly), but the dog got sicker and sicker. Eventually it crept away and hid for a while, and when it came back, it was in agony, paralyzed throughout the head and neck. It could not swallow or blink, and its eyes bulged and watered, and saliva ran in ropes from its lips. Brother Webster, who travelled by canoe back then, paddled all the way back across the lake with the dog in a blanket at his feet. He got it to his car and laid it on the front seat. Somehow, the dog kissed him. Its tongue snaked out between its seized teeth and licked Brother Webster's hand. The dog died with its tongue on Brother Webster's wrist.

I drew Brother Webster a picture of a bull terrier, and Brother Webster wrote a poem to go with it:

> To Oscar
> His dog was so grateful
> For their time together
> That he held on, stiff & sore
> Prolonging the perfectness
> Of being half-and-half
> With a brother human.

He explained to me that the poem did not have to rhyme to be a poem, and I thought of Kipling's couplets and Service's clappable meter and believed Brother Webster didn't know much about writing poems. But I didn't say anything about that – I only wrote one of my own.

> Oscar Wilde was a very good dog
> He lived with his friend and ate like a hog.
> His friend was a human who cried and cried
> The very sad day when Oscar Wilde died.

I gave it to Brother Webster, and he taped it onto the fridge alongside the picture. His own poem he put into an accordion folder, where he kept things he believed he wanted to keep forever. He showed me some of the contents once. In among his own work were a pressed and waxed maple leaf from a kindergarten-aged Theresa, pages of sheet music from David, and several of my stories (which I did not even recall writing, so many things had I written). He said that everything we Graham children had ever given him was inside it.

"I won't ever have kids, so you kids are my surrogates," he said. "I keep these things, because some day, someone might misunderstand my motives, and keep you away from me."

"Who would do that? What motives? What's a surrogate?"

He answered only the last question, explaining for many minutes the word *surrogate*. "So, who's your favourite of us kids, then?" I asked.

"Well," he said, cryptically. "It's not Theresa."

Since David was never around, I assumed, of course, that his favourite must therefore be me. I forgot that other people's experience wasn't limited to my own.

As soon as we landed at Brother Webster's dock, some of the thrilling spell that I had lacked that summer cast itself at me, pouring over my shoulders and down my back in a tingling mantle of anticipation. Brother Webster was its instrument;

as we ascended the dozens of wood-and-earth steps to his cabin, he said we must proceed slowly and cautiously, for the faeries were watching.

"Not faeries," I said. "Tigers."

"Tyger, tyger, burning bright," he said, then recited the entire poem, with great flourishes of arm and tosses of head. I knew the last line well, and chorused it with him: "Did he who made the lamb, make *thee?*"

"Let's go upstairs and change into our swimsuits," Brother Webster said, as we finished. "We'll go find Atlantis."

He waited, patiently, while I struggled with all the stairs, for by the summit I was gasping for wind, and held his hand out to me to allow me to pass onto the porch before him.

"By the way, I got Pillsbury cookie dough," he said. "But don't tell the Dad."

I could have wept with gratitude. I dismissed the idea of swimming in favour of baking cookies. As we split the plastic on the sausagelike roll of cookie dough, he recited, in full burr, the *Address to the Haggis*, brandishing a very intimidating knife. And although he frowned, he did not comment when I ate chunks of raw dough, not even bothering to be surreptitious. I ate so much dough, in fact, that we only had half-a-dozen cookies to eat when we were finished.

Brother Webster put the half-dozen survivors on a plate, and sat me down at the coffee table, with stacks of foolscap and old magazines. We ate cookies and cut out pictures and pasted collages. I rifled through everything, looking for a bull terrier for him, but he'd got to them all long ago.

It grew warm in the cottage in midafternoon, and as a thunderhead began to climb skyward in the distance, we donned snorkelling gear and went searching for underwater civilizations, and in lieu of those, smallmouth bass nests. I then suggested we play Castaway, which he agreed to, and we both dragged our spent bodies up onto the rocky shore, speaking in the best Defoe we could muster.

"Where might we be, on this strange and verdant land?"

"It matters not, dear friend, for we are spared from the wreckage and must learn to survive. Come, let us search for a site for our home."

"Watch out for tygers."

"Watch out for nutty eighteenth-century poets."

The thunderstorm came in slowly, in a vertical misty wall of rain falling from the flat and sinister base of the thunderhead. We sat comfortably watching its journey across the lake, from the safety of Brother Webster's dock. Then the air cooled suddenly, although not unexpectedly, and lightning spiked from the mushrooming cloud's curvy, billowing depths. Moments later came the thunder. Brother Webster said if we counted the seconds between the flash of light and the sound of thunder, we would know about the distance between us and the rain.

"Because light travels faster than sound," I said.

"Right. Dee, soon I won't be able to teach you anything."

When the first heavy drop fell, we packed up our lawn chairs and climbed up to the cabin again, well ahead of the downpour. There was no taking me back to the island while the storm was still blowing, so we sat in the cabin, having lit a small, merely picturesque fire in Brother Webster's round red acorn fireplace. He showed me how to light the kindling, starting with the very small shreds of wood, teepee'd together so that the air rushing in from the base would form a candling effect, and then accumulating larger pieces on top of that, until the fire was powerful enough to engage a single log.

"You can't just hold a match to a log," he said. "You'll never get it going. You need little bits. If you're ever lost in the woods, and it's raining, you can find dry kindling on pine trees. Don't search the ground for kindling, because...my God, Dee, what did I say?"

"What?" I said. "You didn't say anything."

"You just looked so sad, suddenly. Did something I say bother you? I'm sorry if it did, but I don't know what..."

He stopped talking and came over to sit beside me on the floor, where I had my work spread out on the coffee table. "Nice picture," he said, running his hairy-backed fingers over what I'd been drawing in ballpoint pen, which was an illustration of a cabin in a clearing, beside a running stream, with many trees and a field of corn. As he watched, I drew into the picture a seated doglike form.

"That's my pet wolf," I explained.

"What's his name?"

"Grey Brother," I said.

"Not Akela."

"No, this is a friend wolf, not a boss wolf."

He nodded, and leaned forward a little so he could look into my face. Whatever he saw there satisfied him, and he rose from the floor and stretched, shaking back his frizzy hair, which he had told me had him in deep Dutch with the status quo. They wanted him to cut his hair and shave off his neat little beard, but he wouldn't do it. He'd go to court, he said, if he had to.

Evening fell and on it rained. The thunderstorm intensified, blowing air and wind down the chimney, raising the spirit of the single-log fire, and rattling the ancient windows in their frames. The screen door blew open and slammed shut, and Brother Webster began to recite *The Raven*, which I'd never heard before, and didn't understand.

"It's about losing someone you love and not being able to forget it," he said. "Oh, shit."

The lights went out, as the hydro failed, and the small glow of the fire was all the light we had. "We need candles, or the lantern," I said, but

Brother Webster said no.

"It'll come back on soon, and in the meantime, let's pretend we're really stranded somewhere, with no power and no lights and no heat." He drew his feet up onto the sofa, curling them beneath him. "Our ship sank, and..."

"We did that one already." I yawned.

"Are you sleepy? You had a busy day."

"Yeah. I had a lot of fun." I drew another, clean sheet of paper from the pile of newsprint and foolscap, and in the shivering glow of the fire, began to draw an island, trying to render in pen the leaning pines and mica-peppered rocks, and the smash of waves.

"You'll ruin your eyes, Dee," he said.

"So what? Everything else is ruined."

In the dark there was no sound but the rain on the shingles, heavy drops filtered through the cover of the leaves and branches above the cabin. Faintly, I could hear Brother Webster breathing evenly, but he didn't speak for a long time. I drew several trees before he spoke again.

"You're having a rough time nowadays, eh?"

"Noooo," I said.

"Lots of changes, physical, mental, emotional."

"Mr. Big Guidance Counsellor Guy," I said. "Look. Does this look like the island?"

"It's great, Dee, but I can hardly see it," he said. "Leave it and I'll put it on the fridge. Dee, I know you're in a lot of pain."

I started to deny it, but couldn't find a voice

that didn't have a sob clinging to it, so I took another page and began to draw and draw. A wolf's curved skull, his proud ruff of fur, his muzzle pointed to the sky in a howl.

"It will get better, Dee. Trust me."

Trust him, trust him. With head still inclined over the page I dared to peek up at him, from beneath my animal brow, and there he was, cross-legged now, with his arms extended along the sofa-back, fingers toying with the loose threads of the sofa's upholstery. He saw me looking at him and did not take away his gaze, but softened his expression to such welcome – such acceptance – that for a moment I thought *he's pretending. No one cares about me that much.*

It was his expression that started something slow and nascent, a burgeoning swell of longing, of desire: the familiar urge to reach for an object and consume it. Brother Webster unwrapped his legs, which were clad in fashionable flag-of-Canada denim jeans, red-and-white maple leaves all over, down to the floor. His shirt, white suedette, was one of his favourites; it had fringes down the arms with beads at their ends. They rattled as he stood and stepped right over the coffee table, so that he was beside me, and I was looking up at him. He lowered his hands to me, in a gesture that meant *stand up.*

Taking his hands, I brought myself to my feet, with effort, as it always took. I was as tall as he was. There, standing, he embraced me, as my hands hung at my side, feeling the tickle of the fabric-and-bead fringe against my bare biceps.

"Dee, you are going to be the most incredible woman some day," he said. "You just can't let the bastards get you down."

"But, Mr. Webster," I said, "there are so *many* bastards."

He laughed and hugged me tighter, rocking me somewhat, then pulled back and held me by the upper arms, so that he could look me up and down. "Yep, there's a whole world of them, but you don't have to give them any power over you. Keep yourself precious and rare, Dee. Keep yourself electric."

The power came back on, shockingly, like a bad joke in a variety show. I wanted to dismiss what Brother Webster had said, because it was so corny and so stupid. Electric my big fat ass.

But the fact was, when he had raised me to my feet, and looked into my face without grimacing or finding there a single stroke of horror, I had thought, I had hoped, I had imagined, that he might kiss me. A race of current flowed through me still, placing itself low, in the small of my back and across my hips, a hunger that was not a hunger. If he had come to me at that moment, instead of turning away to go out the door to check the rain, I would have fallen against him, and into him; I would have lifted my face to his, like the drawings in the romance comics, and felt lips against lips.

I could not imagine, beyond that mere comic-book notion, what lips on lips would be like.

Later that night he drove me home across a calm, post-storm lake, a flat black sheet of gleaming mica, steam rising from the bays and coves, where the water was shallow and likely to be warm. The mist and fog bathed itself in moonlight, rolling out into open water and blowing away in the openness and breezes. Slowly we went, the red-and-green eye of the boat's bowlight warning others that we were there: me in the prow, like a wooden invention, and Brother Webster in the stern, steering and providing all the power. I wore a sweater he'd loaned me, and it smelled of his cabin and Dial soap. The collar caressed my throat and neck, and I drew it closed around my chin.

All the way back to the island, propelled by Brother Webster, I split the night world open with my smile.

Theresa was sitting on the dock, in the sun, leaf-
ing through some back issues of *Seventeen*, wildly out-of-date, so old they were like wartime
*National Geographic*s. The *Seventeen*s were from
1962 or so, and they had articles on how to do the
latest dance step, illustrated with line-drawings of
footprints – men's shoes and women's high heels.
Broken-line arrows and swooping ink semi-cir-
cles, telling us where to step and stand. I cautiously sat down beside her.

"Whatcha reading?"

She dangled the magazine like a dead rat by its
tail, but did not speak. Then she spread it back out
in front of her, between her splayed legs.

"Look at those spike heels!" she said, not
quite to me.

"Yeah," I replied. "Can you believe what they
wore back then!"

Theresa ignored this, and read on. "You think
you know stuff, do ya?" she said.

"No," I replied. "Not really." I watched as she
turned the page, to the glossy full-page cosmetics
ad. *When it comes to being beautiful, the fun is in
learning how...*

She tossed that one aside and reached for
another from the pile. The magazine she extract-
ed I had previously only seen at the corner store in
Toronto. Our minister had denounced it from the
pulpit. It had on its cover a woman whose expres-

sion reminded me of the women on the covers of *Playboy*.

"Wanna see?" said Theresa.

The magazine – *Cosmopolitan* – seized me by the throat and dragged me in, as much as if a strong, bared arm had leaped from the cleft between the pages. I saw there a half-naked woman, not in a *Playboy* pose, but draped in a towel and standing before a mirror, contemplating her body. *What He Really Sees When You Undress.*

"Are they allowed to show, like, tits in girls' magazines?" I asked.

"It's not for girls, it's for women. And yeah, they can show tits. But it was *banned* once, you know. Stopped at the border."

"Like, you could get arrested for reading it?"

"Uh-huh." She turned the pages slowly, exposing to me the magazine's stories. The text was rife with those eerie, half-forbidden words: sex, seduction, arousal, orgasm. The Big O. Passion. Turn him on. Sensual. Sensitive. Sexual. Sibilant, hissing words.

"Look at this," she said, turning the pages hurriedly to an article towards the back. "It's about birth control."

I snorted with false bravado. "So?" I said. "I know about that stuff. The Pill and stuff."

"Yeah, but do you know about what you have done...before they'll *give* you the Pill?"

And so I learned about the dreaded *internal*:

the horrifying prospect, the unbelievable proce-
dure, of the Pap Smear. The magazine, calmly and
coldly, said every woman had to have one, if they
wanted the Pill.

"I don't want the Pill, though," I said, remembering the doctor with his rubber gloves, the
meaning of which suddenly coming clear.

Theresa hesitated before she answered, speaking softly, in recollection.

"It doesn't matter," she said. "You gotta have
it done anyway."

"It happened to you?" I said, awestruck by her
bravery.

She nodded. "Yeah, in Grade 9, when my period started. Soon as the doctor found out I'd started, that was it. He called in the nurse, and...they
like, did it."

"What was it like?" I whispered, for she had
grown small, and was bent over the magazine
with her hair draping along the sides of her face,
veiling it.

"Don't ask," she said, not showing her face.
"Just read the article. I'm doing you a favour, so
you won't get the shock I got, okay?"

I read on, about how a nurse would come in
the room, and I would lie on my back, with no
pants on, and they would put my feet in metal
stirrups and maybe, in case I reflexively kicked,
there would be loosely tied restraining straps. If I
was scared, the nurse would hold my hand. Then
the doctor (described as "he") would pry open

my...*vagina!*...with a...*speculum*...and take a *swab*.

"No way," I said. "I'm not doing it. No way."

Theresa said, "We have to," and chewed her lower lip.

We both stared at the illustration of the half-naked woman, draped classically in a sheet, and then Theresa slapped the magazine shut. "Change of subject!" she yelled. "Let's talk about necking. Do you know necking, Dee?"

"Yeaaah," I said, huffily.

"How about 'horny'?"

"Of course I do."

"Then what's it mean?"

"It means, 'wants to screw,'" I said.

"Okay." She narrowed her eyes. "You ever screw, Dee?"

"Don't be ridiculous."

"Don't you call me ridiculous," she said, but then she settled back on her hands, and crossed her legs lengthways in front of her. "How about necking? You ever neck?"

"No," I admitted, humiliated without knowing why.

Well, she exclaimed, necking was great. It was soooo great, she told me, rolling her eyes and tossing back her hair, drawing the "o" in "so" out to sensual, sexual, orgasmic lengths, just like in *Cosmo*. Then she shivered all over, shivered and shimmered, and clasped her hands together. There was this guy, you see, up here at the lake, and he was so cute and so cool and just the biggest hunk.

"What about Colin?" I reminded her.

"Well, Colin's not here," said Theresa. "And Guy is *nineteen*, Dee. He has really dark brown hair, and he's such a good kisser."

"What makes him a good kisser?"

She looked at me as if I'd lost my mind, but then she sighed and started from the beginning. "He's like gorgeous, okay? So I want him kissing me. You've wanted someone to kiss you, right, Dee?"

"No," I lied, thinking of the moment with Brother Webster, and then thinking, all of a sudden, of Richard.

"Liar. You gotta want to kiss someone."

"No. I don't want to kiss any boys."

"Dee, this is so abnormal. You're a lezzie."

"I am not!" I knew what lezzies were. Lezzies were like men. They were big, loud, hairy-legged, didn't want babies, and wanted to have jobs as bus drivers or policemen. They played sports – not stuff like badminton or volleyball in gym, which everybody had to put up with, but baseball and football. They threw the shot put.

I'd never met a lezzie, but Theresa had. One of the phys-ed teachers at the collegiate was a lezzie. She would try to make the girls take showers, Theresa explained, even when they weren't even sweaty. She'd stand there and demand they take showers.

"Lezzies stare, and you stare," said Theresa slyly.

"I tell you I'm not a lezzie." Big. Loud. Hairy-legged. Didn't want babies. Stared. Did lezzies write stories? What if lezzies wrote stories? I might be one.

"If you're not a lezzie, prove it."

"Okay." I sat, waiting for the test.

Nothing came, and Theresa threw up her hands in frustration. "Go on, tell me about a guy you like."

"Okay," I said, for I was learning to talk fast, before thinking got in the way. "Richard, then."

She grunted and nodded. "Him. Yeah. No surprise there. He's okay."

"Okay!" I cried. "He's beautiful!"

Suddenly I was reeling off a list of Richard's attributes: his amazing hair, his amazing smile, his amazing smooth-skinned tanned-as-a-walnut glossy bare chest. Theresa leaned forward and listened, grinning with encouragement and nodding.

"And his eyes," she said. "They're so blue."

I frowned. "How do you know his eyes are blue? He wears those glasses..."

"Not all the time, he doesn't," she growled.

All my blood washed away in a torrent of cold, and I sat, ears ringing from shock, as she leaned back on her hands and crossed and re-crossed her long legs in front of her. She ran her tiny tongue over her upper lip, from one corner of her mouth to another, and raised her eyebrows at me, smiling, as if we were both in on a very dirty secret.

"You kissed him?" I whispered.

She raised one shoulder in a noncommittal shrug. "Everybody kisses," she said.

"What, what, what do you mean?"

"Oh, please don't stutter. God. If you stutter, you're doomed. If you're going to stutter, don't say anything." She levelled her pedagogical gaze my way. "This is the way it is. At parties, we turn out the lights and we kiss. You find a partner and you kiss."

"Is it, like, soft kissing, with lips?"

She rolled her eyes. "God, what a stupid question. Yeah, sort of. But then there's French kissing. Tongues."

"Like, tongues at church? Speaking in tongues?"

"Dee, try to be normal, okay? Church is out, man. It's establishment bullshit. French is they put their tongue in your mouth."

"Eww." I didn't want Richard's tongue in my mouth, or any boy's.

"It's not eww, once you get used to it. It's not eww at all. And they bite you, they suck on you. Look." She pulled away her throat scarf, and there on her neck were three fading bruises, in a neat row, one nearly the size of a quarter. "Those are hickies. From Guy," she sighed.

"But not from Richard. You didn't ever kiss Richard?"

"I may have kissed him, and maybe I didn't. But I won't kiss him anymore. I have Guy." She sighed again and performed once more her shimmering shudder. "I love him! He's so great!"

"Is Richard...a good kisser?"

"Richard? I told you, I have Guy. Who cares about Richard? Not me."

"So he doesn't have...have...have..."

"Have what? Geez, out with it!"

"A girlfriend?"

"He's gone out with a couple of girls. It's kinda hard, because of that blind thing. It's like they gotta be careful of him. He can't drive a boat while they water-ski, for instance, and he can't drive a car. Well, he couldn't anyway, because he's just fourteen. That's another thing. We're all much more mature. Nobody seventeen or eighteen is gonna go around steady with a fourteen year old, even if he's really mature, like Richard is. I'll say that. Richard is very mature."

I had no idea what mature meant, except for the dictionary definition, as it applied to barnyard animals and oak trees. But whatever mature was, it was another thing I didn't have, and Theresa and the others (and Richard, too), did. So I would have to be mature, as well. I remembered my mother's purchases for me, from the catalogues – how my size had been 24 1/2, for the "mature woman's figure." Yet lately even that seemed inconstant. There was a sag to the buttocks of my cotton trousers that I attributed to stretching of the fabric.

Theresa closed her magazine and returned it to the centre of the pile, then drew all of them to her and sighed, staring out at the grey, mobile water. The day was overcast and not very warm, although it was the height of summer, the halfway point even. Whenever a boat buzzed in the distance, Theresa perked up and listened to see if it was coming our way.

"If you want to go to the mainland, you could take the canoe," I said.

"Too windy," she replied. "Besides, someone will come for me." Then, as if she realized she'd been nice to me for too long, she said, "Don't think I wanna hang around here with you all day."

I lay down, on my back, on the boards of the dock, listening to the riverlike roar of the wind through the pines. I wondered what Richard was doing. Not reading; not with those crippled eyes. More likely hanging around the porch with the other kids. I tried to picture him as he was to me – skinny, bespectacled, shivering in the cold, his swimshorts hanging on his tiny, buttockless hips – but the sight of the sun-drenched man-boy kept overtaking the thought. I could not even properly conjure the memory of the forest walks anymore.

Theresa drew her knees to her chest and put her head on her forearms. "Are you okay?" I asked.

"I'm just bored," she said. "I'm so bored, I could die. This is the ultimate dullsville. Hanging around a stupid island in the middle of nowhere. I want to go home. I hate it here. One day I'll just go psychotic. I will. Trust me."

It did not surprise me that Theresa would say

this, for she had often said she hated the island, and the cottage, and the cabin, and the lake, and that she wanted to do things that other kids did in the summer, like go to the Exhibition, or get a job to earn money for cool stuff, or go to the 7-27 Drive-In, or even Yorkville (although her mention of Yorkville had caused the Dad to grow pop-eyed with agitation, reminding her of just how dangerous druggies were). She sat, rolled into a ball, bewildered by the lack of activity around her.

Trust me.

"We could read comics," I suggested, sitting up. "Or you wanna go swimming? We could do tire tube dives and stuff."

She peeked up at me from the corner of her elbow. "'We'?" she said. "What's this 'we'?"

"Well, you know..."

"Oh, forget it. Never mind. No, Dee, I do not want to read comics or go swimming. God, you're so out of it. You've always been out of it and you always will be out of it."

"Well, you said you were bored."

"Enough already," said Theresa, waving a hand dismissively. "As if there's anything you'd do I'd be like, un-bored by. You're hopeless."

"I am not. I do cool things."

"You do not. You are the biggest uncool thing in the world."

"Oh, yeah?" I said, prodding the tiger. "What makes me so uncool, and you so perfect?"

"I didn't say I was perfect. But you! You look

like a beachball and you act like a baby. You can't take a joke. Someone says something to you the least bit funny and you burst into tears. You couldn't go to a party or anything, because you'd do something like sit there in a corner, hanging your head like a retard, at least until someone gave you a bag of chips and then, *woof!* Now, see, you're crying, and I was just telling you the truth."

"I'm not crying!"

"Dee, you've got tears in your eyes. Bawling your eyes out already. Fuck, Dee. You gotta be able to take the truth, because people tell it like it is. Get used to it."

I hadn't recognized or felt that I was crying, but when I put my fingers to my eyelids I found that they were wet. I hadn't the power to recognize when I was crying. Had I spent that much of my life in tears?

Don't let the bastards get you down. Dee has been fighting. Trust me.

"Theresa," I said. "Why do you have to be so mean?"

"Why do you have to be such a loser? Do you have any idea what it's like to have you hanging around me like a ghost, like some sort of punishment? I heard about reincarnation, ya know, and I heard that stuff comes back to haunt you, like for life after life. I bet that's you. You're always right behind me, coming up from the rear, snorting and snuffling and stuttering. I can't have my own life,

I've always got to look out for you."

"You do not. You do not."

"I do too. I spend my whole life trying to get away from *you*."

I lay back again onto the boards of the dock, thinking of how many ways I could deny that I pursued her, but on this day I had done exactly that: I had come to her and read her magazines, talked to her, listened to her. I had stolen the story of the Pap Smear she'd suffered. I lay staring at the grey unflagging wall of the sky above me. Was I hurting her? Had I that power?

"I don't chase you around," I said at last. "You're too mean to chase around."

"You do too. You hang around me and Cathy. You touch my stuff. And I wouldn't be so mean if you weren't such a waste. If you helped yourself a little, I might help you too."

"Help myself?"

"Like, go on a diet or something."

"Great," I said bitterly, "So, like, if I lost like fifty pounds..."

"Try a hundred," she snorted.

"A hundred, yeah, okay. If I lost like a hundred pounds, you'd stop being mean."

"I'm *not* mean," she said, her voice full of warning. "Stop saying that."

I adjusted my tone. "Sorry. But if I lost weight, you might be, like my friend?"

"Gimme a break," she said. "I'd never be your *friend*."

"But I'd be less weird, if I lost weight."

"Yeah. Sure. I guess. But there's so much other stuff. The tall thing, and the clothes. Even the way you talk. You stammer and you say stupid things. It's like some kinda *My Fair Lady* or something."

"What's that?"

"A fucking movie, Dee, see? You don't ever go out, you're just like Mum, all goody-goody. You don't do anything right. You...are...*out of it*."

"I'm not!" I said, clambering from my recumbent posture to a half-seated one. I grabbed her arm. My fingers encircled her entire bicep easily, and she and I both looked at the joining of our flesh, amazed by it. But I did not let go. In fact, I gave her a small, gentle shake.

"I can change," I said. "You can make me change."

The voice that emerged from her lips was as sinister as a demon's, but seductive as well. "Let go of my arm, pig," she said evenly, and I did, but not before I let a beat of time pass, as if to let her know I was not obeying, but choosing.

"That's better," she said, brushing her fingers absent-mindedly over the spot where I'd touched her. "Okay, let's just say I was going to make you change. What would I change?"

She was not asking me, but rounding up her thoughts to itemize a list. "The first thing's the size of you," she said, standing up and brushing her palms together, to rid herself of the sandy dust. "You've gotta lose a lot of weight. The skin is good. The clothes – God! But we can do something about that. Once you've lost weight, we can get new stuff. But lose weight first. Nothing we can do about the height thing, though. But maybe there's like a tall boy somewhere. He'd have to be really tall, though, like a giant."

"The Friendly Giant."

She glared at me and then went on, on her feet while I stayed down. She continued to itemize, counting on her fingers, rocking back and forth on her soles.

"I don't know about that hair. It's like an Afro. Maybe that's what we should do. Just give you an Afro."

I did not want an Afro, for I had seen from her magazines that they involved going to the hair-dresser's, and then had to be picked at with a vicious-looking comb. But I said, "Okay."

"And your fingernails are dirty, and your eyes are all red," she said.

"I'm sorry," I said. "I'm sorry…"

"Stop bawling! Stop crying!" she shrieked at me. "That's the first thing – at least most ugly girls have good personalities! But not you! We have to change everything! *Everything!*"

"But what if – if I lost weight – and you did my hair – and I learned how to do my face pretty nice, because I don't have pimples…"

"You don't have pimples because you haven't hit puberty all the way," she interrupted. She picked up a handful of stones and threw them into the water, then sank to a squat, tucking her feet beneath her. "No boobs, no figure. Just a big baby..."

A huge, never-heard-before noise, like the cracking of metal, shot between us. Theresa jumped and froze, looking around to place its nature and its source, but somehow I knew what it was at once.

"Theresa," I said, "That was the gun."

The Dad stood in the doorway, carrying the gun at chest level, as if prepared to raise it, but reluctant. Big Dick was right behind him. He pointed at the treetops, there, there, there, his finger as aggressive as the gun itself.

The Dad worked the rifle's action and then aimed it, squinting down its length.

"Dad, don't!" I yelled, and at the same time Theresa broke into a run and charged up the path, running like an athlete, arms pumping and feet digging into the soil.

"Daddy, don't, don't!" she cried.

Too late. The gun went off again, surprising all of us. Theresa clapped her hands over her eyes and wailed. Almost at my feet, a squirrel fell, its russet fur ripped by a black and dark red hole. Pinkish worms – its innards – caught against the pine needles as it struggled once or twice, then stiffened, quivering, and died.

"Little bastard!" cried Big Dick.

"Get back, Theresa," the Dad said, just before she hit him with the full force of her slight body, leaping onto him, grabbing the gun with both hands. She pulled, and almost wrenched it free, but he wasn't surprised enough and easily held onto the gun.

Big Dick brought his foot down on the squirrel's head, grinding it. Then he picked it up by the tail and tossed it into the brush.

"Daddy, I hate you!" Theresa was weeping, unembarrassed and unashamed. She fell back, but stayed on her feet, crying as I thought only I could cry. "You – big – big pricks! You – you buggers!"

"That's enough, Theresa," said the Dad sadly. "I'm sorry, but they're all over the place..."

"They're vermin," said Dick. "They had babies. Theresa, Jesus Murphy, take it easy."

The Dad nodded and cracked the gun open, discharging the spent shells into his palm. They were hot, and he jostled them in his palm. They clicked together like pulled teeth.

"You said there were babies," I said, not crying, not even that angry. The squirrel was dead and I didn't feel much sorrow for it, since dead was dead and all. But the babies left behind – they would wonder where their mother was, they would be hungry – that bothered me.

"A nest of 'em, behind the icebox," said Big Dick.

"Oh!" cried Theresa. "We can feed them with an eyedropper, keep them in a box and let them go on the mainland, sort of like *Born Free*..."

"Terry-Bear, Uncle Dick looked after them already." He glanced at Dick, and the phrase *looked after* took on a diabolical tone. "I'm sorry, Sweetie. I'm so sorry."

"Dad," said Big Dick. "Don't you be apologizing. Girls, listen – sometimes, when you're a man, you gotta do stuff that's not very nice, and it's all very well and good for you girls to be weeping and wailing, but that little beggar was in the cupboard, right in the bag of Lancia pasta! Lucky no one got bitten. It woulda been buzzsaw time, I tell you."

"I hate you, Uncle Dick," said Theresa, and he shrugged.

"Sorry you feel that way, Theresa."

The Dad, however, couldn't seem to raise his head, and the gun hung at his side, dangled by one limp arm. He took a step towards Theresa, but she did something rare and amazing: she spat at him, complete with a dollop of mucous drawn with a *horrch* from her nose. The gob hit him on his shirt front, and the Dad recoiled noticeably, dropping the gun and grabbing at the material, holding it out in a tent to stare at it, unbelieving.

"Jesus," breathed Big Dick.

"Oh, Honey," said the Dad.

As Theresa stood, defiant before her father, my mother came drifting like a spirit along the path from the island's far end. She had the blanket and Thermos beneath one arm, and a book in her hand.

"Mum, Mum, he shot the squirrel!" Theresa and I cried, rushing to her. "Mum, the poor squirrel!"

"I know, we heard the gun. Theresa, if that's the worst thing you ever see in this world, count yourself lucky."

"Then I hate you too!" Theresa screamed, and she whirled and ran, not down the path but straight into the woods, over the picked-clean berry bushes and low, prickly, juniper shrubs.

"You better get that pony under control," said Big Dick. "Jane, where's Alice?"

"In the ladies'."

Big Dick had picked up the rifle and was cleaning the dirt off it, scolding the Dad for letting it drop and get earth in its moving parts. The Dad didn't seem to hear, for he was staring off in the direction Theresa had vanished, as if he could still see her.

"What is that on your shirt?" said my mother.

"Nothing," muttered the Dad.

Alice arrived, and immediately demanded to know who'd fired the shots: Dick or the Dad? She shook her head and clucked her tongue when the Dad said that he had done the shooting, and that he'd killed one of the squirrels.

"Aw, poor ol' Dad," said Alice. "Y'okay? That musta been hard."

"We can't have squirrels in the cottage," said my mother.

"Yeah, but it doesn't make it easier to kill 'em. Unless of course you're Dick."

"What's that supposed to mean?" said Dick.

"Just that you're the Great White Hunter–type," said Alice, "and Dad's more Gentle Ben."

The Dad sank down onto the cabin's stone step, and he lay the gun down beside him. Then he put his face in his hands, and rubbed and rubbed.

"Aw," said Alice, but this time, the sound was unpleasant, tinged with exaggeration. The Dad paused in his rubbing, but did not reveal his eyes.

I kicked the dirt where the squirrel had lain, and stepped into the shrubs to find the tossed-away corpse. I told myself that I would need to see the corpse, and get used to dead things, were I ever going to go live in the woods. I'd have to learn to skin and eat them.

And even my own mind said, *as if*.

I found the body, strung up in the upper branches of a small sapling birch, and stood beside it, looking into its empty black bead of an eye. Its little face was so darling and familiar, like the hamsters' in science class, and like the favoured chipmunks' too. I saw along its damaged belly a couple of teats, and realized that it had indeed left babies behind. Poor babies – but they were dead, too. I did not want to think about how Dick had done them in. Had he, perhaps, thrown them into the woodstove, where they would suffocate and die, frightened and confused and motherless, in the cast-iron cavern?

My own mind could come up with a dozen horrible deaths for the squirrel babies, but my body could not bring itself to touch the ripped little form in front of me. My hand went out and came back, and went out, and came back, and once it approached within an inch of the matted fur, but in the end I had to give up. I could not touch it, let alone skin and eat it.

I came out of the woods, not really surprised by my failure. The Plan, which until then had staggered along beside me, refusing to give up in full, now fell flat on its face. I could not kill for food: another thing that had changed, in the Plan's voyage from story to reality.

I walked up the path towards the cabin, but the adults were arguing up there, and I spun in midstride, heading away from them as quickly as I could. I could still hear them, as I moved into the bushes, on my way to my surviving house.

"You're so out of line, Alice," said Big Dick. "Jane's happy. Leave her alone. You're like, contributing to her delinquency or something."

"Aw, fuck you, Dick."

The Dad's voice spoke. "Well, actually, Alice, these last few months, even a year or so, I've noticed a change in Jane…"

"So, your wife's growing up at last? Did you think you could keep her around, your pet retard, forever?"

"Hey!" protested the Dad. "She's no retard!"

"I'm sure Alice didn't mean it that way," said my mother.

"You bet she did, Janey, don't you trust this broad," Dick roared. "She's not normal. She gets her kicks putting other people down, you know, intellectually. You're just some big experiment to her. Some kinda project, ya know, like she's building a sculpture and she's gonna pump it fulla air – her air – and make it live. That's what these women's libbers do, Janey, they're poisoning the whole Western world…"

I kept moving, over the crest of rock that formed the island's spine. Down in the valley below it lay my little house.

Behind me, Big Dick was still shouting. "I shoulda divorced this dame years ago, and got myself a real wife. But there was the kid, I've got my duty to Richard, you don't walk out on your son..."

To my house – that was the only thing to do, the only place to go. To my little hut. I could recover there. I could, perhaps, even stand to remember Richard. I would pretend him. I could talk to him; I was still good at pretend; Brother Webster had shown me I was. And I would think differently. I would imagine, for instance, dancing with him. I didn't know how to dance yet, but I could learn. I could dance with the new Richard, and I would be the new Dee, and although much had been taken, I was not dead yet, not at all.

I made my way down the partings in the shrubs, down the rocky incline. As soon as I approached, however, I knew. It was occupied. I could see, through the cracks and gaps in my construction of its walls, the form of a person inside.

Richard had come after all, with his parents he had come, and he was waiting! "Richard," I said, "Richard, did you bring..."

"Fuck, Dee," said Theresa, from inside my house. "It's me, you big idiot."

She came out of the opening, on her hands and knees, and peered up at me. "You know what, though? This place is cool. You did a good job. Maybe you're not completely useless."

I didn't know what else to say, so I thanked her. She backed up, and I followed her inside.

There, with her face still chafed red from tears, she told me how evil our parents were, particularly the Dad, and how they deserved to die in exchange for what they'd done to the poor squirrels. I listened, hypnotized by the flow of her voice as she spoke to me, communing with me about the faults of someone else; as if I were a collateral and not a subordinate.

Eventually, she ran out of words and anger, and she leaned against one of the trees that formed the cornerposts of my house, and nodded to herself with relief and satisfaction.

"Cool little pad, Dee," she said, looking at the patchwork ceiling above her.

"Thanks. Theresa?"

"What?"

"Can I ask you something?"

She frowned, but did not look at me. Her otherwhere-gaze gave me strength. "Okay," she said, guardedly.

"How come you were so upset about the squirrels and yet you're so mean to me?"

"I told you," she said, running her fingers along the cracks in the planks behind her. "I'm not mean. You could change. All the stuff that happens to you, you do it to yourself. It's your own stupid fault."

"I can't help it..."

"Aw, bullshit, Dee. Change. That's all you gotta do. You just gotta put your mind to it. Have a little willpower."

Now she looked at me, and with more strength than it took to touch a dead squirrel, I kept my eyes on hers. There, staring into my eyes, she seemed to transform, and I could see what others saw in her. She wasn't merely pretty. She had spirit and flair in her face. I saw this, because she smiled at me.

"Okay, what the fuck, this might be interesting. But you gotta follow the rules, Dee, or man, I'll make your life a living hell."

That I could believe. I nodded, accepting the bargain, but could not keep from asking one more thing of her.

"Theresa, like, why would you help me, eh?"

There is no true altruism in nature, and Theresa proved it. "Hey, in like a month, man, you're gonna be in my school. I am sick of watching this crippled fuckup drag itself through life. You're sadder than that dead squirrel, with its guts hanging out, but you're not sad, either – you're like, angry-making. Because it can't help being a squirrel. You, you're doing this to yourself. So, like, I can make you stop. I can do anything, even fix you."

"So," I said, and my voice trembled, "you'll fix me?"

She smiled again, but this time, it was the

fox's smile. "Yeah, I'll fix you," she said, "or man...I'll fix you. Get it?"

"Got it," I said.

We both leaned back against the walls of my little hut, which held firm, for I had learned some carpentry over the years I'd been alone with Richard. I knew I could learn. I had learned how to hammer, how to haul, how to plan, how to write, how to read, how to survive. Could it be so hard, then, to learn to be a *girl?*

Eight

VAGINA DENTATA ON HER MOTHER
MARCH OF DAMES COMEDY NIGHT, TORONTO

You wouldn't have believed my mother. God all freakin' mighty, you never saw such an invertebrate. Seriously. She followed my father around like a gnat behind a gnu, doing everything he said, but buzzin' at him all the time. Do this, dear, do this, dear, do this dear. She was his fetchit girl. I don't know why she thought this was desirable. I bet that when men go looking for wives, they don't rank scrubbing floors above giving head. Or maybe they do, I dunno. But I suspect they'd never say, "Hey, I'll marry the first girl who can scrub a toilet until she exfoliates herself right up to the elbows." They're much more interested in someone who can fellate them until their eyes pop.

Ewww. I just talked about cocksucking and my parents in the same monologue. Definitely time to change tangents.

I used to think my mother was the single most stupid broad that ever slipped a pair of mulies onto her size sixes. Scary, somehow. My Dad shoulda been the scary one. He was like a Douglas fir with legs. Big sun-nuvabitch. The kind of guy over whom cops pull their guns when he gets out of the car. "Hold it right there, fella." But it turned out my old lady was scarier. She had the patience of Gollum, and them same big eyes, washed-out cave-dweller blue. With liner, mascara and eyebrow pencil. Fooled us all cold...

But she does rebel. Even if at first she was impressed by male prestige, her bedazzlement soon evaporates...she sees no reason to be under his thumb; he seems to her to represent no more than an unpleasant and unjust duty...

Simone de Beauvoir
The Second Sex

The next day, I expected Theresa to get started on my lessons, but she said not one word to me. Then I remembered: it was a Saturday, a day of a dance at Ashleigh's. With that on her mind, there was no room for me, and when (shortly after 10 a.m.) a dark-haired man in a fibreglass powerboat cruised into our dock, she leaped aboard and told me to tell the Dad she'd be staying at Laurie Packard's and would be back in the morning.

"What if I don't want to?" I said.

"Hey, then kiss our plan goodbye, and stay what you are – you big toad!"

The boat spurted away, with the dark-haired Guy standing behind the wheel, and Theresa nestled upright beside him.

At lunchtime Dick and Alice arrived, and disembarked without speaking to each other, but Alice greeted me warmly as she passed my sunning-spot on the deck.

"Good book?" she asked.

"The same as always," I replied. "Got the

damn thing memorized by now."

She laughed very loud. "God, sweetie, you're growing up."

The Dad and Dick got involved in a project, which they soon discarded in favour of sitting by the firepit, looking over the lake, and drinking beer. I could hear what they were discussing, and it interfered with my concentration on the book, irritating me beyond necessity. I threw the book down on the deck, but even the slap of its binding striking the boards didn't rouse the men's notice and quiet them down. So I strode up to the cabin, thinking I might try to find something to eat, which would not be missed. Alice had brought marshmallows; I had seen the bag in her hand. Perhaps I could figure out a way to eat a few, without discovery.

My mother and Alice were not in the cabin, of course, but the marshmallows were on the counter. I tore a nickel-sized hole in the plastic, away from the seam, and was manoeuvering a marshmallow through it when I heard female voices on the path. I quickly abandoned the bag and dived onto my bed, scrambling to pick up a comic and thrust my attention into it.

The women were like the song sparrows, a pattern of giggle and treble-pitched murmur. "Dee, are you in here?" my mother asked, even though I was clearly visible, on the bed.

"Yes. Where else would I be?"

"I'm sure I can't imagine," she said, and Alice blew

out a guttural laugh.

"What's so funny?" I demanded.

"Nothing is funny, Dee. But Auntie Alice is going to give me a lesson in driving the boat. We thought you might like to come, too."

Was this really my mother talking? "Uncle Dick's gonna let you drive the boat?"

"Uncle Dick can take a long walk off a short pier," said my mother, then inhaled a shocked laugh. "A very long walk! A very long walk!" she sang.

"Okay, okay, Janey," said Alice. "Settle down. Nothing to be afraid of. Dee, are you coming or not?"

"Where are we gonna go?" I said, setting my feet on the floor in search of my flip-flops.

Alice rolled her eyes. "I don't know, Dee, just around the lake. We'll try not to hit any rocks."

"I just don't want to see anybody, okay? As long as we don't see anybody."

Alice shook her head and sighed. "I promise we won't see anybody. Good grief, Dee, you're as antisocial as your mother. C'mon!"

So I slipped on my rubber sandals and joined them, following behind, looking at the parts in the tops of their hairdos. Alice's hair was greying dark-brown, and my mother's part was straightly set with a comb. She no longer had the flip, though – her hair hung straight and fine to her shoulders, and floated about without the stricture of hairspray.

"Shhh," said Alice, as we approached the end of the path and firepit clearing.

Dad and Big Dick were seated on lawn chairs, facing the water, away from the path. They had their legs crossed, ankle resting on knee, and the Dad had his pipe lit, and Uncle Dick a cigarillo. He had lately begun to smoke wine-dipped cigarillos, which stank of cheap cigar, because he'd seen an advertisement for them on TV and liked the look of the woman who purred over the smoking man. "She's a living doll," he'd said.

The men were talking, more or less: I heard the Dad say, "I'll keep working on him. Money talks..." and Big Dick nodded.

Alice and my mother were moving forward, nonchalance personified, trying not to look as if they were sneaking. They had their arms folded across their breasts, chins high and gazes forward, and they did not speak but kept moving without meander or delay. I thought of *I Spy* and *Hogan's Heroes* and followed them, praying I wouldn't snap a twig in passing.

"Good girl," Alice mouthed, as I reached the dock. "Get the ropes."

I knew how to untie the boat, but Mum did not, so she stood there while Alice and I unmoored Big Dick's precious bowrider. From their vantage, of course, the men could see us, so we moved very quickly, snatching at the cords, our fingers fumbling.

"Hey, girls!" Big Dick yelled. "Whatcha up

to?" Alice laughed a squealing, panicky little laugh and yanked hard at the bowline. My mother danced from one foot to the other, shaking her hands. "Hurryhurry," she urged.

"Get in, quick, both of you," said Alice.

The men were both on their feet. "Whaddya doin'!" yelled Dick, not pleasantly at all, and the Dad shielded his eyes with his hand and stood, legs apart like the Colossus of Rhodes, frowning at us.

"Girls! Where are you going?"

"Dee, Dee, get in!" said Mum, who had already climbed into the stern, and without her usual helping hand from the Dad. She leaned over and tugged on my trousers, and they pulled right down several inches, exposing my panties.

"Mum!" I gasped, tightening my drawstring.

The men were on their way. "Wait, wait!" Dick called. "What the hell are you doing! Wait!" They scrambled across the uneven rocks, and Alice began to push clear of the dock.

"Now or never, Dee," she barked at me. I took one look at the men as they arrived on the planks of the dock, then turned and jumped into the boat. It was a longish leap, perhaps only two feet but still difficult for me, and when I landed the boat tipped dramatically under my weight, then swayed back into place. Alice, behind the wheel, turned the key, and the clicking thrum of the starter sounded from the engine. We were still within reach of the dock, and Dick, who was at its lip, leaned out over the gap and tried to grab the stern's light standard. He missed, so he lunged for a bumper, catching its cord in his fingertips.

"Girls, the bumpers!" cried Alice.

Mum snatched the bumper out of Dick's fingers, then smacked his hand as if he'd been fresh.

"Start, you whoreson," muttered Alice, as the engine coughed and cranked itself over.

"Alice Holmes, that's my boat, and don't you fucking forget it!" screamed Uncle Dick, standing on the dock's end. He was only a few feet from us, but he could not bridge that span. The engine caught, and Alice put the boat into gear, standing up to see over the windshield. She drove straight out into the channel, slowly, still being proper and prudent, even demonstratively so, to give Mum – and me – a chance to settle into our seats. We waved cheerfully at the Dad and Dick, who pursued us along the shore as we puttered away, the big 90-horse Johnson straining to be opened up full throttle.

Alice had lit a cigarette, and was steering the boat clear from between the reef and the wall of Bald Face. Bald Face fell away to our left, and the island to our right, as the channel opened into lake. Away from the shore and the cliff, we had free sailing for miles.

"You guys seated? Good." She turned and looked at us, over her shoulder. What a striking figure she was: captain at the prow, standing with her hand on the wheel, like Bligh or Ahab, cigarette clasped between prehensile lips. Her greying hair whipped around her face, blowing into her eyes, and her eyes squinted against the smoke and the blow.

"When do I get to drive?" said my mother.

"Soon as we're far away. Any second. So, shall we go back to my place? We can have a drinkey-poo, Janey-poo."

"That's the first place they'll come for us, in the Dad's boat."

"Okay, where else then?"

Mum was about to answer, but I interrupted, before I could mind my manners. "Let's go see Mr. Webster!"

She and Alice looked at each other, and then at me. Concurrence passed between them. "Okay," said Alice, nodding and turning back to face the full-blown lake. "Let's open her up."

Two hundred yards away, calling from the shore of the island, stood Big Dick, raging and blowing and waving his hands.

"I'll kill you if there's so much as a scratch, Alice! So much as a scratch!"

"Aww, tell it to the marines," said Alice, and kicked the throttle fully open. Up went our nose, down went our stern, and the churning V-wake behind us thrust white foam into the calm.

My odd little mother read my mind. "Look, Dee," she said. "That's V for Victory."

We hit the water at full steam ahead. Out in the middle of the lake, my Aunt Alice let my mother take the wheel, and together they stood leaning on the windshield, driving at low throttle, while I rode in the nose of the boat, where the bowriders' seats were luxurious white leatherette. We cruised, lazily, across the rolling, rippling waves, rising up and sinking down, warmed by the sun, rocking in the lap of the lake, three foolish women who'd stolen a boat, and lived to tell the tale.

"Janey Graham, is that you?" called Brother Webster from his dock. "This is a surprise. Uh, careful, girls, you have to stay away from that buoy!"

Brother Webster's bay – past the sandbar – was a treacherous, submarine field of boulders, beautiful to explore with a snorkel but difficult to navigate through. The rocks all bore tattoos of paint and aluminum, scars of the blows from various boats who had missed the narrow pathways where there was enough draw for a boat to pass. The routes changed, too, as the spring runoff drained away. A good route in June was impassable in August. A matter of an inch could mean the difference between cruising pleasantly by, and disembowelling your craft.

Mum, at Alice's direction, stayed outside the furthermost lip of the reef, where the water was at least twenty feet deep. Even then, when I peered over the side, I could see that the lake floor was peppered with large rocks, some as round as bowling balls (and not much bigger), and others massive boulders that nearly broached the surface, stone leviathans lying asleep on the sand. I watched them pass beneath me, imagining how long they'd been there, and how they'd got there, and what, if anything, would ever cause them to move.

"Careful!" screeched Brother Webster, as we steered too close to one of the bleach-bottle buoys, which Brother Webster had painted with yellow-and-green peace signs.

"This wasn't such a good idea, maybe," said Alice. "I never thought about docking this thing. Damn."

"Girls, you better let me do it!" called Brother Webster. "Put her in neutral!"

So Brother Webster pulled off his shirt and dived into the lake in his denim shorts, slicing a shallow dive that barely creased the surface. It was not very safe to dive or jump off his dock, for the boulders there were only five or six feet down, and in many places I could stand on one and still have my head above water, from the earlobes up. But Brother Webster knew what he was doing.

He swam out to us and climbed monkeylike into the boat. He was a slender man, with a patch of grey hair poufed precisely between his nipples. His leg hair was grey, too. Dripping, he excused himself and took the wheel from Alice.

On shore, he helped us all out of the boat, offering each of us his hand, and then he tied up Dick's fancy fibreglass cruiser beside his own little cedarstrip. "This is an unexpected pleasure," he said, as we gathered before him on the dock, pulling our hair back behind our ears. "You're lucky you caught me in. A wandering minstrel I, you know."

"Yeah, that's you all over. So, shall we go up and have a beer?" said Alice.

"Uh, let's just stay down here, in the sun,"

said Brother Webster. "I'll throw together some crudités, just a few light bits, and we'll have a nice picnic here on the dock."

"It's not sunny here on the dock," I announced. It wasn't, either; none of Brother Webster's property was sunny. It was more like a fern-covered cavern, so deep did his cove cut into the shore.

"The cabin's a mess. I'm not ready for company. So you just make yourself comfortable on the deck chairs here, and I'll be right back," burbled Brother Webster. "I'm going to towel off and whip us up some manna."

Mum and Alice shrugged and sat down in two of the big, white-painted, wooden chairs that Brother Webster had set up on the dock around a low, circular table. The table was an industrial spool for thick cable or heavy-gauge rope, and he'd painted it white to match the chairs. Alice put her feet up and lit a cigarette, smiling to herself. My mother glanced at her and then put her feet up, too. Alice laughed with pleasure.

"God," I said, disgusted. "Copycat her or what, Mum."

"Imitation is the sincerest form of flattery," said my mother.

"Good one, Janey." Alice put her hand out and patted her on the arm.

"Bleah," I said, and decided to go help Brother Webster. I steeled myself for the long haul up the stairs, and concentrated in passing on the lovely flowerbeds that lined the sides of the hundred log-and-soil steps. The flowers were shade-dwellers, petunias and nasturtiums, but even then they were sparse, for despite the clearing-away of trees to make the broad staircase, the trees still blocked out most light. The temperature dropped notice-ably in the forest, perhaps by as much as five degrees, and the bugs came out in little, singing swarms.

Yet by the top of the stairs, I still had breath. I noticed my pants were drooping, and tightened up my drawstring again. My body seemed differ-ent. I was panting a little, but still had wind to get me up the four stairs of Brother Webster's porch.

I creaked open the door of the cabin, calling his name. "Mr. Webster," I began, but got no fur-ther. I froze in the portal, unable to say another word.

"Dee," Brother Webster said sadly. "You were supposed to stay with the ladies."

He was on the sofa, not quite sitting, with his arm around the back of David's neck, and his other arm beneath David's bent knees. David lay across his lap, flaccid-spined, inert, and deathly pale-grey, draped over Brother Webster like Jesus across Mary in a *Pietà*. David's head lolled and he looked up, and said, "Oh, shit, Dee." Then his head dropped back, heavy as a lake boulder, and seemingly as dead.

I almost called for my mother, and my mouth had even opened to make the cry, but something desperately conspiratorial in Brother Webster's face stopped me. My mouth snapped shut and I waited for instructions.

"He's okay. He's okay," said Brother Webster. "Help me, Dee. He's heavy."

Brother Webster showed me how to take David's ankles, and he wriggled beneath David's back and seized him under the armpits. Together, we carried him into Brother Webster's one bedroom, and with effort got him onto the bed. David smelled terrible, like sour milk and pee, but his shorts were dry. The pee-smell was oozing from his skin.

I was about to ask what was wrong with him, and then I saw the answer on the bedtable. It was a shock – the idea that David, too, had been struck with that disease – and I had a score of questions about it. Why hadn't David told us? And what was he doing at Brother Webster's? I looked between my grey, sweating, shivering brother, and then to the bedtable, on which lay his belt and, beside that, the syringe (which had told me in an instant what was wrong with my brother). Beside the syringe, a spoon with a residue of icing sugar on it.

"Did he have enough sugar? Maybe he needs more," I said.

"What?" said Brother Webster.

"He's having a diabetic coma thing. Get him some juice maybe. Hurry, Mr. Webster."

"Oh," said Brother Webster. "Oh. Yes, of course. Well, I gave him some, Dee, and he has a different type of...diabetes. He's had his shot and he'll be okay."

He ushered me, not gently and with both hands on my back, out of the bedroom, and closed the door behind him. I noticed now that there was a tin pail beside the sofa where David had been lying, and I gagged inwardly at the notion of my brother's vomit.

"I better get Mum," I said.

"Dee, sit down." I did, in a corner armchair by a bookshelf, far away from the ominous pail. "Don't tell your mum. Don't tell anyone. You're just about an adult, now, Dee, and you've always been very mature."

"I have?"

He went on, as if he hadn't heard me. "Brilliant, mature, stalwart, head-and-shoulders above the ordinary. What you deal with on a daily basis, Dee, amazes me. And you can deal with this. You must keep it a secret. If David had wanted the family to know he was...sick...he would have told them. You have secrets, don't you? That you wouldn't want anyone to know?"

"Well, not really," I lied, thinking of the eating attacks, and the myths I'd written, and of the old, spent dream of running away to live in the woods. The kissing thoughts. The chance I was a lezzie. And the gun in my mouth. All of them were secrets.

"Even if you don't have any secrets, Dee, other people do, and they're entitled to their privacy. David's not a little boy. He doesn't need his mummy and daddy to look after him. He's been through a lot this year. So many changes. So many changes of mind."

"But..."

"Listen!" He froze, like a rabbit scenting a hound. "Damn, there's a boat coming through the narrows."

I went over to the window and peered through the trees, trying to see the lake. All that was visible were patches of blue water, shimmering in the sun, and the shadowy movement of my mother and Alice as they walked around the dock and shore together. "Are you sure it's coming this way?" I asked Brother Webster.

"I know the sound." Down at the dock, there was shouting, with Big Dick's voice soaring above all. "To the moon, Alice!" he yelled, but it didn't sound funny.

"We better go down there before they start bombing Hanoi," said Brother Webster. "You and I will talk later. We'll work out a plan of action. I'm glad to see the diet is working, by the way. You're looking positively Twiggy, my dear."

I stood staring at him as he walked to the door, and when he arrived there without me, he gestured with a beckoning hand. "C'mon, Dick's going bonkers down there. Poor Alice."

Never mind Alice, I thought. What diet? It hadn't been a diet, they had assured me it wasn't a diet. I longed to run into Brother Webster's room, where I knew there was a big oval mirror, four feet high, on a frame above the chest of drawers, but I didn't dare. For Brother Webster was now on the porch and Big Dick and Auntie Alice were screaming at each other. I could hear the voices beginning to ascend the earthen staircase, and I did not want anyone to wake David, or see the vomit pail.

I hurried after Brother Webster, full of information, and full of new prospect. Positively Twiggy. I was Positively Twiggy. I had walked up a flight of stairs and had air to spare.

"Air to spare!" I sang, as I danced down the stairs behind Brother Webster, into the maelstrom of the Holmes family uprising. "Up the stairs with air to spare!"

"Dee, shh," said Brother Webster, not understanding. That was all right, for I didn't understand either. It didn't matter. If I was Positively Twiggy, with air to spare, things could be very different. I could dance. I could wear blue jeans with appliqué patches. I could sit on a lap in a convertible car. I would be able to walk, right out in public, anywhere I wanted. If I was Positively Twiggy With Air To Spare, there was a chance I might survive after all.

I skipped – yes, I skipped – past Big Dick and Alice, who were hurling anger at each other, venomous bags of hot words, one after the other. The forest dripped, fouled with their poison. But even still, despite the heat of the battle, Big Dick couldn't resist. He paused in his invective long enough to whistle "Baby Elephant Walk" as I passed.

I whirled around with Air To Spare. "If you ever sing that at me again, Uncle Dick, I'll punch you right in the nose," I said cheerfully. Then off I bounced, down the steps to the dock, and to the purloined boat.

Alice's bray stripped the bark from the trees. "Dick," she cried, "I do believe she means it!"

My sister and I. Me and my sister. It had never been this way, and it felt like a hot, scented bath (perhaps one just that shade too hot, that nearly scalds, but to which the skin becomes accustomed). It was cleansing and arousing, to have her not chase me away. To have her sit me down and look me over. Like Alice before a lump of clay, she stood and made her plans.

She had her research material: her pattern books, her bibles. *Glamour*, *Vogue*, *Seventeen*. A hardback textbook with a glossy yellow-and-red cover, called *So You're Going to Be a Teen*. Ready for me, ready for us.

For us! That there was an "us" between her and me, was as odd as snow on Labour Day: not unthinkable, but not likely. The alignment of our desire – our mutual goal – had brought us into the same sphere, the same space. Theresa did not let me forget that it was a sacrifice for her to be there: a sacrifice of time. For the day we started work on me, the Dad and our mother had gone to the mainland for ice and groceries, and were even thinking of going into town. Theresa could have been with her friends; they might have caught a lift to Bracebridge in the Dad's wagon; there were all sorts of things Theresa could have been doing, but she was here with me.

"I dunno, I" she said. "Where even to start? With the hair, maybe? I just... don't...know!"

Her bottom was so pretty. Her tight shorts rode above the cup of her gluteus, their frayed hem fringed with a string of ricrac. The ricrac was yellow, like a lemon sucker, and so was her halter top, and so was the puffy cord of yarn that she had wrapped around her ponytail. She stood with the pile of magazines at her feet, faithful dogs, and with me directly before her, in one of the cabin's armless cane-bottom chairs, the ones that groaned whenever the Dad pulled them to him, and which didn't particularly like me, either. I kept my knees together and my hands on my lap, at the crest of the flood of my stomach.

It didn't seem possible, that my stomach could be removed. It was too large, too much. It was attached to me and it was mine. It had always been there, from my earliest naked-baby days. I couldn't imagine myself without it. If only excision were possible. I could just take a pair of shears and slice across it, at the root, where it met my buried ribcage.

Theresa, legs akimbo and pinky finger pressed against her lips, flipped one-handed through a *Seventeen*. She glanced from the pages to me as if she were doing my portrait.

"God almighty," she observed.

Okay, I could take that. I knew that sitting there, with my thighs spreading like a landscape, overflowing the chair, that I was not something that would draw compliments. No one would ever crow at me, how wonderfully fat you are! How marvellous are your threefold thighs! I knew I was (as she said) *in terrible shape*. I *was* a terrible shape.

"Well," sighed Theresa, still thumbing through her mag, "the biggest size here is a 15. I don't know if we can get you down to a 15 by the time school starts, but..."

Here she trailed off, and suppressed a shudder.

"Okay," she said, tossing the *Seventeen* aside. "This is what we'll do. We can't tell what to do with your hair until we get the shape of your face. Which is now just a big blob, right? And we can't do a wardrobe and we can't do a makeup routine yet either. Everything is useless until we get you slimmed down. So we're gonna do the best, best diet. The quickest. There are some, you know, you can lose ten pounds in two weeks. Geez, I wish we had a scale. I bet you weigh two hundred pounds."

I bit my lip and said nothing.

"Two hundred pounds!" Theresa sagged to the floor dramatically, sitting cross-legged, and began to paw through her material, looking for references on the covers, to diets and shaping up and slimming down. "Here, and here," she said, setting aside a couple of magazines. "How tall are you?"

"I think about five-ten," I lied.

"Holy cow, that's huge! That's as big as a guy! Wow. Okay, here." She flipped a magazine open at me, and there was a familiar chart – a height-weight chart, onto which I knew I would never fit. Theresa came over, walking on her knees, to my side, and leaned against me while she ran her finger down the 5′ 9″ column (that was as far as it went).

"Small-boned," she said. "Small-boned is right. Big bones is just cheating. You should weigh 125. So you gotta lose seventy-five pounds! Wow, that's three-quarters of what I weigh."

"You weigh just a hundred pounds?" I said. I hadn't weighed that since Grade 2.

"I'm a *junior petite*," she said proudly. "Yep. One hundred pounds."

"I think my left arm weighs that much," I said, and to my shock, Theresa burst out laughing.

"Hey, that's funny! I didn't know you had a sense of humour. Cool. That's good."

Over the next hour, she tore from the magazines every reference to every diet she could find. There were advertisements and articles, charts and programs, the Campbell's soup diet and the Metracal weight-loss plan. The ice-water diet ("chill your stomach so you don't feel hungry!"). We particularly relished the Wayde's Diet Candy ads, which featured before-and-after pictures. The woman in the before picture always looked very much like me, even though she was always much, much older:

MY HUSBAND CALLED ME LUMPY
UNTIL WAYDE'S DIET HELPED ME

200 pounds! I knew that since the birth of my beautiful son, I had been gaining

*weight, but now the scale read 200
pounds! I was even heavier than my husband! How could I have let it happen?*

*It was because of my bad eating
habits. I ate cereal with cream and sugar
for breakfast, toast with jam and butter,
and sugar in my coffee, and a glass of
juice. Lunch was greasy food, like french
fried potatoes and hamburgers, and sometimes a grilled cheese sandwich. I would
have pickles or fry myself up a snack of
onions. For dinner, I made a sensible
meal, because my husband liked broiled
steak or chops, but as I prepared the
evening meal, I snacked on cookies and
potato chips.*

*Then came the day. He came home
from work with a friend, who said he was
very glad to meet me, and shook my hand.
But as I was leaving the room, I heard my
husband's friend remark, "I see why you
call her 'Lumpy'"*…

The lady in the story said that she lost eighty
pounds by eating the candies. "I wonder how
much they cost," Theresa mused.

"We'll never be able to buy them, all the way
up here," I said. "The general store won't carry
them."

"You're right." She sighed mightily. "We'll
have to make a diet up ourselves."

"I've got paper," I said.

I got my Playtime Doodler, and tore from it the few pages I'd filled since the beginning of the summer. There were a few lines from a myth in which I'd lost interest, and a poison-pen letter to Richard, which began "Undear Richard, you big Nixon you." I crumpled up the pages and threw them into the firebox, handing Theresa the Doodler as I passed by.

"What's that?" she asked.

"Old stories and drawings and stuff," I said, praying she wouldn't ask to see.

But she merely nodded, opening the Doodler and smoothing out a page. She took a pen from her pile of research material, and at the centre of the top of a pale pink sheet, she wrote in block capitals, THE DIET. Then she sat back and admired the words, cocking her head as if she'd never done anything so clever in her life. Which, I thought (in spite of myself), she hadn't.

"Give me your hand," she said, her eyes on the page, but her hand reaching out to me. I sat down, thump, and reached for her fingers. She seized me, prayerfully, and said, "You gotta make a vow. You gotta stick to this."

"Okay, sure," I said, and she squeezed my hand so hard that her little claws pierced me.

"This is a holy vow," she said, mostly to herself. Her eyes were tight closed, and her hand rested heavily on the page that said THE DIET. "Dee will stick to this. Dee will stick to this. Dee will stick to this. Say it three times, Dee. It'll be like a chain letter."

I agreed, but not quickly enough, for her nails sank in even deeper. "Dee will stick to this, Dee will stick to this, Dee will stick to this! Oww!" I cried, but Theresa stayed fixed in place, her hand trapping me, her other hand covering the pastel paper, which I'd always thought of as strawberry-coloured. Now I looked past the sweet flavour of the page and saw the word that Theresa had partly concealed beneath her hand. The word, the command, the threat, the *or else* at the centre of my Playtime Doodler: DIE.

Theresa released me, so she might hold the page while she wrote. Her hand moved, adding more words – breakfast, cereal, grapefruit – but I remembered what I'd seen. Die. Diet or die. I wanted to laugh at it, to make fun of it, to rip its foolishness apart. But for that, I needed someone who didn't think it was important. And there wasn't a soul in the world who didn't agree: Dee must diet. Or Dee must die.

The Dad noticed the difference right away. "Why's my little darling so unhappy?" he asked, time and again, day after day. "You're so sad, Jane. Cheer up. It's for your own good."

My mother had lapsed into a soggy state, limp as old celery. For the Dad and Big Dick had decided that she and Alice should spend some time apart.

"You have a delicate nature," he said, "and she's got you all excited and upset. You just need a little time to yourself. That's what you like, isn't it, dear?"

But my mother didn't answer. She merely went on, making dinners of hamburgers or steak on the barbecue grill, or a fish the Dad had caught. Night after night, the same thing. Burgers, steak, a fish the Dad had caught. Burgers, steak, a fish.

"Help me to plan the Labour Day bash, Jane?" asked the Dad. "How much corn do you think we'll need? Shall we invite other folks? Make it a popular do, rival the Ashleigh's?"

Mum, when he spoke to her, turned her back and walked away. Picked up a dishrag. Cleaned off the table. Hung the sleeping bags on the line, for airing.

"Jane, c'mon, Honey, please talk to me."

She would not.

Big Dick would come over, by himself, but not as often, for he reported it wasn't worth the

flak he got from the wife to try. He suggested the
Dad come over there, which the Dad did, dropping by in the mornings on his fishing trips,
when the water was glass-flat and steaming in
the cool dawn, to visit Dick and have a cup of
instant. Alice was refusing to make coffee, and
since Dick hated the messiness of the percolator
and its grounds, he just made instant, using hot
water from the tap. Alice would try and jump
into the boat when he'd leave to visit Blueberry,
and he'd had to hide the keys. She tried to start
the engine by pulling the pull-rope, which on a
90-horse is man's work, for sure. He sat on the
dock and watched her pull and pull and pull, hair
straggling in her red face, all her bulk useless to
get that engine started. Then he'd caught her trying to rent a boat at Ashleigh's. He'd told
Ashleigh not to let her use the water taxi, and
they'd said no problem, they wouldn't, and she
couldn't use Mackenzie's taxi or his barge service
because Mackenzie hated her, and what's more,
he didn't rent his boats to women without their
husbands' permission. Despite all this, she'd still
tried. He'd caught her, marching down the
Lakeshore Road as he was coming back early
from a trip to Huntsville, heading off to
Ashleigh's when he'd expressly forbid it.
Expressly. He didn't think she'd try it again,
though. There'd been a hell of a row. He'd had it,
he told the Dad, with her and her women's lib
and her big mouth. He wanted a normal life and

a normal wife. Jesus Murphy, what a woman. What a life.

Brother Webster thought the whole thing was ridiculous. "You two are behaving like a couple of Cro-Magnons," he said, sitting cross-legged on the soil while they sat in lawn chairs, and I hovered on the outskirts, adding and re-adding my calories in my Playtime Doodler.

"Whats?" said the Dad.

"Cavemen," said Big Dick. "Hey, Webby, some day, when you're married, you'll see that's the best way to treat 'em. The only way to deal with them. A good club to the head and drag 'em out of harm's way."

"Well, I don't know about that," mused the Dad. "That might be a little extreme."

"Bloody Neanderthals," said Webster. "Goddamned chauvinist pigs."

"That's us," said Dick, and he saluted the Dad with his beer. The Dad, haltingly, saluted him back.

Brother Webster gave up and asked what I was writing now. Could he see it? I shook my head and covered up the figures. I was trying to calculate if I had any calories left today, so that I could have a saltine and a glass of ice water. I wondered if there were any ice chips left. I'd been raiding the icebox, and when the chips were all gone, I would chisel new ones free.

Theresa said if I put food colouring on them, I could pretend they were ice cream.

Nobody noticed I wasn't eating, except for Theresa, who promised me everything: the moon, the stars, the sun, that I could come to the mainland and even, perhaps, to a dance (one of the informal ones, with the record player – not one with a live band, which was out of the question – next year, maybe, next year!) if I would just not eat. She employed police power, raiding my bed at night, lifting the mattress to check for a slice of processed cheese, or going through my box of comics to see if I'd hidden any Ritz crackers. I was no longer allowed my bedsheet curtain, for I might be eating back there, and if I said I wanted to go off for a time in the woods, she would pat me down like Julie on *Mod Squad*, frisking me, looking for contraband.

Everything I ate, I was to write down, and she reviewed it and added up the calories. I was allowed 600 calories a day at first, which she reduced to 500 when she didn't see immediate results. The loss of that 100 calories was noticeable to me: it meant I didn't get my slice of toast and half an apple at three in the afternoon. It meant that my stomach roared at times, and I more than once doubled over from pain, as stabs of hunger tried to force me to eat.

"It's okay," said Theresa. "That's normal."

Theresa monitored the food in the cupboard, even counting the saltines in their waxpaper columns, and measuring the Quaker Oats in the bag. She accompanied the Dad to the mainland, to make sure he bought only certain types of food. He complained, because he wanted Peek Freans cookies and he wanted a Sara Lee pound cake, and he wanted butter on his spuds.

"I put Dee on a diet," Theresa told the Dad.

"Oh. That explains *that*."

The Dad had no other interest in the subject, although he did, at one point in mid-August, frown at me as if he'd seen a ghost, and then mutter something about how I was *lookin' pretty good there*. Otherwise, he was too occupied trying to make my mother speak. I had never noticed that my mother really *did* speak, until she collapsed into this state of nonresponse. She continued to tend to us, though: listlessly, mechanically, at an unvarying pace.

"Okay, you made your point already, Jane!" the Dad said. "Look, what did you two girls expect? Can we have an end to the silent treatment now!"

Theresa thought it was funny. "They're like Betty and Wilma!" she said, and returned to monitoring me. Her only regret was that she did not have a scale, and had to judge my progress by measuring my stomach. My girth was greater than forty inches when we first taped me into Mum's numbered ribbon. She also measured herself. She was twenty and one-half inches around.

But there was camaraderie in this. There was touching. Every day, she spent time with me. If I hid, she searched me out, calling, "Dee, you better not be eating! Dee, I'm coming for you!" Even though she still left me every day to go to the shore with her friends, there was the promise that some day, I could go too.

She was inspiration. When her blood was up with the importance of the project – when we discovered my girth was down to thirty-seven inches – she leaped around on her tiptoes, crying, "We did it! Way to go!" but not mentioning my name. She was brown as butterscotch pudding, but smelled of lemon shampoo; active as a volcano, swinging her arms and knowing she had the space to swing them.

She claimed we were alike. She exposed her midriff to me and told me that she, too, had to watch her weight – that it was part of being a woman. I wasn't sure about the word. I was trying more to be a girl. Not a woman, and not a child, but a girl, who could date the boys, like in the *Archie*s. I knew I had to get thin, but I wasn't sure how that would make me a girl. And I did not really *want* to be a woman, who had periods and Pap tests and babies. That was not what I was doing this for.

"You be good while I'm gone," Theresa would say to me, when her friends came to pick her up for the Saturday dance. Everyone else waved and smiled artificially, saying *hi Dee, hi Mr. & Mrs. Graham.*

My mother would sit on the end of the dock, in a fold-down deck chair, staring at the distant shore. When the Dad asked for a beer, she went and got it. She brought it back, on a tray, opened and poured it into a glass.

"That's my girl," he said, in an unhappy, unnatural, almost-shout.

And Bald Face shouted, "Girl!"

The squirrels were back. They launched their revenge, insidious and unstoppable, performing their tiny outrages. We would go to the mainland, the Dad and Mum and I, for a day trip to Bracebridge, and come back to discover a trail of poo on the kitchen table; upended canisters; shredded hems on the bedspreads. We would catch sight of them in the rafters, right in the corner where the joists met the eaves, chirring and glaring at us. Only one squirrel at a time, for they were ferociously territorial.

Outdoors, they taunted the Dad by making their constant presence known. They would chase each other wildly through the clearing, screaming threats. The Dad would leap for his gun, but they were always too fast – by the time he returned with his gun (still struggling with the shells), they'd have disappeared into the arboreal canopy, shrilling machine-gun screams of rodent outrage from the inaccessible maelstrom of pine branches and oak boughs.

The Dad had promised Theresa (and me), after the first squirrel death, that he would never shoot another. He said he had hated to do it, and indeed his eyes watered and welled as he assured us that there would be no more death. But when he lifted a spoonful of oatmeal to his lips one morning, only to find both a fragment of acorn shell and a melting squirrel turd in among the porridge, he grew tightly aggressive, and we knew that sabotage was the only answer.

First we hid the gun. That got us both grounded (and for me, the added punishment of nothing to eat until I confessed). So we revealed that the gun was beneath the cabin, and the Dad retrieved it, grumbling about the dirt in the magazine and how Mackenzie would be furious. He was still anxious to stay in Mackenzie's good books, for he assured us that despite Mackenzie having refused to sell us Blueberry, he would eventually come around if the Dad played his cards right. The Dad's money was burning a hole in his pocket, and even though Brother Webster tried with disproportionate desperation to convince him that other property was available, the Dad assured him he only wanted Blueberry. He'd been there so long, and he had such plans for it. He loved its privacy, its little beach, its deep cold fishing trough right off the promontory. The peace of the island, the silence of it, the comfort of the cabin filled with the lantern-light, the late summer evenings when he had to build a fire to keep his family warm. It had been his summer home for seven years. How could he buy anything else?

That whole month, to me, was as ragged and blowing as the trees, and as infested with mania and uncontrollable notions as the trees were with squirrels. Theresa assured me I was losing weight. I asked if I could have more food. No, I could not. She restricted my swimming, too, for she said that exercise would make me hungry and muscle-bound. Muscle weighed more than fat, so it had to be avoided at all costs. I should sit still and not eat. I could read, if I wanted, but none of that browner stuff and no DC comics, which were (a) lame and (b) for boys. I did what I was told. After all, it was something to do.

I also begged her to prepare me for the day I could come to the mainland, not just in the same boat with her, but to stay with her and see her friends. She reiterated that there was no way I was ready for such a thing – probably not this year, even. Nevertheless, she started to teach me to dance, in preparation for the future day. I thought I was doing well, for I had been listening to music for years, and could sing along and clap a beat as well as anyone. But when I stood up and began to do the Monkey (a dance Richard and I had prac-tised, along with the Twist), Theresa shrieked in dismay.

"Oh, God, you look completely spastic!" She twisted her spine and bent from the waist, gri-macing like Quasimodo, and then flailed her arms around. "This is you," she explained.

Learning to dance was harder than not eating, for I found that I could get used to being painfully hungry, and that if I ate nothing at all it was some-thing I could handle. I was used to pain. It was craving – need – that I couldn't stand, and some-times eating that half-a-cup of Special K with four ounces of milk merely served to trigger a ferocious, screaming, demon of craving. So there were days I ate nothing at all. Theresa was frankly stunned with admiration at this ability.

"Wow," she said. "I wish I could do that."

In the third week of August, I went three days without eating. Dizzy, with stomach sizzling from acid, I dived in off the end of the dock and submerged to the bottom, confused by the environment, forgetting that I was in water. I saw a beautiful woman swim up to me, a pale green woman, covered with lake mosses. Then I realized she was one of the lake bottom's resident logs. This struck me as funny, and before I could stop myself, I laughed.

The water, in my nose and throat and lungs, exploded into pain. I kicked hard, trying to surface, but there were flashing lights in my vision, and I had no sense of *up*. I swam right into the rocks of the drop-off, not ascending but moving laterally. Nevertheless, I could locate myself by the rock wall's presence, and I pulled my body up along it, clearing the surface at last.

I hung onto the dock, warm water pouring from my nose and lips. There was no one close enough to help me out of the lake, and I had no air to yell with. So I hung onto the wood, barking the breath back into me, and finally I found myself breathing again. My chest, throat, and sinuses all stung as if whipped. Serves you right if you'd died, dummy, I thought. Don'tcha remember your Red Cross rules – never swim without a buddy?

At last I felt the dock vibrate, and heard the Dad's self-involved, tuneless whistle. Then, the trilling paused.

"Whatcha doin', Darlin'?" he said. "Having fun?"

"Uh-huh."

"Diving for treasure?"

Asshole. As if I'd be diving for treasure. "Yeah," I said.

"You wanna come help me make a shopping list? I'm going into town."

"Bracebridge? When? What for?"

"Tomorrow. I want to start picking stuff up for the corn roast." He had started calling the Labour Day Barbecue the Corn Roast, having fixed on the idea that he would boil up several dozen cobs of corn, and that would be enough to coax Theresa – and David, if he showed up – to stay for the Labour Day party, instead of heading off to the mainland for the Ashleigh's dance, or to do whatever they truly wanted to do.

I put one foot up onto the dock and rolled my body out of the water. I had never been able to just pop up onto the dock, like Theresa or David or Richard, using my arms as levers. I had always either had to drag and roll myself, or swim over to the rocks and climb out there. It bothered me that I was thinner – definitely thinner – and yet I still couldn't drag myself out of the lake. It didn't seem fair that I was still weak.

"Dee, you gonna come to Bracebridge?"

I lay on my back, staring at the rich, blank, blue sky and thinking. Calculating. Only two more weeks left in summer. Everything, absolutely everything, had turned out differently from what I'd expected. I hadn't looked at the Plan since early July. I was not going to run away and live in the woods. I was going to go to high school with my sister. No wave of a magic wand could have made things turn out more strangely.

"Yeah, sure I'll come," I said.

In the distance, on the open-water side of the island, I heard a small motorboat approaching. The Dad heard it too, and immediately trotted off down the path to the beach, where he could see the open lake and wave at whoever it was. My head was pounding, with a noise like the waves against the rocks on a very rough day.

The Dad's heavy feet struck the dock, and he stepped over me to reach the end of the dock. Brother Webster called from his boat as it rounded the point and entered the channel. "Ahoy, Daddy-O!"

"Ahoy, Brother Webster!" The Dad nudged me with his toe. "Dee, you're in the way. Mr. Webster's trying to dock."

I groaned outlandishly and rolled over three or four times, until I was clear of the dock's end, and lay on the cozy wood while the Dad and Brother Webster moored the little punt. I listened for David's voice, but as with every other visit Brother Webster had made since that day I discovered David in his bedroom, there had been no David. I longed to tell the Dad – *David's got diabetes and he's living over at Brother Webster's* – and rid myself of the irritation and responsibility of carrying around someone else's secret.

"Hello, there, Dee," said Brother Webster. He stood over me, casting his dark shadow, and I opened my eyes and looked up at him, shielding my eyes.

"Hiya," I said.

"Writing any good stories?"

"That's baby stuff."

"So it is." He crouched down beside me, as the Dad carried his case of beer into the woods and up the path to the cabin. "How are you?"

"I'm fine. Why shouldn't I be?"

His silhouette shrugged. I couldn't see his face, but I could smell his Hai Karate aftershave. "Just everything."

"I'm fine," I said, ignoring the flashing lights that had started up again in my vision. "Where is David? Is he at your cottage?"

"He went back to the city, but he's coming back by the long weekend. He has some appointments."

"Gigs," I said knowingly.

"Yes. Gigs. And appointments." He coughed a little nervously. "You haven't said anything to the Dad about seeing David, have you?"

"No."

"Thank you. Dee, you know how sometimes,

in life, there are misunderstandings?"

"Yeah," I said, not knowing at all.

"Well, I'm afraid there's been a misunder-
standing, and your Dad – well, your Dad is going
to be very hurt, but I did what I thought was best
at the time. For David."

"I think the Dad should know about David's
diabetes."

He frowned. "You definitely haven't said anything, have you?"

"No. You told me not to."

"Good girl, Dee. Thank you. But actually, it's
more complicated than that." His voice drifted
off, but then he cleared his throat and regained his
straightforward way of speaking. "I suppose I
acted inappropriately, but I had no idea the Dad
was so determined."

I shrugged, for I did not know what he was
talking about, and for once didn't have the curiosity to poke further. I had decided, after the log-
lady incident, that maybe I ought to eat. I would
have lunch in half an hour. I'd get an apple, a pick-
le, and three Premium crackers.

"But David will be better soon, and..." said
Brother Webster.

That I listened to. I sat up, angry at his igno-
rance. "Mr. Webster, you don't get better from diabetes. It's forever. Geez. How could you not know
that, especially with Richard and all?"

I got up, and as I did, I saw another expression
pass over Brother Webster's face – one of shock,

even dismay. "Good lord, Dee, how much have you lost?"

How much? I couldn't answer that question. How much had I lost? It was too big to measure. I had lost everything. I was left scrabbling for calories and colour schemes. I had to go back to the city in two weeks. I had to go back to school. I had abandoned hope and was about to enter, but when I did, I would be the right size to fit through the gates.

"I bet fifty pounds. Have you been on a scale?" Brother Webster stood up and put his arms around me, hugging me tightly to him. He was still smaller than I was, although about the same height. "Dee, I'm so proud of you. This is going to make all the difference in the world to you. Every girl likes pretty things. Every girl likes to be pretty."

"And I wasn't pretty." I could draw the truth from him quite easily, I knew.

"Not in an ordinary sort of way. You had panache, though, my dear! Flair! You had tremendous individualism! Guts! Strength! You always were something, Dee Graham, so you didn't need to be pretty!"

"I see." And I did see – I had already seen, and Brother Webster confirmed it. Now that I wasn't *something*, I better be pretty.

"Are you going to the Ashleigh's dance?" said Brother Webster, threading my arm through the crook of his. "I hope so. If David gets back in time, he's going to play during the band breaks. I thought

I'd do a little something, too. Why don't you come, Dee? We can have a nice dance together."

The realization that I had just been asked to dance – albeit by an old man and a teacher to boot – flew away as it faced something very distressing. The Dad, and his corn roast, which he'd been making lists over, and stacking firewood, and picking up the branches and windblown flotsam from the firepit clearing – the Dad was expecting Brother Webster, and me, and even Theresa and David. He had plans for fireworks and for renting Mackenzie's generator for a hi-fi and the patio lanterns. There'd be polkas and singalongs and ice-cold beer straight from the bottle. Porterhouse steaks with A-1 sauce, and baked potatoes in their jackets. The last weekend of summer required such a salute.

And Brother Webster was not coming. He was going to the Ashleigh's dance. He had *never* not come to the island on Labour Day.

I couldn't see myself at the Dad's party, one of only five people there – four if Big Dick didn't allow Alice to come – all of us sitting on lawn chairs or the benches the Dad had built, staring into the bonfire and saying, "Great corn. Really sweet and tasty." It was too awful to think about. I did not want to polka around the firepit, or watch the Dad glance repeatedly and compulsively at his watch, as if more company would come anytime now, while the hi-fi played taps for the summer of 1970.

I scented in the wind the onset of another explosive change – a reward for my stalwart, blinkered procession through these late-summer days. I could hear fireworks going off, bangbang-bang, as I kissed Richard full on the lips. We'd be seated together, wearing our frayed denims, and he would take off his glasses. His eyes would see me. I would see him, approaching, closer and closer, with those parted lips. He would slide his arms around my neck and back, and he'd be more than just soft and hard and warm and cool. He'd be there. He'd be beside me, inside me. The gunfire sounds, the sky rings with colour and sprinkles of sparks, and he puts himself into me, where he always belonged.

Yes, I'm going to the dance at Ashleigh's, Brother Webster.

With those words, I ruined everything.

The chickadees had started their fall cry. Theresa had a new magazine, the October issue of *Seventeen*, available in August so that we might all be prepared. The colours for the fall were chocolate brown, deep golden yellow, and a smashing tone of orange. The look for the face was a red-russet shade above the eyes, with emphasis on those stunning high cheekbones (dust yourself with a beautiful tone of ochre, just in the hollow of your cheeks – think svelte, svelte, svelte!). And the time has never been better to be a brunette. You dark beauties can come out into the autumn sun and celebrate the change of season, taking the frosty limelight from those beach-blanket blondes! Celebrate, for the world is coming out in colour, colour, colour!

In less than four days, I would be walking up to Bloor Street, past my old schools. With whom would I walk? Theresa? When the door knocker sounded Tuesday morning at the house on Lindsey, and a duet or trio of teenage girls stood waiting, chewing their 8:30 a.m. wad of Wrigley's, would I be allowed to come too? Theresa might cast a quick glance my way and with a tiny, nearly imperceptible, jerk of the head, summon me to attend. And the other girls might shrug and accept me, the way Cathy accepted her sisters, and I would be allowed to pass through the portals of high school in the company of Theresa Graham.

For now, however, the only thing going was the Ashleigh's dance. I had to tell Theresa I wanted to go; I needed her endorsement. Without her willing acceptance of my presence, the dance would be just another trial. But I could not find the way to say it; I couldn't risk her saying *no way. You're not ready.*

Theresa went through her chest of drawers, and lay out one trousseau after another, in preparation for Saturday. The pale lemon blouse would not do. Sailor shirts were out as well. She could not wear the halter, either, for she might bounce out of it. It's sleazy, she said. She loved her pale-blue, wide-wale, corduroy hiphuggers, but she had worn them to two dances already. She wanted a peasant blouse, a new peasant blouse, with an empire waist and a Ukrainian pattern along the collar. She wanted a new set of Lee Riders.

"We'll have to go to town," she said, and I wriggled inside at the word *we.*

But then she said, "Guy can drive me. He has a really sharp car. It's a '67 Mustang. It was his mother's but now she has a... Dee, are you listening to me?"

"Yes." I realized that the "we" had not meant she and I. "A Mustang. It's really sharp, eh?"

She looked at me, and blew an exasperated sigh. "You look like a bag of potatoes."

"I'm sorry. I'm trying."

"It's those clothes. Gawd. Look at you. Do you have anything at home in the city – anything at all – to wear to school on Tuesday?"

I thought of my wardrobe of polyester suits of armour, all several sizes too big, but still probably close to the right size. I now had a 35-inch waist, and a 44-inch bust, and 42-inch hips. I knew exactly what that made me. A women's size 20. Even a 22. And then there were my shoes, the orthopedic duty shoes in the size 11 triple-E, designed for nurses whose feet had been pressed into pancakes by years of serving others. Mum had dyed them pink or black or brown, but they were still clodhoppers and I was still going to have to wear them to high school on Tuesday.

"I guess I'd never really thought too hard about it – about what it would be really, truly like to have you in my school. I suppose I thought that you'd straighten out naturally or something. But you just got worse and worse. And you know what's really weird?"

"What?"

"I had this feeling you'd go away somehow. Like, poof, you'd just disappear. Maybe I've got extrasensory perception. I just never really figured you'd end up in my high school."

So that's what it would be. I would walk up the road, past the Brockton stadium where the football players slammed into one another, and the track stars stole batons from teammates' hands, to the collegiate itself. The front doors were written above with ABANDON HOPE; the windows were frosted black; there was a groaning from the basement and a cackling from the wash-rooms. The boys were narrow as snakes, the girls as scrawny as rats, and their bright colours were warnings of poison flesh and viperish fangs. Pretty, pretty people, sailing like catamarans down the crimson-tiled hallways, seething with sneers. When they saw me come in, the explosion of laughter and horror and anger and insult would rock me back on the heels of my duty shoes.

"Oh shit, Dee, you're at it again. Fucking cry-ing."

"I'm not," I said. "I'm just sitting here."

"Tuesday, you stay away from me," Theresa said. "I don't know you."

She put all her clothes away, neatly, and left me completely alone.

Nine

Suffering brings change. If we did not suffer, we would not adapt, or make amends. We want to change, so we seek out suffering. We look for the heavy weight to drop on our toes, the hot stove to lay our bare palm across (feel the sizzle of our white skin as it heats and melts into grease). If we are in enough pain, if we cause enough grief, do enough things wrong, then we might stop, we might change. We'll have to, or we won't survive.

Did we ruin this earth to return to our roots, in that same warm earth, the mother-stuff beneath our tired, worldly feet? Did we roll big cigars and smoke them, so that we could be eaten alive by cancers that took hold in the fleshy inner bulge of our lips? "She doesn't look herself at all, now that her tongue and jaw are gone." On the corner of this street there was once a house with a window box of pansies, and the lamplighter used to pause here and take a pinch of snuff; his sneeze was the sign to me that I was about to fall asleep. That house, those pansies, that man and me: we all passed away, we didn't matter. But we did change.

Nothing is lost on this earth; it only changes. All the water on this earth is all the water there ever was here. The tears that tumble down your wife's cheek as you admit to infidelity are of the same stuff that Louis XIV pissed onto the draperies. They are the same drink that lubricated the tract of an Australopithecus. Tomorrow they will fall as part of the first precipitation to grace the Transvaal since September 14th. Next year, hockey players will skate on them at Boston Gardens.

Your body sprouts hair, loses hair. Your dog dies and you feed its corpse to your hungry garden. The handmade marker – Best Dog in the World, Goodbye! – fades under the tears of King Louis. In a hundred years your house is gone, and so is the man who reads the gas meter, who was the faithless husband, who was you.

Sometimes, I lose time: I lose the ground and go astral, way up high, wouldn't it be nice, the swing, the swing, up in the sky! When I'm up I'm woman, I'm fast, and I fit, and I can fight back and front. Everyone listens to me. And then down it goes, drawn by the pull of the timebound planet, that swing goes back with me in it, and I recede into the arc of air, back in time, back in my time: my arms grow long, I sprout a snout and lose my articulate tongue and Aeolian larynx. I snort around, one of Circe's pigs, driven into the ocean of my own suffering, and I surface only when the swing drags me clear. Then back again to a summit, a high point. I can see the other floundering changelings.

We're the same water we always were...

Author's Introduction
from The Kitchen Counter *by J.E. Graham*

– Why are you crying, Miss?
– I'm Gertie Shultz! The girls in my Grad Class hate me...they say I dress badly and I have no style! They voted me "Class Wipeout"...because I have no money, and I'm not an A student, like them! But I never wanted a career! I don't care about women's liberation! I just want to marry someone nice, and have children, and live in a nice house...but I have no hope of that ever happening! Because nobody asked me to the Senior Prom! And even if I could go, what would I wear? I haven't got any nice clothes...

Cosmo Man Comics #22
July 1968

Dee, why are you crying?

Because the chickadees were crying, because summer was over, because school starts Tuesday, because I hadn't done what I planned with this summer, because my only friend hates me, because soon the world will be a city covered with grey hideous snow instead of a glorious ancient rock bathed in warm earth and surrounded by cool water, because I have the face (I am told) of the southward end of a northbound mule, because I cannot sing in tune, or dance to a beat, or write a good story, or save a squirrel, or love my mother and father. Because I haven't seen my Auntie

Alice in weeks. Because I have to swim without a buddy. Because I'm lonely. Because sometimes I'm so hungry I think I'm going to die. Sometimes I'm so hungry. I think. I'm going to die.

David, beside me on the beach, up high where the sand was dry, put his long arms around me and his forehead against mine and held me, because so many things were pouring out of me, hideous things with wings and tails and cloven feet. They were truths. They crawled down my legs and scuttled off into the earth like centipedes. David said nothing, not to a single one of them. He just let them run out and away, resting his bearded chin on my shoulder. I cried until I had to lie down, because there was so much water in my eyes and nose, that I seemed to be drowning, like the day the lady at the lake bottom pointed me upward, and I nearly went the wrong way.

"Poor Dee," he said, at last, "you poor, wonderful kid. Do you know how wonderful you are?"

I shook my head. "How wonderful?" I asked, sitting back up, my forehead on my arms, my arms on my knees, my knees against my chest, my ass on the ground, shinbone connected to the anklebone, God I wanted a Pepsi, an ice cream. I wanted to suck in my svelte cheeks and paint myself peasant brown.

"Look how good you look," he said, not moving his face. His lips moved in my ear, as he whispered to me, an endearment. "You've lost a ton. That's so wonderful, Dee."

I nodded, thanking him. He, too, looked wonderful: very thin, and untanned, with a yellow tint to the whites of his eyes, but he was clean-smelling again and his breath smelled only of Pepsodent. Only because of my promise to Brother Webster – not to let David know what I'd seen, to confront him about his sickness, to make him tell Mum and the Dad – did I not say more than, "You look great, too."

I inhaled through my mouth and dragged tears and wet down into my throat. And David patted me and stroked me until all the crying was gone, which by then was evening, and Theresa was coming home for dinner. Her chariot had arrived.

I don't know why I said it; why I was so clever. But I had been with Theresa for a month, and perhaps I had learned more from her than the counting of calories. Quickly, I said it, so that it would be fresh on the heels of my pain, and David would be roused to protect me. To defend me. To help wonderful-lost-a-ton-me with her passage through the portal.

"David, Theresa won't let me go to the dance at Ashleigh's on Saturday."

David, never one to move quickly, nodded his head. "I see," he said. But he watched Theresa waltzing up the path from the dock, swinging her string-and-bead beachbag and wiggling her pert little tail. She spotted us hugging on the beach, across the little bay that the beach curled partway around, and put her hands on her hips, pouty with disgust.

"You guys look like perverts!" she said. "God, what if my friends had seen! God!"

"Ignore her," David said. "That's the best thing to do with bullies." Then he got up, brushed the sand from his jeans, and ruffled my hair. "I'm gonna go have a beer with the Dad," he said. Nonchalant as a terrorist, he ambled, half-naked, off into the forest, and up to the cabin, to slaughter the dragons in my – his little sister's! – way.

Evening, on the island, on Barebones Lake: the birds asleep, except for the loons, who were less bird than spirit. A calm night coming. There would be sounds from the entire waterfront, from the lake's complete circumference. Owls, and the cry of a nighthawk. Catcalls and war shouts from cottagers; splashes as they hit the dark night water, skinny dipping with impunity. Boat engines sputtering to life, then revving to a whining pitch, approaching, departing. The mutter of ripples against the rocky shoreline, broken into the rhythm of boat wake, measured wave action smacking into land. The creak of the dock wood. The crickets' chirps which, if counted properly and prodded with a formula, would reveal the temperature of the air. Seventy-two degrees. Room temperature.

I had skipped dinner, and lunch, and had only had applesauce for breakfast. Too late I saw that the sauce contained sugar, and I stopped eating it at once, panicked as badly as if I'd been poisoned.

I remembered something Richard had once told me – about the Roman vomitoria, and how at orgies the guests would force themselves to puke so they could go back and eat more. I wanted to puke up the applesauce. But I had no idea how to do such a thing. So I suffered the containment and digestion of the sugared invasion.

Morning was so long ago. Now night settled in, blue-black and fretted with golden fire, as Brother Webster observed, to me and Richard, every time he sat with us and sought the constellations. "This brave, o'erhanging firmament," he would say. "This majestical roof."

Why it appears no other thing to me but a foul and pestilent congregation of vapours...

I knew many things by heart. Losing so much had not caused me to lose the little marks of code, of data, which I had absorbed into me during my life alone with Richard. I did not understand what I'd read, but I remembered it.

Lend me your ears. It meant listen, Auntie Alice explained, not a Laugh-In or Wayne & Shuster moment, where a crowd of toga'd extras would hurl foam-rubber ears at the actor playing Brutus. And the speech about the firmament was about suicidal sadness.

"How do you know this stuff, Auntie Alice?" I asked.

She shrugged. "They teach you. High school. You'll see."

High school. Listen. You'll see. The night

crooned to me, as I sat still on the beach, cold despite the warm temperature. My feet were in the lake water, my bottom on the damp sand. Thursday night. Far across the bay, I heard music start up at Ashleigh's. Someone was playing the jukebox. The Beatles, singing about secrets, and promising not to tell. Often the waves and wind would not allow the Ashleigh's jukebox sound to travel this far across the lake. But tonight I could even hear voices on the Mackenzie dock. Put her over there, buddyboy. And a single call, for *Maureen!*

But I had not heard a word from up at the cabin.

I shivered. My feet, dipped in the water, shuddered and shifted in its refraction. I pulled them clear and then stood up, using my hands for help. There, standing in the dark, I looked down at my white feet, and I saw them: my toes, peeping out like the little mice-feet that had snuck out from beneath Theresa's prom-gown hem. Newly discovered stars. I pressed my stomach flat and pulled the elastic waist of my cotton trousers away from me. I could see my pubic hair. I could see that my skin was striped with angry red lines, like bait worms. Stretch marks. My own body had torn my skin, like a cocoon. How much bigger could I have gotten, before it ripped open completely?

I pulled my trousers up beneath my breasts. Yes, breasts too. Clinging to my clothes, carrying my skin, I saw how much I'd lost.

I began my way back to the cabin. David's campaign, perhaps, was at an end, and I would learn the results. I was strangely unexcited by the prospect of his having won: what would I do at a dance, only two days away? I didn't really know how to dance, despite Theresa's lessons, and there was of course the biggest rule: I was not allowed to dance unless a boy asked me, something I was assured would not happen. So why not stay with the Dad, on the island, and eat two dozen cobs of corn with butter, and set fire to the schoolhouse, and line my Barbies up on the rocks so that they too could come to the party? Why not listen to David sing "Puff" and "Leaving on a Jet Plane"?

My bags are packed. I'm ready to go.

The cabin regarded me with its yellow eyes and its yellow door, its whitewashed walls gleaming against the dark pines and the fettered sky beyond. Up on the hill, the island's occiput, it had sat for my whole life, for all my memory. Suddenly, seeing it glare at me, I knew that this weekend would be my last here, with it, after all – I would not be back again.

I had to stop to absorb this shock, for unlike my sense of knowing when I played with the Plan and with running away, this was a premonition as firm as faith itself. After this weekend, I would never stand on this island again.

"Shhh," I heard David say. "She's right outside."

How long had I been standing there, looking at my happy little cottage in the woods, which had suddenly seemed like the witch's in a fairy tale, the home of cannibalism and cages? How could I have made such a mistake, and seen something sinister in the glow of the lanterns that poured through the windows and the glass of the door? Now my cabin shook itself free of threat and offered only welcome. I could see the Dad through one window, and Jane through the other, and the Dad had his pipe to his lips, and Mum her fingers to hers. David and Theresa were at the table, and as soon as I reached the front stoop, I saw that David looked exhausted, surprisingly like the Dad. As if he'd been working overtime for days and days and days, and there was nothing left ahead but overtime either.

When I came in, they all looked up, excessively cheery. "Hi, Dee!"

"Hello." The topic of me floated in the room like the Dad's pipe smoke.

"Precious, sit down a little moment," said the Dad.

"What's going on?" I wasn't sitting until I knew I could get up again easily. Someone might come and put their hands on my shoulders and press me into a chair.

"Nothing's going on," said David brightly. "We wanted to ask you about this Saturday night."

Theresa exhaled, a breath full of hoptoads and

lizards, and pushed herself away from the table. Her chair's feet screamed on the linoleum tiles.

"What about it?" I asked, trying to catch Theresa's eye. But she would not look at me.

The Dad sat down and patted his knee, as if to invite me to sit, which I of course did not. He sucked on his pipe, and then spoke in his every-one-will-do-what-they're-told voice. It was the herald of an impenetrable decision.

"Saturday night is very important to me. I have been planning all month for this. As has your mother." He looked at my mother, who had seat-ed herself on the edge of the bed, in her Royal Family pose, and fixed her gaze on a framed print of the trout fisherman that had hung forever and ever from a joist behind the daybed.

"In any event," he continued, "This is a fam-ily party and an annual tradition. This year, I have made special arrangements, at no small bother. I will be cooking corn, and have arranged for a prop-er hi-fi, and for Mr. Mackenzie and Miss Mackenzie to come as guests. Mr. Mackenzie will be bringing a generator so we can have the proper hi-fi. And Mr. Webster and Uncle Dick and Auntie Alice and Richard are all coming."

"Auntie Alice...?"

"Sure, yeah, of course, Auntie Alice. I want to show Mr. Mackenzie an especially good time. Do you understand me? I want him to see how beloved this place is to me. When he sees what it means to us all, he will surely name his price."

David appeared to wince, and said quietly, "Oh, Dad." I opened my mouth to say something, but the Dad put his hand up to both of us, in a policeman's stop-right-there gesture.

"Excuse me, young lady, I'm speaking," he said. "Now, I understand from David and Theresa that there is also a special event at Ashleigh's Marina that night."

"That's right!" Theresa began. "And..."

"Shh, Theresa," said David quietly.

"Thank you." The Dad sucked on his pipe, exhaled a blue blast, and continued. "I understand that Dee is invited to this event, as well."

I gasped in spite of myself, but my gasp was absorbed in Theresa's moan. Both the Dad and David shot her a strangely identical glare of disapproval, and she put her head down on the kitchen table and began to cry.

"Mum, Mum, it's not fair! It's my party! They're my friends! Why does she have to come!"

Our mother re-crossed her ankles, so that the left ankle now pressed against the right, and said nothing. The Dad shook his pipe hand at Theresa, as if it were his fist.

"One more word out of you, young lady, and you won't be going to Ashleigh's at all. This is the deal."

I knew from David's tenseness, from his fingers drumming on the table, that this deal had been negotiated with some effort on his part, and that it was a strained peace. As Theresa pounded the tabletop with her fist, crying *boohoo, boohoo,* the Dad explained what we were to do.

"If Dee doesn't go to the dance, Theresa doesn't go. Because Dee is only thirteen, Theresa is in charge of chaperoning her. If Theresa doesn't like this, then Theresa can stay here for the evening. Furthermore, I understand that David is playing his guitar at this gag."

"Gig," said David quietly.

"Thank you. Gig. I don't want to be a big square. I know young people need to let it all hang down. But you have to understand the importance of having a family. Of little family traditions and moments. You have to understand that my party, my last weekend of the summer, is important to me. I like to look at my children's faces as they eat the food my wife has cooked. I like to hear their happy, singing voices. It will not be too long before that'll all be gone. You'll all be gone." He took a long and thoughtful drawl of his pipe. "So, go and have your fun, but you be back by 10 p.m."

"Dad, we said eleven," said David, in that same even, unemotional voice, before Theresa could raise a scream of protest. "The deal was eleven."

"Did I say eleven?"

"You did, you did!" cried Theresa, lifting her careworn face from the table.

"All right. Eleven. I can keep some corn waiting for you."

"Dee can't have any corn!" said Theresa.

"This is a special occasion," said the Dad. "She can have anything she wants on a special occasion. Her first dance. It makes up for missing her graduation. This can be your graduation, Dee. Are you happy?"

The directness of the question, shot at me like a bullet from the blue, left me speechless. Was I happy? About this, or about everything? I answered with a shrug, and sat down at last, feeling now that no one was going to push me into submission. The cabin was so smoky, from the Dad's pipe, that a haze swirled around each of our heads, the one around Theresa disturbed by her movements.

"That's gratitude for you," said the Dad. "I'll have you know that I was against your going. I don't think you're mature enough for a rock 'n' roll dance. If you don't want to go, just say the word. Because I would much prefer you stay here at the corn roast. Your friend Richard is coming."

"He is not," I said. "He'll be at Ashleigh's with everybody else."

"He is coming *here*. Uncle Dick put his foot down about all the carousing. Uncle Dick has had it with all the nonsense he's had to put up with since he moved. Uncle Dick..."

"Oh, do be quiet about Dick," said my mother, without uncrossing or moving.

"The mummy speaks!" cried David, in a Peter Lorre voice.

"David, that's not funny," admonished the

Dad, because Theresa and I laughed right on cue, a couple of trained seals. Theresa stood up and said, "This is Mum! Look, everybody," and began to priss around the cabin, checking surfaces for dust, miming Mum's actions perfectly. My mother never looked away from her focus-point on the wall, and the Dad and David twitched with discomfort, but Theresa's mimicry was uncanny. She put on Mum's apron, tightened her lips into a rosebud, and robot-walked to the fridge to get the Dad a beer.

"Here you are, Master," she said, then slipped into an I-Dream-of-Jeannie dance, humming the theme with a *da-dah, dadadada-dah, da-dah, dadadada-dah*, as she raised her hands above her head, Hindu-goddess style, and waggled her bum in their low-slung shorts. Around the table she went, belly-dancing and shimmying, stopping in front of Mum's line of vision, where she performed an upper-body shoulder shimmy that sent her little boobies quivering in their T-shirt.

"Back in your bottle, Jeannie!" called David, clapping his hands.

The Dad, smiling self-consciously, put his fingers to his head and tried not to look. "Yes, that's enough tormenting your mother, Theresa. Come and sit down."

Theresa hesitated in front of Mum, waiting for a reaction, but my mother might have been a stone image outside an Egyptian temple. An exaggerated, exasperated whuff escaped Theresa, and she flopped down onto the daybed, directly across from Mum. Who still didn't move.

"Uh-oh, somebody broke Mum," I said.

"Okay, okay, that's enough, we said." David pointed a finger at me. "Things can go too far, you know. I think we really pissed her off. Mum, we're sorry. We were kidding."

Our mother still didn't move.

"I think we've passed beyond the silent treatment," said the Dad to the comatose one. "Okay, fine. Jane, go ahead and behave like a child. You want me to tell Dick not to bring Alice on Saturday night? It can be arranged, you know."

"What's this about Alice?" said David.

The Dad explained. Auntie Alice and Jane had been acting out of line all summer. Jane not particularly, although she'd kind of let a few things go around the cottage, and she never did get a vegetable garden planted, although of course that veggie patch never accounted for much, but the Dad missed having it. There hadn't been a single pie all summer, and the meals – cripes! Inedible. Lots of women sitting around talking, but not a hell of a lot of help around the place, that's what was going on. Lots of little critical remarks, too, from Alice – Alice had started some sort of Women's Lib group and now the mouth on her! You wouldn't believe it – all sorts of gibes about chauvinist this and sexist that. Dick's always given her every last thing she needed, anything she asked for. Did anything she wanted, and she's going on about getting a job. Going to night school, too, so that when Dick comes home, there's nobody there.

"What the hell has this got to do with Mum?" said David.

"Well, they stole the boat, see. Dick's big bowrider. That's his baby. They joyrode it over to Webby's, in among those rocks! They could have torn that big boat to pieces!"

"They made it over just fine," said David.

"How the hell would you know? You were off gallivanting, Mr. Happy Wanderer, bloody irresponsible nomad, you make me crazy!"

"So they dared drive the boat, and so? They get to stand in the corner?"

"They were seriously out of line, David. Dangerously. That is not Alice's property. It's a question of property."

"'All my worldly goods with thee I share...'"

"It was a sneaky, dirty trick, David. And then the lipping off Alice gave Dick over it. I'm surprised he didn't haul off and let her have it, right there, right in front of everybody."

"Pow, right to the moon," said David acidly.

"Don't get me wrong. I don't agree with hitting women," said the Dad. "Even women like Alice."

Silence crept through the room, ghostly in the pipesmoke, and when Mum rose from the bed I nearly jumped out of my skin. She moved over to the door and stood, looking out into the black, her reflection sliced into rectangles by the glass. Then she turned to me.

"Do you want an outfit?" she asked.

"An outfit?"

"For this dance. Do you want some sort of outfit?"

Theresa thrust her hand into the air, as if volunteering to clean erasers or deliver a note to the office. "Mum! Mum! I'll go with her! Bracebridge, right!"

"Huntsville would be better for a dress," said the Dad.

"A dress!" Theresa and I squawked.

"Apparently not a dress, Dad," said David. "I think she'll need jeans."

"And a haircut," said Theresa.

"A nice blouse," said Mum, without heart. "Decent shoes."

"Shoes might be a problem," I said, holding out my spatulate feet.

"We'll find sandals," said David.

"We'll do fine," said the Dad. "Don't you worry, Princess." He sighed and leaned back, taking a final drag on his pipe, and exhaling one last puff of dragon's breath. "Ah, my two girls, all grown up, and going off together, friends at last. I knew that once you were both teenagers, you'd be inseparable. Look at you. Look at you both. My wonderful family. My wonderful, beautiful kids, and my beautiful, beautiful woman."

"'My wife,'" said David, in the commercial's monotone. "'I think I'll keep her.'"

My mother's reflection closed its eyes. It reached up and touched her fingers. The women's hands met at the fingertips, and although they did not see each other, they knew the other was there.

The day of the trip to Huntsville to buy me my outfit might have been the happiest of my life. The morning broke, Friday, sunny and warm as the weathermen say, but on the island it was fresh as new life, as crisp carrots, of the first notes of a much-loved guitar song. David was to come with us. He had someone to see in Huntsville, about playing in one of the several taverns there.

Mum and the Dad made a list of things to buy for the party the next day. Mum wrote while the Dad talked. Steaks, from the butcher's, not from the supermarket, and fresh corn from one of the roadside stands, and two cases of beer (one 50, one Red Cap). Also, a bottle of Scotch, another of gin, three of tonic water, two of soda water, three big bags of Humpty Dumpty, as well as pretzels, sour cream, and Lipton's Onion Soup Mix so Mum could make a dip.

The Dad folded the list and slipped it into his shirt pocket. "I can't believe summer's over," he said.

"Not a moment too soon," said Mum, but he didn't seem to hear her.

"C'mon, let's go!" he hollered at me and Theresa, although we were only a few feet away, discussing rules for the trip. "Girls! Move!"

"It's like the army," sniffed Theresa, "living with these people."

Mum had dressed in town wear, her face put on

in front of the washstand mirror. She had tried to curl her hair, by weaving a few sponge rollers in its dampened ends, but it hadn't worked. The moist strands drooped, like the ears of a disappointed dog, and by the time we reached the mainland her face was draped in wind-whipped, beaten strings.

Theresa had been thoroughly over the protocol for the trip. We would find a store that sold jeans. Lees and Levi's. They were the only acceptable brands, and they might have my size. They had to be hiphuggers and they had to be blue denim. For a shirt, it was hard to say what to buy. A peasant blouse, with an elastic/scooped neck, might do. A belt, too, perhaps in woven suede. We only had $50, though, and a suede belt would be hard to find. Expensive, too.

If we saw anyone Theresa knew, I was not to speak to them, unless they spoke to me, and in that case I was not to say anything stupid. "Like what?" I asked, and Theresa said, "Like that." If we met Guy, which wasn't likely but was possible (since his parents often came up early on Fridays and always did their shopping in Huntsville), then I was to walk quickly away and not say a word. In all cases, I was to be prepared to both disappear at once, and to act completely normal.

Members of the Porch Gang sat, half-a-dozen of them, not on the porch but on the edge of the government dock. The boys were smoking. The girls were leaning back, on their hands, dangling their bare feet above the water, displaying their breasts in their bikini tops. This sextet, who had been at the lake all summer under their mothers' care, were known to me by sight, although not by name. Theresa saw that they had seen her, and she elbowed me sharply as we proceeded from the boat towards shore. David and the Dad lingered behind, having somehow en route started a Byzantine argument over David's whereabouts for the last month, which now had expanded to incorporate the Vietnam War, Henry Kissinger, the Beatles, Cesar Chavez, and every offence on the part of each of them, dating from the moment of David's birth. My mother, however, was forging on ahead, marching down the dock, her arms and straggly hair swinging. She passed the six kids without answering them when they said, "Hiya, Mrs. Graham," and when she reached land she did a military turn to the right, and headed off along the road towards the laneway to the parking lot.

I fell in beside Theresa, leaving the Dad and David to their dispute, which had now gravitated to knot-tying methodology. Theresa pushed me away.

"Don't walk with me!"

"I'll walk wherever I want."

"Not if you want to go to the dance tomorrow."

"You can't stop me," I cried, and she shooshed me and paused, causing me to pause too, or to go ahead without her.

"See?" she said.

"See what?"

"I can make you do anything."

"Fine!" I said, and started off ahead of her, so that I would pass her friends first. I saw them looking at me, their six faces blank and fixed, like a row of mannequin-heads in a hat shop window. I bowed my own head and proceeded, but then I remembered what Theresa had shown me about walking. She had put a book on my head and made me walk "like a model." My posture was appalling; I slouched; I was the Hunchback of Notre Dame, and I looked like a dweeb. Knowing she was behind me, and watching, pressured me more than the weighty gaze of the jury of six.

Then, the oddest thing. I had no sooner reached the first girl than she spoke: to me, she spoke, and the effect was like having a statue speak, or a formal portrait. I choked when I tried to reply, although all I needed to say (Theresa had told me) was what the girl herself had said:

"Hi."

I should have kept moving, but I couldn't. The greeting – the summons – had run up a line before me, which caught me in the throat. Standing there, looking at this beautiful girl and her five beautiful friends, I strained to respond. My mouth moved, my gullet worked, but no sound came out.

Theresa, instantly, was behind me, pinching me none-too-gently in one of the diminished rolls of fat above my pants' waistband. I yelped, and the six exchanged confused glances, then returned their gaze to me, and now to Theresa as well.

"Move," Theresa snarled at me, very low in her throat. "Don't talk to my friends."

"Hi, Terry," said the same girl as had spoken to me. I still could not take my eyes off her. She had pale green beads dangling from her earlobes, beads of light and sparkle, and her sunglasses did not quite conceal the shadows of her eyes. She wore no lipstick, and her nails were painted frosty pink. I loved her.

"Hi, Gail," said Theresa. "I can't hang out. I gotta go to town with my stupid family."

"Oh, is that your little sister!" said Gail, as if reciting a line from an etiquette book.

Little sister, little! And the acknowledgement, the smile, the glittering genuine jewel of a smile, not chasing me away with a collie's bared teeth. She may not have meant it (it could be a trap), but it looked so real, so model-perfect, as if she were smiling from the cover of a *Mademoiselle* I was about to buy.

"Little, huh!" said Theresa, but without real conviction. I saw, or heard, that she was taken off guard by Gail's acknowledgement, by the drawing of a connection between us.

"You've lost weight," Gail went on. She turned to the others, the boys sucking on their cigarettes, squinting through the smoke, and the girls, sunglasses-less, wrinkling their noses in the blinding sun. "Hasn't she lost a ton, you guys?"

She had the same generous tone that Cathy

had. The other girls said, "yeah," and giggled (those giggles were as loaded as artillery). The boys laughed out loud – manly, seventeen-year-old laughs, and one of them leaned to the other and said, "Still looks like a pile of shit to me."

Theresa took my elbow and gave me a heavy shove, away from Gail, towards shore. "Go!" she ordered, and I took a step or two, but stopped. I wanted to speak some more to Gail. I wanted more words from her. I was so hungry for them. Like that single cookie which would always trigger a binge, I had heard one moment's thrilling kindness and I wanted to stuff my head with more. What else could she say, what gentle thoughts? She could come shopping with us, instead of Theresa, and under her care I would buy an outfit so perfect that no one would recognize me. I would look not like me, but like Theresa's Little Sister. My hair would be loose and straight, and my dancing would flow like a freshet. I would raise my arms above my head and spin and swirl, like Theresa, like Goldie on *Laugh-In*, with a flower or MAKE LOVE NOT WAR painted on my flat, exposed tummy. All because Gail said so.

Gail's enlightened face suddenly lightened more. She grabbed the knee of the girl beside her, signalling her, and I realized Gail's gaze had moved past me to the approach of someone behind me, coming from the end of the dock.

"Hiiiii, David," the girls all crooned, in a chorus they'd orchestrated at Gail's signal. Then they crumbled into laughter, and the boys disgustedly tossed their butts, also in unison, into the lake.

"Hey, you!" cried David. "Pick those up!"

"Fuck you, man," said one of the boys.

David, who in previous years would have jumped in himself to retrieve the butts, merely shook his head and snarled "littering, anti-Earth assholes" as he passed. The girls sat very still as he went by, tense with admiration, while the boys exchanged curled-lip silent condemnations of David, their muscled, tanned, bedowned arms crossed over their pectorals.

"He's so gorgeous," sighed one of the girls.

"He's a fairy," replied a boy.

"Hi, kids," said the Dad, making me jump. He had been right on David's heels.

"Hi, Mr. Graham."

"C'mon, Theresa, Dee. Let's hit the road." He put a single beefy finger between my shoulder blades and gave me a push. The spell broken, I moved.

"Where the hell is your mother?" said the Dad, when we reached the car, and our mother was not there waiting.

We all looked around, equivalently amazed by her not-being-there.

"Where could she be?" said the Dad, opening the driver's side door to let the hot, trapped air flow out. "The ladies' room, maybe?"

"You mean the backhouse," said David. "Tell it like it is...hey!"

"Hey what?"

David was grinning – the cat that ate the cream indeed. "She's gone to Auntie Alice's, I bet you anything." He punched the air with his fist and danced a little simian tarantella in the dust of the parking lot. "Way to go, Mum!" he cried.

"What a lot of bullroar," said the Dad angrily, making ushering motions towards me and Theresa, swooping us towards the car. "Fine, so she went to Alice's. I give up. She's a grown girl. She can do anything she wants..."

"No, she can't, you never let her!" crowed David. He climbed into the car, into the very back where he preferred to be, leaving me the back seat. Theresa sat up front, with the Dad, pouncing on Mum's empty seat.

"Are we gonna go pick up Mum?" I asked.

"No reason to. No reason to have her along, sulking and pouting like a child."

"Treat her like a child, a child is what you'll get," said David.

"Comments from the cheap seats," said the Dad, trying to sound uncaring. "The peanut gallery speaks."

Theresa patted the Dad's hand. "It's okay, Daddy, don't be hurt," she said.

"Hurt! Why would I be hurt?"

Dust kicked up from the tires and we careened through the landing's narrow drive, out towards the main Lake Road. Even though we were far out of range of any station, the Dad switched on the radio, and without letting it warm up began to punch the tuning buttons one after another, top to bottom and back again. All he got was static.

I settled down in my entire back seat, and realized that in a matter of days I would be heading down this road again, this time with a car full of the summer's remains: the same sleeping bags, one summer older, and the same cooler and Coleman lamps and first-aid kit and rubberized air mattresses and suitcases and my cardboard box of writing pads and doodlers and comic books. I had blinked, it seemed, and summer had gone. All my plans, as Brother Webster would say, had *aft ganged aglay*, and now all I had was the round-backed nightmare of Tuesday morning, crouched like a malevolent sun, on the other side of the weekend.

The last weekend of summer. When I was little and the last to come down to breakfast, having slept in, the Dad would sometimes greet me with a big smile and the remark that I was arriving like the last rose of summer. This summer had held no roses; it had seemed more like a few hours of very hard work, like the thirteen times tables, or polishing silver, or getting a hem to hang perfectly. I had not expected to reach the autumn so unprepared, with no house built in the woods, and no secret lake discovered. I was not packed and ready to go; I had not learned to make pemmican or chop down a tree. I had skinned no squirrels. I had not so much as caught a single fish.

If I had been told two months ago that I would, on the Friday before Labour Day, be heading into Huntsville with my brother and sister, to buy an outfit for the Ashleigh's Dance, I would have not understood the language. I would have referred to my pads of paper, with their elaborate lists and schematics; I would have waved my hand over the history of Richard's fidelity and devotion, and over the remains of our forts and playhouses, and shown them that we had been working on this for years, and of course it was possible. As for Theresa helping me, I would have explained her ferocity and cunning, and shown that the jackal cannot be trusted. The weight loss – the thinning-out – was also beyond possibility. That I had learned to not eat – to live without eating – so that I might please my sister and go to a dance...these were things I could never have seen coming. Or imagined wanting.

Here I was, in the back seat, and although there was no one beside me, there was room for two other people. My thighs did not take up half the upholstered bench. I did not have a fifteen-cent box of Rosebud chocolates in my hand; I had not eaten half a gallon of oatmeal porridge with milk and maple syrup for breakfast. My belly did not smother the territory between my crotch and my knees, like a flow of flesh. I needed new clothes and was going to a dance. I may as well have been walking on the moon.

The moonwalks, the men who'd been there:

they wore air-suits and their feet were weighted, so that they would not fly off the atmosphereless rock. The moon, at that moment, was still visible in the sky, and it flashed through the trees as we spun along the highway, white as albumen. Soon it would vanish as the Earth turned away for the day. I wondered if Richard still looked at the moon, forgetting, as I often did, that he was blind. Perhaps, then, he remembered looking at the moon, and knew what it was like to stand on the grey-skinned, pocky surface, the rocks, the empty space that hadn't even the weight of air, with nothing to hold you down. And the voyage there: days and days in a confined drum, trapped in a can of processed oxygen mix, wires, and pasty space food, everything measured out and measured in, living with people you barely knew but on whom you depended completely.

The trees whirled by, some of them already frosted with yellow, a branch here or there, the harbinger of fall. The temperature was eighty degrees but the trees knew, the trees knew. It was coming to an end, again.

When we arrived in Huntsville, approaching from the curved access road that crested the hill over the Lake of Bays, the Dad had brightened enough to repeat his story about how, when he'd first come to Huntsville, he used to see the log booms in the lake below: acres of slain trees coating the water, and men scampering across them like insects or playground children. There were logging camps all around, in Algonquin and farther up Highway 11. Now they use trucks, said the Dad, not the water or the rails.

"Logging is another rape of the ecology," said David. "The logging companies strip away entire forests, ruining the drainage of the land, and they don't replant. We use too much paper. We're wasters. We have to learn to not use so much paper...We're destroying the world, slowly but surely...in twenty years all of this will be gone, it'll be covered in apartment buildings and the lake will be dirty and there'll be motorboats, motorboats, motorboats...litter...sewage..."

David's voice trailed off. He ran his hand over his face, which I saw had gone grey and moist, like a mushroom. "You'll have lots to sing about," I offered, twisting around in my seat to try to address him alone, but of course the Dad heard me.

"And lots of places to sing it," said the Dad. "You kids go on about progress, how it's such a bad thing. Think about it, David. These buildings here – they're progress. This used to be nothing but Injun land. You wouldn't be here if it wasn't for progress!"

David, his head now buried in his hands, didn't reply.

"Did you hear me, son!" the Dad almost shouted.

"Yes, yes, I heard you. Let me out here, wouldja?"

"Here! Why here?"

"There's a tavern down the hill a bit, used to be a railway hotel or something. Jesus, Dad, just let me out?"

"It would be nice if you spent one little minute with your family," said the Dad, but he pulled over to the shoulder and let David out.

"I'll see you later," said David, swinging his guitar over his back by the strap.

"Wait! How will you get back?"

David lifted his thumb to indicate hitchhiking, and the Dad shook his head mightily. "Dirty hippie freeloading habit," he said.

I looked back through the wagon's glass box and watched David crossing the highway to reach a run-down, barnboard-and-planking tavern onto which someone had hung a psychedelic, daisy-swirled sign reading LIVE BANDS FOLK ROCK HAPPENING HERE THURSDAYS FRIDAYS SATERDAYS. I saw him light a cigarette, and somehow that was more shocking to me than learning he was a diabetic too. The Dad would be furious that David had started smoking. It caused cancer; they'd proven it now. The Dad was glad that he only smoked a pipe, which was safe. How could David start smoking, when he knew it was dangerous?

My big brother, breathing out smoke, shook back his hair and settled his floppy-brimmed leather hat onto his head, straightened his shirt, and started down the driveway, his guitar on his back.

The next time I saw him was also the last.

The radio, which had been broadcasting static, suddenly fell upon the local station, and Doris Day warbled a single line, then vanished again into the ether. "Aw, darn," said the Dad, "I liked that song!" And he tried to tune her back in. But she was gone.

"I'll sing it, Daddy," chimed Theresa. She did, too, the whole song where the little girl begs to know what's to become of her.

"Princess," said the Dad, "you have a way of just brightening my day right up."

I rolled down the window completely, and hung my head out of it like a dog. We were now right in town, before the river and the more up-to-date business section, where there were gas stations, and motels, and a hotdog restaurant that sold wickedly creamy soft ice cream, better than the Dairy Queen's even. But we were to stay in the old town, Theresa and I, and go to the Eaton's. The Eaton's, unlike the ones in Toronto (which were huge, multistoreyed department stores), was a squat, one-storey building across from the Dominion grocer's. Down the street was a string of turn-of-the-century, three- and four-storey Victorian stores, with apartments above, their facades decorated with stone scroll-work and dingy brick, selling hardware, duck decoys, crepe-soled black leather shoes, local real estate, insurance, and candy floss–coloured beach toys. Not a single Smart Set or Very Very Terry Jerry; no Big Steel or Thrifty's Just Pants. We were stuck with Eaton's, but Eaton's carried jeans and it carried large sizes. We had been shopping from its catalogue for years. I associated it with thick, drenching, old-woman clothes, not with the chic new outfit Theresa was going to help me find.

The Dad pulled over and handed to Theresa the fifty dollars in mixed bills, fives and tens and a twenty, the tens and the twenty in unfamiliar colours. Theresa put them carefully into her wallet and then into her fringed, yellow suede purse, promising the Dad that she would never let that bag out of her hand. Yes, she assured him, she remembered that everything had tax on it, so it would be more expensive when we actually got to the till.

"Daddy, stop fussing," she said at last, and he pulled away, to go to the big A&P and to the butcher's. We were alone, unsupervised, and we were about to go shopping.

"Let's go, Lardbucket," she said cheerfully.

I trotted after her, through the open-sesame doors, like Lenny in *Of Mice and Men*, like Herman Munster behind his beautiful, crepe-hung wife. How silly, I thought, when I could knock her head off, with one blow of my paw. Her decapitated body would collapse among the dress carousels, and her ponytail would impede the smooth rolling of the struck-off skull.

"What are you laughing at?" said Theresa suddenly.

"I wasn't laughing." I didn't think I had been.

"You're making this grunty-gulpy sound. Everybody's staring."

I looked around, and sure enough, there was a saleslady looking at us from over at the cashier's desk, with that slightly disapproving glare of the past-middle-age woman – an age group that generally liked to stomp up to me and demand why I hadn't slimmed down. If I had been laughing, the saleslady's gimlet glare certainly put an end to it. Suddenly, I was looking at the floor, at the linoleum tiles and the hems of the garments on their racks around us.

"That's better. God, Dee, you're such a retard. Try not to be so weird!"

We moved through men's shirts and ties and shoes and into the Young Teen Shoppe, where we got some ideas, but as the saleslady-denizen at that locale reminded us, they only carried Junior Petites. "We're just looking," said Theresa, which seemed to signal to the salesladies that we were to be watched, for we were shadowed thereafter by shrivelled women in Eaton's smocks, offering suggestions.

"Perhaps something in the Women's section? What size are you, dear? 20?"

I couldn't speak. A huge wall of cold seemed to engulf me, a familiar one though, water-heavy and wobbling with light. Never, ever, in my entire life had I fainted, although Theresa had done so three times (twice in gym, and once in church).

Now I thought it might happen to me. I thought I might go down, when the salesladies brought a knee-length polyester dress in mauve, with what they assured us was a fashionable front zipper.

"No, thank you, no," Theresa said firmly. "We are looking for hiphugger jeans."

"Maybe you had better try Men's," sniffed the saleslady. "You could do that unisex thing that the young people like so much."

We found the men's section, and were tended to by a pimply man who fell so madly in love with Theresa that he couldn't listen to her instructions, thereby earning a few cutting remarks. "I said Levis!" she said. "Weren't you listening?"

He brought us Levi's, Wranglers, Lees, and Eaton's own brand, in sizes 32 through 42, which he said weren't the real waist sizes. He brought out a tape measure and began to string it around my waist, but I pushed his hands away. I couldn't bear to be measured by this stranger.

As he and Theresa went over the jeans, sorting them, I stood and waited among the trees of clothes, and the shelves of folded, packaged shirts. I kept seeing little boys through the racks, various elven figures peering at me, as if from a forest; bespectacled, scrawny, their incisors too big for their faces. I would look again and see that they were only folds in fabrics, or metal signs on waist-high stands, advertising specials for back-to-school, or 50 percent off housedresses. I had worn housedresses many times, since they went up to

triple-extra-large. Theresa had said that a housedress was just the thing for someone as big as a
house.

The myopic little boys darted in and out, like
crayfish from rock to rock, minnows in the granite-
edged pools along the shore at Richard's cottage.

"Dee, I'm talking to you!" Theresa shrilled.
"Oh my god – why are you crying? Now what?
Quick, get in a change room; take these pants.
You're ridiculous. You're unbelievable."

Ah, but she had found clothes for me. With
devotion she searched, and she would not take
second-best. In the women's section the "jeans"
were of fake, stretchy, denim-coloured acrylic, but
she fit me into a pair of men's Levi's, size 38, and
although my belly lunged over the low-slung
waistband, they were hiphugger jeans and they
were what everyone else was wearing. To hide the
dangle of my stomach, she chose a series of gaily
printed, scoop-necked peasant blouses, with golds
and greens and yellows, and said that we were
going for the gypsy look, which would work out
okay with my wild hair. We'd work on the hair
tomorrow, she said, as she leaped around me in
front of a three-way mirror, a hummingbird serv-
icing an enormous flower. She chirred to herself.
"If we tuck it in, your gut sticks out, but if we
leave it out, you're all bulb-shaped! What are we
going to do about that gut!"

We tried a sash, a big pink satin pirate sash,
but that didn't work, so we looped it around my

throat, and that gave the outfit (she said) a nice long line. The salesladies were back; there was nothing to do on a Friday morning except watch Theresa throwing beads around my neck and strapping belts around my middle (for it could not be said that I had a waist). She sent the pimple-boy for sandals, explaining to him that I wore a men's size, and could he please try to find as faggy a pair as possible? Soon they were slipping shoes onto my feet, and the salesladies found me a little purple satin purse on a long spaghetti strap, which I loved, and wanted, but Theresa said satin was outsville. They brought me a plain brown leather bag with a fringe.

"Perfect," said Theresa.

At one point, I stood there as perhaps half-a-dozen people – Theresa, the pimple-boy, the salesladies, and perhaps the elves I'd been imagining – flapped and fluttered around me, running their hands up my legs ("we can take up these jeans while you wait, dear") and across my shoulders ("does she have a proper bra?") and lifting my hair from my neck ("perhaps you should try wearing it up – oh, it needs a wash!"). They opened their hope chests and their Pandora's boxes and their Cinderella closets and their Mary Poppins carpet bags, and they flung fabric over my arms and legs and torso and buttocks, and they strung me like a Christmas tree, or the dress mannequin in Jane's kitchen back home. At the end, they told me to close my eyes, and I did, and then to count to ten, which I couldn't, because I couldn't speak. So Theresa did, backwards. Ten, nine, eight, seven, six, five, four, three, two, one. Blast off. Dee, open your eyes.

There I stood. It was not bad, and it was very different. They had fluffed my hair out and stuck a flowered band in it, drawing my bangs off my face, and the scoop neck of the blouse rounded the curves of what were definitely breasts. Knotted casually down my front was the long pink scarf, and Theresa had decided that tucked in was best for the shirt. My belly was not so bad after all, with the blouse's fabric fluffed out to cover it. The shoes were thin straps of brown leather, and my naked toes were exposed. Theresa said we could paint the nails.

Over the backs of my feet the jeans' fabric draped. They would not be "taken up." The jeans' hems were supposed to drag on the ground. They were huge, cumbersome bellbottoms, tight to the knee and then flared out foolishly, almost like a dress's skirt from a tight waist. I saw that my feet were peeking out, like mice, just like they were supposed to.

"Thank you, Theresa," I said.

Theresa made a face, an exaggerated look of surprise, over my manners. "That's okay. It was fun, I guess," she said. Then she clapped her hands, to clear away the spell. "Okay, take it all off, let's go, before it gets wrinkled."

The final bill was $48.75. The change was

exactly enough to buy us each an ice cream, and still have a quarter for Dubble Bubble. For a moment I thought Theresa might give in and let us have one, even though I didn't ask, for as we crossed the old metal bridge over the broad, dark-watered river, heading to the supermarket where the Dad would be shopping, we could both see the ice cream store, plain as day, and blocking our path.

"No ice cream, Dee," she said, quietly, holding up the clothes in their Eaton's bag. "This is your reward."

We found the Dad, who was in the liquor store, having already been to the Brewer's Retail and the butcher's. "Finished already? Did you get a pretty dress?" he asked.

"Daddy, no dress," said Theresa. "But yeah, we got her something okay, I think."

On the way home I sat with the big paper Eaton's bag on my lap, afraid to touch my costume. I could feel it beneath the paper, breathing and moving. Then I realized that it was just my body, shivering under the cloth. It must have been nearly eighty-five degrees, but my whole body was shaking. I closed the window and huddled down, letting the scenery flash by, clutching my clothes to my chest for warmth, unable to shake the feeling that I was sinking into cold, desperate waters, and that no one had even noticed.

Mum was on the dock, waiting for us, when we returned. She sat on the dock's icebreaker apron, warming her calves against the sun-heated steel, her sandals beside her on the wood. Her head was tilted back, with her face towards the glow, and I could have sworn she was smiling.

But I was mistaken. When she turned around and rose to her feet, her face was the same solemn mask it had been all month.

"We missed you, Mum," I said.

"Did you get a nice outfit?"

"Yeah. Jeans."

She pulled her sunglasses down along the bridge of her nose, and looked up at me piercingly. "Jeans? I thought this was a special occasion dance. Certainly enough fuss has been made over it."

"Jeans are what we wear," said Theresa.

The Dad came along with a boxful of groceries and liquor bottles balanced on the cases of beer. It was a towering load, and he struggled. "Thanks, girls, for helping," he said snidely. He saw my mother and said, as if in passing, "Hello, Jane."

"David." She never called him David – nobody did. He was the Dad.

It seemed to have escaped him that she'd called him by his son's name. Or perhaps he wasn't listening, for he went straight into the boat and started her up, leaning forward to tug at the free ends of the mooring ropes. In a second he'd be away, and Theresa and I clambered quickly aboard.

"If you're coming, then come," said the Dad.

Mum let two beats pass before she moved. In that time, the Dad pulled the boat forward, but not too far away from the dock, so that there was perhaps eighteen inches of space between its gunnels and my mother. He did not stand up and balance himself to offer her his hand; in fact, he stared ahead from the rear seat, over the nose of the boat, his face as clenched shut as if he were smoking his pipe.

She jumped. She stepped off the side of the dock and dropped the three feet to the boat's floor, landing in a crouch. The boat shuddered and swayed, but righted itself quickly as she settled onto one of the benches. I handed her a life preserver. She had always worn her life preserver.

She slipped it under her buttocks and settled onto it. "Thank you, Dee," she said.

The Dad was still idling the engine in low gear, bubbling us along in the bay. We were past the zone where there would be swimmers or smaller boats (not that there were boats much smaller than ours). He could have gunned us and taken off, and Theresa was frowning, crossing and uncrossing her arms, miffed by the delay.

The Dad said, "So you had a nice little visit, did you?"

"I did," she replied.

"Fun, was it, taking off on us like that?"

She raised an eyebrow at him. "Productive," she said.

"Oh-ho, productive!" The Dad cranked the throttle full open, and the boat reared up like a spurred horse, then spurted ahead over the water. "She had a productive visit with the Women's Lipper!"

The wind came up and snatched away the rest of his words, but they were nothing I wanted to hear. Neither did Mum, it seemed, for though she had been facing him, she swivelled on her life preserver to face the front, and the spray and the blow. She and Theresa and I formed a triangle, with she and I on the bench, and Theresa in the prow-seat, her feet curled beneath her.

It may have just been a reaction to the wind, but I thought I saw it again: my mother's furtive, sneaky, subversive little smile.

I went to my little house, to say goodbye. For after spreading my clothes out on my bunk for the admiration of the Dad and Mum, I suddenly saw the bodiless clothes as distorted flags – tents, even – and a feeling like stage fright swept over me. It was the same anxious, distressed sensation that I felt when I had to enter a room, or face a group of people, or cross the schoolyard. My pretty, pretty clothes twisted themselves into a uniform of sorts, and I did not want to see them anymore. Having no place I'd rather go, I excused myself (Theresa had taught me that I was not to just run off in tears – it was grotesque) and went to my little house.

I could not pin down what it was I was supposed to be doing. I sat and peeled bits of bark off the supports of my hut, and felt the emptiness of sitting inside what I'd built. Richard and I could have fit in here very well together, with a pile of books and comics and a cellophane bag of Cheesies. Richard and I could have lain out in the sun until we were sparkling with sweat, and then we'd tumble down to the lake and straight off the end of the dock, cannonball! Richard and I could have stayed up late and if it was calm, paddled the canoe to the foot of Bald Face and looked at the stars as they spilled over the edge of the massive cliff, marvelling at the line between the rock's end and the stars' beginning. We would never worry about what we wore, or how we moved, or what we said, or how it sounded. We could howl and giggle and scream and scream, and there was nothing wrong with any of it, because there was only us, and we were only kids.

I thought about screaming. I used to howl. I would howl for fun. Sitting on a rock's edge, I would howl to summon Wolfgirl, who was now just a scrap of a memory, something I used to play at. Only months ago I could metamorph into her, and now she was a wraith, not even a full-fledged recollection. She had become a story I told myself: *I used to pretend to be a werewolf, isn't that silly?* I could see myself telling Gail and my new friends how I once crawled around in the pine needles, willing myself to grow fangs and fur. They had never done such things. They had never believed in Mowgli, or White Fang, or Sam McGee surviving the Lake of Fire. I would, from now on, only be able to speak their language.

So, considering carefully that I might want to let loose with one last ritual howl, I suddenly heard Theresa wail. *Daddy don't you dare. Daddy! Daddy!*

I was slow to move, to react. It was only curiosity that propelled me, and a longing to see Theresa get in serious trouble, for whatever reason. But then I heard the crack of the rifle, and the Dad yelling.

"Dammit, girl, dammit! Look what you made me do!"

What Theresa had made him do got me running, over the rough ground and rocks, to the path. Theresa could make people do things, and this sounded serious. Through the trees I saw the Dad stooped over and searching the underbrush, with Theresa standing beside him, soldier-straight and criminally defiant.

I crashed my way over, crushing the underbrush. "What happened?"

"Nosy," hissed Theresa.

"She grabbed the gun when I took aim," said the Dad bitterly. "I wounded the little brute. Goddamn, goddamn. Theresa, you could at least help me look."

"No, you'll kill it." Theresa's eyes were shining and shrewish, but she'd also been crying. I could see the residual tracks of tears on her cheeks.

"I have to kill it, Theresa, it's wounded. It's suffering. I have to put it out of its misery."

"No," said Theresa.

"I'll help," I said. I began to shuffle around through the bushes, kicking aside the juniper shrubs and blueberry bushes, lifting dead branches out of the way. From another tree, twenty yards away, another squirrel shrilled at us. The Dad straightened up immediately, snapping to attention like a pointer dog, but then he muttered something about out of range and went back to searching for the escapee. No sooner had he bent over than another squirrel, and another, answered the warning call of the first, but these two were closer – one close enough to earn a sweep of the Dad's rifle sight, but it ran around to the opposite end of the trunk of the fat, bushy old cedar. "Rats," said the Dad.

Then I found the squirrel. Its movement caught my eye, as it dragged itself with its front paws along a clear spot no bigger than a shoebox. I almost told the Dad, but then I realized that as soon as I spoke, that squirrel would be killed. I could keep it alive, by saying nothing. I watched it, hauling its ripped lower body along. The .22's bullet had taken off its right rear leg, neatly as a knife, but there were tissues dangling from the wound.

"Dad, here it is," I heard myself say.

The Dad came over at once, but as he passed her, Theresa flung herself on his back. She tore and punched at him as with great determination he lifted his heavy foot above the crawling squirrel, took careful aim, and smashed it with his heel.

Theresa was now screaming at him, and the squirrels in the trees were screaming too. *I hate you, I hate you,* Theresa screamed, and the squirrels screamed it, and the Dad took off his straw hat and wiped his brow. Somewhere, he had dropped the gun, and now (with Theresa still piggy-backed on him), he returned to where he'd left it. "That's enough, Theresa," he said quietly, still ignoring the blows that she rained on his head and neck, and the kicks she delivered to his calves.

She dropped from him and sank to the ground, weeping. I wanted to ask her, yet again, how could she weep for the squirrel? Why was she so distraught, so beside-herself, when she had seen me suffering all these years, and never fallen to the ground wailing? I had been crawling my entire life, and she had never wept for me. What was it about me that I had not earned her agonized sympathies?

Mea culpa.

I stood there, watching, as she rolled into a ball and got dirt in her hair and on her shirt, bawling *poor little thing how could you daddy.* The

Dad, who was grey around the lips and shaking, retrieved the .22 unhappily, handling it as one might something decayed. He broke it open and peered down the barrel, then worked the lever to discharge the half-a-dozen unspent shells. These he threw in the dirt.

Theresa snatched them up and, making a fist, shook them at him.

"You'll never do this again!" she said. "I won't let you!"

He didn't look at her, but snapped the gun closed with finality. Then he went to the squirrel, but didn't look at it, either, as he kicked it into the bushes. A funereal screech came from the trees: a ululating cry, which was taken up, as always, by the others. The Dad didn't cock the gun, though. He just walked away, back to the cabin, and inside.

Theresa, eventually, got to her feet, her hands still clenched into fists. She saw me watching her and snarled, "Take a picture, why don't you?" before stomping off, grim-faced, through the trees to the path. I watched her descend to the firepit, where she crouched down by the edge, as if praying. I honestly thought she was praying, for she stayed there long enough, and I saw her hands move in front of her, as if she were – like Catholic Cathy – making the sign of the cross. I realized she was digging in the dirt of the firepit, and her hand moved above the disturbed ashes, as she seeded them with the shells.

We ate a tense dinner. The Dad could hardly speak, but he ate a large meal, trying to make small talk but forgetting to finish his sentences. Theresa just glared at him. He proposed a game of four-handed crib, which Mum declined, and Theresa said she wouldn't play with a murderer.

"Excuse me, young lady," said the Dad. "I'm the one who gets to do the filthy, unpleasant jobs, so that you can have a nice, safe, clean, squirrel-less life. C'mon, Dee, let's play cards."

So the Dad and I played two-handed crib, while Theresa lay on the old daybed, reading the *Mademoiselle* she'd bought in Huntsville, and Mum sat in the big cane chair and stared at nothing. The Dad had confiscated Mum's reading material and returned it to Alice through Big Dick. She had a Bible, which she held closed in her lap, tracing her finger over the cover, but not opening it. There were other things she could have done, though: she could have taken in a dart in the back waistband of my jeans, so that it wouldn't hang out as men's jeans do on women's bodies, or she could have straightened or tidied or washed. She could have played cribbage. But she just sat and stared, spooky as a robot, lurking as a spider.

"Mum, you're giving me the creeps," Theresa said suddenly, after night had fallen completely.

"Am I? I'm just thinking."

David did not come home. Nobody comment-ed on this. The Dad tried to spark some enthusi-

asm for the big night we were all to have tomorrow – Saturday night, and the corn roast, and the
dance – and to engage us in making plans. Uncle
Dick and Auntie Alice and Richard would be
coming in the late afternoon, somewhere before
dinner, and Brother Webster would come at seven
or so, although he never was much for being punc-
tual. "Won't it be nice," the Dad said, to me and
Mum, "to have your friends over for a party?"

"What friends?" I said. "Besides, I'm going to
the dance."

The Dad said *yes yes of course you are I'd forgotten*, and went on about how Mackenzie was
bringing over the gas-powered generator, and would
stay for dinner and not just a beer. I found myself
staring at the glowing cloth mantle of the Coleman
lantern, which burned with an intense white light,
the colour of the moon. The Dad's pointless dron-
ing soothed me, and I forgot that I was playing
cards and that it was my turn to count the crib. I
put my head on my arms on the table, and felt the
coolness of my own skin. I heard the Dad say,
"Jane, look at Dee, she's fallen asleep at the table!
She looks just like the little girl she used to be…"
and then I was gone, and I was dreaming.

I know I dreamed, and I know I went to bed, but
the dream and the voyage from the table to my
bunk are gone. The next thing, I was awake, it was
Saturday, and I was having breakfast. An envelope
of instant oatmeal, chosen instead of the cooked
version because with the packets I could make no

mistake of measuring. I could not cheat when the food was sealed and offered up in that insistently small amount.

I ate it with water and without milk or sugar. I ate it on the tippy-tip of my spoon. I ate it with Theresa sitting across from me, running her fingernail dreamily over the squares in the gingham-print vinyl tablecloth. She looked up at me, and saw me sucking the treasured porridge from the spoon, and offered me a smile.

"Atta girl," she said.

A wave of tears and gratitude surged from my chest to my throat, and I lowered my face so that she wouldn't see me struggling not to weep. She hated the way I cried all the time, and I would not, could not, would not, could not betray her now. So I swallowed the whole horrid lump of emotion and within a few seconds, I had looked up at her again, renewed and polished and smiling.

"Thanks," I said. She said. The girl who was me said.

As part of the deal for being allowed to go to the dance, Theresa and I had to help set up for the party. "It's not much of a party," Theresa observed, as we swept the flagstones of the pathway, and cleared fallen branches from the firepit area. "There's only the Holmeses and that old creep."

"Mackenzie," I agreed.

"No, not Mr. Mackenzie – boy, you're so out of it. Mr. Webster. The *fag*."

Although I knew lezzies, and that fags were like them, I didn't entirely understand the word any further than its status as an insult. My new sandals were faggy, Theresa had said. Faggy was girl-like, and Mr. Webster wasn't girl-like. He wasn't an old creep. He liked my stories.

"I like Mr. Webster," I said.

"You would. Creeps of a feather stick together."

"Girls can't be fags. Boys are fags," I said.

Theresa looked at me, long and hard, as if deciding whether she really wanted to get into something big, when we still had the chairs to set up and the firewood to stack. Then she decided, and motioned for me to sit down. We did, together, on the benches the Dad had built so long ago. There, Theresa set out to me an entirely new set of rules, beyond the health class lectures about penises being inserted into vaginas, Tab A into Slot B.

Girls could like girls, and they were lezzies, or dykes, and boys could like boys, and they were fags. Fags are sick. In high school, there are two teachers who are fags. You could tell. The fag teachers were the drama teacher and one of the modern languages teachers. Fags looked girly, just as dykes looked like boys. Dykes had boys for friends. Fags had girls for friends.

"I don't get it," I said. "Wouldn't they have, like, guy-guy and girl-girl?"

"That's just for sex."

"Sex! They have sex!"

So she explained that to me. My head reeled. Then something else occurred to me. If this business about Brother Webster was true, then Brother Webster had ess-ee-ex with *guys*.

"Like I said," Theresa pronounced. "He's an old creep."

I thought of him sitting beneath limp, sickly David, who had been in his underwear, and how David's nearly nude form had been draped across Brother Webster's arms and lap. The look on Brother Webster's face had been the sort of look I rarely, if ever, had seen before. No person I knew ever showed themselves that way, when faced with the agony of another human being. No wonder David preferred to spend time with Brother Webster. It seemed very certain that they would indeed have kissed.

My puzzlement, and perhaps shock, at this revelation must have shown on my expression, because Theresa's eyes narrowed.

"You know something," she said. "What do you know?"

"Nothing," I replied, which was true. It seemed to me that there were oceans of things I did not know, which had been unfolding and growing while I planned my escape and wrote my myths and lived on my various islands. All the spying I had done – all the notes I had taken – and yet so many things I had missed entirely. Looks of love. The meaning of a kiss. Sex that didn't involve *the man inserts his erect penis into the woman's vagina and ejaculates his semen...*

All at once understanding dawned – what the boys in the schoolyards were really saying when they squealed at each other, *suck my dick you big fag*, just before a fistfight broke out. And Richard – Richard had been called a fag, so many times I could not count. Was he a fag? I walked on dangerous ground, thinking about these things.

"You're keeping a secret. Tell me what it is," demanded Theresa, drawing me from my wondering.

"There's nothing to tell."

"Tell me, or I'll tell on you."

I laughed at this, I really did. "Like tell what? Who to?"

"I'll tell Richard you're a dyke."

"I don't care what Richard thinks," I said. This was largely true. The Richard who had once been my friend would never have cared about such things, and the Richard who existed now didn't really exist at all. He was no one I knew. Pile it on, Theresa – I can take it, I thought.

Theresa seemed momentarily thwarted, but then she brightened. "Tell me or I'll tell the Dad – about David."

"What about David?" My voice, despite my attempt to control it, had gone up an octave, into that pitch where it's evident the speaker is lying. Somehow, Theresa knew about David's diabetes. Perhaps she'd seen him giving himself a needle. I could see him, begging her to keep it quiet. Not to tell on him.

"His big secret. I'll *tell*." She reached over and pinched me. "C'mon, Piggy, you can stop me. Just tell me what you found out."

I tried another tactic. "But you know already."

"Yeah, I know something, but I want to know if it's the same thing you know."

"This is *so* stupid," I said. "I don't know any-thing."

"You are lying," she said. She thought about the paradox. "Okay, I'll make a deal. You tell me what you know and I'll tell what I know, and then we're even and we're sure." Her voice was actual-ly friendly, so similar to the tone she used with Cathy on the phone that I felt for a moment part of their little, inward-facing circle.

"Okay, but it's already what you know," I said. "David's a diabetic."

"What!"

Her rocked disbelief sent a chill up my back. I had made a mistake. "I was kidding," I said, "I take it back."

But there was no such doing. Theresa latched onto it. "He's not diabetic, no way, he'd be dead. Diabetics have to do all sorts of fancy things." She rolled her eyes. "Don't I know, after all that Richard-this, Richard-that stuff all summer, with everybody all clingy to him...you idiot, why did you think David was diabetic?"

I resented being called an idiot, and also being so wrong. "He is too diabetic," I said. "I saw the needle and the insulin."

She mulled this over. "Where?"

"Brother Webster's. The day Auntie Alice stole the boat. You were at the mainland or something, off with your friends, but you know that Mum and Aunt Alice..."

"Yeah, yeah, booooring," she said, miming a yawn. "C'mon, what happened?"

So I told her about going up to see Brother Webster and finding him with a very sick David, and how we carried David to bed, and how there was a needle on the end table. I didn't mention the spoon and the icing sugar, which seemed very irrelevant to me, but Theresa's eyes were wide with something not unlike horror. "My fucking God," she said, a strong curse, even for her.

"Told you so," I said. "Diabetes."

She shook her head, quickly. "Did you see

any, like, vials, you know, whaddya call 'em, the ampoule things? The little bottles?"

"No." Something warned me not to mention the spoon, but Theresa, strangely enough, seemed to know. "Was there like, anything else? Like, a spoon, or something?"

"Yeah," I said. "He'd been eating sugar. For his diabetes."

"Holy fuck," said Theresa. "That fucking explains it."

"What? Explains what?"

"Just why he quit school, and why he's so hot on going to the city all the time, and why he doesn't live with us even though he could, you know. Why he was gone for like fucking years, and then now that he's here he's over at Brother Webster's all the time, instead of with us. He's trying to break the habit."

"What habit?"

"Never mind," she said. "Fuck, that's fucking amazing."

I'd never heard her curse in this tone before, and I realized that I had been wrong about David, although I didn't know how. When I probed, she shook her head and said, "Don't worry about it, never mind," just like an adult. I had made a grievous error, mentioning the spoon, but I didn't know why. I tore at a hardy, lonely clump of tape grass, growing from between the rocks, and struggled to figure out the key to finding out more.

"So I guess I gotta tell you what I know," she said.

Oh, God, there's *more?* I thought. "I don't wanna know. Tell me what *habit!*"

"Never mind that. Besides, this is even bigger."

I looked up, into her wide-pupiled eyes. She was smiling devilishly. "Our big brother is an eff ay gee."

"An effigy?"

"A what?"

We got that sorted out, but of course I refused to believe David was a fag. Theresa was just a mean old shit-for-brains peckermouth, and I told her that through copious tears, and she told me to settle the fuck down because the parents would hear and then we'd have some explaining to do. She said that she'd made a mistake telling me something so adult as David-is-a-fag, because obviously I wasn't mature enough to handle it, and I better keep my mouth shut and not tell anyone.

"Like, who am I going to tell?" I said.

She laughed, a sound like a cat's spitting hiss. "Pah! Good point."

The interview was over. We continued as if nothing had happened, and Theresa took special care to arrange the wood in the firepit in a floral motif, which was not something we'd been requested to do. The Dad wandered by to check the dock ropes and to look out for Mackenzie, who should have arrived by now with the generator, and when he saw my tear-splotched face he frowned, and perhaps thought he should enquire as to why I'd been crying again. But then he went along his way instead.

The day charged ahead, insisting on getting itself over with, and Mum never lifted a finger to help. She stayed in the cabin the whole day, and the Dad never told her to get up and do something; he acted as if she weren't there. When Mackenzie and his prune-faced, swallow-murdering sister showed up with the barge and the generator, the Dad brought them their beers himself, and asked that they please excuse his wife, who wasn't feeling well.

Maureen plunked herself down in one of the webbed chaise longues, silent as a fish on ice, her knees spread, her only movement that of bringing her bottle periodically to her lips. The Dad and Mackenzie powered up the generator, and hooked it up to the strings of patio and Christmas lights the Dad had hung from the pines and maples, and along the railing of the upper deck of the dock. There was much fussing from the Dad when they did not light, and Mackenzie rose from his chair like Boris Karloff and lumbered over to help argue with the dirty connections that were impeding the flow of power. The sun sank lower, and the Holmeses did not come and neither did Brother Webster and neither did David.

It was after the dinner hour when Mackenzie

finished his third beer, having managed to wrangle the lighting system into functioning. The Dad had rented from a Rent-It-All in Huntsville a portable hi-fi, and borrowed from Big Dick a milk crate containing a selection of hi-fi albums: Nat King Cole and Tommy Dorsey and Judy Garland Live at the Met. Theresa and I examined these with the good humour of two girls who were not going to have to listen to this stuff all night.

Eventually, Mackenzie nodded to his sister and they both stood up, causing the Dad to cry, "You're not going!"

"Looks as if we are," said Mackenzie.

"You'll stay for the party!" said the Dad. "The corn roast – the girls have been shucking corn all day."

Not all day, but all afternoon. Theresa was going to have to spend an hour on re-doing her nails alone.

"Sorry," said Mackenzie, heading to his barge. He began to unloop the mooring ropes. Maureen, still carrying her beer, stepped aboard and sat down on one of the lawn chairs that served as seats.

"Wait, wait, I have business to talk to you," said the Dad.

"No more business between us to talk," said Mackenzie. He stood up from his fiddling with the ropes, and the effect of this was condescension and borderline intolerance. "I told you, place isn't for sale."

"Mackenzie," said the Dad, his voice desperate. "I will pay you anything."

"Place isn't for sale."

"Name your price!" cried the Dad.

Mackenzie sighed and herded the Dad away from the mooring ropes, in a gesture of taking-him-aside, but everything they said was still clearly audible.

"Lookit, it's not a matter of it being not for sale, Graham. I sold it."

"What! When!"

"Late last winter I sold it. Got a good offer. Fella in question wanted a long closing, though. Made me sign sale papers with a lawyer in town, wouldn't take a handshake. So, sorry to say, Graham – that's it for our association. She ain't for rent no more. Less you can come to an arrangement with this fella."

"Look, let me try to better the offer," said the Dad, pleading in his voice.

"You couldn't better it," said Mackenzie. "The man's overbid by ten grand as it is. You got fifty grand, Graham? I doubt it. What you got, fifteen? Twenty? Twenty grand, when I could have fifty? C'mon, a man's gotta have a head on his shoulders."

Mackenzie gave a rope a final yank and pushed off from the dock, letting the big pontoon barge catch the small current and the winds that flowed through the channel. The Dad watched, still saying nothing, and powerlessness flowed from him – from his lowered head and sagging shoulders, and from his arms crossed behind him, as if they were tied.

As Mackenzie started up the barge's engine, and moved off and away, the Dad turned briskly on his heels. He saw us watching him; waiting for the story.

"What are you two staring at? Mind your own little businesses," he said.

"Daddy, what's that about twenty grand?" said Theresa.

"What's this about him selling the island?" I asked. "Does that mean we can't rent it any more?"

"That's exactly what it means, you little stickybeaks," he said. "What a couple of girls you are." There was no affection in his tone. "What I wouldn't do for my son right now, but of course he's off lollygagging, damn him. And my wife's in a coma, all frosted over because I won't let her have her spoiled-rich-kid way." He pointed his finger at Theresa. "And you, you little princess! Don't you be turning out like her. Don't you ever treat your man the way she treats me."

"I won't, Daddy," said Theresa solemnly, dropping entirely the question of the twenty grand. "I really-truly promise."

"Good girl," said the Dad.

He brightened, only slightly, but noticeably. He raised his head, and then I heard it myself – a boat approaching, a big one. Uncle Dick's bowrider. Richard was coming.

I jumped up from where I'd been kneeling with Theresa beside the albums, and ran into the woods, contrary to all the etiquette I'd learned. I headed for my hut, but changed my mind, for he had found me there once, and I could not guarantee he would not try to find me again. Then I realized that if I kept moving, he'd never find me. I could see, and he could not.

So I hung around the firepit, peering through the trees and over the shore's boulders as Big Dick landed the bowrider with precision. Auntie Alice sat in the stern, facing the engine. Richard was not there.

"You didn't bring Richie," said the Dad, as he took from Big Dick the bottles of liquor and mix he'd superfluously imported, and the big gallon tub of Shopsy's potato salad.

"Kid didn't want to come yet," said Dick, disembarking. "I was gonna raise a stink about it, but dammit, you know, the kid's fourteen, and you get tired of all this trouble and strife. And speaking of trouble and strife, Alice – get yer ass outta the boat."

Alice got up slowly. She gingerly put her one foot on the boat's gunnels, and her hand on the rear of one of the upholstered seats, evidently having some trouble with stiffness. "Goddamn arthritis is kicking in," she said, and the Dad immediately moved to help her, taking her by the hand and the elbow.

"Thanks," she said. "You were always a gentleman, Dad."

"And you weren't ever a lady, Alice, so don't think you'd recognize one," said Dick.

Alice, who was wearing a very broad-brimmed straw hat strapped to her head by a floral print scarf, tugged its brim down over her face, as if to bar Dick from her vision. She wore one of her painting shirts over her swimsuit, and a pair of long cotton stovepipe trousers. With the same cautious walk, she headed towards shore. "Hello, Theresa," she said, and Theresa waved hi.

"Dee around anywhere?" Alice asked.

Theresa shrugged. "Dunno. But Mum's in the cabin."

"I know," said Alice. She gave herself a little shake, through the arms and torso, and said she felt better now she was all uncramped. With a little of her normal briskness, she started up the path to the cabin.

"Auntie Alice!" I cried. "Wait up! Wait for me!"

She swept me under her big wing, and together we walked up to meet my mother.

I was wearing a peasant blouse the night I tried to die. Anybody else, writing about that night, would pay attention to the events that pushed me into the lake, and across it, but little attention to the blouse, or to the heavy denim hiphuggers (except insofar as their massive bellbottoms, drenched and sodden, helped to drag me under). But if I were writing about it, I would write this:

Cross-Dressed Teenager Drowns Escaping Debutante Ball.

And my editor would say, "Aww, Dee. Nobody cares. Go find something really awful."

The men stayed down at the dock, the two of them, making their own party to the tunes of the LP records, and unpacking the fireworks, laying them out to discuss which would make the biggest bangs, while we girls got ready for the dance.

Mum poured two glasses of beer, for herself and for Alice, and set them on the table. I had never seen my mother drink before, and she sipped her beer exactly as she sipped tea, holding the glass in two hands as if it were a cup, and extending both pinkies.

Alice lit the Coleman stove and boiled lake water for our hair. In the washstand bowl, and using a ladle, she lathered our hair with Herbal Essence shampoo, so that we smelled of a haymow; she had us wear our swimsuits while she poured water over our necks and scalps, so we wouldn't wet our clothes.

"You're both gonna knock their socks off," said Alice. "Aren't they, Jane?"

Theresa sat and brushed her hair until it was almost completely dry, and I did the same thing with my brush, although my hair would not lie straight, as hers did. Hers was as uncurled and flowing as Cher's, whereas mine was more like Arlo Guthrie's. But Alice produced a magic potion – Curl Free – and sprayed it all over my frizzy-even-when-sodden locks, and commanded me to keep brushing. The scent of the straightening lotion, combined with the Herbal Essence lawn-clippings scent, was bizarre, as if vinegar had been poured over lilacs.

"This is a great product," she said. "I gotta use it on my hair or I just have one big frizzpile. But when Janey told me you were going to the dance, Dee, I thought you kinda might wanna try doing something different with your hair."

"Yeah," I said.

Then she did a curious thing. She cleared her throat, and her voice took on a stentorian tone, and she said, "It's really for Negroes, this stuff. You know, Negroes have stopped trying to look like Caucasians. They're saying 'black is beautiful.'"

She paused, obviously waiting for some sort of reply, but I had nothing to say. There were no Negroes on my street, and only half-a-dozen in the school, and they never said anything like "black is beautiful." I glanced at Theresa, but she was concentrating entirely on brushing any hint of undulation out of her hair. She merely rolled her eyes at Alice, who narrowed her own eyes in reply, daring Theresa to say anything.

So if I had nothing to say, and Theresa was forbidden to comment, that left Mum. I realized it was *she* who was supposed to speak. And she spoke.

"The movement of the Negroes is a lot like the women's movement." She spoke without expression or intonation, as if reciting from the Bible. "They have been kept down, denied the vote, refused the right to property, had their valuable labour stolen from them, and had their voices silenced, ever since they were brought to North America. Women have similar problems to resolve. It has been suggested that the women's movement organize around the Black Power model. Do you think this is a good idea, Alice?"

"I do, Janey, I do. We often have a common oppressor." Alice gave my hair a particularly hearty tug. "God, this stuff is like steel wool."

"How come Negroes don't have to straighten their hair, but I do?" I said.

Alice leaned over and looked into my face, studying me, eyebrows raised with bemused interest. "Well, Dee baby, you *want* straight hair," said Alice. "Negroes don't need it or want it. It's the difference between fashion and cultural prohibition."

"How do you know I want straight hair?"

Alice stopped brushing. "I'm sorry, Pet, I assumed you did. I'll stop."

"No, no!" I cried. "Don't stop!"

Alice laughed and started brushing me again, for the Curl Free was working and even though it stank, having Alice fondle my hair was a marvellous feeling. Not since I was a little girl had anyone brushed my hair, for my mother had made it clear very early on that I was to tend to my own nest. She bought me Tame creme rinse, for the matted tangles that always developed as I washed it, but she hadn't brushed my hair for me in ages.

"Jane," said Alice, "Dee's brought up a good point, don't you think? Why does she want her hair brushed straight?"

"Because she has learned her sex role," said Jane.

Theresa and I both protested, me in a voice that was nearly croaking in its alarm. "I've never had sex!"

"Me neither!" said Theresa.

Alice, for some reason, guffawed at this, but she kept tugging away at my hair. "I agree with Jane. Dee, you've already learned your role. By sex role, Jane means – well, Jane, what do you mean?"

"We women have certain roles that are linked to our sex. We believe that we must be beautiful in order to be women. We have to be beautiful in a way that attracts men. We do not decide about our own beauty because we are objectified. Objectified means that we have become the objects of male desire and that means everything we do becomes a service for the patriarchal status quo. This has been a problem for women who are considered beautiful. We attract an intense gaze that is impossible to avoid, and it inhibits our development as full human beings."

I looked at Theresa, who was frozen in mid-stroke, gawping at our mother. "Mum, are you all right?"

"Yes," said Jane. "See, Alice, what I go through?"

Alice nodded. "Theresa's still young, Jane, and think of the disadvantage being pretty was to *your* life. Like we were discussing awhile back, it's a curse in a lotta ways. You get all wrapped up in the bull, and the sales pitch, and the next thing you know, you're doing nothing but spending half your life trying to look gorgeous. Sit still, Dee."

"Now wait a minute," Theresa started. "What's this about the curse?"

"Never mind, dear. Just brush your hair," said Jane.

"I got something to say," I said, squirming around to look at Alice, who had actually succeeded in calming my hair to a wavy tide of black, very gypsylike, very unlike me. Alice crossed her arms and gave me the attentive-mother look she always used to give Richard, when he had an intelligent question to ask.

"Being pretty is *much* easier than being ugly," I said.

"I'm not disputing that," said Alice. "But what's good about things being easy? Easy gets you nothing except spoiled, and spoiled means rotting, gone bad, you know. Life's no fairy tale. Being a princess is being in prison. You use your head, Dee, your whole life – that'll get you places. This decorate-your-body stuff, it's okay, it's fun, but it's your brains'll get you places. Be glad you got brains instead of looks – aw, shit, I didn't mean it that way. I mean, you keep it up with your writing stories, and your reading, and your good marks, and..."

"Wait, wait, wait!" Theresa slammed her hairbrush down. "Who cares about her good marks! Nobody marries you for good marks!"

"Who says I want to get married!" I spat at her, and Alice slapped me so hard on the back it stung. I thought I'd said something wrong, but then I realized she was congratulating me.

"Ah, Dee, you're a quick ticket, Sweetheart! Isn't she a quick ticket, Jane?"

"I suppose so," said Jane. "She always got good marks. But she was very domestic. She was very good with housework and cooking."

"Excuse me," said Theresa. "But aren't we supposed to be getting ready for a dance? Look at her hair. It's still a mess. And mine's not dry yet. And we're not nearly ready. It's gotta be nearly eight already..."

"Don't fret, Princess," said Alice, with just the slightest hesitation between *fret* and *princess*.

"You're not going to turn into a pumpkin."

She launched into song, the fairy godmother's song: *Bibbidi, Bobbidi, Boo!* She threw her entire body into it, conducting with her arms and bellowing in a tenor-ish voice. Jane hummed along as she helped Theresa put on her foundation and blush, which Jane still called rouge. I was completely bewildered, because both Jane and Alice were tending to Theresa and me as if the talk about ugly and pretty had not gone on, and besides, the talk had got me thinking about itchy, uncomfortable things. Negroes didn't have to change anymore, so why did I? Didn't God make me fat and big and frizzy-haired? How come it was so important to have boys want to kiss me? How come when I danced, I had to dance a certain way, and couldn't just jump around waving my arms, which is what my own rhythm seemed to want? Who, exactly, had declared that I was ugly? That patriarchy thing?

But it wasn't a patriarchy telling me I was ugly. I knew. I saw. I wasn't blind.

"I hah anudder kestion," I said, while Alice painted my lips with shell-pink lip gloss.

"I bet you're full of questions. Attagirl. Shoot." She took away the lipstick, and blotted me, before I spoke.

"How come if this is all just to get the boys to like us, and that's not good because we're supposed to be...well, I dunno, be doing whatever we're supposed to be doing..."

"Reading, writing, thinking," said Alice, filling in the blank.

"Yeah, okay, so. Okay, if it's wrong to be pretty, I mean, to change yourself to be pretty – if pretty is just something the boys came up with and they made all the rules..." I was having a lot of trouble with this, and had to pause to think. "I mean, If I'm only brushing my hair and putting on lipstick so that boys will like me, why do it?"

Alice snapped the lid back on the lipstick. "That is so bright, Dee, for you to notice. Jane, what a bright girl this is. What a smart girl. The answer is big. It goes to anthropology, Dee. Do you know anthropology?"

I knew, from *National Geographic*. "The study of man."

"Yeeesss," said Alice. "That's what men call it. It should be the study of people. But in any event, one of the biggest anthropologists ever was Margaret Mead, and she went and studied tribes all over the world..."

"Boooring!" cried Theresa, from around Jane's attentive, blush-applying form.

"Just ignore her. So Margaret Mead found all sorts of tribes all over that had different ideas about what's feminine and what's masculine. It's culture. What we grow up in."

"Okay, so, yeah?"

"So, what we grew up with is the idea that women are the sex that need to decorate themselves and touch each other. But it's crap. Sorry,

Jane. It's nonsense. Men here in North America would decorate themselves too, and get together and pick fleas off each other's backs like monkeys, except they're afraid it'll make them feminine. Oooh, scary, being feminine, eh, Jane?"

"Oooh, scary," agreed Jane. "Close your eyes, Theresa, your shadow's uneven."

Alice continued. "So, in a way, men have taken over the whole human ritual of body painting, and hair-tending, and decorating yourself with shells and beads and ribbons and penis sheaths..."

"Alice, don't get carried away in front of the girls," said Jane.

"Sorry. But there is a tribe that does, that, Dee, really – they decorate their you-know-whats with..."

"Alice!" snapped Jane.

"I've heard the word *penis*, Mum," I said. "So we're doing something that's not, like, girl stuff, it's like, people stuff, except that because we're not like some tribe in Africa..."

"Mead was more the South Seas, actually," said Alice.

"Auntie Alice, I wanna talk," I said, sharply, because I was rolling along and didn't want to lose it. It seemed important to get this straight. "What you're saying is that the boys control how we dress and stuff and we go along with it, but actually it's just supposed to be, I dunno, it's supposed to be..."

"Fun!" cried Alice. "Fun for everybody, not just the little tiny blondies like your mum and your sister! It's supposed to be way-out, kinky, crazy, out-of-control!"

She grabbed the lipstick and drew a huge garish mouth around her lips, and slashed red lipstick through her eyebrows; then she lifted her shirt and drew an Egyptian-style eye on her soft tummy. She began to belly-dance around the table, holding up her shirt to display the drawing, just as Theresa had danced days before. But from this I turned away, for her stomach was squishy and she looked clownish, not beautiful.

"Stop, stop, Auntie Alice," said Theresa. "You look really stupid!"

Alice roared at her. "Shut up, girl, I'll dance wherever I want to, however I want to!" She turned to me, and her whole face moved as she spoke, emphasized by the paint. "Dee, you aren't ever, ever going to get anywhere because you're cute enough to be somebody's toy! But that is a blessing! That is a blessing! It means you'll never get stuck in the trap your mother did, and I did – for a long time ago, I used to really look good. I did. But goddammit, Dee, it's a lie! Don't fall for it! One day, you wake up and you're thirty, or you're forty, and you've got a kid, and you've got a house, and you've got some dork asshole husband who thinks he knows what's best for you, and you realize – this stinks! This stinks! This stinks!"

These last words she leaned over me to spit into my face, and I held fast, for I had had people shout in my face before. She was acting, however, angry at *me*, when it was Theresa who called her stupid-looking, not me. I had merely thought it.

"Alice, dear, you're overdoing it again," said Jane. "Okay, Theresa, take a look in the mirror and do your touch-ups."

"Theresa could paint her tummy with flowers and dance," said Alice, standing erect and speaking quietly, although somewhat breathlessly. "Why are big, old, heavy women stopped from – Dee, what are you doing?"

I was trying to lift her shirt, for I had seen something odd beside the eye. A shadow of some kind. "I wanna see your eye, it's cool," I lied, and Alice, mollified and flattered, chuckled and lifted her shirt.

"Oh, Alice, oh," said Jane.

Alice frowned, then glanced at herself and understanding dawned. She pulled her shirt down at once, and then tucked it in quickly, as if to lock a door. "Yeah, well, the little fucker can really pack a punch. I should learn to keep my guard up, but that's hard when he always goes for the solar plexus. They never teach us boxing in school – fuck no! They only teach us fucking how to fuck-ing *cook*…"

Alice sank down into a chair and began, dreadfully, to cry. Jane went to her at once, saying nothing about all the fucks, and actually crawled into her lap and looped her arms around her neck. Alice, head lowered to Jane's throat, gave several sobs but quickly pulled herself together, lifting her face away and smiling through the smear of her clown's face. "Sorry, little chickens, sorry. But you're old enough to know. Don't marry in haste. It's hard to get out of. They don't let you get out of it easy."

"You'll get out of it, Auntie Alice," I said, not knowing what else to say. "Don't worry, Auntie Alice."

"Get off me, Janey, you're putting my legs to sleep. Theresa, what's that look for?"

Theresa, hands on hips, was gape-mouthed; shaking her head like a teacher who'd just come back to an unattended class, to find it all in chaos. "You two are pervs," she said. "Mum, you sat on her lap."

"And what if I did?" said Jane, defiantly. "Affection between women is always seen as a heterosexual activity..."

"Homosexual," corrected Alice.

"Homosexual. Yes. Homosexual. But it's not always at all. Women's affection for each other involves much stroking and caressing and physical contact. If men did this, they would not be so violent with each other." She raised her chin, and her next statement was the first that didn't sound read from a script. "They wouldn't punch their wife in the belly!"

"Eww, you guys are grossing me out," said

Theresa, who had stopped listening somewhere around Jane's mention of stroking and caressing. She flung herself at the chest of drawers, snatching up her jeans and her cut-off top, and undressing with almost vicious fervour. "Dee, get your fat bum ready, because I'm going right away. They're going to be here to pick us up and if you're not ready, I don't care what anybody says, I'm going without you."

She threw herself into her jeans and tiny blouse, which would not have covered so much as my upper arm, and slipped her feet into her chunky-heeled sandals. "There," she said, then grabbed her rope of multicoloured beads and draped them over her head, while checking herself in the mirror. "Dee, don't forget your door money. One dollar at the door. Don't think I'm gonna pay for you."

And she was gone, slamming the door behind her, and disappearing immediately into the night. "I better get going," I said.

"Don't you rush on her account," said Alice. "Let's enjoy this."

So Alice dressed me. The mice scuttled along in the rafters, and in the cupboards came their chirps and rustlings, as Jane sat drinking her beer, pinkies extended, watching Alice put a touch of shadow on my eyes, a touch of blush on my cheeks, polish on my short little nails, polish on my piggy little toes. I stood very still while she pulled my blouse over my head, and stepped into my jeans as she held them for me, then pulled them up my legs and did up the button below the still-large shelf of my stomach. She tucked in the tail of the shirt, slowly, walking around me, humming and singing softly to herself, a medley of war songs and show tunes and folk-rock snippets, "We'll Meet Again," and "So Long Marianne." Jane bowed her head, as if praying, and didn't look up; I thought for a moment she was crying, but when I asked her if she was all right, she said something strange, without raising her head.

"I want to look up and see you all at once, in a burst, so I can remember you forever."

Alice, at last, brought me my shoes, the faggy sandals. I put them on and they made me six-foot-one. It couldn't be helped. So I towered there, even taller than Alice, who hung around my neck the sash Theresa and I had chosen, and knotted it daringly, then stepped back and said, "You look great."

"Pretty?" I said, just to make trouble.

My mother looked up, and yes, she had been crying.

"Fuck pretty," she said.

I left them and tottled down the path on my unusual shoes, my lipstick in my purse, which was for decoration and fun, not to please the boys. The path was dark, for Dad and Uncle Dick had not yet lit the fire, which would have thrown light through the forest more than halfway to the cabin, where the illumination from its windows would blend with the fire's glow. Dad and Dick sat on the shore beside the upper landing for the dock, beside the stereo, which was playing a Mills Brothers album. The patio lanterns were burning just fine, spotting the night with anomalous colour.

Theresa stood on the dock's end, arms crossed over herself, teeth chattering in the cold. For the shorty top was not much more cloth than a bikini bra, and the evening was early-September cold.

"Do you want me to get you a sweater?" I offered. I was not cold; both my blouse and my flesh kept me warm.

"These people," she said, not hearing my offer, "make me completely sick. So sick. I hate them all. Auntie Alice belongs in a loony bin. Did you see her dancing around?"

"Of course I did. But Theresa, you yourself danced like I Dream of Jeannie..."

"I'm not some hideous fat old hag!" said Theresa, loud enough for the men to hear, and Dick cried out, "Don't call my wife that!" and laughed gratuitously. I didn't hear a sound from the Dad.

We heard a motor, from a small boat, coming down the channel, and from around the point and the cat's tail string of rocks came a big speedboat, going slow, with one dark figure at its wheel. "Guy!" breathed Theresa, and I looked back at the Dad. He could drive me over, so I would not have to sit in the same boat as my sister and her boyfriend, who would no doubt be cruel and cold and evil, and despoil the evening before it had even begun.

"You girls have a good time," said the Dad, but his voice was lifeless. "I'll hold off on the corn and the bonfire until you get back. Then the party'll really begin, okay? When Webby and Dave and Richie get here, and when you get back, and the girls come down, we'll have a really nice time together..."

His voice trailed off and although Theresa had not noticed anything, but had leaped into the boat and settled in at once beside Guy, I did not like what I'd heard, not at all. "Hang on a second, Theresa," I said, forgetting myself entirely, and I walked back along the dock to where the Dad's dark form sat beside Uncle Dick's, completely in shadow. There were just the two men's shapes, in their chairs, surrounded by the empty chairs in which their friends and their sons and their wives should be sitting...would be sitting.

"Stop there a sec, Dee," said Uncle Dick suddenly, but without too much malice at all. He even sounded gentle, which was not something I'd ever heard from him, not in all the years I'd known him. Then, to my horror, I saw that his hand was on the Dad's arm – circling his bicep – and I could see the connection between them, even in the black night. I saw that my Dad had his head lowered and his other hand on his face, across his eyes. His shoulders shook.

Uncle Dick was a fag. Uncle Dick, Brother Webster, David, Richard, everybody. Numb all over, I turned at once and ran to the end of the dock, where Guy and Theresa were still licking each other hello. The boat lurched as I leaped aboard.

"Guy, this is my sister," said Theresa, much as she might say, *this is a garden slug on my arm.*

"Hi, Dee, you look really pretty," said Guy.

I started laughing, and could not stop. Guy looked at Theresa, who merely shrugged with great, dramatic resignation, and snuggled up against him as he sped us away in his caravel, across the high seas to the light and the action of the Ashleigh's Marina Dance.

Red and green and blue and yellow were the lights from Ashleigh's Marina, and black were the twin mouths of its boat bays, and out from its sides came the arms of its docks, at the points of which stood the gasoline pumps, tall as yours truly and with bulbous glass heads, and clicking meters that measured the essence that poured into the boats' orange-red tanks, and spilled as well across the oil-black water of Barebones Lake. There it loomed, two large storeys high, festooned with Christmas lights that did not flash off and on, but shone their resolute reflections into the water below. The second storey housed the dance hall, and the bar where I craved their 7Up floats; nothing tasted as good as Ashleigh's 7Up floats, which were served in the tin cup and were only fifteen cents! They frothed and bubbled and left a scum of strawberry and cream and sugar on the teeth and the lips, but there would be no floats tonight. Tonight, we will dance, and tonight we will celebrate.

"Celebrate" was the song the band was playing as we ascended the wooden, backless risers of the stairs to the second storey. Inside the marina office, which was a walled-off section of the boat bays, I could hear the Ashleighs' outraged, penned-up Alsatians, King and Rex, tearing at the wooden door, and barking their ferocious, thunderous barks. Even over the music I could hear it, even over the command to celebrate, celebrate, dance to the music.

Theresa and Guy were met on the balcony before they even achieved the pinnacle of the stairs, by a trio of girls not much older than me, who flocked to Theresa like attendants to Venus. None of them was Gail; my heart sank. I considered Gail a friend.

They began their accolades. You look so beautiful, I love your hair, how do you get it so straight, *hiiiii Guy* (this last crooned seductively, followed by giggles and averted faces). Guy reacted by leaving, slipping off into the dance hall without a word, which made them all giggle harder.

I had not been able to leave the second riser down, for Theresa was in my way, so I hung back, waiting for the congestion to clear. Through the brightly lit windows I could see only the backs of the band, and although the lyrics and melody of their song had been identifiable from down below, from here I could understand little, only the wham-wham-wham of the bass and electric guitars. The drummer was thin and dressed in black – he reminded me of a spindly crab, lurking in a hole, behind a reef of steel and circles. He whipped his instruments like a Roman charioteer.

"Let's go in," said one of the girls, but she was looking right at me. Her eyes were at the level of my own, and it took all my strength to hold the gaze. Alice might shout in my face; teachers might thrust their chins against my own and call me insubordinate; but when these girls' eyes hit on me I could not help but cringe. But everything

Alice had said straightened my spine, and I did not look away. I did not have to be pretty; I could dance no matter what I was.

"Who are you?" she said.

"That's Dee. You know…Dee."

Theresa could not even say the word sister, but this girl could. "Oh, your baby sister! Hey, Dee! You lost like a ton of weight! Did you go on a diet?"

"Yes, thank you," I said.

Theresa kicked backward at me and caught me in the shin, but not too hard. I'd realized that the "thank you" was ridiculous the moment I'd said it, so she needn't have kicked me. But the girls didn't seem to mind.

"I'd love to lose ten pounds," said one of them, and I couldn't help but glance at her body. There was nothing there that I could see, so I said, "You don't need to lose anything."

"Oh, I do, I do! I've gained so much weight this summer. I was only one-fifteen in June, but now I'm one-twenty-eight. Can you dig it! One-twenty-eight!"

I had no idea how much I weighed, but two-twenty-eight was not beyond possibility. The discussion, I feared, might turn to me and my weight next, and Theresa had stepped off to the side, motioning me to hurry so that the girls wouldn't drill me any further. She did not want me discovered, it was obvious, but I was obvious too. I didn't know how I could accomplish what she seemed to be expecting: to be this big, and yet be invisible.

"Didn't you used to be taller?" said one of the girls, and then she laughed aloud. "Oh, geez, you're on the step!"

All the girls laughed together, the exact same ah-haha, ah-haha, trailing off to a warbling titter within just a few blows. I nearly turned and ran, but I had come so far, and worked so hard, and besides, David was supposed to be here. He was supposed to play. I wanted, too, to know what about the needle, and what his habit was, and about that other stuff. I needed him to explain, and I knew he would, if I could find him and ask.

So I had to get past the triple-headed harpy, who had stopped laughing all together, like three dolls in a toy shop timed to synchronized display. I realized I had tears in my eyes, and prayed the dimness of the balcony would mean they couldn't see me crying. Crying, as Theresa had told me many times, only made things worse.

"Well, are you coming?" said one of them. "The dance is dy-no-mite."

"The bass player looks just like Paul McCartney."

"Maybe it is Paul McCartney."

"He's dead, you know. That's his double on Sergeant Pepper. You know the car crash in that song, where they sing about reading the news today? Well, that's about the newspaper story about when he died. And the president of his fan club..."

I followed along, listening but not listening, and Theresa fell in beside them. The line of girls curved in on itself, as they approached the door, so that all four of them could listen and talk at once, but when we reached the maw of the dance hall the blasting force of the sound and the smoke and the shouted conversation blew away all talk.

We paid our little green dollar bill, and had marked on our hands an "x" in red ink, so that we might come and go, and pushed our way inside. I had not known that there were this many people on Barebones Lake, or in all of Muskoka. And they were all dancing, so close they were touching, men and women and boys and girls, and halfways in between, many of them naked from the hips up, except that the girls wore bikini tops or halters or cropped low-cut blouses like Theresa's. They whipped their hair around and waved their arms as if swimming, or brachiating through a jungle, or paddling an unruly kayak. Many of them were smoking as they danced. I could not see my way through the crowd, and did not know where we'd sit. The bar where I'd once bought floats and sundaes was blocked by people – a row of backs and fronts, leaning up against it – on the far side of the room. Heads nodded time to the music. The singer, at whom I now looked in the hope it might be David (how could it be? he did not sound like this), was even thinner than the drummer, and so were the two other guitarists. Only the keyboardist, who looked very unhappy beneath his porkpie hat, had any fleshiness to him at all.

They were singing a Doors song that I recognized, but it didn't sound like Jim Morrison's voice, for the lead singer had pressed the microphone up to his lips and was singing into it very wetly, making it crackle. When he moved the mike away a scream of feedback split everyone's ears, and all at once, but just for a moment, the dancing stopped while every soul in the room clapped their hands to their ears. But the band played on, *don't you love her madly, don't you need her badly, want to meet her daddy, don't you love her way, tell me what you say,* slurred over and over, without breaking into the real song.

"Dee!" came a holler in my ear, for I had been standing transfixed.

"What?"

"Come and sit down!"

It was Theresa, of course, making sure I behaved myself, which I was not doing by standing stock-still directly in front of the stage, staring up the lead singer's nostrils. I sighed and followed her once more, fixating on that flaxen mane that fell halfway to her rump. The crowd actually parted as she passed, and many boys and men looked at her as she elbowed and excuse-me'd her way to the booth she'd commandeered: a U-shaped, upholstered, one-piece bench, curving around a table on which sat a Mateus bottle with a melting candle in its spout.

"Sit down there and don't get up all night," she yelled at me.

"What!"

"SIT DOWN THERE AND DON'T GET UP ALL NIGHT!"

At that moment the band crashed its final note, and Theresa's shout managed to fall into that gap completely. Her friends all cracked up, for once all laughing at Theresa, who glared at me as if I were a carrier of contagion.

"C'mon, let's dance," she said, and instantly she and a group of half-a-dozen girls were on the floor, leaving me alone in the booth. The boys (boys? they were not boys, but they weren't men) sat down and all lit cigarettes off the wine-bottle candle. One of them shook his cigarette pack at me. I took it from him, thinking he wanted me to hold it, and he and the others exchanged flummoxed glances before he simply took it back, fairly gently. Only then did I realize he'd been offering me a cigarette.

"I'LL TAKE ONE!" I hollered.

The man-boy shrugged and pulled a cigarette out, which I put in my lips, thank goodness with the filter the right way around. The boy tossed me a pack of matches and, remembering what I'd seen Alice and Dick do a million times, I lit a match and held it to the cigarette. I had heard inhaling was what caused cancer, so I merely sipped a mouthful of smoke, which tasted so appalling I felt both my lips curling. All the boys were watching me, silently in the roomful of din, so I opened my mouth as if to blow a smoke ring (again, something I had seen done). The smoke popped out in a puffy ball.

"THANKS!" I shouted at the boy.

They all turned away, their curiosity satisfied, to watch the girls dance. Oh, I could never have danced like that, with my legs bent at the knee and my head turning coyly, this way and that, and the flat plain of my muscular stomach exposed above a pink shiny-vinyl belt that held up velveteen hiphuggers. I could never have found the strength to raise my hands above my head, so that my arms were straight as flagstaffs, and I could not have found the reason to look down at myself as I danced and admired my own body. My eyes could not have hunted down the faces of the boys, summoning them to come and dance.

"IN A MINUTE, TERRY!" one of them shouted at my sister's silent beckoning.

She mouthed COME ON at him, and then the band swung into *twist & shout*, which caused all the girls to leap around and applaud, as if a celebrity instead of a song had just entered the room. They all planted their feet and began to shimmy, shoulders and hips shivering, and the boys all jumped up with yells like in a game of Cowboys & Indians, bounding each one up to a girl. They paired up and each duo was dichotomy: the man flailed and flung and watched the girl, and the girl stood still, wiggling, barely moving, watching her own body tremble.

Somebody slid in beside me on the empty bench: no one I knew, although I was of course aware of both Richard and David, who had to be here, where else would they be? The boy, who was much like Richard in that he was blond and good-looking, swept his eyes over me, smiled edgily, and then turned away. I took the chance to drop my cigarette on the floor and stamp it out.

I suddenly realized that this was it for me. I was going to sit here all night, with nobody talking to me, except in a sidelong fashion that was bound to broadside me and make me do something laughable. I wanted to go home, right now, except that there was no way. I had brought only three dollars, one of which I had spent getting into the dance, and even if I could get Ashleigh's to provide a water taxi at this hour, it would be at least five dollars. I was stuck, until Theresa made Guy take us home. She might, even, decide to disobey curfew. In which case, I would miss the corn roast, too.

"HEY!" said the boy beside me.

"WHAT?"

"DO YOU KNOW WHAT TIME IT IS?"

"NO."

"OKAY."

He looked around, sighed, and settled back in the bench, almost semi-recumbent. The band seemed to have got hooked on *twist & shout*, for they were playing it again, sounding the long *ahh-hhhhh* crescendo cry for the second time. The

girls who were shimmying had switched to a
modified twist, although Theresa had assured me
during lessons that people did not twist, frug,
monkey, swim, or mashed potato anymore.
Dances with names were *out*. You just danced.
Except you had to just dance just right.

But they seemed to have identifiable names to
me. I could see someone shimmy, someone monkey, someone hitchhike, someone twist. They
could deny that they were following a pattern, but
I could see it. I began to mime some of the movements, sitting in my seat, forgetting that I was not
alone.

"HEY!"

Now what? "YEAH!" I shouted back.

"YOU DANCE?"

I went cold. I had been asked. It wasn't possible. Theresa had said that it might happen, just
maybe, but I shouldn't count on it, because I really didn't have a snowball's chance in hell. I tried
to remember what I was supposed to do, if someone asked, but I could only think of one answer.

"YEAH, I DANCE," I said.

"THEN FUCKING GET UP AND DANCE,
AND QUIT BOBBING AROUND ON THE
FUCKING SEAT. IT'S MAKING ME CRAZY."

I shouldn't have been surprised, or disappointed, or crushed, but it was as shocking as being
dropped off a building. Up, and then down, and
my stomach stayed in the same place despite my
fall. I stayed with it. I sat, I stayed, and eventual-

ly the others came back, for the band was taking a break. They chased away the interloper (THAT SEAT'S TAKEN MAN) and rejoined me.

"Don't you dance, Dee?" one of the girls asked me.

"NO," I snapped.

"Geez, no reason to be rude. Theresa, she's so rude."

"I know. Dee, stop it. Try to act normal – please."

Everyone on the floor who did not have a seat went out onto the balcony, and the Wurlitzer jukebox, which had been hidden by the crowd, was now visible against the far wall, between two groups of benches. A tall blond boy and a group of girls in shorts and halters stood before it, but I could still see its lovely, mysterious lights, and the curved glass rainbow of its upper casing, with its lush, almost cathedral-esque lighting, below which the moving platters were fed 45s, layered like a roll of candy.

Only when I saw the boy reach behind himself and scratch between his shoulderblades did I realize that it was Richard. The girls were telling him what records he could choose, and moving his hands across the buttons, so he could press them, and the girls could say they held his hand.

I turned away, looking back up on the empty stage, where the bandsmen had left their instruments. There, to my surprise, was Brother Webster, setting up a stool and a collapsible music stand. I was about to leap to my feet and wave at him, but then I realized he'd already seen me, perhaps some time before, for he was assembling the music stand without really looking at it, using practised motions, but his eyes were right on me. He smiled when our eyes met, and his Mark Twain mustache raised one arm as he folded the one side of his face into a wink.

"Theresa, Theresa, there's Mr. Webster," I said happily, but she shooshed me.

Too late. "That old faggot," said one of the boys. I had not learned any of their names, for none of them had been introduced, but I knew I was somehow expected to know who they were. Without knowing their names, I didn't feel I could argue with them, but not saying something in Brother Webster's defence seemed like the lowest of cowardices. I had never been brave, not on anyone's behalf. I couldn't start now, among this crew of strangers.

"He's not a faggot," I said, under my breath, the best I could do.

No one heard me, not even the girl right next to me, who was tête-à-tête with the girl beside her. They were comparing fingernail polishes. I did not repeat myself.

But then Brother Webster spoke into the mike, over the song on the jukebox, shouting to be heard. "Hi, kids, we're gonna do something very groovy while the band's off playing it cool, instead of playing it loud, haha. We're gonna have a very with-it singer come up and give you some of the best in protest, in action and in peace, his own original work and a little Dylan..."

The crowd, which had listened briefly, lost interest and went back to its conversation. With great exaggeration I stayed alert and sitting tall, half-out of my seat, so that I could show Brother Webster my unflagging loyalty. I knew David would be all right, once he got up there; the girls alone would ensure lots of attention, just by their drooling admiration. But poor Brother Webster, he was fighting the crowd, and yet he went on oblivious. "I'm going to read you one of my poems, just before we go on," he said, and I lowered myself a little in my seat. A poem!

"A poem," snickered one of the boys.

"A poem," the rest echoed.

And Brother Webster read his poem about a teenage pregnant girl, which he'd let me read once because it had been published, in a little photocopied magazine that cost a dollar fifty, even though a good magazine like *Chatelaine* only cost a buck. The thing was that the poem didn't even mention the girl, or the pregnancy, and Brother Webster had had to explain it to me.

> *A matter of fact and solidity*
> *in amongst digestion and diversion*
> *and not knowing any better*
> *despite what they all say and said*
> *and continue to say, because these things*
> *should not happen, they should not in this*
> *day and age*

He went on above the brou-ha-ha, and beyond the peals of irrelevant laughter and Polish jokes being told at the bar. I applauded furiously, as soon as he'd done, but he didn't seem to hear. He folded up the paper and slipped it into his pocket, smiling to himself, and set aside the girl and her baby, who had a poem about them in which they never appeared.

From nowhere, behind a speaker perhaps, my brother stepped up onto the stage. The stage was only a series of flat, low boxes, elevating the performers a mere foot above the rest of the floor, but David seemed to be a yard above the rest of us. He wore a black, long-sleeved, suede shirt, and black-and-white striped bellbottoms, and sunglasses even though it was dim in the dance hall. He set aside the music stand, on which Brother Webster had placed his poem, for David knew his songs by heart.

"Oh, god, your brother's so cute," said one of the girls.

The first song David sang was an original work (as Brother Webster had said), and he began with only the introduction, "This is called 'Denial.'"

Fool me, and pretend, and say that it can be
Pretend again and look across the empty galaxy
The stars are not there, lover, they died so long ago
That measurement's beyond us

Their ghosts are all we know
Lover, you can fool me. I beg you, let's
pretend...

Some protest song," said one of the boys at our table.

"What's he protesting? Lack of chicks to ball?" another said.

"How do you know he's into chicks?" replied the first.

"Don't be ridiculous," one of the girls piped in, "you're just saying that because you're jealous. Any time a guy thinks another guy's better than him, he calls him a faggot."

"You said it, I didn't," replied the first boy.

I didn't know their names, but they knew more about my brother than I did. David's first song ended, and people applauded; there was attention being paid. The next song was "Blowing in the Wind," which was out, and so was the next Dylan number, to which nobody really listened either, to protest the notion of protest. So then David played "Sit Down Young Stranger" by Lightfoot. His voice was thready throughout it. He even lost his key at the line where the prodigal son carves *does anyone love me?* into the treebark.

That David might sing a song like that – that David might wonder who loved him, too – convinced me only of his acting talent, not that he had any area of his life that pained him. For he was David, my peregrinating big brother, who slammed into our family from time to time, bringing news of the outside world and scary ideas and stories about Communism and DDT and the Chicago 7. He was not the boy of the song, who visited his parents after a long prodigal leave, to find that they knew nothing about him and didn't really want him there at all. Our parents had never turned David away; how could he feel that he wasn't at home. It was such a clever act, that my brother put on.

When the applause died from that song, David did one more, looking at me all the while.

You're lost, little one, lost in the woods
But you like it, you like it, it's home
You're lost, my wee giant, my ancient-eyed Druid
You're afloat in the gloom and the gloam...

By halfway through the song, the audience had lost interest again. When David finished, he packed up his guitar and case without thanking the audience, who by then had returned completely to their private conversations. He did not even say goodnight. Brother Webster met and greeted him as he stepped off the stage, and I saw Brother Webster's arm slip around David's waist, and David turned his face to Brother Webster's with a grin that was full of gratitude and intimacy. David's hand rose like a ghost and settled briefly onto Brother Webster's cheek. The touches

were so brief, so furtive, that they passed as swift-
ly as baseball coaches' signals, but I saw them.

"Excuse me," I said, standing up. I had to see
David.

"Dee, sit down," said Theresa. "The band's
about to start."

"I have to pee," I pronounced, very loudly,
which did exactly what I thought it would do – a
path cleared at once as the boys almost leaped out
of my way. I sidled down the bench, and the
moment I was free and upright I determined I was
not sitting down again. No way.

I ran across the dance floor, and to my horror
the floor actually shook beneath me: the boathouse floor was no more than plywood over
rafters. I had not noticed it trembling when it was
full of dancers, but when I passed over it, the
reverberations were audible. I heard a voice give
the Fat Albert call, *heyheyhey*, and I kept moving,
bursting out onto the balcony with such impetus
that I ended up belly-first against the opposite rail.

I looked this way and that, but could not see
David or Brother Webster. The balcony was a
widow's walk, extending all around the boathouse,
and I hurried along the one side, and then the
other, certain they could not have gone far. Then,
in a corner of the parking lot below, where the forest edged up against the cleared gravel field on
which the Ashleighs' customers parked, I saw the
interior lights of a car. And just before the band
struck up again, I heard David's voice.

"I'll miss you so much," he said.

Where was Brother Webster going? I shouted *hi you guys*, as lightly as I could, for something about their moving in the semi-dark, in secret, told me they did not want to be discovered. They looked up and David said, "Oh, shit," mildly but sadly.

"Hello, Dee," said Brother Webster, calling up to me. "C'mon down."

So down I went, careful not to trip on the hems of my bellbottoms, which swam over my feet like a gown. I ran across the parking lot and threw my arms around Brother Webster, who hugged me back for much longer than he ever had. Then he pushed me from him and held me at arm's-length, my shoulders in his hands, smiling, his eyes gleaming in the glow from the car's dome light, and the light from its open trunk.

"You look beautiful," he said.

"I do not, but thanks anyway," I said. "Where are you going, Brother Webster? This isn't your car."

Brother Webster's car was a sports model, red and shiny and foreign, and unusual enough to gather the neighbourhood boys in a circle around it when he came to visit in the city. This car was a Rambler four-door sedan, very sedate, pale yellow but looking white in the darkness. It was an old-woman car, reliable, and it had in its open trunk and rear seat the duffle bag, the boxes of music, the big hat, the sheepskin coat, the knapsack, the notebooks, and the guitar which belonged to my brother.

I realized whose car it was. I didn't care how he'd got it, only that he was going away in it, again. "David, David, where are you going?" I said. "David, you only just got back, why do you always have to go?"

"Aw, poor Dee, don't cry," he said.

But for once I was not crying. Crying was for the Fat Albert call and for the laughter; what David was doing did not make me cry. If anything, I was angry: he was leaving, and he hadn't proven Theresa a liar about the faggot thing, or come to the Dad's party. The poor Dad, who would be waiting at the corn roast, expecting him to come home, counting on it.

"The Dad's gonna be so mad next time you come back, I betcha he doesn't let you back in," I said.

"Dee, honey, listen very carefully. I'm not coming back. Ever, ever. I'm going to California, and I'm not coming back." He looked at Brother Webster, who had covered his eyes with his hand, as if it were the brow of a cap. "I have a little money and I have some songs, and I cannot, cannot, cannot stay here one more minute."

"Not here? What here? What do you mean by here?"

"Dee, I could take a hundred years to explain. But you're gonna hear from me, or about me anyway…"

At this Brother Webster gave a choked sob, and I looked at him and saw his inclined head and his shaking shoulders. David made a cooing sound and went to him, putting his arms around him and letting him sink his face against his collar. "I thought I could keep you, I was so wrong to think that," Brother Webster said, and David hushed him, *shhh*.

There in the dimness, bitten by mosquitoes, shielded by the glowering black maples that stalked around the parking lot, rustling and muttering, they held onto each other and cried in man-sounds, which were much like chuckles, and their hard strong hands sunk into one another's backs, tearing at their shirts.

"You saved me," said David. "You know that. I'm sorry I can't stay, I'm sorry we won't be together…"

"Shhh," said Brother Webster. "Just don't forget me, David, no matter what, please. As long as I'm in your head, I'll know I exist."

"Never forget you," said David as he pulled away, and stood before Brother Webster, face both red and wet. They held each other's hands and met each other's eyes, and touched each other's faces, not crying with sobs but crying with a worse pain, a sort of silent tear-drenched smiling agony that was the prelude to their finally letting go. Something had to break them apart; someone had to trigger their separation.

At that moment, the band upstairs blew into

massive life. A screaming electric chord, and "Wild Thing."

"I'm gonna kill the battery on your gift if I keep those lights running like that," said David. "I gotta go, this is killing me."

He pulled his hands away and Brother Webster let him. Suddenly Webster grabbed me around the shoulder and drew me against him, his arm around my shoulder, crushing me. I was as tall as he was and I realized that he needed to hold on to something while David closed the trunk and the car's back door, and climbed behind the wheel.

When David touched the key, Brother Webster inhaled a strength-giving breath. David turned the key. Brother Webster's arm held me tight against him.

"Hey, Dee," said David. "Don't forget to tell Theresa I said goodbye."

And suddenly, the penny dropped. Somehow Theresa had done this. This had to be her doing: David's precipitate flight. She had scared him away, with her talk of faggots and sneaky habits. I remembered the boy on the dock who'd called David a fairy. All her friends she would have told, and soon the Dad and Mum would know, and this was her revenge on him: her revenge for making her take me to the dance. *She had told.*

As the red taillights of the Rambler bounced down the lane and into the tunnel of trees that hung around the lakeshore road, I stood seized by

Brother Webster, shivering as if with cold. The mosquitoes landed on my neck and throat; I felt their velvety displacement of air as they fluttered their wings over my cheeks. Theresa's power lurked above it all, over the marina, over the parking lot, and over us. It laughed in the dust of the departing yellow car. Her tongue and her trickery had blown away my brother, like so much fluff from a late-summer dandelion, after you make a wish.

I pulled myself away roughly from Brother Webster, and he shook himself all over like a wet dog. "Sorry, Dee, did I hurt you?"

"No, you didn't hurt me," I said, starting back to the dance hall. "I don't get hurt by stuff like that."

I started up the stairs, holding up my bellbottoms so I could watch my toes on the risers. He had said to tell her he said goodbye. So I had a message to deliver, from our brother. And possibly, if I could find the courage, one from me as well.

I plunged back into the storm of souls, looking for my sister. The folks at the door wanted to see my hand, and the red mark that would make me one of the crowd, and I flashed it at them on the back of my fist. I could see no one I knew, no one at all, and the booth where my sister had been seated was now filled with a different crowd. I pushed and shoved and tumbled around the room, while the band played "Bad Moon Rising." I thought of Richard, and wondered if he could dance blind. He was not where he'd been, at the jukebox, but I saw Gail and the other girls who had been at the dock that day.

"HI!" Gail shouted when she saw me. "IT'S A BLAST, ISN'T IT! ARE YOU HAVING FUN AT YOUR FIRST DANCE?"

"YES. DO YOU KNOW WHERE THERESA IS?"

Gail shook her head. I thought she meant "no," but she meant she hadn't heard. I had to shout it again, leaning into her ear, and then she leaned back to me and said that Terry – their name for my sister – had gone out to Guy's car a few minutes ago.

"YOU JUST MISSED THEM," she said. She glanced at the other girls. "WE'RE GONNA DANCE. YOU WANNA DANCE?"

She looked up at me, so guileless and trust-worthy. The other girls hung back, chewing gum and quietly assessing the moment.

I did want to dance. I had been practising all summer, and "Bad Moon Rising" had been a song I'd liked from the first time I'd heard it on my portable radio – it reminded me of werewolves, and I would have, had it been a song of other times, used it as part of my conjuring of Wolfgirl. I could dance to this, I knew I could, with Gail-who-could-be-trusted.

"C'MON, IT'S OKAY, DEE," she shouted, leaning in to me so that the shout had the feel of a whispered aside. She put her hand on my arm, and said, barely loud enough to be heard, "Pretty blouse," and so that way she lured me to the dance floor, a distance of only a few steps, and yet as far as the moon.

How do you start to dance? What motion thrusts you into the movement and particulars of a dance that has no name, which is not supposed to mean anything or have any recognizable actions? We were to be free, and to dance inter-pretively, Theresa had said, but it seemed to me that the others knew what they were supposed to be doing, and I did not. There, out there, the beat and the pulse of the music was exactly the beat and the pulse of the dancers; they flung their arms up when the music demanded, and swayed their hips and shrugged their shoulders, and their feet moved so fast and with such clever use of toe and heel and leaping. I was not used to moving. I shirked, I skulked, but I did not move.

All I had to go on was the tricks Theresa had

taught me. To move my hands before my chest, as if I were milking a cow; to move my feet in a side-to-side shuffle, "in time" with the music. But how did I launch this, how did I get off the ground?

"CUT LOOSE, DEE, YOU'RE NOT MOVING!" cried Gail. She raised her hands above her and writhed.

I lifted one hand to collarbone level, and lowered it, and then raised the other, then lowered it. I moved my feet from side to side in a movement that felt like lumbering. But Gail shouted, "THAT'S IT, SHAKE IT, DEE!" and she began to do a hop, a pony-trot bounce, with her knees up like a hackney horse's, and her arms to her sides, hands at right angles. I almost stopped lumbering to watch, for it was as if she were in a ring at the circus, with a headdress of pink feathers, although that was just the effect of the lights on her hair. She wasn't really all elastic and candy floss; she was only human, as I was about to discover.

I moved, I did, taking my feet from the ground, feeling their weight, setting them down again. The beat, the beat is the key, Theresa had said, as we listened to song after song on the wind-up 45 rpm record player, and practised clapping our hands (or rather, mine) to the rhythm. Moving my feet was just like clapping my hands, but I was to remember that clapping my hands or snapping my fingers was out. I was not to do anything that was out.

Gail and her two girls leaped around me in a circle, shaking their serious heads of seriously straightened hair, and around us the crowd made a little room. They were smiling, but I did not feel malice in their smiles. I moved my feet with more height and raised my hands with more determination, and then they were over my head and I swung them back at forth. The band went on to its next song, "Mama Told Me Not to Come," which the girls knew by heart, and they roared out the words, audible even over the band. A song about a crazy party.

You were warned not to come...

They were rollicking around me. None of them was more than shoulder-height on me; in fact, I could see over the heads of most of the crowd, for they were, after all, only kids. Just teenagers. Just having fun.

I could not see Richard anywhere, although Theresa, I saw, was back, and standing in the doorway. Guy stood right behind her, bending over very far so he could thrust his face into her neck. Her hair was tousled. Absent-mindedly Guy showed the gatekeeper his mark, as did Theresa, and in they came, and the crowd let them in. Theresa met and greeted, and I saw her lips pull back over her teeth in a grin which no doubt also formed a squeal: she had seen someone she knew and was greeting them. I saw the other person – a girl – hug her.

"DEE, DON'T JUST STAND THERE, DANCE!" Gail was hollering at me, and guiltily I started to dance once more, milking the cow and shuffling my feet. But I kept my eye on Theresa as she moved into the melee, shaking her elevated hands in time with the music, and singing along with abandon. *Mama told me not to come...* She made her way to the centre of the hall, below the pink-and-yellow floodlights which the Ashleighs had hung years ago, when they started doing dances. Jaundiced, infected, she pushed away the others, saying give me space, give me room. And they did.

The girls around me filed away, off in a line through the crowd, drawn to Theresa, who saw them approaching (dancing as they walked), and she gave them her welcome of split-faced grins and monkeylike screeching. Horrible, horrible she was: liar, betrayer, dangerous girl. My head spun; I had not eaten since morning, in an effort to get my belly to lie flat over my jeans. It had not worked. I was still bulging and obese and bigger than them all. Nothing would ever change that; I would always be a giant. I would always surge; I would always loom. There was nothing I could do about my own monstrosity. Starvation had left me only thinner; my feet and my hair and my face and my hands and my mind and my soul were all unchanged. Theresa had merely dressed a troglodyte in finery, and taught it to do a jig.

As I came closer, I heard Gail say to Theresa, "YOUR SISTER LOOKS SO COOL! YOU'VE DONE SO MUCH FOR HER!"

Bitch betrayer, just like Theresa, I thought, as I swung my hand to push her aside. She fell back and may have fallen over, but she collided with another dancer, who broke her impetus. There was a scream, more a bellow, from the girls around Theresa, although Theresa did not scream. She had her eyes on mine, her lion-tamer eyes, and she said, "DEE, WHAT THE FUCK ARE YOU DOING!" But she backed away a single step, into Guy, who also backed away a step.

"HEY, YOU FUCKING FREAK, SETTLE THE FUCK DOWN!" he said.

I was to tell Theresa goodbye, from David, but I couldn't speak. All I knew was that Theresa had driven him off, with her secrets and her sneering about fags and spoons of sugar. Now my voice shrivelled in the cigarettes and loss. I watched my huge hands grab Theresa's hair, and then she did scream, as she sunk her fingers, nails first, into my wrists. The sensation of those nails punching through my skin, and into the flesh below, held no pain, only fascination, as did the odd, almost crunchy feeling of tearing her hair away from her scalp.

She was full of words. "MY HAIR, MY HAIR!" And hanging from my hands, she kicked at me, in the shins, and she sank her claws in deeper, and she horked and spat like the boys back home in the city, who would draw a hefty wad of snot from their sinuses and leave glistening smears on the sidewalk. Mum said only the basest of people spat, but Theresa knew how to do it. *Hochptui*, they said in *Mad* magazine, and this was the sound Theresa made, which I heard because the band had stopped playing, and the crowd was chanting *fight fight fight*. The spit dribbling down along my jowls did not make me drop her.

In the schoolyard, when a fight broke out, the kids would flock like iron filings to a magnet. Here, the crowd parted, giving lots of room. I should have fallen, for I was weak and dizzy, and my run up the stairs and my dancing had drained me without my knowing it. But I had Theresa by the ears and hair and I was shaking her like I might have shaken a doll that had transgressed in some imaginary game. Her feet were flailing above the tiles that covered the plywood that had trembled beneath my tread. She did not cry for help, but she called me my names: *fatso, pig, idiot, cow, jerk*. And she gave me my orders: *let go of me, let go, let go*.

I did not obey. It seemed to go on forever. Then the band struck up a number from *Orpheus in the Underworld*, and I shook her in time to the music. Only a few shakes, for my arms were weakening, and suddenly her feet found purchase on the ground. She released my wrists and began to punch me in the face and the stomach. She was a cheerleader and she played field hockey; she swam and she romped and she water-skied. She was twice the girl I was, when it came to striking blows. A punch landed right in my diaphragm, just as Guy grabbed her and several men grabbed me, and they separated us. I heard them laughing about cat fights.

"Cat fights *cow*," someone corrected.

The men holding me – three of them, including Mr. Ashleigh, who was a big bald man of fifty, with a belly much larger than my own – all laughed. "They're sisters," said Mr. Ashleigh. "Believe it or not, those two are related."

"The princess and the pig!" someone said.

Lots of laughter. Theresa was crying or pretending to cry, covering the bald patch I'd left in her hair, as Guy cradled her and helped her away from me and into one of the booths, soothing her. The blonde lock itself lay on the ground, and I heard Gail say, "Look what she did. She's crazy." I glanced at the sound of her voice and saw her watching me, from the protective nest of the other girls and one or two boys, and she had her hand to her cheek, nursing it.

I had bloody half-moons in my wrists, three on one and two on the other, where Theresa had managed to pierce me.

"Ya settled down yet?" one of the men said. They were not teenagers, but as old as my father, perhaps older. They had come from nowhere, and they were dressed in polyester shorts, and short-sleeved shirts of different prints of plaid. They smelled of aftershave and Brylcreem.

I said nothing, as the wildness left me. All

around me, a throng of staring faces, and the lights were turned up as is done when a fight breaks out at a dance. The musicians were unconcerned, taking the opportunity to re-tune their battered instruments. The dancers were amused. They stood with their arms crossed, tossing their long sweaty hair away from their faces, waiting to see what would become of me.

"I said, ya settled down?" Tentatively, the men's grips on my arms loosened, and they began to herd me towards the door. I saw now that one of them was the gatekeeper, who had abandoned his post to come break up the fight. I knew that my red mark would not be getting me back inside.

"I'm gonna call your parents," said Mr. Ashleigh. "I'm tellin' them what trouble you are. Big thing like you, hittin' your little sister."

"You can't call them," I said, and my voice sounded muffled to me, as if shouted down a long cardboard tube, such as comes wrapped in Christmas paper. "They're on an island."

"Don't you mouth off to me, you. Go settle yourself down somewhere that you can't cause trouble." The music started up, a slow number that I didn't recognize at first. Keyboard notes. "Don't know how you're gettin' back. If I were your sister, I sure wouldn't be taking you."

They left me on the balcony, and returned to the dance. Many people had followed us, and were hovering around the entrance, watching to see what I'd do next. I turned my back on them and headed for the stairs. Standing there, at the top, I counted them as the song unfolded. There were thirty-eight steps. It was a long, not-very-steep, wooden set of stairs. Down to the lake, it took me.

The last song I heard, sitting down by the water, was called "Easy." One last song, asking me – me, who couldn't answer – how people could be so heartless. How they could be so cold.

Easy. Easy to be cold.

I was cold. I was so cold. There on the dock's end, behind the looming metal form of the gas pump, my toes in the water, my shoes thrown away. Faggy shoes. Poor faggots, no one wanted them. They had to hide and leave, poor faggots. But it was their own fault. All they had to do was not be faggots.

How can people have no feelings?

The gas pump was rusty and painted green, with a big BP insignia on it and a single rubber arm that hung down in a loop at its side. I strung the rubber hose around my throat, where my pretty scarf lay against my skin, and the band asked why it was so easy to say no.

The lake wobbled like a gelatinous thing, like the Blob in the movie, dark water that I might have walked on, had I been weightless. Black and pseudo-solid, it wrapped around my feet to the ankles, warm as bouillon left to sit in a mug on the counter back home in the city, where I would be going tomorrow night. Packing – tomorrow we would be packing. The whole day would pass in the sorrowful activity, but first I would have to explain how I had torn apart Theresa. Would anyone understand? No. There was no one.

I need a friend...

Richard, once, would have understood, but if Richard had been the boy he once was, if he'd been with me all summer, I would not be at this dance. I would be leaving for the woods...but no, I knew now it would never have happened. But perhaps, all the growing I might have done, in the arms and eyes of someone who loved me, might have involved something else. Less shrinking. Less starving. More building. What might have been, if only I'd had one friend.

Up above me the sky festered with stars. Oh, what remarkable things they were, considering that they were dead – dead they glittered, dead they shone, dead they danced with one another. Some of them, dead as the rest, raced across the sky. They raced that way a million years ago; they burned into cinder but the news of it only reached me now. I was always a little behind that way. I was always so out of it.

Red taillights moved away from me, in my recent memory. Gone, too.

How would I cope on Tuesday, walking into that school where Theresa would have to explain the bald spot in her hairdo. She'd hide it with a flower, but expose it to certain souls, who would shrill a sympathy at her having a crazy sister.

Maybe she'd make up a story – *my sister's epileptic and she doesn't know what she's doing* – so that I would be sick and crazy as well as fat. I could see the faces of those others already, and behind me on the balcony, in the real and present moment, a girl's voice said *oh Terry it was awful poor Terry are you okaaaayyyy....*

Across the black wobbling water with its stars and its moon trapped in its glue there lay my island. I could see only the corner of it, from around the point of the Bald Face, from which Richard and I had once imagined we might dive. We would dive from its hundred-foot summit; we would be like the man on the Timex commercial who did daredevil things but kept on ticking. When we hit the lake we'd be like swords slicing into it, and we'd go down very far and come up very fast.

I wanted to swim to the foot of Bald Face. The real foot, the foot two hundred feet beneath the surface. I was a good swimmer, buoyant and insulated. I never sank and I never got cold. My island was only across the water, only across the bay. A big bay, a bay that sometimes filled so high with waves that we would be stranded until it settled down. A bay that the fog rolled across on June mornings, when the water was still cold but the air had grown so warm. Now the air was cold and the water was warm.

Easy...

...so cold...

I edged my way off the end of the dock, sinking into the morass of warmth. It only feels warm, Richard would have said; it's because the air is cool. Autumn is coming. Don't be fooled, that water's actually pretty cold. Let's get a thermometer and check the temperature. Let's make charts and see how warm the water gets in different parts of the lake. Let's lower a thermometer down and see how cold it is down deep. It feels colder down deep, doesn't it, Dee?

Yes, it does, Richard, it feels a lot colder.

I began to swim, in my beautiful party clothes, which dragged like sodden towels. I could see the island's tip, and imagine the bonfire and the sweet corn with butter. David singing and Brother Webster clapping his hands and the Dad smoking his pipe and Mum beneath her blanket in a lawn chair and Alice at her feet and Richard bringing me a bullfrog he'd found and hypnotized with a flashlight. My island, my island, my island, I chanted, as I swam my personal stroke – part sidestroke, part breaststroke, but always with my head where I could breathe – out into the bay, towards home.

I knew not to swim without a buddy. But there was another piece of nautical advice of which I was unaware: *land is always farther away than you think*.

I knew things about swimming. I trusted it. I knew that if my canoe were to flip I was to stay with it, clinging to its upended hull, and not to attempt to make it to shore. But I was such a good swimmer. So buoyant. So I never paid any attention to the admonition that we shouldn't leave the boat. Instead, Richard and I would flip it on purpose, to feel the joy of hitting the water. And we always swam to shore. We righted our canoe and – with its body full of water – we'd drag it to the beach and empty it, then climb aboard again, paddling out deep enough that the lake was no longer see-the-bottom-green but deeper-than-deep blue. Ready, set, go, we called. I always did the tipping because I was the biggest and could get the boat swaying more easily. We hit the water together, we came up together, we floated on our backs and listened to the Dad yelling from the dock that if we sunk that canoe, it was coming out of our allowances, did we hear?

But now my jeans were pulling me down. I couldn't kick very well. The bellbottoms – sailors' garb – slapped and wrapped around my calves. I paused, to see how far I was, but I was less than halfway there. I could swim to Bald Face, but there was no place to climb onto shore at Bald Face. There was no land closer than my island.

Where was the fire? The Dad should have lit it by now, and the flames on the point should be visible. Fireworks, too, he would have lit, as he had on Dominion Day. But the island was dark except for the patio lanterns, which were no larger in my sight than were the pinpricks of Christmas lights back at Ashleigh's. Why was the Dad waiting? I treaded water, and my head sank to the lips. I was not floating the way I was used to. The scarf tangled around my elbows. I flipped onto my back, and kept swimming.

For a few minutes I tried kicking along on my back, but when I turned over to check my progress I found I had swum the wrong way, and quite a ways wrong as well. I had been watching the stars, waiting for a comet, so I could make a wish.

I wish I was back on the island and this had never happened.

Nothing to do but keep going. What a strange substance water is, running over your fingers and over your face; nothing else like it anywhere. A whole lake of it, a huge tub carved in the Earth and filled with billions of gallons of the stuff. Wonderful water, to sink into; I tilted my head back to see what would happen next. I floated still, just enough, my face the only thing exposed to air. The water drifted into my eye sockets. The water seemed warm as a bath, and my face began to slide beneath the surface. A single strong kick brought me to air again, but I had to keep the kicking going to stay above water.

It was then it struck me: I was not strong enough to kick all the way to shore.

"Help," I said, and louder: "Help!" The stars all stared from their coffins a zillion miles away. News of my drowning wouldn't reach them for years. Under I went once more. How could it be, that when I dived, the water forced me up, but when I wanted to swim, the water pulled me down?

The Reverend's voice rang in my ears, through the crackling invasion of water. "You're bound for the Lake of Fire, Dee," he said. "That's where suicides go."

"I'm not a suicide," I said, "it's a mistake." But the shock of the imagined voice pushed me to keep kicking, with my dragging sodden clothes pulling at my limbs. I could see that I was not so very far from the island's far end, the tip where Auntie Alice and Jane would have their girl-talks, where the Dad parked his fishing canoe. I knew a rocky reef extended out from that promontory. I could make it that far; find a submerged rock to stand on. I thought, it was only a little ways more.

It's farther than you think. I was so close to the island, suspended by the water over the reef: the water that would let me sink so I could touch those rocks, but would not let me float so I could touch the air. The boulders were just inches below my feet; when I slipped beneath the water my toes kicked their solid forms. I was dangling over them like a condemned man in the gallows.

Dad help, daddy, help. I struggled, smashing the surface now with just my arms, because my legs were being pulled below by the clutching water. Another betrayal: I had always been friends with this stuff. *Stop it,* I told the lake. *Let me go.* Slapping it for its treachery. Useless. Weak. Drowning.

"Richard," I said, with my last loudness. My arms drifted out from my sides. My legs pointed downward. My head slipped back; the water tugged my drenched, well-brushed hair.

"I'm right here," he said.

The prow of a canoe loomed out of the black of the lake. It came right out of the water, made of water it seemed, and it headed straight for me. No one was driving it. It was an empty canoe, made of night sky and black water, and it had Richard's voice propelling it.

It went right by me as I watched. Now I could see, when it passed alongside, that Richard was in its stern, paddling. He wore his dark glasses.

"Jesus," he said. "Jesus, Dee, where are you?"

"Here," I said.

He backpaddled. "Where? Keep talking. Fuck, this is scary. Dee, keep talking."

"I can't."

"Then splash. Fuck, Dee, splash or something. Where are you?"

I'll swim to you, I thought, but could not say

it, and I couldn't swim either. Richard lifted the paddle from the water; I could see the diamond-tinted water droplets plunging from the blade, seizing moonlight as they went. I slid through the water towards him. He heard me. He sunk the paddle into the lake and steadied the boat, waiting, trying to stay still and not drift.

"C'mon, Dee," he said.

I'm coming, I'm coming.

My hand touched the sweet, silky gloss of the canoe's lacquer. The canoe tilted as I clutched it, and Richard said, "Can you hold on?"

I lifted my other hand out of the water, into the now-cold air. Both hands trembled in the chill. "I can, I think," I said.

At the sound of my voice, Richard threw back his head and exhaled a huge breath, the sort that would earn him a cloud of white and a WHEW in the *Archie*s. I didn't, however, have the strength to hold myself away from the canoe's flank, so that I could watch him. All I could do was hold onto the gunnel and kick, feebly, at the grasping, thwarted lake.

"Which way is the island?" he said.

I myself could hardly tell. "Sort of behind you."

"Okay." He sank his paddle and turned us, and although his trajectory was off, before long my feet struck rock again, and my toenail dragged across the rough surface of the submerged guard. I let go of the boat when the water hit waist-deep, and

Richard, slowly, kept paddling. I heard the boat's keel grind against rock, and Richard climbed out into the lake, which was still knee-deep, to drag the boat to shore.

"Dee, say something, so I know where you are," he said. In the night, with everything wrapping up, I could hear his soft voice as if it were beside me.

"I'm coming. Slowly."

"Keep talking, Dee, I told you keep talking."

"In a sec. I'm outta breath." I came slowly out of the deep, not like Venus born from the waves, but like a primordial candidate for life as an airbreather. Richard stood on the rocky shore, beside the canoe which he'd dragged onto land, his head tilted in a posture of listening.

"Hurry up," he said. "I want you safe on shore."

I was knee-deep, but crawling in the kneedeep. The water nudged my dangling belly. *I'm right here, at your feet,* I said, but not out loud. I turned over, and sat back in the water, on the lessgargantuan rocks of the island's far end.

Richard sat down beside me. We were both in the water, sitting on the rocks which had been there for a million years, and would be there for a million more.

"That dance sucked," I said.

"I thought it was just okay," said Richard, taking off his sunglasses and wiping the water off them.

"Can you see at all?"

"Not at night. At night I'm blind as a bat. Dee, what the fuck were you doing? Were you really in trouble? Man, you scared me! I thought it was some hurt animal or something, the biggest beaver in the world, and then I heard your voice. What happened?"

I put my head down on my knees and sat there, like a pear in pudding, unable to begin, and unwilling to say a word about what happened. "What happened" was not something that could be put into a few sentences, spilled out in a matter of ordinary discourse. It was as numerous and as dead as the stars, and as indescribable. And pointless, too – aren't the stars pointless, when you think about it?

"What's the point?" I said. "Oh, Richard."

"Never mind, Dee. Never mind."

We sat, me blinded by my knees and him just ordinary, run-of-the-mill blind, and he said he'd not much cared for the dance, either. He'd come back with Brother Webster, and then the adults had got into a fight, which Brother Webster had started by saying it was him bought the place. Richard didn't know what that was all about, but he sure wasn't going to listen to all that yelling. He came down to the island's far end to get away, and to listen to the loons on the water instead of the loons on the dock, haha.

He still wasn't much good at jokes. It didn't matter; I wouldn't have been able to laugh anyway. Something in me had broken, as clearly and as painfully as a bone might. I tried to identify precisely where it was, that massive injury, but it seemed to have no locus. My skin tingled – had I been burned? Perhaps not. What about my heart? It was drumming hard and slow, as if it were being squeezed. And my guts were liquid. Had I anything in them, my bowels would have let go. I was held together only by the pressure of the air around me, like the weight of a mile of water.

Rising in the night was the sound of argument, from the adults' end of the island. Raised voices talking all at once. Alice crying, "You can't stop us!" Richard shuddered so hard I could feel it, and I tore my head away from its resting place, raising my eyes to the lake. The night, I saw now, had clouded over. It was starless and dark, and the wind had come up.

The Dad's voice, louder than all of them: "I just wanted a goddamn goodbye party! Just one little goddamn party! And look!"

"We better go down there," said Richard.

"Why?"

"To help, I guess. I dunno. He's your dad and he sounds upset. Aren't you worried?"

I shook my head, just once, because that was all I had in me to do.

"Dee, c'mon, get up. I know your life stinks. I know, I know. I was there. I saw."

"How could you see," I growled, thinking he meant what happened at the dance.

"Every day I saw, Dee."

Ah. He meant our whole lives. "But it was bad for you, too."

He shrugged. "Yeah, but it got better. Dee, a lot of that stuff wasn't that bad...now don't make a snorty noise like that. Worse things happen to people. And we did bring a lot of it on ourselves."

"It was *not* my fault," I said bitterly. "And look what happened when I tried."

"What did you try?"

"To change. I tried to change."

Richard shrugged. "You changed."

His tone alarmed me. It sounded accusing. "What's that supposed to mean?"

"You changed. You got mean. And I changed. I didn't need you that badly. I'm sorry, though, for this whole summer – that we never saw each other, you know, that you didn't come hang out with the other guys and stuff. All those years, we were so scared of those kids, and you know, they're okay kids, they're kinda cool..."

"Yeah, if you're a hunk. Jesus, Richard, you really are blind."

Richard laughed. "See what I mean about you getting mean?"

From the far end of the island, Auntie Alice roared, "Forget it, Dad, and just start the fire! It's over! It's fucking over!"

"I guess the Dad's party bombed," I said.

"He was hoping Theresa and David would show. He was practically crying about it, when I pulled up with Webby, and it was only just us two."

"He didn't cry for me."

"He knew you'd come back with Theresa. Dee, you're so paranoid. You think everybody hates you."

There was an obvious reply to that, but I didn't make it. I didn't want to talk to him anymore, but talking to him, hearing his voice, changed as it was...it was what I'd spent the summer missing. How odd to have him here, at the season's end. Did it mean we could be friends again?

"So," he said, "can we be friends again?"

I started a little – just a sharp intake of breath – and he said, "Read your mind, eh?"

"Yes. God, Richard. I missed you so much."

And then I was crying, but not for myself. For the future. For the many days and years I had spread before me, like a carpet of nails to cross. How could I do it, in this body, with this wretched soul, this incompetence? I had never cried like this before; always the tears had been for some sting or some hurt that was as easy to pin as a chloroformed butterfly. *He said, she said, I'm fat, I'm ugly.* But this was a fearful, lost-fawn cry. It was a knowledgeable one. I could hear in my sobs the agonies of the damned, and knew I was one myself. Damned and doomed. Alone my whole life. It would happen, I could see it. It would never be better.

A whippoorwill sang out in the bushes behind

us: the song of an entire species, conjuring pain again and again. The bird would sing that tune for hours, and I could see poor Will; I could feel the whip.

"Poor Dee," said Richard.

How silly, in the water like that: how ridiculous to climb aboard me, across me, as if I were a boat. Richard, sliding himself over across the rocks, and across me next, straddling me. I could not tell, as his leg swung over my hips, that he might have been shorter than me, and that he may have been lighter, but who knows, who knows? It was dark, and I'd been crying. He sat on his knees above me, and I leaned back not from expectation but confusion, what game was this? Richard, astride me; Richard, moving in on me like on the television programs, the movies where the men and women kiss. He was going to kiss me, and I was going to let it happen.

I lay back slowly, catching myself on my elbows, and Richard put his weight on his hands. He was above me, on all fours, and I was on my back in the shallow water, on a bed of stones. I did not care; I had been in worse discomfort. My eyes were open, and even in the cloudy dark I could see him, all those carrots I suppose had enhanced my night vision. Or perhaps I imagined him. Perhaps I imagined it all.

There were explosions and we thought we should get up. He was cold. It was dangerous for him to be so careless with his schedule. He should check his blood sugar, get something to eat. Would I like something to eat?

"Yes," I said.

We stood together, slowly, dripping in the dark, our clothes clinging to us. My scarf a wet noose. His T-shirt diaphanous against his skin. The ecology symbol like a tattoo beneath its drenched cloth. His hand slid into mine. Man fingers, thick with difference.

The explosions were the Dad, setting off the fireworks. As we came down the path, hands still linked, I saw the activity, the five of them, moving around on the dock like a pantomime: Jane and Alice strangely stiff in their lawn chairs, Brother Webster cross-legged at their feet, staring at nothing, his face stony and grim, and the Dad and Big Dick bickering over what device to set off next. Big Dick waved a yard-long paper-and-cardboard tube like a sword, or a teacher's pointer: he wanted *this* one next. They had got a pail of sand from the beach, into which they had stuck the fireworks: phosphorescent supernovas, balls of blue and red, cones of sparkling lava. Whatever the argument had been, it had died down.

Across the water, beyond the booms and cracks of the fireworks, there came the hum of a boat: a powerboat, Guy's fibreglass speedster. The Dad snapped to attention, a pointer scenting a partridge. He peered across the moonless water, his hands in fists of hope.

"Theresa's back!" he cried. "Okay, now we can light the fire!"

He came running up the dock and saw us, coming down the path. I tried to loosen Richard's hand, but he held on.

"Kids, you're soaking," the Dad said, "you been swimming, you little crazies?"

"Yeah. What was all that yelling?"

"Nothing. Nothing. Forget it. Everything's hunky-dory. Hold it right there a sec – don't come any closer – I'm just gonna start up the fire – Theresa's back and the party can start..."

He took the tin of lighter fluid and poured it onto the logs. He was singing a made-up song, *Theresa's here, baby light my fire*, and he sounded quite insane. I watched, feeling Richard's hand in mine, as my father danced around the firepit, sprinkling fluid onto the logs. I could smell its cutting, mildly stomach-churning odour: my head spun all the more from the fumes. He emptied the can completely. Beside me, Richard's nose wrinkled at the stink.

As he danced around the pit, the Dad cried *woowoowoo*, as if playing Indians. I heard the speedster's motor cut down at the dock. Theresa's tattling voice rose clear, preceding her arrival, as she ran to the firepit clearing. No one else was speaking.

"Mum, Dad, everyone!" she trumpeted, triumphant. "You won't *believe* what Dee did..."

Then other things, all at once. The Dad throwing a lit match on the fire. *Woowoowoo*, he yelled, and the pit mushroomed into flame. *Woosh*, said the pit, and at the same time, a big cracking sound from the fireworks on the dock. Then another, far too big, from the firepit, and another, and another, as the shells Theresa had buried there exploded. There were cracks in the night, cracks in the universe, Richard let go of my hand and fell down. Diabetic coma, I thought, but then I saw his glasses were gone, and his face had two eyes open, and one eye more. A strange black hole. Richard twitched, lying there in the path, on the path Theresa and I had swept clear of needles that morning, when we had also organized the whole island for the party, and we had tended to the firepit, and Theresa had prayed beside it. Seemed to pray.

Two more cracks and the bark of a tree exploded, pine sap bleeding, and with the last crack I also heard a whine of ricochet. The last .22 slug must have hit a rock. I stood and stared at Richard's flopping body, at the hole between his blind blank eyes, and the Dad said, from behind the ten-foot blaze in the pit, "Dee, is he all right? What happened?"

And then I remember nothing.

Now Again

I am so tired of this process. I just want it to be over. But I'm afraid. The Lake of Fire hasn't disappeared for me. Is Richard there? Surely not. He was a good boy. Or am I only remembering him that way? Those "happy" memories: they're slippery things. They smile at us, trapped in the liquidy circuits of our brains, bugs in amber staring out at us. Golden memories.

If I die, will I see Richard again? Do I want to? He will still be just a boy. Will he say again that I have changed? That I got mean? That I'm not the person he once knew?

I have to work this out. I have to be strong.

TANTALIZER REPORTER STALKS SISTER. SLAUGHTERS HER IN HONKYTONK.

I forgot my exclamation points.

After that summer of 1970, starting on Labour Day, I spent nearly a year recovering in hospital. I had minor kidney damage: my only traceable physical problem. But as the doctors told the Dad, I was still *mentally sick.* That scared him so much. He didn't know what to do. So he left me in their care, and went home to wait for me to get better.

I did get better. But I never did get back the knack of eating. For a while I ate what they gave me – diet meals, of course, because I was fat, and they felt bound to fix that – but it was like eating dust. And what I ate, I threw up. Bulimia was an ailment unheard of back then, but Richard had heard of it. He once told me about Roman vomitoria. I got the idea from him.

While I was in hospital, Theresa left home, leaving the Dad all alone in that pristine little house on Lindsey. He tried to find her, handing out flyers on Yonge Street, and by putting advertisements in the "personal" column in all three dailies, but she simply didn't come back.

My father never abandoned me, nor I him. Once I was on my feet, he placed me in a private school for girls. He used his Barebones money on my education. I was a year behind everyone else, but since I was born in November, it wasn't noticed. There were two other six-foot girls in the school, and many other ugly ones, and many bright ones. And of course, I was no longer fat. I kept my own counsel, and was left in peace.

After university, I started sending stories out to magazines, freelance writing. Some of Jane's recipes and cleaning tips. A few humorous poems. Short stories, while they were still popular. It wasn't much money, but I didn't need money: I was home, looking after the Dad. In no time I fell into the *Tantalizer* gig. And stayed there.

The Dad never forgave Webster for buying the island, but I did. I met him now and then, for a Tab at the St. Clair subway station coffee shoppe. He had not intended for things to work out like that, he told me. He never thought the Dad would get the money together; he was afraid Mackenzie would sell the island to someone else and then some stranger would have the "little jewel." He wanted to stay forever at Barebones, and build a lovenest for his David.

"Like all old men in love," he said, "I did a foolish thing." But I could see why he'd done it. I would have stolen the island, too, had I had the power.

My mother left with Alice shortly after Richard's funeral. She didn't even come to say goodbye, although Alice, I hear, tried to see me and they wouldn't let her because she wasn't family. At first she and Mum moved into a feminist vegetarian co-op boarding house, until they could find part-time work and enrol Jane at school. They made a large group of friends at once. Alice showed up at the house in Bolton with a U-haul and a crew of consciousness-raising, hairy-pitted harpies, as the Dad reported Dick had called them. She cleaned out all her art and took nothing else. It took five women to hoist Alice's kiln onto the truck, and when they'd done, they all did a ritual pissing on Big Dick's lawn.

My mother earned her high school equivalency, her Bachelor's, her Master's, her PhD, tenure,

and the Orange Prize for literature. She is the
author of five novels, an anthology of essays on
social and literary criticism, hundreds of articles,
and the Governor General's Award for the collection of poetry, *The Kitchen Counter*. Jane's books
are dense but readable, but Alice's work is down-
right angry. I have a print of hers, over my fireplace. It's a pen-and-ink illustration called
Carpathian Christ, and Christ is a woman,
fondling her bulbous yoni in one hand while she
brandishes an exacto knife with the other. They
send me a card on my birthdays.

David met with some small success as a
musician. He lives in San Francisco with his partner. We exchange email from time to time. And of
course, he came to the Dad's funeral.

Richard is buried in Mount Pleasant
Cemetery. I have never visited his grave.

And we all know what became of Theresa.

This morning, Saturday, I woke up at home, in
Toronto. Barebones Lake was behind me.

I went to the gym and worked out, running
two miles, doing an hour of weights, until I was
red-faced and frighteningly sweaty, like a wet
tomato. My grey flannel track suit black at the
armpits, breastbone and crotch. Wet, hot, Amazon
woman.

It's noon. In seven hours I will go to the bar
where she's playing tonight, so as to ensure that I
get a front row table. There is a $2 cover. All that

work on the road, and she still only rates a $2 cover.

I wonder where she lives. How she pays the rent. If she has a boyfriend. A girlfriend. A family.

I should feel sorry. But I don't. It's like I'm eating dust again. Jaw sore. Bones like glass. A pain like a sinus headache beneath my temple. And a mind that circles around a single plan: to stand before her, point the gun, and fire. Stand up. Point the gun. Fire. Standuppointthegunfire. *Stop her.*

Outside, the children in the street are playing loud games. *You're out I said you're out stamped it no rubs out. No rubs out* means that what's said, is done. It's the same as Amen, or So Be It. *Dee has the cooties. Stamped it. No rubs out.*

I get a coffee and a cigarette and my newspapers, and my Theresa/Vagina Dentata file, setting myself up to watch out the window. The phone rings. I don't answer. It's my editor. He leaves voicemails. *Dee, c'mon, it's been five weeks…we don't want to let you go…*

The kitchen fills with smoke. I flip through the pages of Theresa's file. Transcripts I've typed of her routines. The occasional clipping of an interview, from local entertainment rags. And the review of her play from the *Globe and Mail.*

Before me on the table is the .22 pistol. I pick it up and aim it, through the glass of my front window. I have some details to consider. If I go for the head, the human skull is thick, and a small target for a .22 pistol. If I shoot her in the gut, I will need more than one shot. Even squirrels can survive a shot from a .22. I will shoot her in both, then. Two shots. At least.

But I don't know what I will do afterward. I should prepare myself for a trial. Formulate a defence. I can't claim loss of reason. I have my reason. I know what I'm doing.

I might claim I was sleepwalking. It has worked before.

But do I really want to go on, after it's done? Should I turn the gun on myself? I will go to hell one way or the other – live or die. To what level of hell does sororicide confine one? Someone once said that hell is other people. Someone who understood.

Maybe I will put the gun in my mouth, and fire. But that doesn't always work. I should press the barrel between my eyes, against the well-plucked patch between my eyebrows, where the skin is downy. That should work. After all, it was good enough for Richard.

Happiness, as the Beatles said, is a warm gun.

Before I know it, it's past 8 p.m. Time to go and see my sister.

So how sane do I look? I am sane. "Sane" once meant "clean." My hands are clean. I know what's fair.

I pay my $2 cover charge and move to the front row, where there are black plywood tables with rough undersides that tear at your nylons. I have been in places like this enough to know: wear jeans.

The room begins to fill. I turn around to see who's here for the show. Limping and dragging and lurching they come, all the victims of my stories: the vampire fish boy, the armless farmer, the conjoined twins (leaning up against each other, like Jane and Alice used to do). The jawless man, the bereaved parents with their bloody-faced mastiff on a tight leash. And the girl with her heart outside her body. She's a grown woman now, very pretty, and she's wearing Jane's graduation gown, except that bulging on her sternum is her red and pumping heart. The cloth has been cut away to allow for its beating, pulsing, jelliform bulb.

Do it, they all whisper to me. *Do it for us. Who have never much liked to hear laughing.*

The gun, somehow, is in my lap. I don't remember putting it there. I don't remember loading it. I wish I could just go home. I'm so tired. I'm so tired. Can't I please change my mind?

But the lights – such as they are – are going down. And here is the emcee. And here is the show.

So like, syndromes. They're not even bona fide ailments, man. They're just tendencies. Carpal tunnel syndrome. Irritable bowel syndrome. Like, it's not really sick, it's just irritable. It got up on the wrong side of the bowel bed this morning. Man, today I just don't give a shit.

And the disorders. My favourite is panic disorder. Of course panic is disordered. You want orderly panic? Imagine someone saying, we're going to start the panic –

Hey, you getting a little excited there in the front row? Here, folks, this lady here, standing there like a hydro pole – she's my stalker. She's been following me for months. How're ya doin', stalker?

Hey. Fucking put that thing down. Is that real? Is that a real gun? Hey, this is not funny. Hey, fuck, stop it, lady, that's not *funny*...

Bedlam.

I rise from my chair like Venus from the waves, and fire that first shot. *Look out!* someone screams. *She's got a gun!* Then, random panic: people scrambling under and over the tables, toppling chairs and overfilled ashtrays, rums-and-cokes flying through the air in parabolas of fluid and glass, screams of fright replacing the laughter (although, if you will, the sounds are basically the same).

Theresa falls. But she does not crumple. She drops, belly to the stage. I watch my arm descend, with the gun in its hand, trying to level it at her. The first shot was wild by several feet. Now I have her cold. She is worming across the stage, trying to get to cover. *Grab her,* someone yells, *stop her*. I think they mean Theresa. But I realize they mean me. I have to do it, right now, for I won't get another chance.

I raise the gun's muzzle to the ceiling. Bang,

it says, sending the recoil-shock down my upright arm. A powder of ceiling dust showers on my hair and face.

Suddenly there is a massive push between my shoulderblades, from someone very strong, and the gun flies from my hand. It spins through the air, strikes a pot light with a clang, plummets to the stage like a dead swallow. It doesn't go off again. Theresa is lying still, on the stage, with her hands over the back of her head.

There are people all over me. The bouncer who pushed me is shorter than me, but a man of substance. Others, unnecessarily, drag me to my knees. Everyone wants a piece of me. Theresa dares to pull her head up from the stage's painted plywood, and for a moment, with me on the floor and she on the dais, our eyes are at the same level. They meet. There is a flash of recognition, like the burst of fireworks.

"Dee," she says. "Good God. *Dee.*"

She crawls to the edge of the stage, slips over it, murmurs something to someone who's on a cell to 911. "Part of the act," I hear her say, very quietly, in a voice that sounds like our mother's putting-us-to-bed voice. "Experimental meta-humour," she is saying, still soothingly. "Improv...high camp...audience involvement..."

The bouncers hold me tight, on my knees, unconvinced by her calm. Theresa kneels down on the floor beside me, puts her hands on my face, thumbs wiping away the tears that I (as always) haven't even felt fall. She puts her arms around me. Her face against mine.

"Dee," she says. "What happened?"

THE CUNT SHOWS HER TEETH
(INTERVIEW WITH VAGINA DENTATA,
NOW MAGAZINE)

She looks like hell, she says (or admits), as she squeezes herself into a seat at our table at the Rivoli. It's a new material night, the organizers tell me, but Vagina Dentata doesn't have any new material.

"I'm working on some," she says, gulping back an entire can of Pepsi, which she's brought in her handbag (to avoid paying $2 at the bar, she explains).

I comment on the calories in the Pepsi, but she waves me off. "Don't bother me with calories," she says. "I'm 45. I eat a lot. I'm fat. Such is life."

Her hands are surprisingly small and delicate, but puffed with flesh, as if she had edema. It's hard to get by the impression that this is the quintessential thin-woman-inside-fat-struggling-to-get-out scenario. Visible beneath the chubby, moonlike halo around her face is what might have once been prettiness. But when I ask her what she was like as a child (she performs a successful spiel about how she was a fat kid), she says I've got it all wrong.

"This is an act," she explains. "I was never a fat kid. When I was young, I was a knockout. This character's based on my kid sister, who was *huge*. She ate everything that wasn't nailed down or running away. It was scary."

It seems we've got it wrong. Vagina Dentata embraces some aspects of herself, but she – Theresa Graham – is a very separate individual, with a parallel but distinct history. So although yes, it is indeed her family in her routines, it is her family reconstructed.

"Believe me, my family was not funny. My brother was gay, which was no cakewalk back then. My mother was disowned when she was 17 – she 'had to get married,' as they used to say – and eventually she ran off with her lesbian lover. Then my sister was carted off to the loony bin when she was only 13."

Is this the sister on whom Vagina Dentata is based, I ask?

"Yeah, that's her. Vagina is what I imagine my sister's like now: a powerful, spitting, in-your-face *broad*, free to say exactly what she pleases, and not to care about how she *looks*."

Do looks matter, then? She thinks it's an interesting question. "I find being an ugly woman less confining. As a girl, I was confined by my looks. I *looked* so adorable. I couldn't get anyone to take me seriously."

It gives one pause, I must admit. Are we, as they say nowadays, *lookists*? While I rarely find her routines very funny – that Phyllis Diller/Totie Fields shtick has been done to *death* – I do wonder whether I might like her more, were she as pretty as Rita Rudner?

Vagina Dentata, in person, offstage, is actually very nice. She thanks me for the opportunity for some publicity and struggles up out of her chair. As she clomps up the stage steps, her pants straining across her elephantine behind, I wonder under what circumstances she could ever have been a knockout. She grabs the mike and starts right in on the audience, all trace of that ghostly sweet face consumed by vindictive. We're assholes, we're fools, and we have no idea what it's like to truly suffer...

I am sitting on Theresa's sofa, wrapped in Theresa's blanket, reading Theresa's clipping scrapbook. This is one from last year, so I did not have it in my file. She has a lot of clippings I don't have. Now there'll be a new one: *Prop Mixup Claimed in Nightclub Shooting.*

I spent a night in jail, in a detention centre. Theresa joked, as she bailed me out, that it sounded like I was being kept after school.

I have been charged with *weapons dangerous* and *pointing a firearm*. It would have been attempted murder or assault with a weapon except that Theresa managed to convince the police that it was all her idea; part of her wacky crazy-comic act. We hadn't known the gun was real; it belonged to her ex-husband, and he was an actor; he'd always said it was a prop and they were blanks and *oh my god, officer, I can't believe it, someone might have been killed!* Theresa goggled and fawned; one cop even laughed at her stupidity. She has been charged, too: public mischief and possession of an unregistered weapon.

"Public mischief," she said to me in the car,

musing. "I can work that into a routine."

All the way to her place she played whale sounds music; wisecracked that she spoke fluent Beluga. Wordlessly handed me tissues for my streaming eyes. Helped me out of the car, wrapped me in a checkered car blanket, as if I were coming home from the hospital after giving birth. Helped me up the stairs. I leaned on her, towered over her, all the way into her home.

Her house is in east Riverdale, a turn-of-the-century rowhouse. She's divorced. Rents out the basement and second floor to tenants, one of whom has a yapping dog that barked a hysterical alarm from the upper window as we approached. On the front door hung a placard: *Theresa Marie Graham, RMT.* Registered Massage Therapist.

"I thought you were a comedian," I said. "I thought that was what you did."

"Comedy doesn't pay the rent."

She settled me into a narrow, spongy sofa with wooden arms, and urged me to put my feet on the coffee table, then stuffed an Obus-forme back support behind me. Tall women, she explained, often have disk problems.

"No," I said. "I have lots of other problems, but my disks are fine."

She laughed. "Good ol' Dee. You always had a great sense of humour."

I wondered what Dee she was remembering. I don't remember being funny.

And now I am sitting on her sofa, with her

clipping scrapbook on the floor, by our feet. She has brought me black tea, no sugar, and there is a plate of Peek Freans shortbreads on the coffee table. Upstairs, the tenant's shower is running. On Theresa's walls are framed prints – Matisse and Cézanne – and a door leads to her office and examining room. She has put a Gordon Lightfoot CD on, because she remembers that I liked him. *Sit down, young stranger.*

"So," she says. "Why did you try to kill me?"

I don't reply. Anything I could say would be foolish.

In the silence, she takes one of the cookies, slipping the whole thing into her mouth at once. Chews it to death. Swallows the crumbs.

"Come on," she says. "Tell me."

And in a blink, the words are out, in a freshet, like the hoptoads (or the diamonds) from the fairy tale sisters' mouths. After all these years, the grief should be gone, but it thrashes around inside me, headless, deformed, striking out with heavy limbs. It has survived, and I have kept it happy and warm, fed it through the toothed mouth of its angry belly.

You ruined my life, I tell her. You ruined everything, you made me feel like dirt, you stole my life, you stole me, Theresa, you stole every chance I had. I was just a kid, just a little girl, but you took all that away. You took everything. You took everything I had.

She puts her head briefly in her hands, thrusting her fingers into her dyed and permed mop of hair. I can see that the roots are blonde-grey. There are cookie crumbs in her lap.

"Dee," she says. "Can I say something?"

Here it comes: the denial. The justifications. It didn't happen, she'll say, and besides it was no big deal anyway, get over it, get some therapy, it was years ago, and in the long run who cares, because here you are thin and here I am fat, isn't that just a killer?

"Go ahead," I say.

"I know how hard it was for you. We all knew. Even then."

I shake my head. She didn't know. Nobody could have known what it was like.

"We were all worried about you."

"You were not *worried*. You were *inhuman*."

"Dee, forgive me. I was just a kid. And we change. People change. You changed, didn't you?"

"No," I said. "I only look like I have."

She reaches for the cookie plate. "Have a cookie?" she says.

"I never eat cookies."

"But you're thin as a rail..."

"That's because I *don't...eat...cookies.*"

My voice sounds furious; I'm embarrassed by it. I pick up my teacup and it clatters against the saucer. Theresa won't stop looking at me. I don't look back, but let my eyes fall over the pictures on the walls. There are no photos of any of our family, but that makes sense: how would she have any pictures of us, when all that ended so long ago?

But on a corner table, beside a tiny laughing Buddha and a Chinese waving cat, is a fold-out brass triptych. I can see there three faces, of children, but cannot tell their ages; cannot tell their sexes. Two are blonde, though, and one is dark, like me. My nieces and nephews?

"Yes," she says, when I enquire. Eats yet another cookie.

"Where are they? Are they grown? At university…"

There is only one cookie left on the plate. Theresa addresses it.

"Well," she tells it. "It's like this."

Gerry and I came home around 2 a.m.; we'd been at a party, and we were a little drunk and looking forward to rolling around with each other, somehow that makes me feel guilty, that I had sex on the mind when I opened that door and heard that silence and smelled that smell. The odd thing is that I felt the silence was wrong, before I smelled anything. I remember I was two or three steps inside, propelled by that sense of something bad. It was like we'd opened the seal on a tomb. And Gerry grabbed me, and stopped me. I was screaming for the kids. Then we heard sirens.

The leak was from the main; it was very large. Someone else on the street was awake and had smelled it and called the police. We were all evacuated, the whole street could have been blown flat. But only the four kids died. Our three, and the girl we'd hired to sit for us. She died, too.

Funny thing is: sometimes I remember it differently. I am sure I remember going up the inside stairs, running from doorway to doorway of the kids' rooms, clapping my hands and calling for them to wake up, wake up! But that never happened. I never made it upstairs, because Gerry was holding me, and then the firemen came. So I remember something that didn't happen at all.

What's even stranger is that I have a dream, even nowadays I have it, that's come so often it's like a memory now too. In the dream, when I clap my hands, they all sit up, rubbing their eyes in big stagey gestures, and they grin at me and toss their blankets aside, and they all get up and run past me down the stairs. And they're safe.

Sometimes, I deliberately remember it that way. I pretend they're all still alive. Like you said. At university, or in Europe, or something. I pretend none of it ever happened. That's the best way, sometimes, don't you think...

I look up. She is not crying. How can she not cry?

It is hard for me to say. I'm so...*sorry.*

I was going to ask about Richard. I was going to give her hell. But I can't find the opening. What should I say? *Speaking of dead children?*

Gordon Lightfoot is singing "If You Could Read My Mind." And Theresa says, "I think we should talk about what happened to Richard."

And suddenly, there's a howl, and for a moment I think it's that yappy dog upstairs, but my *God* it's *me*. I'm making so much noise, the man in the cellar bangs on the pipes, and I hear the upstairs tenant come to the head of the stairs, and pause there. But Theresa comes and sits beside me and wraps the blankets around me tighter, and rests her head on my shoulder as noises rocket out of me, ghosts and hobgoblins now, not just little toads and salamanders. Big throbbing behemoths of pain. Theresa's hands dig into my arms, down to the thinly covered bone.

When I open my eyes again, and the silence has spread around us, I see the late afternoon sun slanting across her carpet. It will be dark soon. I have to go home.

"No," says Theresa. "Stay here. We have so much to talk about. All those years of not-talking. Dee, did you know you talked early?"

I shake my head, no. I don't remember anyone telling me that.

"I remember you as a little, little baby. Talking. Do you know what your first word was?"

"No," I say again, my voice nearly gone.

Theresa strokes my short, clipped hair. "Tee-ah," she says.

"Tee-ah?"

"Yes," she says. "Tee-ah."

Theresa.

She picks up the plate with its one little cookie, and she brings it to me, both hands on the saucer's rim, her fingers fat and her nails short, and bangles on her wrist, and skin mottled and sagging already, from the weight of the world no doubt.

"Have a cookie," she says.

And I do.

That night, I dream.

Richard comes to me where I lie in a yellow bed. The walls are the amber sap of pines, and Richard has three bright eyes, and then only one, like Kipling's little idol. I try to raise myself, to sit and follow, but I'm too heavy. I am adhered.

Help me, I say.

Okay, he replies. He comes to me, straddles me, and the yellow melts to blue. The heat grows cool, the fire is water, we are on the stones of Barebones Lake.

Now turn over, he says.

He is now on my back. *Yeehah*, he cries, riding me bareback.

I am the Black Stallion, I am a wild wolf, he is Silverheels on his pony, we are the centaur of Sagittarius, the sign of the galaxy with a spine of bright stars. With a chuckle he moves me forward, off and away from this place, these moments. The ground drops away like a bomb. The lake disappears. We rise, rise, rise.

We do not stop, not even when we reach the moon.